Harry's Trees

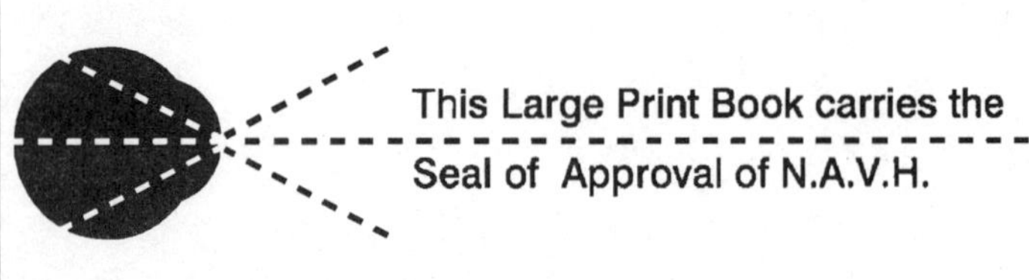
This Large Print Book carries the
Seal of Approval of N.A.V.H.

Harry's Trees

Jon Cohen

THORNDIKE PRESS
A part of Gale, a Cengage Company

Farmington Hills, Mich • San Francisco • New York • Waterville, Maine
Meriden, Conn • Mason, Ohio • Chicago

Grum illustration by Anthony Spay.
Thorndike Press, a part of Gale, a Cengage Company.

Thorndike Press® Large Print Bill's Bookshelf.
The text of this Large Print edition is unabridged.
Other aspects of the book may vary from the original edition.
Set in 16 pt. Plantin.

**LIBRARY OF CONGRESS CIP DATA ON FILE.
CATALOGUING IN PUBLICATION FOR THIS BOOK
IS AVAILABLE FROM THE LIBRARY OF CONGRESS**

ISBN-13: 978-1-4328-5847-6 (hardcover)

Published in 2018 by arrangement with Harlequin Books S.A.

Printed in the United States of America
1 2 3 4 5 6 7 22 21 20 19 18

For Mary

1

The Weekly

Friday, March 11, 2016

$100 MILLION BOUQUET

Essington, PA - After claiming Wednesday's multi-state MegaMillions ticket worth $110.3 million, seven employees of Staslin's Florist Shoppe on First Street talked about their win.

"We're stunned," said Katherine Keefe, one of the employees and the buyer of the winning ticket at a bar in York "We've played the lottery, you know, always together, for five years."

"Six!" shouted fellow florist, Ellen Meriwether, as the rest of the winners laughed.

If the women opt to take the cash payout option, each will receive $11.9 million after taxes.

"Our friendship and camaraderie paid off big time," Keefe said. "I call us the Fortunate Florists."

"Really, really fortunate!" Meriwether chimed in.

Rer foll imp

The that rela the beh of a exp in I its beh con or v

It m

The memorial service for Beth, Harry Crane's wife of fourteen years, was held in the Leiper Friends Meeting House in Waverly, just outside Philadelphia. The large, unadorned room was packed with relatives, friends, neighbors and coworkers. A woman's whisper rose from their midst. "Oh, look at him. Poor Harry." Grief-haunted and pale in his rumpled blue suit, Harry sat in the front row propped between his imposing older brother, Wolf, and Beth's father, Stan.

A deep quiet fell over the gathering. In a Quaker memorial service, the mourners sit in ungoverned silence until someone is moved to say a few words, recite poetry or even sing. A long minute passed. The cold March wind clicked a tree branch against the window at the end of Harry's row. A baby fussed. An old man coughed. Kleenex white as dove wings fluttered into view about the room.

Sandy Maynard was the first to rise. Sandy played tennis with Beth every other Tuesday evening at the Healthplex. "Beth," she said. She gripped the back of the pew in front of her. "Beth, I want to tell you something. You were a wonderful friend." Tears streamed down Sandy's cheeks. "You were a wonderful friend, and I will miss you every day of my life." Sandy's husband slid another Kleenex into her hand and helped her sit back down.

Harry stared straight ahead.

Carl Bachman, owner of Bachman's Deli Cafe, lumbered to his feet. "So," he said. He paused to wipe his forehead with a handkerchief and clear his throat. Carl was not a man accustomed to oratory. "So, I just want to say Beth was a great customer. And Harry, I know you were a great husband. And this — this is a great tragedy. Obviously. So. So, God who *also* is pretty great, well, He works in mysterious ways. Thank you." Carl looked around in a panic as if suddenly thinking, Are you allowed to say *God* in a Quaker service, what are the darn rules? He ducked back down into his seat.

The mourners turned their gaze back to Harry. Outside, a heavy truck pulled down a side street. The deep engine throb filled the meeting house. Harry shifted and blinked. The room tensed, but he went still again.

A woman to Harry's left popped up like a meerkat and raised a silver flute into view. "I'd like to play a song for you, Beth. I tried to compose something original but I was too sad to think, so I'm going to play a

Beatles song because the Beatles cover every single emotion there could possibly be. I'm going to play 'Hello, Goodbye.' " She lifted the flute to her lips and gave it a nervous off-key toot. "Um, hold on, I have to adjust. Something." She fiddled with the tuning slide, gave things a twist, pressed the flute to her lips again. She closed her eyes and played the first note, this time perfectly. The simple pop melody hit the mourners with the emotional wallop of a Bach cello suite. Loud sobs detonated around the room.

But not a sound from the front pew, where Harry sat.

Someone in the back of the room stood and began to speak in a steady, elderly voice. "Well, my name is Bill Belson and I live over on Guernsey Road, and I want to speak a moment about Beth and my Jack Russell terrier, Bud. Every morning, I tie Bud to the cherry tree in my front yard so he can watch what's going on. And Beth, on her way to the train, would always stop to give him a head scratch or a belly rub. When she'd step into the yard, she'd say, 'Hello, Bud.' And when she'd leave, she'd say, 'Goodbye, Bud.' "

Bill Belson paused. "I'd hear Beth's voice from an open window or maybe I'd be out back raking leaves, and it brought me pleasure, this little thing between the two of them. This little 'Hello, Goodbye.' " Bill's deep sigh filled the room. "I'm sure going to miss that moment. Because that's why we're here on this planet. You know? To speak to dogs. To be *alive* in the world. That's what Beth was. Alive in the world."

For the first time since Stan and Wolf had led him into the room, Harry moved. He slowly turned to look at this man, Bill Belson. But Bill had taken his seat.

Harry's eyes cut to a teenager rising to his feet. Jason Luder. Nice kid, lived next door, mowed their lawn when they went on vacation. "Yeah, well," Jason began, "kinda followin' up on what Mr. Belson said, and the lady with the flute. We just read *Slaughterhouse-Five* in class and there's, like, this phrase that Billy Pilgrim uses, 'Farewell, hello, farewell, hello,' because he's, like, unstuck in time. So maybe in a way Mrs. Crane's still kind of here, okay? In a way, she's just unstuck in time." Jason sat down.

And Harry stood up. The assembly held its collective breath. Harry was going to speak. He said two words, but in a voice so quiet no one could make them out. He looked at the floor, then at the ceiling, and said them again. "Wait here."

Two hundred people exchanged furtive, puzzled looks.

Harry stepped past Wolf. Wolf gripped Harry's coat sleeve. Harry shook free, stood for a teetering moment, then took off down the center of the aisle. He banged open the meeting house doors, ran down the stone steps and out onto the lawn, accelerating toward some unreachable escape. Wolf, large as a locomotive and huffing steam in the cold air, caught him from behind. They crashed to the frozen ground.

Crushed beneath his brother, Harry felt the relief of obliteration. But he heard himself groan — there would be no escape — and his left eye opened. He blinked and stared at his hand, pinned inches in front of his face. The fingers slowly uncurled and revealed, crumpled and sweaty after five days of clutching it in his fist, a lottery ticket.

"Wait here," he whispered, and saw Beth standing before him, Beth five days ago, standing on Market Street.

Wait here.

They'd been hurrying along Market Street in Philadelphia, hand in hand, late for a movie. Waiting for the light on Sixth Street, he turned and looked at her. Exquisite wifely details pierced him. The smile lines at the sides of her mouth. The lock of hair above her right ear set aglow by the late-afternoon light. The pleasure of her hand secure in his. Harry was always most alive when Beth was beside him. He drew her close and kissed her. A good solid kiss.

She leaned back from him and smiled. "Hello?"

"Heads up," he said. "That could happen again." He took in the faded Sixth Street sign. "It'll definitely happen again. Every even-numbered street."

"Yeah? Like, an OCD thing? Compulsive spousal kissing?"

"Compulsive *even-numbered* spousal kissing."

"You're a very odd man," she said.

"No, a very even man." He planted another kiss.

Beth laughed and pushed him away. "You know, you could use a little OCD. I was just thinking about your sock drawer." They were in front of Old Navy. There were rows of men's socks in the window display.

Harry shook his head. "Wow. You're thinking socks while I'm thinking of your amazingness."

"Your sock drawer's amazing, Harry."

"I don't have a sock drawer."

"Right. You throw your socks into your *underwear* drawer."

"I have an underwear drawer?" He pointed at the street sign again. "Seriously, you've been warned."

Numbers were very much on his mind. Why? He took in street signs, the distant clock on City Hall, the route numbers on the front of the city buses roaring by.

Wait here.

Beth nudged him. "We really do need to hurry. You hate to be late for a movie."

"Right. Let's go."

They went another block. He kissed her.

Her laughter, bright as the sun. "Seventh Street," she said. "Odd-numbered! You cheated."

They turned in unison, drawn by a sudden noise two blocks up. Mammoth machines, louder than battling dinosaurs, were tearing down an old brick warehouse. The roar and push of the city — when they stepped off the curb, Harry stumbled. Beth steadied him. "I'm all right," he said. We're on our way to a movie, he thought, that's all. The sidewalk is crowded. It's cold. They're tearing down a warehouse.

Averting his eyes as another section of wall tumbled to the ground — the impermanence of all things — he focused again on the miraculous constant at his side. Blue eyes, brown hair, honey scent, white teeth, bright laughter, strong hand. Look at her, in her red wool coat. "The coat," he said. It was new. She'd gotten it yesterday.

"Too red?"

"No, it's just — you look so great in it."

She studied him. "You're in an interesting mood, Harry. Kinda here, there and everywhere."

And then his eyes found it. He fixed on the green neon Pennsylvania Lottery sign above the door of a convenience store across the street. It winked at him. *Numbers.*

"Oh, hey," he said.

Beth followed his gaze to the neon lottery sign. "Okay, *that's* what's going on." She tugged his arm. "No, come on. The movie starts in five minutes."

Harry let her lead him forward. He glanced back at the convenience store. Stopped abruptly in front of the plywood barrier along the demolition site like a stubborn dog jerking its leash. "Just wait here a minute. All right?" he said. He had to raise his voice above the diesel chug of the machines. "All I want is a Snickers. Really. You can never get a Snickers at the movies."

Beth reached into her coat pocket and

pulled out a couple of mini Snickers. They had bought too many bags last Halloween. The golden wrappers glittered in the sunlight.

Harry stared, turned without taking one and peered through an observation hole in the plywood. He looked quickly away as the wrecking ball swung. He didn't like to watch things fall, didn't get that thrill you were supposed to get.

Beth reached out and raised the collar on his jacket. "You don't need a hundred million dollars to open Harry's Trees."

You couldn't hide anything from her. Why did he ever bother to try?

"I didn't buy a ticket," he said.

"Great. Let's go to the movie."

Harry's cheeks flushed.

"If you go across the street, we'll be late," she said.

"The drawing's at six. I'll miss it."

Beth looked into his eyes. "*Skip* the ticket. Just this once? Please?"

He felt ill. *They cut down my eastern hemlock, Beth,* he wanted to say. But he'd told her that already. Another chunk of the warehouse crashed down on the other side of the barrier. Harry heard his eastern hemlock fall. He began to stress, as he did too often, about his job at the USDA Forest

Service. How the vibrant trees of his youth had withered in his late thirties into green smudges on satellite maps and brain-numbing data graphics. How his cubicle smelled not of pine sap or oak leaves but the nothingness of plastic. How he'd devoted his life to forest preservation yet worked in a building utterly bereft of wood. Forest preservation? Harry tightened. Who was he kidding? He was unable to preserve even a single tree. Despite weeks of protest, and Harry was not a man to protest, they had cut down his eastern hemlock. Yesterday, in less than two hours, the only tree visible in the small window at the end of his row — the tree that got him through his day — had been chopped, chipped and hauled away in a black dump truck. More spaces were needed in parking lot A-3. Harry sat in his cubicle all morning, a treeless forestry bureaucrat.

"You don't need the lottery," Beth said.

Harry tried not to look at the neon lottery sign, flashing so brightly at him now it made him squint. He shook his head. "Nobody quits their job, not these days. They just don't. It's a crazy idea."

She looked into his eyes. "Not crazy if you're miserable."

"No, hey, I'm not miserable," he said

quickly. "The job's miserable . . . but me, I'm, you know, happy." Except when the job was on his mind. Which was too often these days.

He looked at her looking at him. No, not at him — for him. Beth searching for her Harry. He'd done the same thing this morning, shaving. There he was in the mirror, but only sort of. He touched at the shaving cream on his face, as if it were a thing obscuring the true Harry. He quickly rinsed his face and looked again, but he was still not . . . himself. Your good looks, Beth would say to him. It's all about your eyes. They smile, she said. They light your face. The first time they kissed, long ago, she kissed his mouth, and then she kissed the corner of each eye and drew back from him.

Your eyes, she whispered, bring the whole thing together.

Thing? Harry had said.

The Harry thing, she said. You're a very nice-looking guy — that dark hair with those wavy swoops, that good square chin, those eyebrows like bird wings — but when your eyes smile. *Wow.* She kissed him again. His whole body smiled.

But this morning in the mirror: lightless eyes, defeated chin, short and swoopless hair — unhappy Harry, the slumped man who dreaded going to work. The Harry Beth saw now, as they stood on Market Street.

"Really, I'm not miserable," he said miserably. Blinking and squinting, he tried to make his eyes smile.

Now she was really staring at him. Her eyes reflecting his undeniable misery.

"It's just the *job,*" he said. When he leaned in to kiss her cheek, he glanced past her to the neon sign.

She turned away.

"Oh come on. It'll take one second." He was speaking loudly to make himself heard over the machines. "It's such a small thing, Beth."

She spun around. "Small? Hanging everything on a lottery ticket? No, that's a big thing, Harry. Sweetheart, just *quit* the Forest Service. We don't have kids, our mortgage is doable, I'll work more hours." Beth was a grant-writing consultant for several city nonprofits, a professional optimist undaunted by long odds.

"You're not working more hours," Harry said.

"You'll work a lot more hours, too." She smiled at him. "At your new job."

"At Harry's Trees," he said, a hint of a smile in his eyes. Such a great name. So unfussy. So unbureaucratic. In desperate moments at the office he'd lean back in his chair, close his eyes and see the website logo — a big *H* shaded by the wide canopy of an American beech.

"No," Beth said. "At Baylor Arboretum. They love you there. And in a few years, with the money we save up, you'll start Harry's Trees."

"Come on. What could they even pay me? Ten bucks an hour? Eight?"

"But it's a job that would make you happy, Harry. Happy at work. For the first time in —"

The word leaped out of his mouth. "Forever."

Beth moved close to him. "We can do it. We'll figure out a way. We'll do this thing. Together."

They really would. It was so simple. He could see it. Planting and tending real trees instead of moving them around on a computer screen. Working outdoors, the rich scent of soil and leaves. Tired at the end of the day instead of drained. No more cubicle, no more meetings. And Baylor Arboretum *was* looking for an arborist. Jim Massinger was about to retire. Harry brightened. Then frowned. No benefits, no government pension, no guarantees. "No," he said. "It's crazy."

"Harry —"

"No. Just. Wait here!"

He didn't mean to shout, but he did. Against the noise of the demolition, against Beth making impossible things seem possible. He glanced over his shoulder as he crossed the street. She was pressed in her red coat against the plywood barrier, as if nailed there by his outburst.

Wait here.

He almost turned back. No, if he hurried, they could make the movie. And she wouldn't stay mad at him, not for this dumb little thing. Besides. What if he won? Because wasn't that the strange dreadful excitement he suddenly felt in his gut, the almost physical premonition all lottery winners described? *I knew I was going to win. This time I just knew it.* And who hits these jackpots? The taxi driver from Bangladesh, the secretary in the auto parts store, the Forest Service bureaucrat in his cubicle. Yes, the bureaucrat — he wins the lottery this time and everything changes like magic.

Harry rushed into the cramped convenience store. A stroke of luck, only two other people in line, an old woman in a mottled fur coat and a construction worker.

The woman gathered up a fistful of tickets and turned to the construction worker and said in a sly cigarette wheeze, "Sorry pal, I got the winner right here."

The construction worker laughed and replied in a thick Philly accent, "You know, that many tickets, you don't seem so sure of your luck."

"Oh, I'm sure," she teased.

Harry swallowed. These people, so casual with millions at stake. The construction worker reached for his wallet and Harry, aping the move, reached for his own. The construction worker pulled out a five and slapped it down on the counter. Harry patted his back pockets. Empty. Oh shit. He'd left his wallet at home.

A flood of people came and got in line behind him. He shoved his hands deep into his coat pockets. Change clinked against his fingernails and he pulled out four quarters. The exact price of a ticket. A sign. His heart thumped.

"Next," muttered the clerk.

Harry stepped forward. "One, please. One ticket."

The bored clerk waited a beat and lifted his eyes. "You got some numbers for me or what?"

Harry froze. He felt the press of people behind him, as if there were thousands lined up now. His number, his all-important, make-or-break *lucky number.* But his mind was blank. His lucky number was a mix of Beth's birthday, their wedding anniversary, his own birthday — but he couldn't remember any of them.

"You want the computer should pick?" the clerk said.

Harry gripped his forehead and squinted.

"Yo pal," the clerk said.

Harry looked out the window and saw Beth across the busy street where he'd planted her, going up and down on her toes in the cold. Behind her in the lot, the wrecking ball high up on the demolition crane swung back and forth like a pendulum on a great clock.

"The computer, sure, yes," Harry breathed.

The clerk hit a button.

A number came rushing back into Harry's head. "May 23, 1980. Beth's birthday is May 23!"

The ticket machine churned out his lottery ticket. The clerk caught it in his hand like a cop catching an abruptly birthed baby. Harry had a sudden, absolutely terrifying sensation as the clerk handed him the flimsy square of paper.

"Oh God," said the woman behind them.

Clutching his ticket, Harry pivoted and

looked at her. She was staring wide-eyed out the window facing Market Street. Everyone in line turned in unison, like startled cattle. Harry caught the last second of it, the warehouse wall tumbling down in slow motion, the shattered bricks scattering like pigeons, the demolition crane buckling. A steel strut the length of a train rail snapped free from the collapsing center of the crane and sailed toward the street, turning end over end like a giant cheerleader's baton.

What might Beth have seen in her final moments?

The woman with a phone to her ear pushing a stroller? Steam rising from the manhole cover in the middle of the street? Harry in the convenience store clutching his lottery ticket?

The immense rusty length of metal crashed through the plywood barrier behind her.

Stumbling out of the store, all Harry could see was rubble, a rising plume of ghostly white dust and, fluttering across the sidewalk, a large torn piece of Beth's red wool coat.

2

Harry stared at the cardboard box on the kitchen table. It was two weeks after the memorial service, a cold March afternoon. He was still in his pajamas.

Breathe.

He gulped air like a drowning man. Circled the kitchen table. His legs were weak, he wasn't eating properly. And sleep? Hideous. Impossible. He couldn't even get into the bed at night, lay at the foot of it like a dog and trembled until sunrise. He placed one hand on the box.

Breathe.

He placed his other hand on the box. Oh Beth, how playfully we tossed around the notion of death, like a party balloon, batting it back and forth over the years of our marriage.

"I'm freezing to death, Harry, stop hogging the quilt," she said one cold winter night.

"Sorry," he said, then yanked the entire quilt

off her and wrapped himself in it like a mummy, laughing wickedly as she shrieked and pummeled him with a pillow.

Another time:

"I'm dead on my feet, Harry, let's go up to bed," she said, walking past the couch.

He lowered his book. "Hey, thanks for asking. Yes, I'd love to have sex with you."

She stopped and stared at him. "Seriously? I say 'dead on my feet' and you hear 'sex'?"

"Did the sentence contain 'bed'?"

"Ha!"

He chased her up the stairs and they fell into bed.

Breathe, Harry, he told himself. He slid a paring knife along the taped edges of the box and lifted the flaps. And there she was, inside a clear, heavy-gauge plastic bag, Beth turned into ashes. "Oh," he said, and closed his eyes, unstuck in time. He was standing in another kitchen, in their first apartment, five blocks south of the Ohio State campus on Pugh Street. They were both in graduate school, just married, twenty-three years old and vibrating with adoration and desire. Naked and slinky as a cat, Beth walked across the kitchen and slid her arms around him, her breath hot in his ear.

Unstuck, Harry saw Beth on Market Street, the crane collapsing behind her in the same instant he saw her young and naked and alive as they laughed, sexing around in that tiny kitchen on Pugh Street, bumping into chairs and cabinet doors.

That they had been so absolutely physical. That they could, anytime they wanted, reach out and touch each other. Confirm each other with a look, a smile. He shook his head and stared at the ashes. You can't be in a bag. I have to get you out of there. I have to get you *out.* He paced the empty rooms of his empty house.

At midnight, he rushed out to the garage and placed the bag of ashes in the basket on the front of his old three-speed bicycle. Unstuck again, he saw young Beth perched on the handlebars, just after they had bought the bike at a yard sale. Her laughter, as he pedaled down Kirlsen Hill toward campus.

He blinked away the memory and set off through the streets of Waverly, pedaling in and out of the glare of the streetlights, like flares that lit up his guilt. Inside all the houses, husbands were pulling their wives close, kissing them good-night. No, not good-night or goodbye or *wait here.* No, these husbands were holding their wives tight. These husbands would never let go, never turn their backs. They were holding on for dear life, because that's what you do, you hold on to her and never let go. Beth, why did I let you go? The wheels on the rusty bike emitted desolate squeaks.

A cold sliver of moon followed overhead as Harry circled the town. "What am I going to do with you?" he whispered hoarsely to the bag in the basket. Which couldn't possibly contain the remains of his wife, could it? Surely he hadn't done this? But he had.

Clouds swallowed the moon. The dark night grew darker. He pedaled up the long, steep hill at the end of Springer Avenue, faster and faster. The bike veered wildly. "Widower Bicycles Self to Death," *The Weekly Waverly* would report, below the pet-grooming and duct-cleaning ads. But the hill failed to deliver a heart attack.

Sweat-soaked and gasping, Harry peeled off his coat and let it flap away into the street behind him. He turned onto Guernsey Road. A jagged pothole loomed and he swerved, smacking into the granite curb in front of a large Tudor house. The bag of ashes bounced out of the basket and sailed into the air.

Barks of delight pierced the night. A Jack Russell terrier burst out of the dark, crossing the wide front lawn in grasshopper leaps. Intruder! The dog skidded to a halt and looked up at the rising bag. Balloon!

On the ground, entangled in his bike, Harry watched in horror as the bag dropped back toward earth, and the little dog — jaws agape, tongue lolling — leaped.

"No! No, no, no!"

The dog sank its teeth into the bag, jerked its head back and forth, then raced across the yard in a wild zigzag, a berserk canine comet with a billowing tail of ash. A door opened on the side of the house and someone called out. "Bud! Bud, what the hell?"

Bright-eyed little Bud ran up to Harry and dropped the empty bag like he'd just retrieved a ball. The dog sneezed and shook himself, coating Harry in ashes and white grit.

"Bud!" Footsteps clunked down a side porch. Bud galloped away.

Harry grabbed the empty bag and took off in the other direction. Five blocks later he collapsed against a telephone pole, heart slamming in his chest. Oh God!

But wait, why was this a catastrophe? Beth hadn't been scattered by just any dog. No, it was good ol' Bud from Beth's daily walk to the train.

Harry stared at the plastic bag, torn and slobbery with dog spit. Oh God!

He clutched it to his chest and staggered into the black remains of the night. Every so often he bumped into a mailbox or a streetlight and gave off a little poof of ash. Just before dawn he stood in a daze before his empty house. It was as welcoming as a mausoleum.

The house suddenly cleared its throat. "Harry," it growled. This did not startle Harry. It was right that the house should growl at him. The house had been fond of Beth. She had been its life and light. Now look at it. Pathetic and dark. "I'm sorry," he said. "For everything. I'm so sorry."

"Yo, *Harry.*"

Harry saw the glowing tip of a cigarette, then the outline of intimidating male bulk sitting on the front porch steps.

He advanced cautiously. "Wolf?"

Slit-eyed behind his cigarette smoke, his brother stood up. Wolf's real name was Gerald Wolford Crane. The nickname came in the fifth grade when Wolf's voice dropped two octaves and he began to shave.

"Come closer, Harry," Wolf said.

Harry inched forward.

Wolf squinted at him. "What's that all over you? You look like a powdered donut." He reached out a large hand and slapped ashes off Harry's shoulder. Harry grabbed the front porch post to keep from toppling over.

Wolf studied a piece of white grit on his fingertip, then noticed the empty plastic bag in Harry's fist. He slapped his hand against his pants. "Shit, Harry! What'd you do?"

What I did, Wolf, by the very blackest of magic, was turn sweet Beth into ashes. Harry slipped his hand into his pants pocket. It was just a piece of paper, but the losing lottery ticket weighted his pocket, heavy as death. He curled his fingers around the ticket and gripped it tightly, as one might a talisman. Yes, his unlucky talisman. He carried it with him everywhere. He would leave instructions in his will to have the ticket placed in his mouth and his lips sewn shut so that he could taste its curse throughout eternity.

Harry smoothed the bag and folded it. "Pretty obvious, isn't it?" he said. "I scattered Beth's ashes." Actually, Wolf, I outsourced the job to a dog. Come spring, Bill Belson's Beth-fertilized lawn would be greener than a golf course. The dog, the fatal lottery ticket — there was so much to confess. Harry started to speak, but Wolf broke in.

"Scattered? She's in your *hair.* For fuck's sake, Harry, that was your wife, not a bag of confetti!"

Harry gently brushed a white flake from the forearm of his coat and watched it fall. He eased it into the frozen dirt with the toe of his shoe and looked up at his brother, who was shaking his big head.

"It's not as easy as you think," Harry said. And confessing anything to Wolf, *impossible.* He'd momentarily forgotten the first rule of Being Younger Brother to Wolf: give him nothing. Wolf fed on human frailty.

"Yeah, well, you should've let me come with you. It could've been done right."

What else was Wolf here to do right? He was supposed to be back in Virginia in his own empty house. Wolf was in the process of divorcing his third wife, whom Harry had never met. The Crane brothers were shedding wives like dogs shed hair. Like Jack Russells shed ashes.

"Up kind of early, aren't you, Wolf? And, you know, in the wrong state."

Wolf flicked his cigarette onto the frozen lawn. "I've been doing some legwork, Harry. I've been looking into things."

Harry tensed. Wolf looking into things was never, ever good.

Harry plucked from his memory a random and typically unpleasant Wolfian moment. The year: 1992. The place: Plover, Wisconsin. The event: a pale and trembling eleventh grader stopping Harry, a lowly ninth grader, in the hallway of Plover Central High School.

"Excuse me, Mr. Crane," the eleventh grader said, unable to meet Harry's startled eyes. "May I have your permission to open my locker?" For a week the kid would anxiously reappear. "Mr. Crane, may I eat my lunch?"

"Want an ice cream sandwich, Mr. Crane? Want two?"

Wolf, of course, was behind it. God only knew what the kid had done. Glanced at Wolf in the lunchroom, brushed his shoulder in the gym, breathed in a way Wolf didn't like. Existed on the planet. Younger brother of a legendary high school gorilla, Harry was perpetually furious and helpless. "What's going to happen to me when you graduate?" he'd say. "They'll string me up."

Smoking openly in the school parking lot, Wolf snorted. "I doubt it. I think it's going to take this place a few years to get over me." His flicked cigarette butt sparked against a teacher's car door.

What was the source of Wolf's unremitting need to stamp his boot print upon the world, when Harry trod so gingerly? Harry was eight and Wolf was ten when their father, middle-aged and mild-mannered, walked out on the family. Drove, actually. Jeffrey Crane worked in sales at Bingham's Chevrolet in North Plover, and one day he didn't come home at five o'clock. They were told he had purchased a Chevy Citation X-11 in cash, 3 percent off with his employee discount, and had driven off the lot with a jaunty wave. Two days later, an envelope arrived addressed "To: Barbara Crane & Family." Inside was a note written on the back of a Bingham's Chevrolet sales slip: "I'm off to try something else. The change will do me good. Best of luck everybody, JC."

Soon after, Barbara Crane began to disappear, too, day by day, sigh by sigh, going through the motions of motherhood, cooking, cleaning, signing report cards, but no longer there.

And the two boys? Harry went quiet and Wolf went wild.

Harry selected another moment from the stockpile of his brother's exploits: Wolf pantsing the star quarterback of the Plover High School football team on the field during the second quarter. Harry, along with several hundred people sitting in the stands, watched openmouthed as the quarterback stood in the klieg lights frantically attempting to reinstate his sweaty jockstrap. Wolf was given fifty detentions. Never enforced, of course. The principal, like everyone else, was afraid of him.

Another time, hidden behind a stand of trees, Wolf gripped a stolen baseball bat and homered a blazing, gasoline-soaked tennis ball into Windham Park, where volunteer firefighters were prepping for Fire Prevention Day, igniting the back end of Ladder Truck Number One. Pushing always to a limit just short of incarceration, Wolf in his youth was an action movie with way too much action. By the time he left Plover, his audience was exhausted.

Wolf attacked, Harry demurred. It was the yin and yang of their brotherly existence. After their mother read their father's goodbye letter out loud in stunned amazement, Wolf slapped a framed photograph of his father off the mantelpiece and stormed out of the room.

Harry said softly, "Mom. Mom?" When she finally looked up, he said, "Is it all right if I go outside?" Upstairs, Wolf was clawing apart his room. The house heaved, things crashed. "Mom," Harry said again. "I'll just be out in the front yard, okay?"

His shell-shocked mother could only nod.

Young Harry opened the front door and looked up into a sky of deep, dappled green.

A glorious American beech, the largest tree on the block, stood in the front yard. The massed leaves made a dome over their entire yard, as vast as the dome of St. Paul's Cathedral in London, which Harry had seen once in a book.

A year earlier, Harry had discovered that his father had carved "JC" into the tree, in letters so tiny that only a person who spent a great deal of time with the tree would ever see them. His father was gone, but he had left something behind, something that only Harry knew about. Harry walked over to the tree, making sure to avoid even glancing at the initials, which were about five feet up, just above the collar of the first branch. If Wolf ever discovered his father's initials, he would surely hack them into oblivion.

Harry positioned himself so that the beech was between him and the house. The tree blocked the sound of Wolf busting things in his room. Harry pressed his back and his hands hard to the wide trunk and closed his eyes, filling his senses with it, so that all there was in the world was Harry Crane and his tree. The tree was fixed to the solid ground. Maybe its roots went all the way down to the center of the earth. It would never go anywhere. It would be there at night and in the morning when he woke up.

It would be there under blue skies and in the rain, and for all his birthdays. The beech tree was eternal and true.

Young Harry mourned quietly, high up in its branches. If there were tears, he never let Wolf or his mother see them. Staring out over the leafy tops of neighborhood maples, pines and hickory, he imagined himself a dweller in a serene place he called *Harry's Trees.* Floating in the sea of green, safe among friends, some of whom had wonderfully strange names like fire cherry, pignut hickory, shagbark hickory. When he was a teenager, too old for climbing, Harry would still sit in the branches, the childhood names giving way to a deeper understanding. The American beech was *Fagus grandifolia.* The pine in the Lanfords' yard was a *Pinus strobus.* The perpetually bark-shedding sycamore beside the Smiths' garage was a *Platanus occidentalis.* By high school, he knew everything about trees. Harry pondered the biology of taproots, boles, crowns and radicles.

"Hey! Asshole in the tree!" Wolf would call from a window, when the phone was for Harry or it was time for supper, before their mother gave up cooking supper, before Wolf dropped out of high school and moved to an apartment in North Plover.

By the time Harry went off to college, the branch above those carved initials had snapped off in a windstorm. An injured tree undergoes a healing process called rapid callus production. JC was calloused over, but it would always be there.

Harry and Wolf carried their childhood personas into adulthood. Craving stability, Harry married young and went to work for the Forest Service, a place where time peacefully accrued, like the rings in a tree. Peacefully, that is, until he realized he had wandered deeply into a forest that had no trees. But he was unable to accept Beth's offer of escape, insisting on his own, less risky plan for change — betting their future on a weekly lottery ticket. What harm could possibly come from a one-dollar lottery ticket?

Wolf took jobs where you had to push and shove. You imagine the thugs of high school all end up dead or in prison, but they don't. Most of them become salesmen — unsettled, belligerent, always needing to convince, to dominate. Civilized wolves. In the twenty years since high school, Wolf had sold appliances, real estate and insurance, all aggressively and well. Wolf chased money, often caught it, and just as often lost it. The hunt, the devouring, then back on the hunt. The restless cycle of risk and unquenchable appetite.

Now the two brothers stood staring at each other in the cold dawn of middle age, Harry a widower, and Wolf — what exactly? Harry sniffed at the air between them, an old habit, trying to take the measure of his alpha brother so that he might prepare an appropriate defensive posture. Wolf lit another cigarette. Harry waved away the smoke. "I'm going inside," he said, maneuvering past Wolf to unlock the front door. Harry hoped that when he turned to close the door, Wolf would be walking down the sidewalk and away.

Wolf followed him in and surveyed Harry's disheveled living room. "That Turk that cleaned for you," he said. "They deport her or what?"

Harry didn't answer. Why was Wolf here? Not to comfort, certainly.

Harry placed the plastic bag that had held Beth's ashes in a desk drawer in the den, for what reason, he did not know. To pull over his head one long night after a fifth or two of vodka and a bottle of sleeping pills? He eased the drawer closed and turned to his brother, who was shaking his head and pursing his lips.

"You back to work yet?" Wolf said.

"Tomorrow. Everything back to —" Harry choked on the next words "— normal tomorrow."

Wolf positioned himself in front of Harry and looked him in the eye with a sudden and dangerous focus Harry had seen too many times. "We need to talk," Wolf said.

Harry didn't meet that gaze, he never did. "I'm really tired. Can it wait?"

"No, because we have an appointment at ten in the city."

Harry gripped the back of a kitchen chair. "Oh?"

Wolf reached out to touch Harry's shoulder. Harry leaned back. Wolf's flick of a smile showed teeth as he let the hand drop. He shrugged. "Okay, obviously we're not exactly close. But we're brothers, Harry. And I always protected you."

"That's one way of looking at it."

"Hey. You ever get beat up in school? Ever? How many guys get to go through high school without getting smacked around?"

"Most, actually."

Wolf shook his head in pity. "You just don't get the world, Harry. You never have. You don't understand about pushing back. That's why I'm your big brother. To watch out for you because you don't know how to watch out for yourself."

"I've done all right."

Wolf let out a snort. "Yeah? I hate to be brutal here. But they just stole your life."

Harry inhaled sharply.

Wolf softened his tone, but only for effect. "Isn't that what happened? If you think about it?"

It was exactly what had happened. Harry could not have put it better. Life had been stolen from him.

"Beth dying the way she did," Wolf pressed. "We gotta do something about it. We gotta act."

Harry's stomach lurched. Wolf was about to complicate his life in some unstoppable way. The mighty force that was Wolf was about to unite with the staggering death of Beth. At ten this morning.

"Listen to me," Wolf said. "You're this, I don't know, this decent, quiet guy. A thinker, not a doer. You count trees. Harry — this is not a moment to count trees. Okay? This is a moment to take an ax and cut them the *fuck* down."

The ferocity of Wolf's words dazzled, like a blow to the head.

Expert salesman that he was, Wolf threw another changeup pitch, his voice coming over the plate soft and low. "What I'm saying is, in that quiet life of yours, amazingly, you managed to achieve one great thing. And it was called *Harry and Beth.*"

Harry sat down hard on a kitchen chair. Wolf saw the truth of it, with merciless clarity. Amazingly, Harry had achieved Beth. And without her — his one great thing — he was nothing.

Wolf circled behind the chair and leaned over his brother's shoulder. "Harry and Beth. Beth and Harry. And you know what? You're not going to believe this. But I wanted that, Harry. I wanted what you had. I wanted the great thing that you guys were. You guys were always there for each other."

Wolf and his three wretched marriages, doomed heir to his father's restless search for "something else." Wolf's domestic crime? Serial divorce.

But Harry? He had turned his own marriage into literal ashes.

"Wolf," he said. He fingered the hidden lottery ticket, opened his mouth, again ready to confess. But Wolf plowed over him.

"No kids, guess you were shooting blanks or something, but still, you and Beth were a *family.*"

Actually, it was Beth's hormone levels, but when they found out they couldn't have children, and then the failed attempts at the fertility clinic, Harry had been secretly relieved. His father's shadow was long — Harry was afraid of children. Afraid that he would fail them. It was enough that he had found the gumption to marry Beth. She was his family, his home, his everything. And he had swung a wrecking ball through it.

Wolf leaned even closer, his voice in Harry's ear. "They took away your life. They snatched away Harry Crane's life. They killed it."

Harry blinked and saw the demolition crane buckle, the steel beam twirling through the air. He jumped to his feet. "I'm really tired and —"

Wolf shot out a hand and gripped Harry's wrist like a pair of handcuffs. "We're gonna get them, Harry. We're gonna make them pay."

Wolf stepped back to let Harry out of the elevator first, holding the door open for him. Harry stared at the huge gold names on the burled walnut wall behind the pretty receptionist — *McWilliams, Torrey & Conwell* — each angular letter glowing powerfully as if forged from some fierce god's personal stash of lightning bolts.

The attorney's name was Jeremy Toland. He sat knee to knee with Harry, dangerous with empathy. Sitting in the background, Wolf seemed diminished in Toland's commanding presence.

"Tell me something wonderful about Beth, Harry," Toland said in a basso profundo voice so encompassing it seemed without a point of origin. The room itself was speaking to Harry.

He leaned back as Toland leaned forward.

"It's flooding over you, isn't it?" Toland said. "You are at this moment flooded with thoughts and images of Beth. Shall we run through a few? Beth's hair in the sunlight."

Light golden brown hair, Harry instantly thought, scented with honey-almond shampoo.

"Her laughter."

Constant, Harry thought. Like a meadowlark. And when she laughed it washed over you in glorious waves.

"How much she liked nature."

Loved nature. Trees. Grass. Crickets. Sunlight. Wind. Rain. Lions. Penguins. Mountains, valleys, deserts. Harry's mind racing. Sunset sunrise moonrise night day —

"Your twentieth wedding anniversary."

Harry almost fell off his chair.

Toland's eyes flared. "*Exactly,* Harry. Right? You were married only *fourteen* short years. They took Beth away from you in ways you can't even begin to describe. Well, *we* will certainly describe it to the jury, not that at this juncture and relative to what I'm hearing in a preliminary way in terms of OSHA citations and violations vis-à-vis Carlisle Demolition Company, do I believe it will ever come to that."

What? Harry thought. His eyes flicked toward Wolf, who gave him a nod and said, "He's saying it's an open and shut case."

"Nothing is open and shut," Toland said. "But yes, this is as open and shut as it gets. *Res ipsa loquitur.* Which is a legal term that defines this case in its purest sense, Harry. *Res ipsa loquitur* — the thing speaks for itself. Put simply, the harm would not have occurred absent someone's negligence. A fourteen-foot steel beam does not snap loose from the center of a demolition crane and hurtle into a beautiful human being. *Unless* someone failed to properly inspect said demolition crane. Or worse, *declined* to inspect said demolition crane."

Harry sat there, rigid.

Toland kept his gaze steady. "Now, Harry, in this office we do a terrible thing. We put a price on a loved one. Every second that you will never again enjoy with Beth, is priceless. We put a price on priceless. Carlisle Demolition Company and the City of Philadelphia — we will make. Them. Pay."

"You're goddamn right," Wolf whispered, behind Harry.

"Unfortunately, it can't be an eye for an eye, which in a perfect world is what we'd argue for," Toland added.

Toland's voice echoed inside Harry's head. He gripped the arms of his chair.

"You're pale, Harry." Toland hit a button on his desk and an assistant slid into the office with a glass of water and a napkin. She handed them to Harry and slid away again. The napkin was embossed with *McWilliams, Torrey & Conwell,* and in discreet print at the bottom, a toll-free number.

Harry gulped the water and mopped his forehead with the napkin. "Wolf, can't you take charge of this?"

Toland shook his leonine head. "No, he can't. Your brother's done a fine thing, guiding you to the best attorneys in Philadelphia. But Harry, we need *you,* legally and spiritually. There's a Zen quality to a lawsuit. I firmly believe that. For your grief to subside, you must transfer it to others. The defendants must directly feel your pain." Toland stood up, gripped Harry's shoulders and looked him in the eyes. "From you. Through me. To them. We're going to Zen the hell out of these bastards."

They were in Toland's office for another hour, but from that moment on the meeting, for Harry, was distant voices in a distant room. It was all a blur — the meeting, the arrival back home. When Wolf at last roared away in his car, Harry sat bolt upright from the living room sofa, lurched into the powder room and vomited, body and soul, into the swirling abyss of the toilet.

And so began Harry Crane's endless year.

3

The way Amanda Jeffers's endless year began? *Impossibly.*

Amanda stood at the kitchen sink rinsing her coffee mug, pondering the rules of life and death as she looked out the window at the line of sun-grazed morning trees dense at the end of the backyard. Amanda was a nurse, and therefore a philosopher. The woods are beautiful, she thought, but they are not without risk. Right now, someone out there among the trees was about to sustain a didn't-see-it-coming injury. A cut from a saw, a broken bone from a fall. Or maybe a young dairy farmer driving one of the gravel back roads that cut through the woods would glance down to check a text message, swerve his truck into a sugar maple and lump his forehead on the steering wheel. Yes, in the woods, on the twisting roads, in the pastures and out in the barns, business was starting to pick up.

Five days a week, Amanda worked in the ER of Susquehanna Hospital in the Endless Mountains, a stretch of the rolling, time-worn Appalachians in the far corner of northeast Pennsylvania where she'd lived all her life. Rural accidents and mishaps in the wild — that was the way of the world.

A kitchen chair creaked heavily behind her. The dry rush of cereal cascading into a bowl. The sound went on and on, half the box emptied. She smiled. Amanda was a clear-eyed and unswervingly practical woman who understood the indisputable rules of life and death. But she believed, absolutely, that they did not apply, could not apply, to her husband, Dean Jeffers. He was too big for mere rules.

Dean was six foot four and weighed 235 pounds. He could cut a cord of wood in an afternoon and raise the front of his pickup truck with his bare hands if it was stuck in the mud — at least it seemed possible. When he had repaired a tumbled-down section of the old stone wall along the perimeter of their backyard, he'd lifted bear-sized fieldstones.

Amanda's gaze moved from the trees to that rebuilt wall, sturdy and strong as Dean, clotted white with March snow. Behind her at the kitchen table, Dean poured cereal again. Shorter pour, smaller bowl. Oriana, their nine-year-old daughter, sitting down to breakfast.

"What do you see out there, hon?" came Dean's voice. "Anything good?"

Amanda started to turn toward him but a remembered moment caught her, a summer memory of Dean hot enough to melt the snow on that distant wall. Dean, wearing one of his ever-present red caps, but shirtless on a July day. Shoulders as broad as the sky.

"Come here and admire my damn wall!" he had called to them, sweaty and triumphant. Amanda and Oriana were on the deck scrubbing off the moss with bristle brushes where it grew thick on the steps and railing every year because the house was shaded by three enormous sugar maples. Dean wanted to cut them down, but they gave good sugar in late winter. "We aren't hurting for sugar maples around here, you know," he'd say. Always wanting to cut something down or build something up.

"Come on, come here!" he called again, his voice booming, even from a distance. It echoed off the barn.

Amanda's pleasures were uncomplicated. She walked behind him atop his rebuilt wall, eyeing the rippling muscles of his shoulders, growing aroused. She reached out and placed both hands on his shoulder blades. They were slick to the touch, which excited her further. In bed, she liked to feel the weight and heat of him, the steady slow beat of his mass.

Dean. The very definition of life.

Giving her coffee mug a final rinse, Amanda blushed — that she was having this memory with Oriana right there behind her at the kitchen table beside Dean. She glanced at her watch. Late!

"See you, guys," she said, grabbing her coat as she rushed past them. She paused to give her daughter a quick kiss on the head. She did not kiss Dean. She would save those kisses, and more, for tonight.

Four hours later, Amanda got the call.

Franny the ER clerk paged her to the nurses' station. Poking her head out of room 4, Amanda asked Franny to take a message. Amanda didn't have time for outside calls. But then she saw that Franny, ghostly white, was holding the phone at arm's length like it was dangerous.

"Amanda, it's for you," said Franny. "It's for *you.*"

Amanda instantly knew that somebody on the other end of that phone was about to tell her that Oriana or Dean was hurt. She hoped it was Dean, thinking like a nurse, pragmatically, that Dean's big body could absorb a wound. Then she was certain it was Dean because he worked with every known type of god-awful dangerous machine. In her mind she heard screeching lumber-mill saws and pounding quarry jackhammers. He must have injured his hand. Her thoughts were spinning, she couldn't remember — of her husband's three jobs, was this the day he was at the sawmill, or was he at Empett's quarry, or was he out on his tractor brush-hogging fields?

She grabbed the phone from Franny, who quickly stepped back. It was brush-hogging day. Amanda swallowed, thinking, His leg? The fields around here were hilly and filled with treacherous rock, so the tractor must have tipped and broken his leg.

Amanda realized how scared she was, because she had completely forgotten. Dean wasn't brush-hogging — the fields were under a foot of March snow. He was doing side work, plowing roads for the county today.

"This is Amanda," she said into the phone. Outside the hospital came the faint wail of an approaching siren.

Somebody on the other end of the phone coughed and in a frightened voice said, "Amanda, this is Ronnie." A long pause, Ronnie trying again. "Jesus, I don't know, I don't know. Amanda, I don't know how to *say* it."

Amanda closed her eyes. Shiftless Ronnie Wilmarth. I hold you personally responsible for the words you are about to speak, because you're a drunk and somehow you've gotten Dean hurt. "Ronnie, they're bringing him in, I hear the siren, I gotta go."

"No, wait, Amanda. He's still here. Dean's still right here. The EMTs are with him."

Not working *on* him. *With* him. Amanda looked around and saw that she was encircled by the other nurses and LPNs. She felt like a gored bull stumbling in a ring. "Which EMT unit is it, Ronnie?" Because the EMTs out of Harford didn't know what the hell they were doing, but the New Milford boys were good. The siren, closing in, became a scream, like in the medical thrillers she read. She'd always thought "scream" a melodramatic description of an ordinary sound, but now she understood. The screaming came up the highway.

"Did they stop the bleeding, Ronnie?" From what wound? A hand? An arm? Maybe Dean got out of his truck to pee and he slipped on the ice and broke his leg. *The EMTs are with him.*

Ronnie began to cry. "Amanda. Oh Amanda, Amanda."

"No!" Amanda dropped the phone, pushed through the white ring of nurses and ran to the ER entrance to meet the ambulance. The Harford EMTs did not at first understand her hysteria when they opened the doors for her, revealing an old woman who'd fallen in her bathroom and broken her hip.

Twenty minutes later, the New Milford crew brought Dean in. Not to the ER, there was no point, but to the hospital morgue. They stepped back as Amanda stared at her husband. There was not a mark on his beautiful bluish-white form. They hadn't even punctured a vein to put in an IV. He'd been dead two hours before the EMTs even arrived. Amanda did not break down again. She held herself together with a fearsome power.

"Get Ronnie," she said.

Ronnie came into the morgue, pale and shaky. He said it happened like this. He and Dean had been in their trucks doing the crisscross of back roads north of Mountain View High School, Ronnie plowing the upper road that went past Maplewood Cemetery, and Dean plowing the lower road along Martin's Creek. They were supposed to meet for lunch at Jim's Diner, but Dean didn't show up and didn't answer his cell phone, which could have just been the reception, always spotty in the valleys. Ronnie ate his lunch and got a hamburger to go and drove along the lower road looking for Dean's truck.

"When I found it, the driver door was open and the motor was running, but Dean wasn't nowhere around. Just his tracks in the snow," Ronnie said in a jittery whisper. He was scared because Dean was dead and Amanda with her thick blond hair and hazel eyes was so beautiful, but dangerous somehow too with her held-in grief. He really wanted a drink, but she made him tell his story right there in the morgue with Dean laid out on the stainless-steel table between them, his red cap at his side. Before Ronnie had entered the morgue, Amanda had combed Dean's wavy brown hair and placed a sheet halfway up his chest and arranged his big hands on top. She would not draw it over his face.

Ronnie couldn't look at Dean, and he couldn't look at Amanda, so he talked to the ceiling, which was low and oppressive, with the steam pipes overhead sighing like it was Dean trying to start up his breathing again.

Ronnie said, "Tracking his footprints in the snow, I had this bad feeling in my stomach, this awful feeling. I musta gone a mile, straight across Martin's Creek then through a patch of scrub woods, then up into the big field below Brian Taylor's place. And that's where he was, Amanda, that's where I found him, on his back in the middle of all that snow with his arms out at his sides."

Ronnie stopped. Amanda was staring straight at him, but she'd reached for Dean's big hand and was holding it. Ronnie was moved almost to tears, thinking how he'd seen them last August strolling hand in hand through the fun and noise of the Harford County Fair.

"Keep going, Ronnie," Amanda said.

Ronnie swallowed. "Like I said, his footprints just stopped, and there he was." Ronnie took a long breath and closed his eyes, seeing it. Trembling, he said, "Laying there in the snow, Amanda, his arms stretched wide like that, Dean looked like a kid, you know what I mean? Like a kid making a snow angel."

Amanda stared at him, then asked him to leave the room. When the morgue door clicked shut, Ronnie leaned against the tiled wall in the hallway and hugged himself as he listened to her muffled, unbearable sobs.

That beautiful, strange detail — snow angel — Ronnie repeated it over and over that night to Walter and Stu and Cliff and the rest of the regulars who sat on their red vinyl stools around the big oval varnished bar in Green Gables Tavern & Restaurant. Soon everyone sitting in the booths in the adjoining restaurant, and then in the blink-and-you-miss-'em towns along the curves of Route 11 and up its dirt road tributaries in the double-wide trailers scattered in the hills and the dairy farms down in the valleys, knew about Dean Jeffers dying like an angel.

At closing time, Ronnie didn't want to leave Green Gables, but Tom the bartender finally placed two hands on Ronnie's thin shoulders and guided him out the door. Ronnie was anxious about the snow, which for this night at least was inextricably linked to Mysterious Death. He tiptoed through the parking lot to his truck, afraid to plant his foot too heavily in the moon be-glittered stuff, as if it might do to him what it had done to Dean. He swerved his way up and down back roads to his little A-frame cabin deep in the woods and stumbled out of his truck. It was the last thing he remembered.

At dawn, he opened his eyes and saw bright sky through the high bare branches of the sugar maples. He sat up, teeth chattering and fingers blue. He had passed out in the snow but somehow didn't freeze to death. Squinting at the snowdrift in front of him, he gasped in amazement. A long tan-and-black feather stood on its tip in the snow like a quill balanced in an inkwell. A feather! Angel Dean had made a visitation and saved his life! Never mind that it was a turkey feather (but who could be certain, because the icy wind whipped it away into the woods) and never mind there were three-toed turkey footprints all around him in the snow. Ronnie had a fresh story to tell that night at Green Gables, and it earned him two free rounds of Genesee Cream Ale (they were out of Yuengling, his regular) and a shot of Mr. Jack Daniel's.

Dean as a snow angel was such a compelling and gentle image that when Amanda told Oriana about Dean, she used it. "The angels came for your father, do you understand what I'm saying, Oriana? Daddy died — we're not sure why yet. The doctors will find out. Daddy lay down in the field like a snow angel to greet the other angels who came for him." Really, it seemed the only way to explain the death of such a powerful, alive man as Dean. He'd been suddenly drawn to angel heaven because they needed him.

But as soon as she saw the look in Oriana's stunned eyes, Amanda regretted her words. It was right there, with that nonsense about angels, that the nine-year-old girl was lost to magical thoughts. Right there, her father was never quite dead for her, or he had died in a manner suggesting he was capable of reappearing in the same way that he left the earth, on wings. Amanda had given Oriana hope where there was no hope. That night, Oriana cried and cried, and Amanda thought, Good, cry yourself dry, sweetheart, that's the way. Thinking, *She understands.*

But the next morning, Oriana was not in bed beside Amanda. Amanda jumped up and searched the house, stopping cold in front of the big picture window in the kitchen. Outside, Oriana was lying on her back in a clean patch of snow making a snow angel.

My God, what have I done? Amanda thought.

No matter how she explained it or how

often, there was no reorienting Oriana. The autopsy revealed that Dean's right cerebral artery had burst. "Daddy was strong, but he had a tiny weak spot there was no way of knowing about," Amanda said. She took out an old nursing textbook and showed Oriana a drawing of the vasculature of the brain. "Right in there, that's the place, do you see?" Oriana nodding yes, but not allowing the medical facts to impede her father's imminent return as an angel.

It was all angels that first month, angel books and angels on the computer and angel stickers on her door. She's working it through, Amanda thought. This will pass. For the last days of winter and into the mountain spring, each time it snowed Oriana spent hours outside making snow angels until she was dazed with the cold. As the weeks went by, her belief that her father had died magically, and that he'd return in some equally magical way, drifted beyond angels. She began to immerse herself in fairy tales and elves and princesses, anything that opened the door between the real and the unreal so that Daddy, be-winged and aglow, might someday return through it.

4

Oriana had lost a book. She'd left a book behind in the forest. And not just any book. *It's very special,* Olive Perkins, the ancient librarian at the Pratt Public Library had told her. Somebody had made it by hand. When Olive gave it to Oriana, she almost couldn't let go of it. There was a look in the old woman's eyes Oriana had never seen before, a fleeting indescribable expression. Then Olive suddenly did the opposite, pushed *The Grum's Ledger* into the young girl's hands and moved her briskly toward the oak doors.

"But there's no due date," Oriana said. Olive still stamped her books the old-fashioned way, with a rubber stamp on the Date Due slip pasted on the last page. She was a tiny, bird-boned woman, but that stamp hit a book like John Henry's hammer.

"It's due when you're done with it, child," Olive said. She dropped her voice to a whisper. "And remember. You are my favorite reader, and now you are my most important secret keeper." The big library doors closed behind Oriana.

It was wonderful. A secret. Tell no one about *The Grum's Ledger.* Oriana loved how Olive trusted her. Most grownups don't know how to trust children.

And now it was lost. Of all the books to lose! Oriana hurried across her backyard toward the forest. Was it up in the birch tree where she often read? A little farther in on the old stone wall? Had she left it by the creek? And what did it mean? Because everything was a possible clue. A book, a special one, had been lost in the forest. Was it a test? You had to pay very close attention. Everything meant something. Something could mean everything.

"Oriana entered the forest," Oriana whispered to herself.

The word she used for the wooded acres behind her house was *forest.* Sometimes she underlined it in very light pencil in the books she borrowed from Pratt Public Library. *Forest.* In the year following her father's death, she had borrowed 112 books. Olive had to scour the county library system to keep up a fresh supply. Oriana didn't care that some of the fairy tales and fantasy books were too young for a ten-year-old and some too grownup. Every story had something to teach her. *Persevere against all obstacles. See what others can't see. Believe what no one else believes.* The best of the stories, the most important ones, took place in the forest.

"Oriana's Forest," she whispered.

"Don't go far," her mother called to her.

Oriana rolled her eyes. That was exactly what they said to you in the stories. *Don't go far into the forest, child.* And of course you went far. How could anything happen if you didn't go far? She felt the quick sting of tears. She'd lost the book. She despised tears. She swiped at her eyes and thrust out her jaw. *Persevere. See. Believe.*

She paused at the dark line of lichen-specked tree trunks at the forest's edge. Glancing back, Oriana could just see the big log house her father had built with his bare hands, and in the side yard her mother hanging a blue bedspread on the clothesline. Her mother's blond hair was blowing in the wind. Like mermaid hair, thought Oriana, tendrils of hair floating in the current. She couldn't remember the title of that one. Good pictures, but it was a sea story. Sea stories, sky stories, castle stories — she had to read them all, just in case, but they weren't as important as forest stories. Or stories that had creatures with wings. She had to find *The Grum's Ledger.* The grum lived in a forest.

A distant truck groaned up the big hill out on Route 11. Oriana raised a hand and waved to her mother and turned and faced the forest again. You knew when you entered the forest because the light changed and the sounds hushed in on you and everything disappeared: the house, your mother, the tree swing, the shed, the truck sounds.

Oriana crunched through the leaves and stepped across the rounded stones dotting a small creek. She walked past the raspy trunk of a tall white oak, brushing it with her hand as she glided by.

". . . half an hour," came her mother's faraway voice.

And then the light shifted and the sounds hushed. Oriana was in the forest.

Amanda collected the laundry flapping on the clothesline, watching as Oriana hopped across the creek. The cold April wind blowing east through the Endless Mountains had stiffened a towel, and when the icy corner whipped Amanda's cheek it stung. That was the cost of living in the Endless Mountains. Endless winters and springs that stung.

"Oriana, half an hour," she called. "Homework before supper." Amanda saw a flash of red sleeve as Oriana waved and disappeared into the woods. That red coat of hers — it stung, too. Oriana had to have it when they saw it on the rack at the Goodwill store last fall.

"If she wants to be Red Riding Hood, then let her be Red Riding Hood," said the therapist up in Montrose. Amanda had sought out a grief therapist for advice. Not for herself, but to discuss Oriana. "Two months from now," said the therapist, "it will be a different coat and a different story."

Well lady, thought Amanda, you said that in the fall and now it's spring. Same damn coat, same tromping off into the woods.

The woods, Amanda thought.

The woods that were sometimes full of hunters. Not huntsmen, like in *Little Red Riding Hood* or *Snow White,* real hunters, with real rifles. Hunters, and tree limbs that fell, and the abandoned quarry a half mile in with big slippery mounds of shale. Well. Amanda tried not to waste time fretting over such dangers. She would not baby Oriana just because things happened. And things did happen; Amanda knew the dangers of the world. But it was not the ordinary dangers of the woods that most worried her.

It was Oriana's consuming need to be in them.

And was Oriana, with all her fairy tale obsession, trying to be Little Red Riding Hood? Or was she wearing red because it had been Dean's favorite color? Red for Dean. It was so hard to figure out her complicated, grieving child.

Amanda squinted in the wind, then reflexively turned her mind as if it were a physical thing she could grab and point in another direction. *Supper.* What would they have for supper? It was a cold afternoon. She had two loaves of sourdough bread baking in the oven. Venison stew would be perfect. Stew and fresh hot bread.

She started across the backyard to the freezer in the garage. Suddenly remembered. They would *not* be eating the venison stew because last week, in one of Oriana's books, there had been an enchanted deer that turned into a woman in a long white dress.

"I don't eat deer meat anymore, Mom," Oriana had said, pushing away her slice of venison roast.

A million deer up here, more deer than oxygen, and now she won't eat venison. Great, Amanda thought, flipping on the garage light. An extra expense, now I'll have to buy more beef. That is, until she reads a story with enchanted cows in it, then there goes hamburgers and chili.

"*I'll* eat the stew then, and you can have grilled cheese," Amanda said out loud. She felt her skin flush. She tried hard not to be upset with Oriana. Amanda stared at the big Frigidaire chest freezer against the back wall of the garage. The heat in her face grew. But this time her daughter was not the cause — it was the thought of pulling the last bag of venison stew out of the freezer. The last of the stew from the last deer Dean had killed over a year ago now.

Amanda hesitated, then raised the heavy lid of the casket-sized freezer. She moved aside bags of frozen peas and wild blackberries, going deeper and deeper, starting to panic, pushing past the Popsicles and the cookie dough and the frost-hazed bags of cut corn. A bag fell to the garage floor and split open. Icy blueberries scattered like marbles.

There it was. On the very bottom, a frozen brown lump in a quart bag, the venison stew. She lifted it slowly into the dim light of the freezer lightbulb and saw in Dean's blocky handwriting, "3/7/2016 V. Stew," and gave a pained little gasp. The rock-hard bag may as well have been Dean's engraved tombstone, because he had died days after recording that date.

What do I do? she thought. Over the last year, with Oriana howling in protest, Amanda had given away her husband's boots and overalls and his arrows and two hunting bows. She had sold his big Stihl chain saw and his quarry tools and his beloved cherry red ATV, getting rid of thing after thing because they were just that, *things.* They were no good to her or Oriana, and they were no good to Dean because he was dead and buried.

It's just supper, Amanda thought, still gripping the bag. Food. A *thing.* She held the bag in her hand so long the frost on the bottom began to melt. A heavy drop of water formed, quivered and fell.

She tossed the bag back into the freezer, buried it beneath the other frosted bags and containers and slammed the lid shut. She leaned back, shivering in the cold, and looked out across the backyard and into the distant trees, the bare branches lit by the afternoon sun.

She pressed her lips together. Oriana, out there wandering among her trees. That's how Amanda perceived Oriana, as a wanderer through the forest of grief.

What of the long year of Amanda's own

grief? Well, what of it? There was no wandering, the line was straight. Dean was gone forever. Yes, she missed him, at times unbearably, but she would not indulge her sadness. Right from the beginning — at Dean's memorial service — even then she would not abide grief. When her mother said, "He was so strong," Amanda's reply was quick. "Not as strong as death, Mom," she said.

And when Pastor Jim said, "If I close my eyes I see him walking through this door. If it's hard for me, I know how hard it is for you and Oriana, Amanda."

Amanda was quiet a moment and then she spoke in an unwavering voice. "Open or closed, my eyes see an ordinary church door, Pastor Jim, which Dean is never walking through again, and I'm not going to spend one second wishing for it."

She squeezed Oriana's hand tight, knowing Oriana was staring at the church door, certain that her father might step from the shimmering magic light into the world again. Amanda would never admit that on some dawnless nights she wished just as hard as Oriana that Dean would come shimmering back to them. But she had to be solid as a rock. Solid and there for her daughter.

And there was a difference between grief

and fixation. Spring, summer, fall, winter and now spring again — and Oriana's hope for that shimmering door had never waned, never flagged. No, not *hope.* Obsession. Oriana in her dense and tangled forest.

"Yes, you're right, it is a kind of obsession, but it's not harmful, Amanda," that therapist had said. "It will take time and it will be uncomfortable. Oriana will go through phases."

"She's just in one phase," Amanda said. "She's stuck in the my-Daddy's-coming-back phase, doing everything normal, trying to trick me so I won't bother her about Dean. About what she knows is true. I got a little believer on my hands."

The therapist said, "She'll move on. And if she needs fantasy for now, even a little obsession, let her have it. Give it time. She's not you. She's Oriana."

"Okay, of course, I get that," Amanda said. "Still." She stared at the floor. "She's taking food to him now. Candy. Cookies. When she thinks I'm not looking, she'll slip something from the table into her pocket. She takes things from the pantry."

"Yes," the therapist said. "She'll do all sorts of things. It's a process."

"She leaves it for him. In the . . . woods."

"In case he visits when she's not there.

Amanda. Just call it the *forest.* Call it what you said she calls it. Don't let it get to you, that fairy tale word."

Amanda sighed and looked away. Oriana and her books. Olive Perkins at the library and now this therapist. Everybody with the make-believe.

"It's a good thing, Amanda. This is what fairy tales have always been for, to guide children through the scary parts of their lives. Oriana needs an explanation for why her father was taken from her. You said that the way Dean died seemed impossible. Imagine it through a child's eyes. A father is already a powerful figure, but Dean, he was special. He built your house at the edge of the forest, hunted with a bow and arrow, he was tall and strong and handsome — he was almost the hero of a fairy tale in real life, don't you see? A man like that can't die. Oriana's certain of it."

A man like that can't die. But he surely did, thought Amanda.

Oh, the convoluted conversations she and Oriana had. Over and over, Oriana molding the straightforward logic of death into the elaborate nonsense of fairy tale, and Amanda, as calmly as she was able, restating the facts — that Dean had an aneurysm and died, that he was in a grave they could see with their eyes, marked with a gravestone with his name spelled out in fresh-chiseled letters they could trace with their fingers.

They went to Maplewood Cemetery often, Amanda trying to cause the simple *truth* of it to sink in, immersing Oriana in the undeniable evidence of Dean gone. Oriana, always trying to outmaneuver her. Last October, perfect example. They were sitting beside Dean's grave. Oriana had picked up a maple leaf from the red and orange fall leaves scattered in the grass. She fluttered it about in the air like it was a bird or a butterfly.

"Mom," she said that day, her eyes intent on the leaf in imaginary flight, "you were almost right about Daddy turning into an angel."

Amanda inhaled sharply. "As soon as I said that, I took it back. You know I did," she said.

Oriana said, "The thing is, if he was an angel in the snow, he couldn't have left a print. Angels don't weigh anything, they don't have bodies. He's something else. Some kind of *real* animal. With wings." She picked up another leaf, one in each hand now. She danced them together like a pair of butterflies in a field. Or swallows swooping and chasing.

"Oriana."

"Wingèd," Oriana said.

"What?"

"He's *wingèd.*"

Amanda pressed her lips tight. Wingèd. Oriana pronouncing it in that way she transformed everything to her single purpose, turning a plain one-syllable word into a magical two syllables.

Her voice rising, Oriana said, "It happens, you know. It happens all the time. People get turned into other creatures all the time. You keep saying Daddy just fell back dead in the snow. But he didn't make a *dead* snow print. Something extra happened. Ronnie — he was right about the wing part, just not the angel part. Angels don't weigh anything. Pastor Jim said that angels are made of light and Heavenly Matter. Daddy was growing some *other* kind of wings in the snow. Real ones. Don't you see?"

Amanda kept her voice even and calm. "All he did was move his arms, Oriana. The wing imprint meant nothing. Why didn't he just vanish? Why did we have a body to bury?"

"He left it behind. Sometimes that happens. The new animal rises from the old body, like the pupa and the butterfly. It happens all kinds of ways."

"So, Daddy sprouted wings and turned into what, a butterfly?"

"Or a bat or even a Japanese beetle. Or an eagle, maybe. Or a hummingbird. Or maybe a moth. He's a wingèd creature of some kind."

"A moth. Okay. All right, so then why haven't we seen a six-foot-four moth buzzing around?"

Oriana reached over and pulled from her mother's knapsack the new book Olive had given Oriana that morning when they stopped at the library before coming to the cemetery, *The Frog Prince.* On the cover was an illustration of a frog wearing a crown sitting on a lily pad. She pointed, as if at a court document. "See how the frog's the right size? The human becomes a real animal, not a monster animal. Daddy would be the size of a real beetle or hummingbird."

Amanda said, "But the wings Daddy left in the snow were big."

"Because he was changing from big down to the right size. Metamorphosis."

Metamorphosis, thought Amanda. Oh great, Oriana scaffolding fantasy with science.

Oriana said, "And then whatever he became, he flew away into the forest. He's in the forest behind our house. He'd stay close. That's where he'd go."

"Oh Lord, Oriana."

"You should be *happy,* Mom! Daddy's not dead and he's not an angel made out of light. He's real, and he's wingèd and we can find him. But first we'll have to figure out what *kind* of wingèd animal he is."

Amanda felt light-headed and sick. Oriana, wild in her forest. She was truly her father's child. Dean, in his way, had been a wild creature of the deep woods. Bow hunting, trout fishing along the hidden, shaded banks of Meshoppen Creek, long hikes until after dark — he could go anywhere in the Endless Mountains and return home as if he'd left a trail of bread crumbs. Where else would the enchanted woodsman return to Oriana, but in the forest? And Oriana had her father's brute patience. Dean could build a wall stone by slow stone, or target shoot until he hit the bull's-eye five times in a row even if it took all afternoon. Oriana would search the forest of the Endless Mountains for a sign of him . . . endlessly.

When Amanda had told the therapist about this new phase, metamorphosis, the therapist said, "It's all good, this talk of transformation. Her thoughts are evolving, moving forward."

Then the therapist made a mistake. "What about your grief, Amanda? We never talk about you." That was the last visit to the damn therapist.

Amanda looked at her watch. Then into the woods, scanning for a flash of red coat. But Oriana would be too far in to see. Always deep in, hiding food, searching for winged Dean. *Wingèd.*

Amanda chopped wood. Stacked it. Looked at her watch again. And at the woods.

Where are you, Oriana? A half hour, that was the deal.

Amanda started across the backyard. When she reached the old stone wall that Dean had rebuilt, she paused to place her hand on it. It's something she always did. Touched the wall. And always, at the electric moment of contact, the immutable memory was conjured: Dean shirtless. July heat. Broad shoulders glistening.

She closed her eyes.

Amanda's grief? What she did not tell the therapist that day? Here was her grief. This wall. This wall was Dean. And the log house behind her. And the venison stew in the freezer — all these things were him. How could she explain that to some stranger?

That what she missed most of all was Dean's physical, solid presence. That Dean had been so physically *present*. That his spirit was always here in some earthly object. He was always here and never here.

Blushing with need, Amanda reached into her pocket for her phone and texted Cliff Blair. Let's get together tomorrow. She wanted Cliff right now, but it would have to wait. Oriana had been gone for almost an hour. There would be tears and nonsense and complicated explanations. She turned to the trees.

"Why do you make this so hard, Oriana?" she said as she stepped across the creek and marched into the forest to find her daughter. "Why does it always have to be so damn hard?"

5

One year after Beth died, Harry received a phone call from God.

One year had passed, four gray, indistinguishable seasons, and Harry had missed not a single day of work, because what was he going to do at home? Home: the place where he ate peanut butter on stale crackers and fell asleep in the wingback chair beside the fireplace that still contained the half-charred log that Beth had tossed onto the grate the night before she was killed. Harry would lurch awake, rise stiffly, shower or not shower and drive to work before dawn.

Really, was there a better way to punish himself? He would work for the Forest Service until he was sixty-five. No, the way the world was going they'd keep raising the age of retirement — he'd work until he was seventy, eighty, ninety. Perfect. Decade upon decade, clacking away on his keyboard until his heart sputtered out, his corpse sitting there for years, no one noticing the gnarled finger frozen above the delete key.

Sometimes he'd screw up and it would be a Saturday or Sunday. Didn't matter. He'd pull into the parking lot of the suburban headquarters of the Northern Research Station of the USDA Forest Service, park in the paved-over spot where the eastern hemlock had once stood, lug himself up the back stairwell to the third floor, then drop into his chair like a sack of sand and start right in on the reports: rangeland management, forest resource utilization, sustainable harvest, regulatory policy, ecoregional protocol monitoring. He took on all the worst assignments, the deadliest of the deadly dull, day in and day out, rolling the bureaucratic shit ball uphill like a Saharan dung beetle.

Even Bob Jackson, who dodged, whined, griped and shirked his way through every workday, felt a smirking pity whenever he emailed Harry a huge batch of files or plopped a fresh stack of fat folders onto his desk.

"Christ, Harry, you're allowed to, like, get up and take a leak once in a while, you know." Bob bit off a sliver of fingernail and swallowed it like an egret gulping a minnow.

How pathetic to be pitied by Bob Jackson, a creature who chewed his nails to slimy nubs, picked his nose with the insouciance of a three-year-old and used spit to finger-smooth the four hairs of his comb-over. But the life-form that was Bob no longer rankled Harry, nor did Harry notice the widening ring of cubicles around him that had gone vacant as his fellow workers jockeyed for less psychologically intense office real estate. Who wanted to sit near a black hole, to be vortexed into that? Sure, the guy's wife had died in a spectacular freak accident but, *yikes.* And although no one actually said it — the upside? Shell-shocked Harry Crane was a bottomless dumpster for crappy assignments. Forest initiatives, SOPA reports? NFS studies, FSI summaries, process predicament reviews? Turf 'em to The Widower!

Harry's relentless dedication impressed his boss, Irv Mickler, who promoted him from a GS 12 to a GS 13. Over the thirty-eight years of his own government career, Irv had sacrificed a not inconsiderable portion of his mind to the intricate convolutions of USDA red tape and most of his eyesight to its small print, so he understood the value of hard work.

Irv blinked behind thick glasses, leaning in for a long squint at Harry's ID badge.

Harry could see Irv's dry, pale lips moving as he read. Irv looked up. "So. Harry Crane. You're certainly the engine that keeps this office forward-moving. Harry. Crane."

Irv reached out to pat Harry's shoulder but stopped a millimeter short. Even addled and half-blind, Irv could perceive Harry's consumingly desolate aura. Irv drew back and cleared his throat.

"I should get back to work," Harry said.

"Yes, right, good idea," Irv replied, leaning out of his doorway to watch until Harry was safely out of sight.

Harry ate lunch at his desk (if he ate at all), worked late and, on occasion, if the cleaning crew didn't shoo him out, slept in his chair. Chairs were good, beds were bad. Bed: the place where Beth was most dreadfully absent. Alone in the office at night, he'd climb up on his desk and stare out over the sea of cubicles, empty white graves stretching into the black beyond.

Then, one blustery early April morning, his cell phone rang. Well, not rang, exactly. As a joke, a few years ago, Beth had snuck a novelty ringtone onto his phone — the sound of a large tree falling to the forest floor.

"Hello?" he said, picking up on the third fall.

"Harry Crane!" boomed the voice of God in his ear.

For who but God spoke at that volume and with such heart-stopping authority?

"Yes, sir?" Harry whispered.

"Harry, speak up. You there?"

Oh, Harry thought, not God, but His super-aggressive lieutenant, Jeremy Toland. Once a month for the last year, Toland called with updates Harry did not wish to hear. He never gave Toland a thought, except during these brief phone calls, never seriously contemplated where all that legal effort might lead. Harry didn't care. The outcome of the lawsuit would not affect him one way or the other. But today there was something extra in Toland's voice, a powerful mix of testosterone and adrenaline. Harry's body began to tingle. "Yes, I'm here," he said.

On Toland's end, a long suck of breath like an approaching tornado takes just before it explodes the windows out of your house. "Give me a 'J,' Harry!" yelled Toland, like an insane cheerleader.

"J?" repeated a stupefied Harry.

"Now give me an A-C-K! And what's that spell? What's that spell?!"

"Jack?" said Harry in a faraway voice. Sweat prickled, his heart accelerated.

"That's right! *Jack!* As in jackpot, Harry! Never, my friend, never ever have we had a defendant in a wrongful death case settle so quickly. This could've gone on for years. For decades! But these pricks were multiple violators, and we had 'em." Toland chortled and growled, "We had Carlisle Demolition by the *balls,* baby, and we squeezed until the bastards said ouch."

Harry winced.

"Oh yes," roared Toland. "We seized 'em and squeezed 'em to the tune of — okay, remember our first meeting when I told you the average award for wrongful death in Pennsylvania is four-point-two million dollars? You ready, Harry? One minute ago, Carlisle Demolition settled for seven million unprecedented dollars!"

Harry left his body and returned to it, the atoms of his brain short-circuited as if struck by lightning. Seemingly on its own, Harry's left hand withdrew the wallet from his back pocket. His fingers groped for the faded lottery ticket inside, the irrefutable evidence of his unforgivable sin.

Toland kept talking, the echoey cascade of words like coins regurgitated from a slot machine. "Of course, this doesn't bring dear Beth back, but I'm telling you, my friend, it's the next best thing. This is her gift to you. From the Other Side, Beth is saying, 'Harry, your life begins again right now. The past is the past, move on, I release you. And I bless your future with this financial windfall!' "

Harry hung up on Toland and held the lottery ticket out in front of him with both hands like Lady Macbeth gripping her dagger. Working at the Forest Service had not been the punishment but only Limbo. Now he grasped why he had allowed the lawsuit to go forward: to deliver absolute guilt. He could never tell himself, *At least I didn't buy a winning ticket that day. At least, there is that.* Because he *had* won. The jackpot just took a little longer to arrive, that's all. Here it was, his millions. It was official, unequivocal: he had given his Beth away for a bag of money. *Jackpot, Harry!*

Suspended in an awful and unnatural calm, Harry stepped out of his cubicle into the cramped aisle. He turned in a slow 360. He heard something, coming from deep within the endless forest of cubicles. Not the hum of computers and printers but the whisper of leaves. *Trees,* he thought.

Trees.

To the forest and the trees.

In a daze, he drifted through the office and away, beckoned by the scent of pine trees and oaks and the distant rustle of leaves in the wind. Outside in the parking lot, Harry walked across the asphalt grave where the eastern hemlock had once stood, got into his car and drove away from the treeless, soul-sucking suburban headquarters of the Northern Research Station of the USDA Forest Service.

Jackpot, Harry!

He didn't choose the roads, the roads chose him, guided him to the Pennsylvania Turnpike. Pointed him north. The outer suburbs of Philadelphia vanished as if plucked away by a great unseen hand and bare trees rose and grew dense along either side of the highway. American larch. His eyes flicked and narrowed as he gauged the shape and possibility of each one. White oak. Sycamore. Honey locust.

He reached the northeast corner of Pennsylvania, the center of the secondary-growth hardwood forests of the Endless Mountains. He had managed this stretch of the Appalachians by computer for over a decade. Of course he would end up here. Treeless words that had crowded his brain for too long — *forest resource utilization, sustainable harvest, inventory and analysis, development and evaluation* — receded.

"Aspen. Birch. Black locust," said Harry,

taking in the deepening forest. "Fire cherry. Pignut hickory. Shagbark hickory." Fire, pignut, shagbark, the old, familiar names summoning the woodland sanctuary of his childhood, when he climbed high up in the branches of the giant beech in his front yard and imagined the trees going on forever in all directions, and he safely in the center. His shaded escape, the forest he had spent a lifetime trying to reach.

North of Scranton, the low-fuel warning flashed at him and he took the next exit, a two-lane state road. He stopped at a ramshackle country hardware store and bought fifteen feet of blue nylon rope, paid and walked away. The clerk ran after him with his change. When the clerk went back into the store, Harry let the meaningless coins slide from his hand onto the blacktop.

He continued along the rural road, driving up and down the rolling hills, his car like an unmoored boat bobbing on the waves. At the top of a high hill he came to a gravel crossroad marked by a faded street sign perched atop a rusty pole poking out of the undergrowth. A single ray of afternoon sun touched the sign, setting it aglow. Harry hit the brakes. *Maple Road.* They were everywhere, a crowded forest of saplings and towering mature trees, rooted fast to the rolling topography, the leafless early spring limbs majestic against the April sky. Sugar maples. *Acer saccharum.*

"Acer saccharum," Harry said, the botanical Latin uttered aloud sounding like an incantation. A requiem. *Saccharum, saccharum, Acer saccharum.*

He pulled onto the gravel road. There was a two-story log frame house set deep in the trees, but after that no other houses. It was all trees now, crowded so thickly along the road they formed a tunnel, the lower branches scratching like fingernails across the roof of his car. On the left side of the road — he almost drove right by it — a sudden opening in the foliage. The overgrown entrance to an abandoned quarry? An old lumber road? Compelled, Harry cut the steering wheel hard and squeezed onto the worn wheel ruts, bouncing along until the wild rhododendron and thick mountain laurel stopped him a half mile in.

He got out of the car, slung the coil of rope over his shoulder and walked into the forest. Cold dry leaves crunched beneath his feet. He didn't feel the cold, didn't feel anything but the presence of the sugar maples. As he trudged forward, brushing his fingers against the wide, furrowed trunks, he raised his eyes to the tangle of overhead branches. Transfixed by the tree canopy and the infinite beckoning blue of the afternoon sky, he smacked into a waist-high stone wall, folding over it with a surprised grunt.

He straightened and stepped back. The wall was about three feet high and ten feet long, the last remains of an old homestead. The rest of the wall had fallen long ago, now just a tumble of moss-covered rocks that snaked through the tree trunks into the distance. An immense sugar maple had pushed its heavy roots in among the rocks at the base of the wall. It would not be long before the roots toppled it.

The forest, thought Harry, takes everything.

He placed his hand on the wall and looked up into the maple tree. And there it was, thick and strong — the branch he'd been searching for. That this one section of stone wall was still standing. That it was exactly the right height to reach the branch. The perfect and terrible inevitability of it.

He climbed onto the wall and set to work with the rope, amazed to see himself tying such a complicated knot. He had forgotten he knew how. Who had taught him? His brother, of course, Harry remembering the long ago moment behind the garage when they were kids, Wolf showing him how to tie a hangman's noose. Wolf knowing such things, privy to the darker arts. With a grin telling Harry, "It might come in handy someday. You never know, right?" His big brother looking out for him.

Harry completed the noose and reached up and tied the other end of the rope to the tree branch. The noose dangled and swayed in the mountain wind. He reached out and took hold of it again and slipped it over his head. A hangman's noose, a sugar maple, a stone wall: Harry Crane on his forest gallows. He took the lottery ticket out of his wallet. Let the wallet drop from his hand. It bounced off the wall and fell to the ground.

Harry gripped the lottery ticket. In his mind, he heard his sentence pronounced: *Condemned bureaucrat. Cowardly husband. Buyer of lottery tickets. From this limb will you hang; and the flesh will fall from your bones, and your bones will molder and turn to dust, and thus will you be scattered and lost forever.*

Wolf's voice suddenly cutting in. *"Scattered? You tossed Beth's ashes like fucking confetti!"*

Harry tightened the noose, his body shaking, the self-damning chatter in his head crazy and nonstop. *All you had to do was take her hand. But you didn't. You didn't take her hand, Harry. Wait here, you said, and crossed the street. Abandoned her. And the crane crashed down. So do it, Harry. Turn out your lights, Harry. Hurry Harry, hurry, do it! Now!*

Harry opened his hand and let the ticket flutter away. He extended his right foot out over the abyss. Froze.

Hey, asshole in the tree. Jump! Again Wolf's voice broke in, like he was right out there among the trees somewhere. Harry twisted his head in the noose, the rough rope digging into his skin as he looked around for his brother. He saw Wolf dart between the tree trunks. But that was impossible, Wolf wasn't really there. Go away, Wolf, you are not there. No one is there.

Harry tensed his body for the jump and lifted his eyes skyward, the final gesture of all who find themselves with a noose around their necks. Craning their doomed necks for that one last look. And in that very last second, Harry saw something — a glint of gold in a knothole just above the branch where he had tied the rope. He squinted. It was a small, rectangular golden object with writing on it.

Wait a minute, he thought. No, that's impossible. A mini Snickers?

And Harry knew the candy bar wasn't real, that it was only one last torture of the mind. A mini Snickers like the one Beth tried to hand him that day on Market Street. It wasn't there, but he reached for it, as if Beth was giving him another chance, handing it to him one more time so that he might repeat the moment, but alter the fatal outcome, stop the catastrophe of that day by taking hold of the candy, and her.

Redemption tucked into the knothole of a tree. It was not really there, but he reached, and in the reaching two things happened. For a split second, he touched an actual mini Snickers with the tips of his fingers. He heard the plastic crinkle of the golden wrapper, felt the cold hard little piece of chocolate within. It was real! But it didn't matter. Reaching, he slipped on the mossy stones.

Harry windmilled his arms, fought to regain his balance. But off the wall he went. He whipped both hands over his head and grabbed the rope just before it snapped taut, the pain in his shoulders instant and searing as he swung out from the wall. Flailing legs, slipping hands, the door to Eternity opening — and one final vision — a pair of great angel wings unfolding inches from his face, followed by one final physical sensation — feathers brushing his cheeks, his eyes closing at the touch.

Then *crack!* His neck snapped.

No.

No!

No, not his neck — but the branch snapping off the tree. The rope went slack as Harry dropped kicking and thrashing to the ground. He landed on his ass, the force of the fall throwing his head backward against the base of the stone wall, hard enough to fracture his skull. A second chance at death.

He saw a flash of golden stars that turned into a galaxy of mini Snickers twinkling and fading into darkness.

His eyes fluttered open.

Closed.

Opened again.

He lay against the base of the wall staring up at the sky, the noose still around his neck, the rope tangled in the tree branch that lay beside him in pieces. His eyes focused, and he saw a large hawk rising through the treetops. Not angel-winged Death — a red-tailed *hawk.* Harry felt the otherworldly pull of the great bird in flight, and in the next instant he felt the equal pull of gravity and the earthly fact of himself. His back ached and his head was killing him. He groaned and touched the back of his skull. Lump, no blood.

Exploring further, his fingers brushed against something flat and smooth that was not stone. He went up on an elbow and turned. It was an old book, and it had saved his head from splitting open on the wall like a dropped watermelon. He held the book, leaned back against the wall and stared into the forest.

He saw something.

Then he saw *a lot* of somethings.

"Holy shit," he said.

In his dazed march through the forest, searching for the perfect tree from which to hang himself, he had not noticed. It was not just the one mini Snickers in a knothole. There was candy *everywhere.* On top of tree stumps. Balanced on branches. Dangling from bushes. Three Musketeers, Hershey Bars, Skittles. And juice pouches, too. And Ziploc snack bags filled with cookies. Much of it was weathered and gnawed on by animals. He squinted at several colorful dots pressed into the craggy bark of a nearby white pine — Peanut M&M's.

But before he could process any of it — book, hawk, candy — another element entered his consciousness: people. On the other side of the wall, voices and footsteps, approaching fast. He scrunched against the wall, yanked the noose from around his neck, and stuffed it in among the rocks and leaves.

The hawk circled directly overhead, around and around the treetops, as if it had laid claim to Harry.

While Harry had been atop the wall busy failing to hang himself, Amanda and Oriana were nearby, making their way through the forest in fits and starts, arguing heatedly. They were not walking. They were stomping. It was a good thing there were a lot of thick tree trunks separating them as they stomped along.

"I didn't know I was gone so long, okay?" shouted Oriana as she passed a white oak. She whapped the trunk with her hand. Glared at her mother.

"You knew," Amanda shouted back at her. Amanda bumped a slender quaking aspen. It dropped a shower of dry yellow leaves in surrender to her anger.

They came to a clearing and faced each other. Circled like sumo wrestlers, eyes narrowing darkly, opponents taking measure.

"We need to get some things straight, young lady," said Amanda.

"I know what you're going to say," said Oriana. "You're going to say I shouldn't steal food and hide it in the woods."

"That's not what I was going to say. But that's correct, you should not steal food."

"It's not stealing. It's giving my portion away."

"You're not giving it away. You're wasting it. You're throwing away *my* money."

They circled.

"And that's *not* what I'm angry about," said Amanda.

"That I lost the library book? I told you I'd find it."

"Did you find it?"

"Not yet."

"Well, that's not what I'm angry about," said Amanda, in a very careful tone.

"So being late for my homework? It's just some math problems. They're easy."

Amanda shook her head. "That's not it. That's not what I'm angry about, Oriana."

Uh-oh. Oriana looked at her mother's face. Amanda's cheeks were flushed. Mom was always under control. But at the moment, she looked dangerous. Oriana held her ground. "Then what terrible, horrible thing did I do exactly?"

The world around them seemed to go suddenly still. The trees held their breath.

Amanda erupted. "It's not one thing, it's *everything*! It's all of it, Oriana! I'm sick of this forest. That you think something big is going to happen out here. Some big, huge magical Daddy event. I'm sick of it!"

"I didn't say what *size* it was."

"Don't you mess with me! It's not the size. It's the *magic.* It's your brain twenty-four hours a day on a nonstop diet of hidden candy and fairy tale crap and forests."

Oriana said nothing. They continued to circle — two warriors fighting an ancient battle — but Amanda was slowly narrowing the circle. She was poised to strike.

"Look around you," she said. "Okay? Look, Oriana. With your two eyes, look. You know what's in these woods? In this enchanted forest of yours? Trees. That's it. Ordinary animals, ordinary bushes and ordinary damn trees!"

Oriana muttered something under her breath. Not muttered. *Incanted.*

The rising red in Amanda's cheeks matched the red of Oriana's jacket. "What did you just say?" But she knew. They both knew. Exactly the words Oriana had said.

Oriana repeated them. "Persevere. See. Believe."

Words to piss off her mother. The little chant, as if Oriana was casting a spell. Words that were a magical defiance.

And, unbelievably, Oriana suddenly said

one *more* word. The one that was absolutely guaranteed to explode her mother's brain. The one with two syllables.

"Wingèd," whispered Oriana. But not to Amanda. To the sky. Because Oriana was looking up.

Amanda was about to pounce, to sweep up her child and carry her forcibly out of the forest and back to the house, where there would be a time-out to end all time-outs. But before she could move a muscle, a large red-tailed hawk swooped low over their heads. Wing shadow, a thumping feathery whoosh of air. Amanda ducked.

But Oriana took off after it. The hawk disappeared into the woods.

Amanda stood and turned as Oriana crossed the clearing — and stopped suddenly at the edge of the woods.

Somebody in the woods cried out. A tree limb snapped.

Amanda ran up behind Oriana, drew her close and peered into a dense stand of sugar maples. She took in details . . .

. . . a section of old stone wall with a broken tree branch draped over it.

. . . an old sugar maple beginning to drip clear sap from a large scar.

. . . from the other side of the wall — a heavy rustling in the dry leaves.

Amanda stepped protectively in front of her daughter. "Hello?" she called out. Her eyes went to an object lying on the ground. A wallet. She picked it up.

Oriana saw something, too, fluttering in the leaves. She reached down and picked up a small, white rectangle of paper. A lottery ticket. She glanced at her mother who was busy with the wallet.

Amanda examined a photo ID card. Stamped in big black letters across the top were the words: *US DEPT OF AGRICULTURE.* And below that: *Forest Service.*

A groan from the other side of the wall. The man on the ID card rose into view.

6

Banged up and woozy, Harry stood before them, holding the book.

Oriana stared at him. Harry stared back. Her eyes flicked to the book. His eyes flicked to the lottery ticket. She closed her fingers over it, looked up at the red-tailed hawk circling overhead, then at Harry again. He could feel her connecting the strange dots — hawk, lottery ticket, book — arranging all of it into something very important. He had never seen such focus, such intensity in a child's face.

Now Harry's eyes went to the young girl's . . . mother? Yes, they had the same blond hair, the same determined faces. The mother was tall, and she looked powerful. And for that matter, the girl looked powerful, too. No, *wild.* There was a wildness in these two. Speak to them, thought Harry. Say something. In case they are about to pounce. They looked like pouncers.

He cleared his throat — understandably quite sore — and said, "Snickers." He raised his arm and pointed at the knothole just above the dripping scar on the sugar maple. Glittering in the sun, the gold wrapper beckoned. "I climbed up on the wall. Slipped. Grabbed the branch . . ." He shrugged, chagrined. "Got a weakness for Snickers."

"Oh my God," Amanda said under her breath, processing. This man — she glanced at the ID again: *Harold F. Crane* — worked for the Forest Service and this land, this forest, was under his protection. These ten thousand acres behind their house, which Oriana spent so many hours in, was a national wilderness tract owned by the federal government. In all her years, Amanda had never seen an employee — agent? — of the government out here. And that the very first one she did meet got hurt by one of Oriana's Snickers . . .

She shot a look at Oriana. "You are in such trouble," Amanda growled.

Harry was swaying on his feet. Amanda vaulted over the broken wall and took hold of him. He looked at her, a little dreamily. Blinked.

"My name's Amanda Jeffers, I'm a nurse,"

she said. "When you fell, did you hit your head?"

Harry reached past Amanda and plucked a Peanut M&M from the bark of the white pine. "Have I landed in Candy Land?"

"I have that game!" Oriana said. She joined them on Harry's side of the wall.

Amanda said to Harry, "I'm sorry, my daughter — it's hard to explain — she kind of feeds the animals."

"Not animals," Oriana said. "It's for —"

"Oriana!" Amanda cut in.

Harry looked from frowning mother to frowning daughter. Time to change the subject. He raised the book. "I found this." He had not really looked at it before. It was an old account ledger from a business or a bank. But someone had altered it. The word *Ledger* was embossed in the soft, faded cover, but the words *The Grum's* had been hand-painted above it in gold. *The Grum's Ledger.*

"Odd book," he said.

"All she reads are odd books," Amanda said.

Oriana nodded. "I'm a reader."

Again, Harry looked at the strange hand-made book, looked at the candy all around him in the trees. Looked at the little girl. "Odd forest," he said.

Oriana nodded even harder.

Amanda stepped between them. "No, no, this is a very *normal* forest. You've bumped your head."

Harry suddenly noticed several inches of the bright blue nylon noose sticking out of the leaves about a foot from where Amanda was standing. The girl, absolutely attuned to him, read the alarm on his face and looked down and saw the rope, too. With the tip of her sneaker, she nudged it deeper into the leaves.

In the same moment, Harry staggered, theatrically, away from the wall. Amanda hurried after him and caught him in her arms. Looking past Amanda, Harry gauged Oriana. Now he knew which one of these two females presented the most danger. He was not sure what the danger *was* exactly, but something way out of his realm of experience was radiating off this little girl.

"Hold on, I have you," said Amanda.

Harry dropped *The Grum's Ledger,* on purpose, as if to break the electric connection between himself and the girl. Oriana scooped it up. She clutched the book, the mother clutched Harry — but it was definitely the girl who had a tighter grip on him.

Amanda took Harry's head in both hands, searched her fingers through his scalp. He closed his eyes. "You have a big lump back there," she said. While his eyes were shut, Amanda quickly studied him. Not a bad face . . . for a federal bureaucrat. Unhealthy, of course. Skin pale from too many hours beneath fluorescent lights. Nice build, but not enough muscle. Again, a side effect of bureaucracy. What he needed was a little mountain sunlight and some meat and potatoes. Not an offer, merely an observation. He winced when her fingers moved across the lump again. It was a large one. If this was Ronnie or Cliff, with their dense skulls, the lump would be nothing to worry about. As her fingers left his scalp, she thought, Good, thick hair. That, too, merely a clinical observation.

Harry opened his eyes, startled that she was leaning so close. "I'm okay," he said.

"Nope. You need to go to the ER."

Harry shook his head. "No, I don't." He did not want to leave this forest. He had come here for something. And he was beginning to think it was not suicide. He had to figure this out. He felt very alert and at the same time fuzzy-headed. And this mother and daughter were very distracting.

"Head wounds are not a joke," Amanda said.

"Yes. No. Right."

"If it's a *concussion,* Mr. Crane, I will put you over my shoulder if I have to and take you to the ER."

Harry looked at her. Excuse me? "Isn't there a test? Don't I have to fail a test first? The neuro test? Before you sling me over your shoulder?"

"You've banged your head before?"

"When I was nine. I fell out of the tree in my front yard. A *Fagus grandifolia.* That's botanical Latin for American beech." Maybe if he was very precise, Amanda the nurse would leave him be.

But on the words *American beech,* Oriana cocked her head. Now what? thought Harry. If she stared any harder at him, she'd bore holes through him. She was about to say something.

But Amanda spoke first. "Who's the president of the United States?"

"James Buchanan," Harry said.

Amanda looked at him.

"That was a *joke.*"

"I don't do jokes," Amanda said.

Oriana watched this man taking on her mother. If that's what he was doing. Whatever was happening, it was refreshing not to be the one in trouble.

"See, the joke is, this is *Pennsylvania,*" Harry said. "James Buchanan was the only president born in Pennsylvania."

"I'm still not laughing."

He really did not want to be taken from these woods. That feeling was turning rapidly into a certainty. A kind of *desperate* certainty. "Penn's . . . sylvania," he murmured.

"You're repeating yourself," Amanda said. Her grip like a vise.

"No, no. *Pennsylvania* means *Penn's woods.* After William Penn, the colonial Quaker guy? And, well, if you think about it, since I work for the Forest Service, and I manage this land, in a way these are *my* woods now."

To Amanda, it was the babble of a man with a concussion.

But to Harry, it was pure revelation. He went pale. "My woods," he said. Because *that's* what was going on. He suddenly understood what this place was, these woods, this specific forest. The wind in the treetops became Beth's voice, whispering. Harry nodded and said the words aloud. "Harry's Trees."

"What?" Amanda said.

"This is Harry's Trees. This place."

"No way," Oriana said. "Wrong. This is Oriana's Forest."

Amanda looked from Harry to Oriana,

and back. She was having her own epiphany. "Say it again," she said to Harry. "What you just said."

"Harry's Trees."

Amanda released him and stepped over to the stone wall, where she'd placed his wallet. She held his ID card out to Oriana. "Meet Harold F. Crane —"

"Harry," Harry said.

"*Harry* Crane. Of the Forest Service. He owns these trees."

"Not owns," he said. "Manages."

"Right. He was out here managing his trees, Oriana."

Perfect! thought Harry. Yes. That's what he was doing out here. Not hanging himself from a sugar maple, but managing his trees. He unleashed the bureaucratic half of his brain. "Rangeland management, forest resource utilization, sustainable harvest, inventory and analysis —"

"Dull, government stuff," Amanda said, cutting him off, a little taken aback by the torrent she had incited.

"Incredibly dull," Harry said. "But that's what I'm up to out here. That's what I do for a living. Boring, unexciting tree stuff."

Oriana arched an eyebrow. Harry avoided her penetrating gaze.

"So, Mr. Crane, let me ask you something," Amanda said. "Other than the large amount of stolen candy and cookies out here, is there anything out of the ordinary about this forest? In your professional opinion — is this in any way an *enchanted* forest?"

What did that question even mean? His head was throbbing. Which he would not admit to this nurse. And . . . wait. Out of the corner of his eye — flashes of light. He must have hit his head hard, because this light he was suddenly seeing was incredibly weird.

"Mom. *Mom,*" said Oriana.

Harry blinked. What the hell? In the distance, multicolored beams of light shot through the forest. Either this was a *very* enchanted forest, or he was dying from a concussion.

"Mom! He sees it!"

Harry broke into a run toward the light.

Amanda didn't react quickly enough. She grabbed for him, but missed. "Goddamn it," she sputtered. Because she'd forgotten. She'd forgotten all about it.

Harry wove in and out of the trees toward the source of the light that was bouncing crazily off branches and tree trunks and rhododendron. Amanda and Oriana were right behind him. Five hundred yards from the wall, where the forest of sugar maples gave way to a large grove of quaking aspen, he stopped short. Stunned and out of breath, he clutched the trunk of a sapling, and looked up at the mighty thing before him.

Oriana and Amanda skidded to a halt right behind him. All three stood staring.

"My tree," he whispered. Because there it was, the one that had been in his childhood yard, a gigantic American beech. It stood now, right in front of him, regal and alone amid a stand of quaking aspens, a giant among spindly attendants. Big gray elephant-thick limbs reaching toward the afternoon sky branched a thousand directions into a massive canopy.

"Fagus grandifolia," said Oriana.

"How did — ?" No, wait, this beech had five limbs branching off its main trunk, and the one in his old front yard had only three. And held within these five immense fingers, as if in the palm of a giant's hand, was something he had only imagined as a child. A staircase with a bent-wood railing curled three times around the tremendous trunk, spiraling forty feet up to an ornate tree house the size of a large shed. It was perfectly imperfect, as if the tree itself had built the house, organically and over time, perhaps with the assistance of a band of carpenter elves. The tree limbs passed through the floor and up out of a multi-gabled roof. The exterior was a lopsided octagon, the sides going off every which way, woven in among the branches. And the source of the light Harry had seen? It was the sun winking off windows of all sizes and shapes — triangles, ovals, rectangles — half of them encrusted with multicolored shards of glass as bright as rubies and emeralds.

"It's illegal. We get it, we know," said Amanda.

"My dad built it. Isn't it amazing?" chimed in Oriana. "The afternoon sun always makes it light up. Like a magic sparkler!"

Amanda cut in. "But we understand this is government land. Definitely this was wrong."

Harry turned to face them. His mouth was dry, and he was dizzy, not just from bumping his head, but from all of it. From everything that had rushed in on him in the last fifteen minutes. But now he knew what to do. He had been handed his get-out-of-jail-free card.

"I would like to sit down," he said. "I see a chimney in that tree house. It looks cozy up there. I'm betting there's a chair. And I would like to sit."

"There's a cot, too," said Oriana. Amanda clapped a hand over her mouth and hugged her close.

"Yeah? A cot? Great. Because actually, I'd like to lie down. Not in an ER, but up there," he said to Amanda. "I would like you to take me up to that large, cozy, *illegal* structure, which is on my government land, and I wish to stretch out and rest. My back hurts, but it is *not* broken. My arms hurt, but they are *not* broken. And yes, there's a bump on my head. I'm bumped and scratched, but I'm fine."

Amanda nodded.

Oriana squeezed free of her mother and said, "There's a stove up there, and water, and whatever you need."

"Excellent. And something else. I'm a little light-headed because I haven't eaten lunch." Harry walked over and plucked a mini Snickers from a nearby laurel bush and held it up. "So if there are no objections . . ." He tore off the wrapper and popped the candy into his mouth. A beam of shimmering light reflecting off one of the windows lit the empty wrapper, bathing his face in a golden light.

Oriana stared at him. The Harry Crane list she was creating in her head got one item longer. Hawk, lottery ticket, book,

Snickers, American beech. Gold.

Harry looked at her. "What? What now?"

Oriana led the way up the spiral staircase.

7

The tree house was a single room, somehow both small and inexplicably large, filled with nooks and crannies, and pierced by the tree itself, the exposed limbs like columns in a Greek temple. A pair of dusty skylights looked into the canopy of the beech, which rose at least a hundred feet above the tree house. In two or three weeks, the branches would bear pale green leaves and the bright sun would give way to dappled light.

The tree house was implausibly shaped and lit by an abundance of odd windows, but it was simply furnished, which somehow enhanced its otherworldliness. A cot. Two hand-hewn Adirondack chairs. A triangle-shaped table, a little kitchen area with an old, cast-iron potbelly stove.

Harry was stretched out on the cot, shivering beneath a wool army blanket. On the other side of the room, Amanda knelt in front of the stove touching a match to a small pyramid of birch bark and pine straw kindling. Oriana sat in one of the Adirondack chairs at the foot of the cot, the *Field Guide to North American Trees: Eastern Region* in her lap. She'd taken it from the low bookcase beside the door. The bookcase was stuffed with field guides of every type: mammals, insects, fish, ferns, geology, stars and planets. She had been quizzing Harry for the last five minutes.

The fire caught and blazed to life. Amanda added larger sticks and a small log, adjusted the flue, and stood up. "That's enough, Oriana. Let Mr. Crane rest."

"It's okay," said Harry. "I like to talk trees." What he actually liked was that the girl's busy brain was occupied and diverted.

"White ash," said Oriana.

"Fraxinus americana," said Harry. She was trying to stump him on Latin names.

"American basswood."

"Tilia americana," said Harry. "Tell you something about basswood. The flowers have a lot of nectar, and honeybees love them. In some parts of the US they're known as the bee-tree. Also, in William Penn's time —"

"Penn's . . . sylvania," said Oriana.

"Right, in Mr. Penn's time they used the inner bark, which is called bast, for weaving baskets and mats."

Amanda listened to the back and forth. "Let him rest, and keep your eye on the stove, Oriana, don't let that fire go out. I'll be back soon." But they barely heard her. Amanda went out the door and down the spiral staircase. She was headed back to her house to get antibiotic ointment, Band-Aids, ibuprofen — the nurse in her could not allow Harry to remain untreated — and something warm for him to eat.

"Pignut hickory," came Oriana's voice.

"Carya glabra," answered Harry. "Pignut hickory, by the way, is also called — you ready? — sweet pignut, coast pignut hickory, smooth bark hickory, swamp hickory and broom hickory. It's got a pear-shaped nut that ripens in midfall. Wild animals love it."

Amanda paused at the base of the big beech, listening with satisfaction, because this was a gift — the tree man introducing a degree of order and reality back into Oriana's forest. And dullness. She didn't want to sound cruel or anything, but really, Harry Crane, federal employee, rattling off his tree facts, was kind of boring. But somebody had married him — he was wearing a wedding ring. Probably another federal employee. Amanda started off through the woods.

Up in the tree house, Harry reached

behind his head and touched one of the big columnar branches that passed through the room. A quality that always amazed him about trees: the constancy of their temperature. In winter, trees are never cold to the touch, and in summer they give off no acquired solar heat. It spoke to their essential aliveness. They were not rocks growing warm in the midday sun or streams that froze over; they were as self-regulating as the human body. It was a small leap to imagine that trees had souls.

He patted the tree and let his eyes drift closed. The girl had stopped peppering him with tree names. He could hear her moving around the room, fiddling with the stove. The room had begun to warm up.

Oriana peeked out an oval-shaped window. She watched her mother disappear through the trees, glanced at Harry, then zipped over to the bookcase. The field guides had belonged to her father, and they were battered and smudged from use, like everything he had owned. Books were not sacred objects, they were useful tools. When Dean went into the forest with Oriana, they'd take one along. He wanted Oriana to be a creature of the forest, but not a dumb creature. He would quiz her, just like she had been quizzing Harry Crane.

She pulled out *The Sibley Guide to Birds.* The illustration on the cover was a magnificent red-tailed hawk in flight. Oriana's heart soared. Over the last year, there were a lot of creatures Oriana thought Dean *might be.* Maybe he's this, maybe he's that. A beetle, a bat, an owl. Now she knew, she had seen him with her own eyes — Daddy, wingèd, was a red-tailed hawk.

She had read so many fairy tale books searching for clues. But the answer had been sitting right here, in one of *his* books. It was so perfect. In flight, wings spread, the great bird on the cover was powerful. Big in the chest, immensely strong in the shoulders. Like Daddy. And the red of the tail. Daddy's red.

Oriana touched her lips to the hawk on the cover of the field guide.

Persevere. See. Believe. For the last year, she had done that, and at last Daddy had rewarded her.

She put down the bird guide and picked up *The Grum's Ledger,* which sat on the armrest of her Adirondack chair. She walked over to the cot, opened the book and held it inches from Harry's nose. She jostled the cot with her foot. "We need to talk fast, before Mom gets back."

Harry's eyes startled open. The grum was

staring at him. Oriana had opened *The Grum's Ledger* to the first page, to its single illustration. In black ink, drawn by the same unsteady hand that had written the text, was an old, hairy goblin-like creature — the grum — sitting atop a mountain of gold coins staring forlornly into the eyes of whoever might read the book.

"Is this you?" she said. "Are you a grum? Tell me yes or no."

Harry pushed the book away and sat up. "Hey. Jeez, what's wrong with you?"

"I mean, it's *possible* you've turned into a grum, that would make sense in a way. But you don't look like a grum. Well, you do in the eyes and maybe the nose, but you're too big. And not hairy enough. But creatures transform into other creatures. Are you a grum?"

"Are we playing a game here? I don't have kids," Harry said. "I don't do kid-speak."

Oriana narrowed her eyes. "You didn't say yes or no. Which I bet is grum-speak for yes."

"Leave me alone, okay? You may have forgotten, but I recently fell from a tree and hit my head." He tapped the back of his skull, gingerly.

"No, you didn't. You didn't *fall*. I saw what happened. I saw everything."

Well, here we go, thought Harry. Now he was in the deep shit. He fought the overwhelming impulse to get out of this tree house and run back to his car, because this Oriana meant business. On the other hand, you know what? So did he. Beth had guided him to this forest. He'd found Harry's Trees, and he was damn well going to stay here. Although if Amanda the nurse discovered he'd tried to string himself up, she'd haul him off to the ER. No, worse. He imagined a rural psych ward. They probably still had straitjackets up here in the mountains.

Oriana stepped back from the cot. Eyeballed Harry like Sherlock Holmes scrutinizing a clue through a magnifying glass, then laid out the facts of the case. "Okay. So. Number one — Harry Crane tries to hang himself and my dad saves his life. Why?"

Her dad saved my life? What? thought Harry.

"Number two — Harry Crane finds *The Grum's Ledger* and Oriana Jeffers finds the lottery ticket. Why?"

Harry's armpits went slick with a sudden cold sweat. The lottery ticket. His unlucky talisman. "No, no! You need to give that back. Don't mess with that thing. Really."

"Why?"

"It's unlucky."

She smacked her fist into her palm in triumph. "I knew it! I knew it had to be magic."

"I said, *unlucky.*"

"Unlucky is a kind of magic." Oriana closed her eyes, as if conjuring, and said, "Eleven, twenty-nine, thirty-six, sixty-seven, fifty-eight." A pause. "And fifteen."

"What is that? What are you doing?"

"You don't know?"

"Hey. Oriana Jeffers. I tried to hang myself. And all I've had to eat is one mini Snickers. And you're talking in riddles."

"It's *your* numbers. On *your* lottery ticket."

"Give. It. Back."

Oriana pulled the pockets of her red jacket inside out, did the same with her pants pockets, looking Harry in the eye the whole time. "I hid it. I'm good at hiding things. I hid it in a tree on the way over here." She pointed out a large triangle-shaped window. "It's out there in Oriana's Forest. And anyway, if there's bad magic in it, it's too late. I touched it and I memorized it. The numbers are *doubly* inside of me."

Harry swallowed.

"Magic usually works fast," Oriana continued. "Like when Sleeping Beauty pricks her finger on the spinning wheel. Or Snow White bites the apple. But I'm not asleep. Or changed or anything different."

Sleeping Beauty? thought Harry. Snow White?

"Which means — its magic works only on you." She paused, pondering deeply. "That must be it. That *has* to be it. The ticket's magic made you try to hang yourself, didn't it?"

Harry gripped the metal edge of the cot. He could almost feel the tree house vibrating from the cogs churning and grinding inside the girl's strange, fervid brain. But my God, in a way, she was *right.* The magic of the lottery ticket, his unlucky talisman, did ultimately lead him to the sugar maple tree, rope in hand.

"And you know what I think?" said Oriana. "I'm supposed to keep it. That's why it came to me. If I keep it, then you won't try any of that noose stuff again."

There was a grain of truth in what she said: she had the ticket — and whatever crazed energy had gotten him atop the wall with a rope around his neck had indeed dissipated.

But something didn't make sense. Well, none of it made sense, but one thing was utterly impossible. "Back up. You said your father saved me." He thought back to the moment on the wall: Noose around his neck. Snickers. Branch breaking. "I was alone. No one saved me, what are you talking about?"

Oriana didn't answer. Instead, she turned and placed her hand on one of the thick columnar branches running up through the floor of the tree house. Harry shivered. Somehow, he felt the silky roughness of the beech bark communicated to his own fingertips.

She kept her hand on the beech, as if she perceived this, intended it, knew that the way to reach Harry was through trees. Trees, their special common language. The tree house swayed in the wind, back and forth like a gently rocked cradle. She said, "When did you fall in love with trees? Did your father teach you about them? My father taught me."

The sensation in his fingertips — real or imagined — abruptly vanished.

"My father wouldn't know a tree if it fell on him." And Harry often wished one had. Specifically, on the Chevy Citation X-11 Jeffrey Crane purchased the day he abandoned his family.

"Your American beech," Oriana said.

"The one in your front yard. Did your father build you a tree house?"

"I told you. He had no interest in trees. And we're not talking about my father, we're talking about yours."

"You had a beech tree when you were a kid, and I have this one. Did your dad build you a tree house? Tell me."

"No. He did not." In his mind, Harry saw his childhood tree. Saw himself safe in its powerful arms. He blinked.

"What?" said Oriana.

Harry reached past her and touched the beech tree branch. Moved his fingers over the bark. Oriana closed her eyes, as if this time she was the one receiving something tactile from him. She said, "Tell me."

"My father never built a tree house for me. But he did this one, tiny thing. And it wasn't even for me. I know it wasn't for me."

"Did your father die when you were little?" Oriana's voice was a whisper.

"No," said Harry. "Well, kind of. He vanished. When I was about your age."

"Vanished."

"Wait. No. Wrong word. Not vanished in some magic way. Not in a puff of smoke. He left us. Drove away in a car and never came back."

Oriana, taking this in. "You never saw him again."

Where in God's name was she leading him, this child? This child who was way, way too much for him.

"Listen to me," he said. "Whatever you think is going on, this magical link between us, whatever you think I am, I'm not. Okay? I'm some guy. A *human* guy. Not a grum, whatever that is, on some kind of secret magic mission. You're making up stories out of . . . nothing."

Oriana persisted. "What did your daddy leave for you in your beech tree?"

"His initials. That's all. JC. He carved them, high up, and one day I found them."

She reached out and took Harry's hand and guided it around to the other side of the beech tree branch. On its smooth bark, he felt two scars, a year or two healed over. They were letters. Harry read them with his fingertips. "D," he said. "J."

"My dad's name is Dean Jeffers."

Harry took a deep breath.

"Mom will be back any minute," she said anxiously. "We have so much to figure out."

"This is not a 'we' thing! It's an 'I' thing. I, Harry Crane, came here to *kill* myself! It had nothing to do with you!"

"The lottery ticket guided you here. So

my father could save you."

"How did he save my life if he wasn't here!"

She stared out of a little oval window for a long moment. Spoke without looking at him. "I came through the trees. You were standing on the stone wall, ready to jump. But you *didn't.* You saw the Snickers. You reached for it."

Now she turned and looked at him with inescapable eyes. "When you saw the Snickers you *didn't want to die.* When you slipped, you grabbed the rope and held on. You held on and kicked with all your might until you broke the branch."

Harry rubbed his neck. "Okay, maybe. That's one interpretation, I guess."

"*That's* how he saved you. I didn't put the Snickers in the knothole. It's too high up." She waved him over to the window. When he was beside her, she pointed and stepped back. He looked out. He could see candy and juice pouches in the trees and bushes around the beech tree. None of it was higher up than what Oriana could reach on her tiptoes.

"He put it up in the knothole," Oriana said. "My dad put that Snickers up there." When Harry turned from the window she handed him *The Sibley Guide to Birds.* On its cover, a red-tailed hawk.

The hawk seemed ready to leap from the page. Harry was instantly drawn back to the stone wall and the sugar maple. He felt the brush of feathers against his cheek, the beat of wings and a fluttering wind. He squinted at the bright glitter of gold.

"Daddy put it in the knothole for you. He brought us together. He guided me right to you."

"Oriana."

"Do you believe me yet?"

"No."

"Well, you have to! You don't have a choice. Because you know why? You know what else?"

Harry steadied himself against the beech tree.

"Your magic lottery ticket!" There were tears in her eyes. Fierce and desperate. "The date on it? The day you bought it? *That's* the day my dad died in the snow. My daddy, Dean Jeffers, made wings in the snow and he turned into a red-tailed hawk and he put that Snickers in the knothole and he saved your life. And you *know* it!"

Harry's mouth opened and closed. He looked up at the skylights into the canopy of the beech tree and beyond it to the cloudless sky. Unstuck in time, he saw Beth in her red coat as she tried to hand him the gold-wrapped mini Snickers. Unstuck, he saw a red-tailed hawk circling, a piece of sunlit gold clutched in its claw.

Oriana grabbed the bird guide from his hands and thrust *The Grum's Ledger* at him. Harry gripped it tight, as if he was holding on for dear life.

"We have to read it," Oriana said. "We have to figure everything out."

They heard Amanda at the base of the tree, starting up the spiral stairs.

Harry thrust the book at Oriana and jumped back into bed. Oriana scrambled over to the Adirondack chair, put *The Grum's Ledger* on the seat and sat on it. Then realized she was holding the bird guide. She rushed over to the bookshelf and put it back and picked up the field guide to trees.

Amanda came in, with a plastic bag full of supplies, out of breath from climbing the steep stairs. She looked at Oriana, thumbing through the tree guide. Then at Harry on the cot, the army blanket pulled up to his chin.

"Well. Has she stumped you yet?"

"A surprising number of times," Harry said.

"Maybe it's that bump on your head."

"Maybe," he said.

Amanda cleaned and disinfected his scrapes, put Band-Aids on them, gave him Advil and now he was finishing a bowl of stew.

"Never had venison stew before," Harry said. "It's good."

"Glad to hear it," Amanda said.

She reached for Harry's empty bowl and handed it to Oriana, who took it to the sink.

"All right," Amanda said. "Let's not beat around the bush. What are you going to do about our illegal little tree house?"

Washing the bowl in the little sink, Oriana listened intently.

"Stay in it."

That caught Amanda by surprise. "What?"

Behind her, Oriana silently punched the air and mouthed, *Yes!*

Harry ignored her and concentrated on Amanda. "I was planning to stay at the Holiday Inn Express in Scranton."

"But now you want to stay here. Out here. I'm sorry, but you look like the office type." She was staring at his hands. Not a callus in sight. Her eyes lingered on his wedding band.

"Yeah, I am. But with sequestration and downsizing, office types have to take on more fieldwork. This tract — Wilderness

Tract A803 — is ten years overdue for on-site evaluation. Photogrammetry and remote sensing has to be overlaid with physical data from trek mapping, clinometrics, increment borers . . ."

Harry watched her eyes glaze over. Good. He hoped he was hypnotizing her. *Harry Crane is not interesting. Harry Crane did not just try to hang himself from a sugar maple. Harry Crane is invisible so leave him alone. Go away and take that relentless daughter of yours with you.*

"Look," he said. "If I'm going to be out in the trees, then what's better than this? And by the way, I wasn't born in an office. Half of my forestry training was outdoors. Obviously. Also, honestly, I do not want to spend one minute in a motel room in Scranton."

"I get it."

"We hate Scranton. Except for the train museum," Oriana said.

"I have a stipend for living expenses," Harry said. "But instead of paying the Holiday Inn, I'll pay you."

"There's no refrigerator," Amanda said. "And no toilet, and no hot water."

"Okay. So maybe you don't get the entire stipend."

She almost, but not quite, smiled. "What will your wife think, you living in a tree house?" she said.

Harry fiddled with his wedding band, then looked up at Amanda. "That it's just what I need. She thinks I've spent too many years behind a desk."

Harry took his phone out of his pocket. As if he intended to put in a call to her. A lie, but really, today he wasn't certain about the truth of anything. Today, there was no terra firma. Stone walls were unsteady, and the thick limbs of a sugar maple did not support. And besides — tell her about Beth? No. It was too much. Amanda had not spoken of her Dean, and he would not offer up Beth.

"So after you leave in . . ."

"Three weeks . . . ?" He pulled the number out of thin air. It seemed enough time to regroup and ponder his next step.

"In three weeks, we won't have to tear this down? Even though it's illegal?"

"In three weeks this tree house becomes officially invisible to the government."

"Mom, let him."

"There *is* one thing," Harry said. And now he looked directly at Oriana. "All the Ziploc bags and candy wrappers — it's called littering. Littering remains illegal."

Now Amanda smiled. "She'll clean it up, every bit of it. Right, Oriana?"

Oriana looked at the two adults. Then, with a nod, agreed to the deal.

Nighttime. Oriana, in her pajamas, stood at her bedroom window looking out into the dark.

"I can just see his light. See it, Mom?"

"Yep."

Amanda tucked Oriana into bed.

When she walked by the window, Amanda paused. The moon, a star and the faint flickering of a distant kerosene lamp. Fine, good. Stay as long as you want, Harry Crane. Frankly, I can use the rent money — and you could use a few weeks in the woods to air out your lungs. And maybe grow your hair a little. You have good hair. Amanda blushed, ever so slightly, remembering her hands moving over Harry's scalp. You have good hair — and I bet your *wife* would like it a little longer. Married, Amanda reminded herself. And *dull.* She glanced at the moon again. But for a dull man, he sure knows how to make a day interesting.

Harry sat in an Adirondack chair. He poked the fire and looked out a window into the forest night. Way off, he could see the light coming from the Jeffers house. The light went out.

Time for bed. He was exhausted and achy. Toland. Beth. This forest and tree house. And God, he'd tried to *hang* himself? Long day. He lay down on the cot and dropped back on the pillow.

For the second time in one day, his head bonked against something. He reached inside the pillow case and pulled out *The Grum's Ledger.* This child, the way her mind worked. Secretive, unyielding. Making sure he'd find it. Oriana wanted what she wanted, whatever that was. And he wanted what he wanted, which was to stay in these woods and . . .

Did they want the same thing? He knew he should not let that thought in, but there it was.

Harry's Trees. Oriana's Forest.

They had arrived in these deep woods by two separate paths. Or was it the same path?

Harry's lottery ticket. Oriana's book.

He opened *The Grum's Ledger* to the first page. There sat the grum, with his doleful eyes. My God. Harry didn't mean to, but the opening words were right there below the creature, on the lined, white page, handwritten in black ink in large shaky letters. Was it age or emotion that shaped them? He read them silently. *Once upon an endless time in the Endless Mountains . . .*

You could almost hear a whispered weariness in them.

No. He shut the book. What he did not need was a grum running around in his brain. If the girl thought he was going to read her damn book, she was mistaken. He tossed it onto the Adirondack chair and turned his back to it. The pages fluttered lightly, as if the grum had breathed across them with a sigh.

Enough, enough. Harry closed his eyes and let the beech tree hold him. Soon he was fast asleep in Oriana's Forest.

8

"Once upon an endless time in the Endless Mountains," said Olive Perkins as she fished around in her frayed cloth book bag and pulled out a large brass key. Olive was a sharp-boned seventy-nine years old. She leaned forward and squinted through her bifocals, guiding the key into the iron keyhole in the center of the absurdly grand oak double doors of the Pratt Public Library like she was threading a needle. Built in 1910, a time when books were holy, the library looked like one of the old neoclassical banks down in Scranton, or maybe a fancy mausoleum in a cemetery for the rich.

Mausoleum. Pratt Library sure felt like one these days. Olive eyed the once glorious limestone facade, streaked green from the sagging copper of the ornate gutters and downspouts. A weathered slate roof tile lay shattered on the wobbly marble steps.

"Once upon an endless time," she said

again with a sigh, nudging the tile aside with her sneakered foot. She dropped the key back into her bag, leaned a skinny shoulder against the door and pushed. She groaned, and the door groaned in greeting back to her. Some days, that was the extent of Olive's worldly dialogue. Two groans to open the library, two groans at the close of the day, with very little sound in between. Olive was the town librarian, or *ghost* librarian as she sometimes put it if she was feeling less than cheerful. *I'm a ghost in a mausoleum of books.* Well, this town made you lose your cheer sometimes. New Milford had almost closed the library back in 2010, but Olive shook her fist in protest at the town council.

That evening, she rose from her folding chair and approached the seven council members. She slammed her hands on the cloth-covered table that was really just three lengths of plywood set on sawhorses, aimed a gimlet eye at each member in turn, then stood back and folded her arms.

"A town that would close its library. Shame on you!" she shouted, but really it wasn't much of a shout because her gravelly voice had been weakened by decades of reading to children and by the meerschaum pipe she smoked, the ivory bowl a hand-carved, blazing-eyed likeness of Mark Twain. She liked to sit on the front steps of her little clapboard house up on Zick Hill and watch the sunset and smoke a bowl of tobacco — or the sunrise if her old bones woke her in the night and she was just too achy and lonesome to fall back to sleep.

The council president was Stu Giptner, an associate agent at Endless Dreams Realty. "We can't maintain the library and pay you a salary, Olive," he said, in that piercingly nasal voice of his. "The state doesn't have the money, and the town don't either. We're just small-town businessmen and dairy farmers and quarrymen." He quickly added, "And Pump N Pantry head clerks," when Blair Peterson leaned out from her end of the table and raised an eyebrow.

Olive said, "So you can't pay me *and* keep the lights and heat on, have I got that right, Stu?" Shrewd with a nickel, that Stu Giptner — she should never have recommended *The Autobiography of Benjamin Franklin* to him when he had that book report back in seventh grade. She knew that Stu had his eye on nurturing the demise of Pratt Library, which sat on a choice piece of land right in the middle of town. She'd caught him out back more than once, pacing off the lot like a mortician measuring a corpse for a coffin.

"I'm sorry to say, but that's exactly right, Olive," Stu replied. He looked about as sorry as a vulture.

"Then just keep the heat and lights on. I don't need the town's money." But she did need the library, more than food or oxygen. And the children needed books, too, whether their parents understood it or not, and so did the old folks up in the hills who still had the wit and capacity to crack open a book even if these fools on town council never read anything more complicated than Twitter twaddle on their cell phones.

So with a bang of Stu's gavel — God did he love the officious sound of that gavel — Olive Perkins went from being a grossly underpaid librarian to the library's sole volunteer. The ghost who kept the library lights burning. The alteration in her lifestyle was not that significant. She bought her sweaters at Goodwill, heated her house with wood, made her own bread, and was grateful for extra venison and turkey from her neighbors during hunting season. And like everyone else, she had a big Kenmore freezer that she filled with wild strawberries and blackberries, and pale-fleshed sunnies she caught down at Acre Lake.

"A fool and an ass," Olive grumbled,

meaning Stu Giptner, thinking back on that meeting as she turned on the library lights. The old fluorescent tubes flickered noncommittally, then buzzed on. Ick, what a glare. She glared back at them. "Fluorescent lights," she said. "Whoever invented the fluorescent lightbulb should be tossed into the Susquehanna."

Being a librarian, and therefore an inveterate looker-upper of facts, Olive had a sudden need to know who invented the fluorescent lightbulb. She went straight to the reference section without hanging up her coat and reached for F in the 1980 twenty-two volume edition of the World Book Encyclopedia, the last major acquisition she had made for the library. She certainly wasn't going to use Wikipedia on the library's single computer, not if she could help it.

She sat down on a step stool and fingered through the pages of the encyclopedia, pausing at "Florence, Italy" to read about the Duomo, and Michelangelo's David. Ten minutes later she suddenly remembered her original task and, chiding herself, flipped briskly through the Fl's to "Fluorescent Lighting."

"Peter Cooper Hewitt." She read out loud in little bursts. " 'Hewitt built on the mid-nineteenth-century work of physicist Julius Plucker and glassblower Heinrich Geissler.' "

Olive raised her eyes to a flickering bulb way up in the deep pitch of the peeling ceiling. "Geissler. Got a Geissler down in Maplewood Cemetery. No. No, that's Geis*czler.* Arnie Geisczler who raised goats. Now *there* was an ornery bastard. Ornery Arnie and his ornery goats." Her eyes cut back to the encyclopedia. " 'Hewitt developed mercury-filled tubes in the late 1890s.' Mmm-hmm. Yes. Oh *dear* — he joined up with Westinghouse. Well, that was the end of you, Mr. Hewitt. You sold your soul and they ate up your good name and now nobody remembers you."

She slid F back in its slot, and with a groan took hold of the bookshelf and pulled herself upright. When she turned, she was startled by an apparition gliding through the morning light of the library entrance. She clutched her book bag tight and swallowed.

Librarian that she was, Olive possessed a deeply organized mind. She went systematically through the possibilities. Was it Death? Olive had always believed that Death, when he came for her, would enter through the front doors of Pratt Library. She touched a hand to her heart. Still beating. Not Death. Another possibility: raccoon? They were up in the joists, the little devils making themselves right at home. Or was it Oriana Jeffers?

"Oriana? Is that you?"

For the last heart-wrenching year, Oriana Jeffers had been Pratt Library's most important patron. That's what Olive should have said to Stu Giptner. "You keep the lights on in a library the same way you keep the lights on in the emergency room of a hospital. Why don't you understand that, you parsimonious dimwit?"

Ordinarily, when the great oak doors groaned open and someone entered Pratt Library (Fred the postman usually, or somebody in quick need of the restroom) there would be a burst of sunlight, a bright harsh intrusion on the dim and quiet. But when Oriana Jeffers came through those doors, the light transmuted into moonbeams and star-shimmer, and all the books on the shelves fluttered awake. Oh joy, they whispered, a *reader*.

Olive would grin and give Oriana a big wave. "Is that my favorite customer?" she called. "Is that Oriana Eagle-Dare Feather-Top Frog-a-lina Cinderella Athena Snow

Queen Jeffers?"

"You can just call me Oriana," Oriana would answer, waving back. She adored Olive Perkins. Olive was all the best things: she was incredibly wrinkly and smelled like pipe tobacco and she had a sudden laugh that scared the spit out of you and she hated the computer, but she'd use it to search the ends of Susquehanna County for an interlibrary-loan copy of the book you wanted if Pratt Library didn't have it on its shelves. Also, she used curse words.

"Oh, *may* I call you Oriana? May I, just?" Olive would reply.

Another thing Oriana liked about Olive was that she greeted you with a handshake like you were a grown-up, and she let you call her by her first name. "That's what names are for," Olive explained. "If you don't use them, they wither and blow away on the western wind." Which was yet *another* thing Oriana liked — Olive talked like a book. *Wither and blow away on the western wind.* Compared to Olive, other adults spoke in grunts.

Olive would come forward and shake Oriana's hand, peering past her to Amanda Jeffers out front in her blue pickup truck. Olive would wave, and Amanda would reciprocate with the smallest possible nod then drive off to do errands. Amanda was not a fan of Olive and her library.

Olive's and Oriana's library ritual was always the same: greeting, handshake and then the echo. Olive knew that ceremony and routine were important to a child engulfed in moonbeams and possessed by grief. Oriana would cross the chipped brown linoleum floor — a travesty from a library makeover in the 1950s — to the circulation desk and slide the books she was carrying in her arms into the returns slot. The sound of the books hitting the metal cart echoed off the marble walls. Off that echo, Oriana would clap her hands to make the library echo again. In Olive's library, Oriana was encouraged to do things like clap her hands loudly.

"You've earned the privilege," Olive told her back when Oriana started coming so frequently after Dean Jeffers's death. "You are now, officially, a Voracious Reader, Second Class. I am a Voracious Reader First Class, which I earned by reading the entire Oxford English Dictionary, which has over 300,000 entries. But it took me eight years, child, so don't be disheartened. As a VR-2, you have certain inalienable rights and privileges, foremost of which is, a VR-2 is allowed to clap her hands in this library whenever the hell the mood strikes her."

Olive then proceeded to lead Oriana around the floor of the library demonstrating the best places to get an echo. Since no one ever came in, there was no one to disturb. They clapped and they hooted.

Olive called out to her, "I'd like to shoot off a pistol in here one day. That'd be an echo! I'd shoot the raccoons that live up in the attic." She pointed to an ever-widening hole in the high ceiling above the nonfiction section. Oriana looked up and saw a pair of glittering eyes peering out from the dark.

"Not a good idea," Oriana said. "You don't know who that raccoon might turn out to be."

Oriana knew all about Actaeon who'd been turned into a stag and Ulysses's men transformed into pigs by Circe, and *The Frog Prince* and *Beauty and the Beast* and *The Enchanted Snake* and *The Golden Crab.*

"Yes, yes, metamorphosis. But I'm pretty certain," Olive said, "that the raccoons running through my walls and ceilings have always been raccoons. Not every animal is an enchanted human, do you think, dear?"

Oriana sucked on her lower lip and tugged at her ponytail. "I don't know. But I think around here a higher amount of them than usual are enchanted. We have lots of forests, you know? And more stars at night. And we have mountains and valleys, though of course our mountains are more like big hills because we live in the Appalachian Basin."

Olive clucked her tongue. "You are a wondrously bright child."

Oriana smiled. "But it *is* special here, don't you think, Olive, because of the mountains and stars? And it's the *Endless* Mountains we live in. Endless means infinite. And infinite means anything could happen."

Olive felt the urge to pick up a magazine from the periodicals rack to fan away the heat of this child, but then she thought, Oriana is on a difficult journey, and as long as she has a book with her she will come to no harm. Olive wished Amanda Jeffers understood that. Well, perhaps she did, the act of continually allowing Oriana to come to this place was an acquiescence.

One rarely knew what Amanda thought, but yes, Olive decided, Amanda's actions spoke for her — she'd entrusted Oriana to Pratt Library. If only Amanda would come in to pick up a book, too, once in a while, it would help ease her own pain. Dean Jeffers dying so young, the abrupt end of life and love — Olive could not bear the thought of it.

■ ■ ■ ■

A scrabbling erupted overhead, followed by an exchange of low yowls and hisses. Olive looked up. "Well, maybe those raccoons were human beings once, like you say. But ornery humans. In fact, I'm pretty certain one of them is Arnie Geisczler, who was before your time." A piece of plaster fluttered down from the edge of the hole. "Those creatures. How can I run a library that has more wildlife than all outdoors?"

Wait, who was she talking to? Oriana had not come into the library.

Not good, not good, talking to yourself, Olive. Don't do that, old girl.

A rustling sound. *Someone* was definitely in here. A shadow moved through the stacks. "Grum? Is that you?" No, of course it wasn't. Why would she even say that?

Because grums were very much on her mind. It had been such an unsettling week. *The Grum's Ledger* had arrived in her home mailbox last Monday. The return address on the big manila envelope was *Shapiro & Pullman, Estate Law, Scranton, PA 18503.* Olive had never received an envelope from a law firm before, and it frightened her. She thought at first that it was some kind of real estate maneuver by Stu Giptner, the sneaky lizard. But that didn't really make sense. Composing herself with a cup of elderberry tea and a few puffs on her meerschaum pipe, she opened the envelope.

Inside was a simple legal letter and an odd book, written by hand on the lined pages of an old accounting ledger. The author had a very unsteady hand, as if it had taken every ounce of his strength to render the tale. On page one there was a large drawing of the grum slumped atop a mountain of gold coins. What a wretched, despondent creature! The look on its face pierced your heart. The eyes filled with such regret, such longing, so unbearably sad.

Olive read the book. It was only a few pages long, a simple story by an amateur author. Over the course of her life she had read a million stories better than this one, more clever, more poetic, more interesting. Yet after reading it Olive cried for two straight hours, smoked three bowls of tobacco and drank a shot of bright green crème de menthe with a spring water chaser to calm her shattered nerves. She stayed awake all night.

What a tale! *Charlotte's Web, Of Mice and Men, Romeo and Juliet, All Quiet on the Western Front, The Yearling, The Lorax, The*

Fault in Our Stars, Tuck Everlasting, Atonement and *Old Yeller* — drop the lot of them into a literary centrifuge, distill out the pure essence of sorrow, and even that devastating extract would be nowhere near as sad as *The Grum's Ledger.*

The next morning, Olive took the book to the library and attempted to lose it on the shelves. You didn't throw a book like that away, and you didn't keep it, you didn't know what to do, you just didn't know.

Oh dear, but what she *did.* Why? Well, it was a fairy tale and she had nothing on hand to give Oriana when the girl came through the doors on Tuesday. So impulsive of you, Olive — you shouldn't have done it!

Olive didn't know whether she'd handed off the book to help the child or to get it out of her library and away, away.

"Miss Perkins," came a close-by voice from the YA stacks.

Olive nearly jumped out of her skin. "Who's that? Who's there?"

A thin man with stringy black hair and dressed in an ill-fitting green suit stepped anxiously before her, the sputtering fluorescent lighting casting his features in uneasy light and shadow.

"Who are you?"

"It's just me, Ronnie Wilmarth, Miss Perkins."

Ronnie tugged at his tie. He wasn't used to being so spruced up. He'd never worn a real tie before, or a suit. Susie Davis at the Goodwill store had helped him tie his tie and told him the suit looked fantastic on him. It smelled like mothballs. And his armpits smelled like Right Guard deodorant, his cheeks like Gillette Lemon-Lime shaving cream and his hair like he didn't know what — he'd just grabbed a thing of shampoo off the shelf at CVS and tossed it into his cart with the rest of the stuff. He'd bought practically every type of human cleansing and purifying agent ever invented, and now here he was, washed, flossed, shaved and combed, standing in the middle of Pratt Public Library coming clean in the most important way of all.

"Ronald Wilmarth," said Olive. "Well." He kept one hand behind his back, she noticed. He was hiding something.

"Just plain *Ronnie* please, ma'am."

She cocked her head. "Not many Wilmarths left around here. Used to be hordes of them up in the hills."

Ronnie nodded. "Yep, Wilmarths have thinned out, pretty much. Died, moved down to Wilkes-Barre and Allentown and what all." And some in prison, he didn't add.

"You Wilmarths weren't big readers."

Ronnie closed his eyes a moment, trying to see a book in any of the cluttered houses and trailers of his aunts and uncles and cousins. Lots of dusty porcelain figurines and crocheted knickknacks on the shelves, no books. Except the Bible of course, though he couldn't recall anyone actually cracking one open for a read.

"Not big readers, no. So, *about* that. Here's the thing, Miss Perkins . . ." He scrunched his face in anxious concentration.

"Yes, dear?"

Ronnie gulped and looked up at the ceiling, as if looking to the stars and beyond. "The thing is, last night I had another visitation from Dean Jeffers who — and everybody around here knows this — I killed because I was off eating a hamburger at Jim's Diner when I should've been beside my buddy when he dropped dead in the middle of Brian Taylor's field and turned into a snow angel."

Olive blinked. "Do you mind if I sit down, Ronnie? That's a lot of plot in one sentence, dear."

Olive walked over to the circulation desk,

removed her coat and sat. Ronnie followed and stood hunched on the other side of the desk. Still hiding whatever it was behind his back.

He said, "See, it's about the feathers. *His* feathers. Last year, after Dean died? Well, I got drunk, and I mean real drunk, and passed out in the snow. And when I opened my eyes next morning, right there beside my head was one of his wing feathers. And these feathers, see, it's been a sort of regular thing, showing-up-in-strange-places-wise."

Holy cow, thought Olive. How had the death of Dean Jeffers come to play such a large part in her life? But she nodded encouragingly. "All right, dear. But there are a lot of birds in the Endless Mountains. Feathers abound."

"Yes, ma'am, there are natural, everyday feathers, but there are also, um . . ."

"*Magic* feathers. Snow-angel feathers."

"That's right! Magic feathers. It's been going on for a year, his magic feathers all over the place. Feather on my windshield one time, another time one on my boot-scrape outside my front door and three weeks ago one sitting right there on the seat of my tractor . . ."

Olive nodded, as if Ronnie was making sense. She felt like a priest hearing a convoluted confession. Except Wilmarths weren't part of her flock — they weren't readers. What was he doing here? In the Church of the Holy Library? But she leaned forward, always a sucker for a narrative.

Ronnie said, "I can't always figure out what a Dean feather means. I know he wants me to help Amanda and Oriana, but sometimes he has other requests. But the feather that came last night? I know exactly what it means. It's about making amends for a crime I committed in the past."

"Oh my," Olive said.

"When I understand what he wants, it's important I do it, Miss Perkins. If I can do for Dean, if I can be a better Ronnie, it's a way of kinda bringing Dean back to life. I mean, I know I can't bring him back, but maybe I can carry out his wishes and desires beyond the grave. If I do what he wants me to do — even if I don't always understand the meaning — that way he'll still be alive a little bit. Through me. Right?" His voice almost a whisper now. "Dean alive, you know what I'm sayin' . . . ?"

Perhaps it was the flicker of the fluorescent light, but the look in Ronnie's eyes was the look of the grum in *The Grum's Ledger.* The eyes drowning in the same sort of bewildered grief.

"This time, Dean has sent me to *you,* Miss Perkins," pleaded Ronnie. "To this place."

Olive craved a steadying puff on her meerschaum and a shot of crème de menthe. "All right, sweetheart. And he did this *how,* precisely?"

Now Ronnie showed her what he was holding behind his back. It was an old hardcover book, worn to pieces from reading. There was a feather bookmarking out of the top of it, like the feather in Robin Hood's cap. Olive couldn't remember loaning a book to Ronald Wilmarth.

"I stole it," said Ronnie.

"*Stole* it?"

"Twenty-seven and a half years ago, when I was a kid, I stole this book. When you were looking the other way. In my dream last night? Dean, he called my name. And when I jumped awake this book fell off the shelf at the foot of my bed. And this feather was on it."

Ronnie placed the book carefully on the desk. Olive squinted at it. "*Treasure Island,* by Robert Louis Stevenson, illustrated by N. C. Wyeth. Wonderful book. One of the best ever written." Then she peered over her bifocals in stern librarian fashion. "And you stole this? This was your first crime?"

"That is correct, yes, ma'am," Ronnie replied in his humblest whisper. Even at a whisper his voice echoed about the walls of Pratt Library. Every move he made in this old marble building echoed back at him like a finger, pointing. "My first crime. And I am here to make amends."

Oh my, thought Olive. This is all so stunningly interesting. Stu Giptner, she wanted to shout, do you see the importance of books? This Wilmarth has been possessed by a book. "Why didn't you just sign it out, Ronnie?"

"My criminal nature, Miss Perkins."

"I see. And you've led a life of crime ever since?"

"I have done things, yes. But the point is, Dean has specifically —"

"Paid you a visit and left his angel-feather bookmark and here you are."

"Yeah!"

As people too often do, Ronnie had confused guilt with crime. Obviously, this was not a man to whom you could sensibly suggest, *Ronnie, you were off eating a hamburger. You did not get drunk and bludgeon your friend in a snowy field.* Maybe she should hand him an edifying copy of *Crime and Punishment.*

Olive examined the feather. The fact-based librarian in her — and amateur birder — wanted to set him straight. The feather was from a red-tailed hawk. Not an angel, but a rather common Pennsylvania mountain hawk. But Ronnie was too far along in his personal narrative. Ronnie needed what he needed. Oriana needed what she needed. And I need what I need, Olive thought.

"So what should I do?" asked Ronnie.

Olive was a survivor and a ruthless pragmatist. Living alone, a rural spinster, she made good use of whatever fortune or misfortune dropped in her path.

Last week, out of hunting season, a fat turkey had crossed her wooded lawn and she shot it. When dinner walks by, you eat it. The crumpled ten-dollar bill she found in the gutter outside the library last month? She did not go to the lost-and-found at town hall. She kept it. If this discombobulated Wilmarth needs to put on a hair shirt, Olive thought, that is very useful to Pratt Library.

"Ronnie," she said. "You must do exactly what Dean Jeffers and the magic feather are telling you to do. Yes, you must make amends."

He leaned in. "How?"

"It won't be easy."

"Good."

"And it will be prolonged."

"Good."

"And it is possible you will contract rabies."

"Absolutely, yes." Then, "Rabies?"

Olive stood up, came around the circulation desk and placed a finger on the center of his chest, tapping his breastbone as she spoke.

"You, Ronald Wilmarth, through the agency of Dean Jeffers, are going to work off your debt. The library fine for a book overdue twenty-seven and a half years is no small matter."

Ronnie punched his fist into his palm and grinned. "All right! Fair's fair!"

Oh, I'm going to work you hard, Ronnie, Olive thought. Shameless of me, to take advantage of your gullible good nature, but what's an old librarian to do? I must seize the day — or in this case, seize the Ronnie — because the building inspectors are due for their annual inspection, and this time no amount of bluster and begging would ward them off. Forward movement was imperative, and no volunteers had stepped up. Libraries were low on people's list of concerns these days.

"Ronnie, this place is in terrible shape, from the shitter to the shingles."

Ronnie blushed. "Yes, ma'am, I gotcha. I understand. I can fix just about anything and everything. Drywall, plumbing, roofing. Shitters."

"I have no money to buy materials."

He just shook his head. "You let Ronnie worry about materials, ma'am. I got a barn full of stuff."

"Now, understand we can't use *stolen* items, Ronnie." She heard a pipe gurgle and a shingle slide off the roof. She dropped to a whisper. "Unless we are absolutely forced to."

"You mentioned *rabies,* Miss Perkins . . ."

Muffled growls and yips in the ceiling above their heads. Olive turned and pointed at the ragged hole in the nonfiction row. A sharp, whiskered nose appeared and vanished. Olive scowled. "I don't know precisely that they have rabies. But they are rabidly present and I rabidly wish their removal."

Ronnie lit up and was already undoing his tie. "I'm absolute hell on raccoons!"

He lurched forward, bumping a bookshelf. Olive snatched hold of the tail of his suit coat. "I don't want you to be *hell* on them, Ronald. This is not the apocalypse, dear. Just trap them and let them go in the forest."

Ronnie reached down and picked up a

book that had fallen when he'd bumped the shelf. It was *The Sibley Guide to Birds.* He slid it back into its spot, then together he and Olive went off to see if there was a stepladder in the storeroom so he could get a better look at the raccoon hole in the ceiling.

9

When Amanda went to check on Harry Crane early in the morning, he was gone. The tree house felt empty, like he was not just gone, but *gone* gone — that he'd changed his mind and he'd be staying down in Scranton. Everything was too neat. The cot perfectly made, the fire in the potbelly stove extinguished and cold, the food she had brought him last night for this morning's breakfast — cereal, powdered milk, a granola bar, apple — untouched.

Well, why would he stay? He was a grown man, it was a tree house, maybe his wife said *too weird.* Who knew how the mind of a federal bureaucrat worked? Maybe they'd bump into him in the woods while he was doing his clinometrics. Or maybe not.

Amanda had a small knot of disappointment in her belly, walking in the early-morning light back to the house. Harry Crane would've been a good thing for Oriana. Maybe he'd already been good enough, the short time that he had literally dropped in on them and laid claim to her forest.

Oriana had been itching to go to the tree house with Amanda, but Amanda had said no, Oriana needed to make herself a bag lunch and get ready for the class trip to the Steamtown train museum in Scranton. When Amanda got back, Oriana was pacing at the edge of the backyard.

"What do you mean, gone?" Oriana said.

"Not there, sweetie. Gone."

"He must be out in the forest. Doing his job."

"Maybe. But he sure did leave the place neat. Just saying, Oriana."

Oriana wanted to ask: Had he read *The Grum's Ledger*? Or taken it with him? He couldn't just *leave.* It was all she could do not to run to the tree house and check for clues her mother would have missed. But Amanda could sense it and hovered like a prison guard. She got Oriana into the pickup and drove her to school.

Amanda worked a six-hour shift in the ER, then came back home to shower. She checked the tree house again, and even went to the old quarry trail to look for Harry Crane's car. She could see where he'd parked it, and the tire tracks where he'd backed up the car and driven away.

I guess that's that, she thought, and got in her truck and went off to have sex with Cliff Blair.

She'd slept with Cliff five times. It was now April, the encounters had begun in February — that is, eleven months A.D.

Life A.D. (*After Dean* as Amanda grimly thought of it) went something like this. Months one to three — bed was for crying in, not wanting to get out of, reaching over to Dean's side and not finding him there. Bed was misery. Months three through six, bed was lonely and too big, but at least she could get in and out of it like a seminormal human being. Something began to change between months six and nine. When she sleepily reached over to Dean's side expecting to find him there and he wasn't, it began to piss her off. "Why aren't you here to hold me, Dean? I want to be held."

After month nine, it was clear. She wanted to be held — by *somebody.* It mortified and upset her, but it was undeniable. She needed a warm body. Bed was for sex and she was in a sexless bed. Sex was life and she needed to get a life. Amanda had a wicked case of widow-fatigue.

So what to do? She didn't want to sleep

with a doctor at the hospital. No way was she going to be the nurse who played doctor with a doctor. Besides, she didn't like doctors as *men.* Indoor men — ugh. She liked outdoor guys, men with calloused hands and the wherewithal to cut a cord of wood or start a truck in a blizzard. She wasn't some silly-ass, truck-posing gal in a country music song. Nope, she was the real deal. Mountains and trees and deer and lakes were what she knew and what she was.

So who was it going to be? There were a lot of outdoor men in New Milford and the other little towns that poked up in this part of the Endless Mountains. But oh brother, when you put on your fuck-goggles, well, you didn't exactly see a male Shangri-La.

But, but, but — stop it, Amanda. It's rural Pennsylvania, you make do. Because face it, after Dean, everything was going to be about making do.

So back in February, Amanda had been eating supper with Oriana at Green Gables, and she forced herself to look around, give New Milford's finest a serious perusal. She was not unaware that the men were looking back. The EMT crews at the hospital had started to sniff around her, and now so were the men sitting around the bar at Green Gables. *Okay, it's been almost a year, start your engines. Amanda Jeffers is up for grabs.*

Tom the bartender had been the first to approach, when she and Oriana sat in a booth eating an early supper at Green Gables. Since Dean's death, Amanda made an effort to take Oriana out to eat every two weeks. They always ordered the same things: Oriana a grilled cheese and tomato, and the ice cream roll for dessert, Amanda the barley-sausage soup and a salad from the uninspired salad bar. She marveled at how pale the iceberg lettuce always was, as if it had been specially grown in a cave for blind albino salamanders. Well, you didn't come to Green Gables for a gourmet feed, you came because it was amiable, and there was plenty of parking and it helped break up the lonesomes.

She looked up as Tom, smiling nervously, approached the booth. "On the house, Amanda," he said, setting a draft Coors Light in front of her and a Pennsylvania Dutch root beer on Oriana's paper place mat.

Oriana lifted her eyes from her book and grinned, waiting a beat for the official mom-okay before she reached for the frosty mug.

Amanda hesitated, then gave a nod.

She was wearing her hospital scrubs, not exactly sexy, but they sure did something for Tom, the way his eyes were busying around.

"Thanks a lot, Tom. What's the occasion?"

Not a question to tax the brain, but Tom went blank and began to rub his bulging forearms nervously, drawing Amanda's attention to them. I absolutely do not want those things wrapped around me in bed, she thought. They *glistened.* Lord — he rubs *oil* on himself. Worse, she detected an almondy scent. Dean had been muscular, but it was an earned, natural muscle, he didn't make a fetish of his body. When Dean glistened, it was with honest sweat.

And something else was deeply unappealing about Tom — he wore his pants too tight, creating one more bulge she'd rather not see.

"No occasion. Just for. I don't know, just for . . ." He stood there a flummoxed moment longer, shrugged, then retreated to the safety of his bar, the other guys flicking their eyes and hunching closer to their beers, feeling his pain.

None of them were exactly lucky with the ladies. Cliff Blair gave Amanda a quick look over his shoulder. Cliff had never found the right woman. And Stu there on Cliff's left — Stu had found the wrong woman and was divorced. Ronnie was dating the bottle, and Tom had been going with Lisa Stark from up Montrose, but that seemed to have piddled out.

Lisa was a bodybuilder, too. Amanda once got a look at her muscled torso when Lisa came into the ER with a torn rotator cuff. Every ounce of body fat had been sweated out of her and replaced by thick veins and sinew.

"You using steroids, Lisa?" Amanda, clipboard in hand, was filling out Lisa's history and physical, so she had to ask.

"Oh, yeah. Nothing dangerous, just enough to keep me toned." Lisa's unsettling voice would not have been out of place in the bass section of the Mount Zion Baptist Church men's choir.

About a week after Tom the bartender had made his move, if you could call it that, Cliff's battered pickup truck pulled in behind Amanda as she was filling up at the Pump N Pantry on Route 11. Well, not *filling* up, because she didn't have that kind of money. Without Dean, she was really beginning to feel the pinch.

Studying Cliff as he got out of his truck, Amanda thought: Cliff Blair, hmm. She returned Cliff's tip of the tractor cap with a small wave.

Oh, but look at you, Cliff. I simply cannot

go to bed with a man who has such an abiding relationship with cow shit. Cliff was wearing his chore boots, and they were encrusted — not unreasonable since he mucked out stalls for a good part of his day. But there was cow shit caked on all four tires of his truck and smeared thick across the front bumper and headlights. The headlights, Cliff! Where do you park your truck at night — in the middle of your manure stack?

When he got closer, she could see the haze of dried brown on both elbows of his Carhartt work coat. He was such a nice guy, really decent, big and kind of handsome, but he was soaked through and through with cow. Whenever Cliff opened his mouth she half expected him to moo.

"Hey there, Amanda Jeffers."

Now this was someone she'd gone to elementary and high school with. "Hey there, Clifford *Blair.*" He didn't get it, that she was trying to tease him out of formality.

"Cold one today," he said.

"How the cows laying, Cliff?"

He grinned as he stuck the gas nozzle into the side of his truck. "Been getting about two dozen eggs a day. Keeping me pretty good in omelets, you know. *Big* omelets."

Cliff reminded himself not to stare at

Amanda, so of course he got befuddled and stared harder at her, his mouth opening slightly at her powerful beauty.

"Sure, sure," Amanda said. "Big omelets. I bet." His teeth are nice, she thought. And he's got all his hair. Wish he didn't stare with those cow eyes.

"ER keeping you busy?" Cliff asked.

Amanda nodded. "Couple hunters from Scranton yesterday came in dinged-up pretty good. Shouldn't mix beers and bird-shot."

"I hear you there. You wouldn't get no dings with a Marlin 336." Which was the deer-hunting rifle Cliff owned. Cliff didn't mess with birds and small game. A man who tends thousand-pound cows is partial to a large target.

"No, a Marlin'll do a person pretty good," Amanda agreed. "Let's see, what else? Oh. Fred Nils came in Wednesday carrying guess what in a cup of ice?"

"His finger." Cliff chuckling when Amanda nodded. "Fred and his traps," he said.

"Catches more fingers than he does musk-rat." She held up her hand and pointed to her fourth finger. "Just down to his first joint. Docs got it back on pretty good, though."

"That's fine, then," Cliff said. "I'll take a look at it next time I see him."

They flicked eyes at each other and went their separate ways.

In desiring Amanda, Cliff was definitely following the herd. Dean Jeffers was a good guy who sometimes joined the fellas at Green Gables, and when he was alive not one man among them would have considered even glancing at Amanda.

No, let's face it, Dean wasn't just a good guy, he was an amazing guy, and in death practically deified. Dean the bow-hunter, Dean who built his own house out of logs he milled himself, Dean's perfect teeth and easy smile. Dean the strong. Tom with all his great big muscles? Dean had once arm wrestled him and smacked Tom's hand down so hard and fast on the bar, it sounded like a pistol crack and dimpled the wood. And of course — and they all pondered this but never spoke of it — Dean the lover. Dean in *bed* with Amanda. Epic, Olympic-level coupling, right? When he imagined it, Cliff heard the wild sounds of the jungle.

Dean's death had thrown them into turmoil. What had been a wistful sexual simmering at the back of their forbidden fantasies was now, almost a year later, chest-tightening, full-bore desire. Not that it mattered a whit. It was pathetic, really. Amanda barely acknowledged the nincompoops hunched around the bar other than to nod at them. Still, they turned into quivering teenagers every time she came into Green Gables with Oriana.

When she crossed the doorstep, they were struck dumb. Cliff, sitting among them, knew exactly what they acted like — cows. The door would open, and they'd turn their heads in unison and freeze, like livestock startling at a sudden noise.

Cliff's mouth would go dry, and he'd turn away from the blaze of Amanda's perfection and eyeball the other guys. Ronnie would gulp his beer down, medicinally. Stu would light his match but forget to bring it to his cigarette, sitting there like the Statue of Liberty grasping a teeny torch. Old Walter would chuckle and shake his head. Tom might actually drop the beer glass he was swabbing out in the sink. Oh yeah, Tom had shattered a few.

As she passed by the long oval of the walnut bar, Amanda would glance over and say, "How those beers going down, guys?" Something neutral like that. Oriana would not speak a word — her nose was always in a book.

They'd all moo at once. "Going down good, Amanda!"

"Amanda, how ya doing?"

"Oh, hey, Amanda." *Oh, hey, Amanda.* That would be Stu, trying to act casual.

And Cliff? He could not speak Amanda's name at all. It would get caught up around his epiglottis and sit there thickly until it emerged a full hour later, when he was in his pickup, a lonely bull heading home, lowing *Amanda.*

Cliff was such a shy, inarticulate man he could get tongue-tied talking to a cow. He talked to them more than he should, and on days when chores overwhelmed, and he was so tired he saw spots (and not just on the cows), he imagined they talked back to him. On occasion, he'd speak to his day worker, Hoop Sloane.

Cliff and Hoop could go for a week without talking. Neither man could confidently express his innermost thoughts, so why bother? Besides, they agreed on everything. Both men loved the smell of hay, loved to repair the electric paddock fences, even loved to troubleshoot the milking machines, which were fussy, especially on the dawn winter milkings. You did not want a vacuum pump to fail you in cold weather because without a constant, even pulse, the wet tip of a cow's teat would rub raw in the teat cup and sometimes, if the pump failed altogether, even freeze. Cliff could not bear the plaintive moos of an uncomfortable cow.

An only child, Cliff had inherited the dairy farm from his folks, both dead and buried in the family plot in Maplewood Cemetery. His dad had run the farm for forty years as a typical grain-feed operation with a hundred penned Holsteins, but Cliff cut back to fifty animals and switched to seasonal rotational grazing. Going organic was the thing to do these days — low maintenance, low cost, and best of all, the cows were much happier. You could see it in their eyes and hear it in their moos.

"That's a good moo," Hoop would say, looking up from fixing a hinge on a stall door or adjusting a solar pump on one of the numerous water pipelines snaking over the rolling fields.

An hour might go by before Cliff answered. "Yeah, that *was* a good moo."

Other men would surely devolve into extended cow riffs and moo jokes to pass the time, but that wasn't Cliff's and Hoop's style.

Cliff forced himself to go to Green Gables because you didn't want to get out of the habit of being among two-legged creatures.

Hoop had gotten out of the habit. He shaved without a mirror, leaving hairy tufts along his jawline, and on hot July days his body odor could stun.

Cliff, though, made an effort to stay in the game, so after he got the cows milked and settled, he'd put on a clean shirt and sit down once or twice a week at the big oval Green Gables bar with Stu, Walter, Ronnie and whoever else might show up, and let Tom serve him a few. He was always the first to leave because his day began in the dawn dark.

Hanging out with other guys was difficult enough for Cliff, but mingling with women was pure torture. He'd fiddled around some when he was younger, but somehow having fifty lives under his constant care — fifty-one if you counted Hoop — Cliff had placed too much life and time between himself and the fairer sex. He'd mulled over the intricacies of the mating dance for too long, and once you've done that, it all becomes impossibly complex and unattainable.

Every woman you encounter you hoist up on a pedestal. And standing atop the tallest pedestal of all, with her arms crossed and her eyebrow warily raised — Amanda Jeffers, widow.

■ ■ ■ ■

So when Amanda Jeffers showed up out of the blue two months ago he'd almost had a heart attack.

That February day, Amanda was almost having a heart attack, too. She drove down the Grand Army of the Republic Highway in her truck to Cliff Blair's dairy farm, because she was going to sleep with him. Her grip on the steering wheel tightened. She was definitely going to sleep with Cliff Blair. It was *time* to sleep with somebody. And Cliff, well, he was a pleasant, decent enough somebody. Amanda gripped the steering wheel hard enough to snap it in two. Oh man, she was so nervous.

She glanced in the rearview mirror. Look at you, she thought. Nervous and frowning. You can't go to Cliff's and frown at the man. She forced a smile. Would he find her attractive, when it really came down to it? Not a woman who spent a lot of time gazing in mirrors, Amanda saw lines around her mouth and eyes she had never noticed before. She drew back. Amanda, what the hell are you doing? You got lines, big goddamn deal. Of course you have lines, you're drying up like a drought-baked river. You need to get your juices flowing again. This isn't just sex, it's for your damn health, too.

No. For Pete's sake, it's for the *sex* and you know it.

It was a late afternoon, an unseasonably warm winter day, and Cliff sat on an old oak three-legged milking stool, hand-stripping a young cow that was suffering from mastitis. He'd inserted antibiotic into the teat canal using the short cannula method. The most important part of that method, he'd learned real quick as a kid, was dodging a cow's kick that could send your head flying over to the next county.

Cliff was trying to be gentle as he stripped the teats, but you did have to get a strong flow going. The tethered cow moaned and kicked out a few more times and finally settled with a shudder of relief. The milk had thick flakes in it and smelled sour from the antibiotic, but it would clear in about three days. He'd have to toss the milk of course, though some dairy farmers tried to sneak bad milk past the inspectors and ended up losing their Grade A. Fools.

Cliff was alone in the barn. Hoop worked from 4:00 a.m. to 4:00 p.m., and had gone home or wherever it was that Hoop went after leaving Cliff's. Cliff listened to the milk hitting the side of the pail and the wind blowing through the bare trees of the mountains and the cow chewing her cud — all the sounds that were as much a part of him as the breath rising and falling from his own lungs.

He tilted his head when he detected a different sound — the scrape of a stranger's foot on the concrete floor of the barn.

In the same heart-stopping instant, he detected, even among the powerful barn smells, the unmistakable scent of Amanda Jeffers. All the guys knew Amanda's clean-soap smell, their noses tilting up slightly to sniff the air as she'd walk by the bar. But this wasn't Green Gables, this was *here.* Still grasping a fistful of teat, Cliff whipped around.

Amanda stood in the double-wide opening of the barn doors, the late-afternoon sun outlining her form and setting her sweptback hair aglow. She wore a pair of tight blue jeans that looked new, and a sweatshirt jacket open to a red cami (in this cold!). She turned a little, her body now in profile, lush curves and bright color framed in barn wood.

Cliff almost fell off his stool. That he was able to speak was a miracle. "Well, hey, Amanda Jeffers." He instantly thought, Dumbass, don't say her name in full like that. She always teases you when you do it.

But all she said was, "Hey, Cliff."

And Cliff thought, Uh-oh, big departure from the norm, what's going on? What is she doing here?

"Can I come in?"

Like it was his house instead of a barn. Cliff willed himself to speak again. "Oh, sure, please." And then a second miracle. He added, "Don't forget to wipe your feet."

Amanda laughed, made a little show of wiping her feet on the barn floor and approached. She stopped about five feet away and gazed down at him. "You practicing for the Harford Fair?" There was an annual hand-milking contest at the fair, which could get comical, since all of the farmers had mechanical milkers and had mostly lost the knack. The retired quarry and lumber guys who had just an acre and a hobby cow and a few chickens, they'd win the contest, hands down every year.

Cliff was trying to think of something to make Amanda laugh again, and his mind went blank. He gripped the teat like it was a lifeline and stared into the pail of milk.

Amanda cleared her throat and said, "Looks like you got yourself a handful."

Which brought Cliff's eyes right up to Amanda's impressive chest, hovering above him like soft pillows where the gods might rest their heads.

Resisting the urge to cross her arms, Amanda let him stare.

Cliff jumped to his feet and willed his gaze to Amanda's face, expecting to see remonstrance, but her smile was bigger than ever. "So, gee, hey. Amanda Jeffers." He winced and shook his head.

The swagger, which had been false anyway, left Amanda. Cliff saw it, her skin flushing, the slight panic in her eyes.

"Everything okay?" he said.

Amanda nodded and rubbed her arms. "Oh yeah, everything's okay. I'm just a little nervous."

"Nervous?" he asked gently.

"Excited nervous," Amanda said almost in a whisper.

Cliff stared at her. "Sorry?"

Amanda got some gumption back into her voice. "I'm excited. To be here and everything." She added, "Got a sitter for Oriana."

"A sitter, huh?" Cliff said.

"One of the Hytner twins, Debbie, nice kid. Yep. But . . . I'm not really here to talk about the twins."

"Oh, okay." Cliff had never stood this close to Amanda before. She was advancing incrementally, and he couldn't back up because he was against a stall post. He began to mouth breathe. Behind him the tethered cow mooed softly, as if to whisper counsel.

"We've always been friends, Cliff."

"Uh-huh."

"And so, that being the case and all, I want to ask you a big, huge favor."

"Oh sure, anything." Cliff gulped. Her breath smelled powerfully of spearmint gum. The minty freshness, her proximity, that red formfitting cami— it was just too much. Cliff felt a thickening down below and hoped to God that his work coat was concealing it. He could not look at her. Could not move.

Amanda took a breath and reached out to touch his arm, but at the last second shyly took hold of the wood post beside his arm. "Okay, here goes," she said. She fixed her eyes on his. "Cliff, I haven't . . . *been* . . . with a man in almost a year. And so the favor I'm asking you is . . . well, you know what I'm asking."

Cliff nodded. It was less in affirmation than that his head felt unmoored from his shoulders, like a bobblehead doll.

"But this offer's conditional, Cliff. And the condition is, if you go inside your house and take a good, hot shower and scrub off that *Eau de Cow* you're wearing — when you come out I'll be waiting in your bed."

Cliff kept nodding.

Amanda smiled. "Are there clean sheets on your bed?"

"It's Tuesday," Cliff whispered hoarsely.

"Yeah, it's Tuesday . . . ?"

"Tuesday is change-the-sheets day."

Amanda reached up and touched the bristle of his strong jaw, and turned toward the door. She paused and looked back over her shoulder. "You coming, Clifford Blair?"

Behind him, the cow mooed loudly and nosed Cliff forward. Amanda held out her unsteady hand. Cliff took it. Across the barnyard they went, toward the little white house on the hill. Cliff winced when Amanda suddenly squeezed his hand so tight he thought she might break the bones. He stole a peek at her, and she didn't look excited or nervous anymore. She looked frighteningly determined. He stumbled, and she gripped him even harder and moved him along toward the house.

In Cliff's bedroom, each time she removed an article of clothing, Amanda paused to name a quality she admired in Cliff. "Good," she said, stepping out of her jeans. "He's a good man." Showering, Cliff couldn't hear her, the water was beating down too furiously. She could hear him, though, his big body bumping heavily against the plastic of the shower stall as he scrubbed himself. She imagined his hand soaping his shoulder and trembled.

"Strong shoulders," Amanda said in a softer voice, slipping off her red cami. She turned and looked in the faded oval mirror of an old dressing table. It would have belonged to Cliff's mother, Mildred Blair. Amanda couldn't imagine that Cliff ever looked at himself in it. She wasn't a mirror person either, but she couldn't resist looking at the strange, exciting sight of Amanda Jeffers standing in her bra and panties in Cliff Blair's bedroom. She blushed because she'd purchased her underwear online from Amazon in anticipation of this moment. The package had arrived yesterday. The bra (*Favorite Lacy Plunge Bra,* bright peach) cost $33, plus shipping. The panties were turquoise, and boy, when they said *Ultra Low Teeny Bikini,* they meant it. Amanda placed a modest hand over her loins and then willed herself to remove it. She stood there in the center of the room. Should she get into Cliff's bed or join him in the shower? She skittered over to the bed.

In the shower, Cliff soaped himself all over

for the third time. He wished he was washing with a bar of Irish Spring, something with a nice scent to it instead of this pale yellow no-name soap from Shop 'n Save. He made a mental note: ask Amanda what brand of soap smell she likes on her man. He gulped at his presumption: *her man.* This whole thing was so unlikely — showering for Amanda Jeffers who was right out there in his bedroom — that he stuck his head outside the shower curtain to make sure she had not run off in embarrassed regret. No, he could hear the creak of bedsprings. It was his parents' bed, part of a matching walnut veneer bedroom set they'd proudly bought mail order from Sears in the late 1950s.

The bed creaked again and he flinched, trying not to imagine his parents' couplings. He'd lived in this house his entire life but had never heard the bed make a sound, although there had been a lot of groans and sighs drifting up the heat vents to his little third-floor room. But that was just Dad rising for the 4:30 a.m. milking.

Cliff turned off the shower and peeped down at his nakedness. Oh gosh, he thought, shivering, would he be enough for her? Because boy, I mean, she's on fire. When Amanda had taken hold of his hand and led him up to the house, he wondered if she was ill, there was such a fever to her flesh. She was revved up and ready to go. He prayed to God he could attend to her properly. He grabbed his towel, wrapped it around his waist, turned to the bathroom door and placed his hand on the chipped porcelain doorknob.

Amanda, waiting in Cliff's bed, saw the doorknob turn. She lay naked atop the soft quilt like an exquisite candy in a tufted box. When the door began to open and steam curled out into the room, it was as if Cliff had been conjured from the mists of her longing. Yikes, she thought, and wiggled under the quilt and clutched it to her chest like Granny in her bed as the wolf made his entrance.

Standing in the open doorway, Cliff made a sheepish wolf, gripping his white towel to his waist even tighter than Amanda clutched her quilt. Cliff's mom, Mildred, had made the quilt. Amanda, glancing at her form naughtily outlined beneath its log cabin block pattern, remembered it hanging in Textile Hall at the Harford Fair, Grand Prize winner, August 1988.

She found the courage to speak. "Well, here I am, Cliff. Waiting in between your nice, clean Tuesday sheets."

Cliff stood frozen to the floorboards, three feet from the foot of the bed.

Amanda gave him a little wave of her fingers like she was greeting him from her pickup truck as he stood outside Nicholson Hardware. "Hey, it's just me."

Cliff gave a dazed little wave back with the hand that was holding up his too small towel. He fumbled for it, but Amanda was quicker. She reached out and pulled the towel free. Wearing nothing but his farmer's tan, Cliff started to cover himself with his hand, but then stopped and stood there for her.

Amanda looked him up and down. "Oh my God," she breathed. "You're really something." She slowly peeled back the quilt and revealed herself to him.

Cliff blinked and his mouth opened.

"Come on, Cliff. Get in this bed before we both die of heart attacks."

Cliff couldn't take his eyes off her. She was slightly thick around the waist, had an old appendectomy scar below her belly button and was blessed with the most beautiful breasts he had ever seen in his life. His admiration was not simply sexual — he was impressed as a professional dairy man.

Cliff floated on that thought to the memory of a painting he had happened on long ago while idly leafing through a dusty art history book in Pratt Public Library while Olive Perkins wasn't looking: Tintoretto's *The Origin of the Milky Way.* In it, Jupiter holds the infant Hercules to the breast of Juno, her milk spurting into the heavens to form the stars of the Milky Way. Cliff loved the idea that milk could be so essential to the order of the cosmos. In his excitement he had showed the picture to his dad, who was standing by the magazine rack reading a farm journal. His dad slapped him.

Cliff got into the old Sears bed beside Amanda. She closed her eyes and pressed the entire length of her body into his, a goddess in his arms. She pulled him tighter and tighter into an embrace so powerful he could hardly breathe.

Afterward, Amanda wept. But she proceeded to have sex with Cliff four more times over the next few months. The encounters were a disorienting comfort.

So now it was April. Today, at Cliff's, Amanda felt uneasy. The arrival (and departure?) of Harry Crane had been disruptive. Something was certainly out of kilter, and she could not say exactly what it was. Cliff came out of the shower as usual. She was in his bed as usual. She was wanting comfort and contact and they were in bed and she was on her back and Cliff was hovering above her doing preliminary things and it was all going fine, but it wasn't quite. Distracted, her eyes roamed the room and —

That's when she spotted it. Almost like the eye of a hawk, a tiny glittering rounded black dot where a black dot shouldn't be — between two books on the dresser. It flickered.

She froze. "What's that?"

Deep in the anticipation of pure pleasure, all set to go, Cliff murmured, "What?"

She pointed at the dresser. Whatever that dot was, it began to seriously malfunction. It blinked madly.

Amanda screamed and shoved Cliff off her. "What the hell is that?"

On the floor where he'd fallen, Cliff turned and looked at the dresser. "No, no, that's just —"

Naked and furious, Amanda tore across the room and found the mini digital video camera, a little black box about the size of a deck of cards tucked between the books. "You've been filming us? Cliff, you dirty shit, you're filming us!"

She hurled the camera into the wall above Cliff's head.

Smashed bits of black plastic rained down on him. "Amanda. It's just — I *knew.*" He got to his feet.

"Knew what? What are you saying? Did you put this online, you prick?"

"No, no, no! No way. It's just for shots of you. From the waist up. For me. For when it was over."

"What?"

"Just from the waist up."

"Stop saying that!"

Cliff's voice was an abashed whisper. "I knew, I mean, we *both* know. It couldn't last. That this was just you getting over Dean."

Amanda took this in.

"And I *never* put them online. Honest. The only other —" He caught himself.

Amanda's look instantly hardened, her eyes drilled into him. "You showed *Hoop.*"

"Only because —"

She crossed the room, stood smiling incredulously in front of Cliff, then slapped him so hard he saw stars. "Where's your computer?"

Sprawled on the bed, shaking his head, trying to clear it, he said, "In the den, but —"

She ran out of the bedroom. Cliff listened to the computer being smashed to bits.

Amanda reappeared in the doorway panting with rage.

From the waist up. She looked down at her breasts. Then out the bedroom window. In the distance stood the huge barn filled with cows with milk-heavy udders. She crossed her arms over her chest and glared at Cliff. "You two are a couple of *dairy perverts.*"

Cliff whispered, "He gets lonely, is all. He never gets to *see.*"

She struggled into her clothes. "You better learn the difference between a woman and a goddamn cow. What's wrong inside your head, Cliff? Your mother didn't breastfeed you or what?"

He blushed deeply.

Fully dressed, she stood before him. "If Dean were alive, he'd grab you by the neck and toss your ass into the middle of your manure pile. Because that's what you are and always will be, Clifford Blair. Steeped in cow shit!"

On the way home, on the long winding curves of Route 11, she passed Stu in his Buick, Tom in his Honda and about four different guys from the EMT crews. It was wall-to-wall man. Amanda thought: *No. Never again. Not in a billion years. Losers and weirdos, the whole damn lot of you.*

The gesture she made after each car went by was not a friendly wave.

10

Back at his office at Endless Dreams Realty, Stu Giptner brooded. Amanda Jeffers giving me the finger. Is that *really* what I saw in my rearview mirror? Yeah, it was. Definitely. Wow. Doesn't that just cap off a perfect friggin' day. Zero sales prospects and Amanda Jeffers giving me the finger. Was she mocking his nothingness? Did failure radiate off him to that degree? Assuredly. Would everybody start giving him the finger now? No doubt. He began to scratch at the scaly patch on the back of his bald head. The patch had been a source of irritation since childhood. In moments of high agitation, he scratched so feverishly the dry rasp sounded like a squirrel gnawing on a walnut. The other realtors down the hall closed their doors when Stu really got going. Scritch, scritch, scritch. He winced. Ow. He was going to draw blood if he wasn't careful. He folded his hands in his lap and went to his mantra. Repeating his mantra helped neutralize the negativity when he'd had a long, fruitless day.

"Six figures," he said. Ahhh, better, yes, the green warmth of potential money washing over him. "Six figures, six figures." Someday soon, very soon, real soon, soonish, he would become a six-figure realtor. Come on, Stu, hold on to that good feeling, he willed himself. Don't let it fade. Oh no, it's fading. Push that mantra *hard.* "Six figures, six, six, six." Soon now, real soon, sooner or later. Later. Late in life. Better late than never. Never. Never, never, never.

He'd never get there, never ever. *Six figures.* It was Stu's endless dream and endless torture. If he could just become a regular six-figure realtor. If he could just . . .

He sighed and scratched, lifted his weary gaze to the Endless Dreams Realty calendar that hung on the light-suckingly dark, fake wood paneling inches in front of his nose. His office was the size of a broom closet. "Yeah, right," he snorted at the calendar photo of an immense log home that surely belonged to some rich mogul. Behind it, the snowcapped Rocky Mountains ascended grandly into a pure blue sky. "Right. Gimme a break."

Endless Dreams Realty handled commercial, residential, lot-land and rental properties in a thirty-mile radius from the epicenter of Stu's unprepossessing office, north to Harford, south to Elkdale, west to Dixon and east to Tanners Falls. The Endless Mountains were not the Rockies. They were not even the Catskills. The Endless Mountains, let's face it, were inglorious hills where rich moguls never built homes. The only moguls were the coal barons down in Scranton, and that was . . . how many years ago?

Stu leaned back in his chair and tried to conjure a date. He was terrible at dates, which reminded him of the torture of Mrs. Kruckewszki's high school history class, which reminded him that his life in general was a string of constant defeats, predictable disappointments and unceasing agitations with an occasional cigarette break in between.

Let's see, he thought, the Pennsylvania coal barons were alive in . . . 1900 or somewheresabout? Stu felt the heat of stupidity rise in his cheeks, just as it used to when he was a stupid kid twenty-five years ago in Mrs. Kruckewszki's classroom. Except he wasn't stupid, not at all — he was *unlucky.* Mrs. Kruckewszki always called on him just when he happened to be daydreaming, usually about how to get money without working too hard. If she were alive today — and thank God, she was six feet under in Maplewood Cemetery — and called on him right this minute, Mrs. Kruckewszki would catch him in the exact same daydream.

He squinted at the calendar photo and wondered: Did coal barons work hard? Probably. So, really, he'd rather be a coal baron's son. And when *were* those damn coal barons anyway? Well, whenever the hell they were, they sure as Suzy didn't build any grand homes in this woeful little corner of the Endless Mountains like the log mansion pictured on that lie of a calendar.

Stu reached for the pack of cigarettes nestled in his coat pocket, slid one between his lips and sucked air through it, savoring the tease of unlit tobacco. After a minute or two, he slid the moist cigarette back into the pack. One cigarette a day right after lunch was all he allowed himself, and if he made it through the day on one, he rewarded himself with half a pack smoked through the course of the evening, which more often than not was spent at the Green Gables bar in the company of Cliff, Tom, Ronnie, Walter and the rest of those winners. At the end of an interminable day working his potential buyers (yeah, right) or sitting slumped in his Endless Dreams Realty soul-devouring office waiting for the phone to ring — a phone that Stu was convinced was connected on the other end to either a graveyard or a desert island — cigarettes and a beer or two was not a reward, but a life-saving goddamn necessity.

"Coal barons. Right," he blurted, fixed now on the subject he'd torture himself with for the next hour. No rich coal barons around here, he thought, only ancient coal miners who in their youth had dug their own black anthracite graves day after day and now sat coughing the remaining hours of their lives away in their decrepit little clapboard homes priced under six figures — the crummy fixer-upper "as is" properties — which was the only real estate that Vince Bromler, head broker and owner of Endless Dreams Realty, ever let Stu sell. Dead coal miner houses and dingy double-wide trailers owned by quarrymen. Never the parceled dairy farms on the rolling hillsides, never the commercial properties along the I-81 corridor, never the lake homes.

Lake homes. "Yeah, right," Stu said.

He lowered himself into the gloom of his thoughts, like a coal miner riding a coal car deeper into the descending dark. Buyers could smell the glum on him. He lifted his eyes to the wall calendar and sighed his patented desultory sigh. Why were they called buyers if they never *bought*? The economy hadn't always sucked. Why was it always so hard, good times or bad?

This afternoon, for example, the little "as is" gem out past Freeman's Corner in Dimock. Clomping up the front porch steps in his menacing black steel-toe work boots, the prospective buyer, a burly unsmiling guy with a buzz cut named Rod Karp, put his foot through the top step and when he grabbed the porch railing, a four-foot section snapped off in his hand. The foreclosed house had been on Stu's listing for a year, and he'd maintained it with threats and pleas and multiple tubes of cheap caulk. He kept a case of caulk in the back of his Buick at all times and a hammer, too, not to fix any of his properties, but to knock off rusty gutters and loose shutters and anything else that might be dangling. Or just to bang repeatedly on the ground after a sale went south, as today's did in less than a minute and a half.

Rod Karp had gone red-faced with anger. His scalp turned red, too. Stu could see it through Karp's buzz cut. Stu had always been scared of buzz cuts, and Rod Karp's looked like a million little nails anchored in boiling blood.

So Stu quickly smiled. It was a rictus grin. "Fifty thousand is a great, great price!" His voice a piglet squeal.

"I just put my foot through the goddamn porch!" Karp yelled.

"Only the top step — fixable — I'll get my men on it!"

Karp raised the piece of busted railing over his head and Stu dropped to the ground and cringed in anticipation of the blow, which he deserved. Instead, Karp hurled it at Stu's car with such force the right headlight vaporized in a sparkling cloud of glass dust. Then he jumped into his black Dodge Ram pickup, circled Stu twice like an Apache on horseback and roared down the dirt road.

Stu had let a minute go by before he sat up. He was shaking and feeling like he might throw up. He flopped back on the ground and stared at the sky. Someday he would just crumple to the ground and never get up again. It would happen because he was pusillanimous. Stu had come across the word a few months back, when he had been idly Googling definitions for "spineless" and "soft" and "lily-livered." *Pusillanimous.* The word impressed him because it seemed to be composed of "pus" and "villainous," which was precisely how he saw himself: made of pus and small-bore villainy. He was the kind of man who would cheat widows and librarians, given the chance. He would steal candy from a baby, except he didn't want to get caught. The mother might slap him. Stu envisioned it. Slapped and falling to the ground in a heap, a sticky lollipop instead of a cigarette in his mouth.

Sequestered in his office now, still trembly from the Karp encounter, Stu whispered, "I'm soft." He scratched his patch and whispered again, "I am a soft man."

He was a soft man in a region of tough men. Even the good guys, the ones nothing like Rod Karp, were tough in a way he could never be. Cliff was as tough as they come, and so was Ronnie and old Walter, too. Virtually all the exhausted, sweaty men hoisting beers in Green Gables were tough and worked in tough jobs Stu knew he wouldn't survive an hour, let alone a lifetime. Truck drivers, tractor mechanics, lumberyard workers, quarrymen. My God, Ronnie slaving away in Empett's quarry with stone saws and dynamite? Or dairy farming, like Cliff, are you kidding me? Stu was afraid of cows. The big dumb half-ton sons of bitches could bump you into a fence post and snap your spine like a potato chip.

Cows got Stu to thinking about deer, and deer led him to a particularly shame-inducing fear — guns. He could barely stand the sound of one going off, hated the smell of the cleaning oil, didn't even like being in the same room with a box of live ammunition. Everybody hunted something up here — even little Olive the librarian owned a .22 for scaring off groundhogs. There you have it, Olive Perkins, no bigger than a sparrow, was tougher than he was. Hell, *all* of the women in his thirty-mile real estate radius were. Including and especially . . . Amanda Jeffers.

Amanda.

Stu sighed, this time with pleasure, settling back in his office chair and raising his feet to his desk, idly massaging the tiny scar on the middle finger of his left hand like he was rubbing a magic lamp to conjure a genie. Maybe Amanda had given him the finger, not *disparagingly,* but in friendly acknowledgment of a finger episode — a crisis — that she had helped him through so wonderfully, three years ago. Sure, of course, yes. *That's* what she'd been doing when she passed his car on Route 11. Stu massaged, and slid into reverie. Sweet Amanda.

Three years ago he'd sliced the finger on the edge of a tuna can, setting off a journey that led him, ultimately and deliciously, to Amanda. Ronnie or Cliff would have bandaged the wound with duct tape and a paper towel and gone right back to work with their dirty cows and dirty jackhammers. A wound was important only if it seriously impaired a trigger finger.

But Stu was pusillanimous, and when he saw blood blossom from a wound that looked to him deep as the Mariana Trench, he cried out and grabbed a dish towel and sat down hard on the floor of his tiny apartment, pale and shaking. Stu was scared of cows and guns and buzz cuts, but what really terrified him was the notion of losing a finger. Half of the men he knew were missing fingers, and now, trying to make a tuna sandwich, he was about to join the club. He peeked at the towel. Blood seeped into view on the lower left corner. His precious blood was flowing abundantly enough to soak through a *towel.* He slid his hand under his armpit and clamped down hard, tourniqueting his wound as he fumbled in his pants pocket for his cell phone. He would call Ruthy, his ex-wife.

He hesitated, remembering their last meeting with a wince, and lowered the phone. Last month, he'd been showing Ruthy around an "as is" up in West Gibson, and when she opened a kitchen cabinet door, a hissing opossum leaped out, teeth bared. With a scream, Stu latched on to Ruthy as the opossum flew past them, skittered twice around the countertops, jumped to the floor and ran into the living room.

Ruthy jerked free of him and narrowed her eyes. "You were gonna sell me this infested piece of crap place? I mean, goddamn, Stu, I knew you'd try to cheat me, but I didn't know you was going to do it this bad!"

"Like I knew a possum was living in there, for chrissakes, Ruthy!" Well, he sort of knew. He'd heard a rodenty noise yesterday when he was caulking a few things around the house, but he was hoping it was just mice.

Ruthy looked him up and down, slowly, like she had lasers for eyes she was using to slice him in two. Above their heads the yowling opossum bounced off the walls of the upstairs bathroom. Suddenly and inexplicably, the toilet flushed.

They both stared at the ceiling. "Least he's toilet trained," Stu joked.

Ruthy shoved him aside and stormed out of the house.

So he couldn't call Ruthy, and he couldn't

dial 911 because not even Stu, scared as he was, would allow men with buzz cuts the opportunity to shake their heads and roll their eyes as they put him in the back of an unnecessary ambulance. *Paper towel and duct tape,* they'd be thinking, *that's all that little skinnick needs.*

The longer he sat on the apartment floor, the deeper the deadly foreign microbes from the tuna lid were burrowing into his wound. He was going to lose the finger, but Christ, he didn't want to lose the arm, so he mustered all his strength (very little) and courage (less) and ran downstairs to his Buick, covering the twenty miles of gravel back roads to Susquehanna Hospital's ER in less than fifteen minutes, steering with one hand.

Sitting in his office, thinking back on all this, Stu came to his favorite part of The-Day-I-Almost-Lost-My-Finger. The Amanda Jeffers part. Amanda when she still had her smile, before Dean up and died on her last year in that snowy field.

Swooning across two chairs in the ER waiting room, Stu had tried not to think about the scalpel that would finish the job the tuna lid had begun. The Susquehanna Hospital doctor would tend to his wound with the brisk, brutal efficiency of a Civil

War field surgeon. *Bite down on this here whisky rag, Corporal Giptner, and feel free to cry out to yer mama, because we gonna start sawing.*

Amanda Jeffers appeared in the hazy distance, an earth angel in scrubs, and even though Stu knew he was going to lose his finger, at least Amanda, luscious, powerful Amanda, would be the one holding him down while they hacked it off. She was so beautiful. Between the booms of his panicked heart, he heard actual angel music as she walked down the corridor toward him. Sweet violins, a babbling brook, celestial birds at dawn.

"Hey there, Stu," she said, looking at his towel-wrapped hand. Her voice had none of the Scranton nasal common to the local women. It was pure velvet, and so was her skin when she took hold of his arm. Everybody in the Endless Mountains was a mix of Polish and German, but Amanda looked like a big Dutch girl or a Swede, that smile, those white teeth, the blond hair, her full hips. She was the epitome of the woman Stu would never, ever have.

"How many fingers and how did you do it?" she asked as she guided him to an ER room. In his erotically laced fear-haze, her voice took on a thick Swedish lilt.

"One finger," he managed to croak. "Tuna lid."

"Ouch," Amanda said. Not mocking, not at all. Wounds didn't have to come from guns and axes and tractor accidents. There were lesser, perfectly legitimate wounds in the world. Stu wanted to kiss her for acknowledging it. He lay back on the stretcher as she carefully unwrapped the dish towel and dropped it into the biohazard trash can. He couldn't feel his finger, and in a moment of panic thought it had been tossed into the trash can along with the bloody towel. He peeked. It was still there. He looked quickly away and tried not to whimper.

Amanda adjusted the exam light. "Aw, that's just a bitty cut, Stu Giptner. It won't even need a stitch, just a couple of Steri-Strips."

For a moment, drenched in sweat, Stu was unable to speak. He closed his eyes and immediately thought of the fallout that would result from this little visit to the ER. "Um," he murmured.

"Yes?"

He opened his eyes again but couldn't look at her. "You won't tell . . . anybody?"

Amanda grinned. "You mean, like Dean, who'd tell Ronnie, who'd tell Tom so that by the time you hit Green Gables tonight, every man at the bar would —"

"Right, right," Stu whispered. "That's exactly what I mean."

Amanda placed a hand on Stu's shoulder. Her eyes were jewels and her breath was spearminty from the gum she slowly chewed as she smiled at him. He remembered her in high school, chewing gum in that way of hers that somehow was not trailer-trashy but a sign of her vigor, the need to keep even the tiniest muscles of her fine powerful body in motion. Dean was like that, too, shifting his weight from leg to leg, rubbing his arms the entire time he talked to you. Both of them too physical to keep still. Stu could only imagine the monumental sex between them.

"Listen to me, Stu. Dean and Cliff and those fools wouldn't even have come in. But you knew to come in — for your tetanus shot. The cows and chickens, the farm dust in the air — around here's a petri dish for tetanus. You get an A for thinking."

Stu blushed and stared in wonder. Mrs. Kruckewszki never gave him an A for thinking. Amanda was kind-hearted and beautiful and she made love like a lioness. Backlit by the powerful glare of the exam light, she appeared heaven-sent. That day, Stu was the happiest man on earth. He would sacrifice a finger a week just to be ministered to by Amanda Jeffers. When she gave him his tetanus shot, he took it like a man.

Now, in his office, he swiveled around to his computer screen and pulled up a file:

Amanda P. Jeffers.
RR 4 Box 4152 Maple Road.
New Milford, PA 18414

Stu felt real bad about what he was going to do to her. What he was hoping to do. What he prayed he'd be able to do. And then he felt real good.

He frowned and squinted his eyes. Because you know what? Screw her for giving him the finger this afternoon. Because that's what she had done. Gone out of her way to reject him. He never stood a chance with her. None, zero, zip.

He scrolled down, his frown lifting into a smirk of conquest. He had a little set of eyes and ears at Susquehanna Mortgage & Loan by the name of Steve Jones. Steve kept him apprised of who was in arrears on their mortgages and home equity loans. And look who made the list last month:

Dean L. Jeffers and Amanda P. Jeffers:
Acct. #382W904
10 YEAR HOME EQUITY LOAN,
INCEPTION JUNE 15, 2008.

Repayment Summary

$265.09 Monthly Payment	$53, 000 Total of 120 Payments
$19,592.27 Total Interest	June, 2018 Completion Date

LOAN IN ARREARS

DECEMBER 15, 2016 $265.09
JANUARY 15, 2017 $265.09
FEBRUARY 15, 2017 $265.09

Stu grinned. The Widow Jeffers had missed three payments. He couldn't have her, but he would get her house. Her lovely six-figure house.

Stu leaned back in his chair and placed his arms behind his bald head. Those arms like flexing wings, that bald head — he looked just like a vulture circling the treetops of the Endless Mountains for easy prey.

Six figures, baby. Off her back, he was going to become a six-figures man. Then we'll see who gives the finger to who. To whom. Whom or who? He blushed, because he could almost hear Mrs. Kruckewszki in her grave, chuckling at his stupidity.

11

After supper and homework Oriana searched the tree house.

There was *The Grum's Ledger,* hidden in the pillowcase. She had left a tiny bit of pileated woodpecker feather fluff in the crease at the binding on page four. If it had been puffed loose, that meant Harry Crane read the book. It was still in place.

How could he leave? She was dizzy with anger. And fear. Harry had to come back. He had to. What if something happened to him? What if — she stopped herself. Took a shivery breath and gulped back tears.

She went to the bookcase and pulled out the tree guide. She turned to "North American Hardwood Trees." Found the maples. Red maple, silver maple . . . sugar maple. She nodded and studied the botanical name. Then she spoke, loud and determined, and cast her spell. The incantation that would bring Harry Crane home to his tree house.

"Acer saccharum," she said. *"Saccharum, saccharum, Acer saccharum."*

She looked out into the woods. Like a curl of invisible smoke, the spell would wend its way sinuously between the tree trunks, find him and compel him back.

It did not compel him back at 8:00 p.m. or 9:00 p.m., when she looked out her bedroom window for his light. Or at 9:01 p.m. or 9:02 p.m. All was dark.

"To bed, Oriana, come on. It is what it is."

You don't know what it is, Mom, she thought. You just don't.

Amanda did not glance out Oriana's window as she passed by. She was not feeling charitably toward men in general, not after today's episode with Cliff. The men who die too young in the snow, or cheat on you with stupid little cameras, or drop into the forest and get your daughter's hopes up.

Back in her own bedroom, though, just before she turned her light out at ten, she looked. The forest, the big fat government wilderness tract, was as dark as her mood. Good night, she said, to the empty tree house, to the empty forest, to the empty side of her bed.

■ ■ ■ ■

But at 10:10 p.m., when Oriana tiptoed over to her window and looked out, she saw the flare of a match in the distant trees and the brighter flare of a kerosene lamp coming to life.

Oriana, queen of secrets and stealth, knew all the squeaky floorboards and just how to go down the stairs quiet as a ghost. She was fully clothed and ready for action. She found the flashlight hanging on the peg in the mudroom, eased open the back door and slid into the night. She advanced through the trees toward the flickering lamplight.

She didn't need a light. All she had to do was follow the sound of Harry cursing.

"Shit. Goddamn it."

He was somewhere close to the base of the beech tree.

"Harry Crane. Where *were* you?"

She flicked on the flashlight and shined it on him. He flung his hands in front of his face. "Hey! You're blinding me." Then, "Your mom know you're out here?"

"Are you kidding?" Quietly, she added, "I thought you ran away."

"I would've, if I had any sense."

Oriana nodded approvingly. "But you don't, do you?"

"No. I lack common sense. Increasingly."

He looked up into the giant beech tree. Lit up by the kerosene lamp, the colored glass in the windows turned the tree house into a floating jewelry box. The tree house seemed a manifestation of his own psyche. His life had changed alarmingly in the last twelve hours — he wouldn't be surprised if he suddenly began to emit the same sort of dizzy, multicolored glow.

"You weren't just doing forest work," said Oriana. She trained her light on a duffel bag and a cooler leaning against the base of the beech.

He pointed up at the tree house. "That's the shelter. This is the food and the clothing. The three always go together."

"Where did you go?"

Where? To the place all escaped forestry bureaucrats who have attempted suicide and then been rescued by a candy bar and a red-tailed hawk go — Scranton.

When he awoke at dawn this morning in the tree house, Harry had thought to himself: *here.* He had not been present anywhere in a year. Sitting on the cot, taking it all in, he heard Beth's words. *Sweetheart, just quit the Forest Service.*

He looked through the dream-strange windows into the forest. I am living in a tree house, he thought, in the middle of a forest. In no version of Harry's Trees had he and Beth ever contemplated running away to a forest and setting up home in a tree house. They were a sensible pair. He'd have quit the Forest Service and worked at Baylor Arboretum. Or become a landscaper or an arborist. And the place he'd come home to — not in a tree, but firmly grounded — Beth would've been there.

Now he was ungrounded, floating almost, in the treetops. He looked out at the tips of the sugar maples and pin oaks. The terminal buds were swollen with the possibility of spring. Much more than a possibility — spring was *inevitable.* It was about to cascade through this forest, the energy building in the trees like the crest of a wave. To be here in the treetops when that wave of green hit — it was going to be stunning.

Oh Beth, he thought, *I wish you were here to see this.* He listened for her reply, but heard now, not her voice, but the wind in the trees, her communication with him not fading exactly, but changing into something else. She was everywhere present, but no longer here.

Harry gripped the windowsill to steady himself. Harry's Trees without Beth. On his own.

A distant flash, from the direction of Amanda's house, the dawn sun glinting. Harry shrank back from the window. No doubt, Oriana flashing a mirror at him. Urgent for contact. The fact was, he was not at all on his own. Because there seemed to be a little girl in his life. A very *overwhelming* sort of little girl. And he had to get her under control so he could remain here, so that he could become whatever kind of tree man he was to become.

He needed to clear his mind, get organized, have a plan. He would commit to the unknown, yes, but he'd do it in a very practical and measured Harry sort of way. After all, he had a job, a house — and millions of dollars to deal with. It was critical he proceed with scrupulous care. If he vanished unaccountably they'd search for him.

Thus, Scranton. He drove twenty miles south to downtown Scranton, because:

(a) the cell phone reception in the forest was spotty and he had a lot of texting and emailing to do,

(b) he needed supplies, and,

(c) Scranton was, well, anonymous.

Scranton was a tired old town. Running north to south, the Lackawanna River bisected the city, filling the air with its sluggish perfume. Coal dust blackened the once-glorious brick municipal buildings. Scrantonians seemed unable to look up from the broken pavement. Really, not one person lifted his or her eyes to look into Harry's face. It was absolutely perfect.

He spent the morning at Home Depot and Hagley's Camping Supply. He paid cash for everything. He bought a cooler and ice and went to the Giant supermarket on Dullun Avenue. Then he went back downtown for lunch — but mostly for a beer.

He sat in a booth in a place off Gunster Avenue called McWhistle's Pub & Eatery and ate a large salad and a hamburger. He ordered a Guinness Extra Stout because he needed extra stouting. He was about to do something he had never done before — cross Wolf.

Harry scrolled through his text messages. There were fifteen from Wolf, from yesterday and this morning, and all of them said, in typically escalating language, essentially the same thing: Where the fuck are you, little brother? Wolf, in his Wolfian way, knew that *McWilliams, Torrey & Conwell* had settled with the construction company, that Harry, as Wolf would perceive it, had struck it rich. Harry smiled in wonder. Here he was, about to hide in the magic forest from a devouring Wolf. And, oh yeah, the girl in this fairy tale — was wearing red.

Harry chugged his stout, wiped a rising line of sweat from his brow and began to type away on his phone. Wolf replied instantaneously.

Harry: Hi Wolf.
Wolf: where are you?
Harry: In a good place.
Wolf: you don't sound right

Harry's phone rang. Harry didn't answer. He texted again.

Harry: I'm not picking up.
Wolf: pick up the phone harry
Harry: No.
Wolf: harry.
Harry: No.
Wolf: where are you?
Harry: In a good place. Safe.
Wolf: safe? what the hell? safe???
Harry: Just a good place, Wolf.
Wolf: come home
Harry: What are you? Dad?
Wolf: dad never came home. cut the

shit, harry. this is big.
Harry: Can't. Know you're there. Sitting on my front step. Smoking.

There was an audible pause in the ether. Wolf probably flicking a butt and lighting another cigarette. Harry could almost hear the angry inhale.

Wolf: I'm here. because you need me
Harry: Listen, I'm not coming home.
Wolf: for fuck's sake, you're going to get scammed, screw up your money. I know investing. this is HUGE, harry. this is the biggest moment in your life.

Wow, thought Harry. Wow, wow, wow.

Harry: Beth's death . . . pretty big moment, Wolf.
Wolf: don't screw with me. you're not in a good place head-wise. the money freeking you out
Harry: Freaking has an "a." Sounds like it's you who's freaked.
Wolf: you come home now

Harry took a deep breath and signaled the waitress for another Guinness.

Wolf: you there? it's seven million dol-

lars, little bro.
Wolf: you there? 7,000,000. look at all those zeroes.
Harry: The thing about zeroes? They equal nothing. Bro.
Wolf: quit fucking with me
Harry: Not to put too fine a point on it, but Toland gets his lawyer third. So, closer to four million.
Wolf: harry
Harry: 4,000,000.
Wolf: harry. jesus. you have to invest it properly. build up your nest egg.
Harry: Smashing all the eggs, Wolf. Getting rid of it as fast as I can.

Harry could just about hear Wolf's head exploding. As for Harry — his heart was imploding. Just seeing the sentence he had just written. All that money, and how it had come to him. Maybe he'd get it in cash and light a bonfire in the forest. He had no idea what he was going to do. But he would do it fast and Wolflessly.

Wolf: please.
Harry: I'm not coming home, Wolf. And I am in a safe place. You got all that?
Wolf: please.

Please. The word had never before come

out of Wolf's mouth. Harry felt a little sick.

Harry: Okay. Signing off.
Wolf: wait. you have a house and a job.
Harry: All handled, Wolf.

This was a lie. Harry had some scrambling to do.

Wolf: please. my dad deserting me. now my brother.

Harry thought, And your too many wives, you forgot to throw that into the emotional pot.

Wolf: and my wife, harry. leaving me. that makes three.
Harry: But all are ALIVE, Wolf. As soon as the check clears, the money is gone.
Wolf: harry!!!
Harry: Will keep you posted. See you.
Wolf: please!!!
Harry: Over and out.

"Fuck, fuck, fuck me!" Wolf stood on Harry's front porch steps, glaring at his cell phone.

A man walking his dog crossed to the other side of the street.

The front yard was littered with Wolf's cigarette butts. He reared back to toss his phone against a tree. Stopped himself. Fuck.

I worked for this money, Wolf thought. Coaxing and coddling Harry, guiding him. I deserve a share. My share. More than my share, because what does he know about money? And now the little shrimp was doing what, exactly? Having a breakdown that was going to screw up everything.

Where was he?

How much time before the check cleared?

Could he have Harry committed? Did they commit people anymore?

Could he hire a PI? Do they have private eyes anymore?

"Fuck." Wolf lit a cigarette, spun around and faced Harry's house. The muscles in his big jaw flexed. He was practically snorting like a bull. I deserve my cut. I watched out for him. I was like a father to the little prick.

His phone rang. Harry? No. Shit. The almost ex-wife down in Virginia. From the moment he'd said "I do" it was over. It was over before he'd even met her. Ashley.

Now she was texting him. Wait, not Ashley. It was *Barb.* Ashley was his second wife. Wolf stared at his screen.

Barb: Where are you? 4 way conference 1 hour. You better be there.

"Fuck," muttered Wolf. I'm hiding from Barb, Harry's hiding from me. The world is one big fucking game of hide-and-seek. Oh, he *would* seek his younger brother. He would seek and find him, but good.

Harry will not walk out on me, thought Wolf. He watched a car go by and instantly thought of his father — not walking out on them, but driving. Wolf hated cars. Wolf hated anybody over sixty behind the wheel of a car, like that guy, because that's how old the prick would be if he was even still alive.

Wolf turned and glared at Harry's house. He could kick the door down, that was an option. I'm gonna huff and puff and kick this door down.

A Waverly police car drove slowly past. Wolf lowered his door-kicking leg as if he was stretching or maybe doing tai chi, and nodded toward the car. The cop wasn't even looking his way. Wolf thought, I should go to the cops, actually. Have them put out an APB on Harry. Because he stole my four million dollars. Do they have APBs anymore?

Wolf half smiled. In a way, he was proud

of little bro. Making a move. Where'd you get the balls to do this, Harry? You're the ball-less wonder.

No, this wasn't about balls, Harry was going truly nuts. I have to find him before he does something stupid. Like donate the money to, oh Christ . . .

1) Greenpeace,

2) The Sierra Club,

3) The Red Cross,

4) Some scammer on Kickstarter inventing a new vegan cheese or a solar flush techno-toilet for some Third World armpit village,

5) UNICEF.

Wolf shuddered in horror. "Fuck!"

Immediately after finishing with Wolf, Harry called *McWilliams, Torrey & Conwell.* In eight days, Toland said, the law firm would receive a check for seven million dollars from Carlisle Demolition Company, then deposit it into the firm's escrow account. After processing suit and attorney fees — this would take four days — they would electronically transfer approximately four million dollars to Harry's money market account at Vanguard. Harry's current balance was $11,431.21.

Toland burbled on, still in the alpha

afterglow of victory. Harry held the phone away from his ear, waited for the noise to subside and then said, "Thank you," and hung up.

Next, he put in a call to Sally Baker, the real estate agent who had sold them the house five years ago. Sally had been at Beth's memorial service.

"Not a problem, Harry. What you're asking for is called property management. We have several properties in Waverly. Rentals. But you're not renting, right?"

No. Not selling, he told her, not renting, haven't made a decision. On a hiatus.

For three hundred dollars a month, her agency would handle everything. Lawn service, cleaning service that would empty the refrigerator, turn down the heat — everything domestic from A to Z. Sally would do a walk-through once every two weeks to make sure everything was in tip-top shape. They set up a plan for tax and mortgage payments.

Harry said, "My brother may be lurking around. We don't get along. We're in the middle of a family thing. Not a big deal, just don't let him in the house, please. He can be . . . persuasive."

Sally understood. She said she'd alert the police for the occasional drive-by. "We see it all in the real estate business, Harry. Families and property — it can get intense."

She added, "So, how *are* you, Harry?"

Harry was ready for this. "Well, Sally, with grieving — you know how they always say the first year is so disorienting? I feel like I'm coming out of a fog. It's been a process. And this is part of it."

This was the notion he wanted to plant in Sally, for surely she would gossip. It's what real estate agents do. She'd say, *Harry is off somewhere getting it together.* He's on an emotional journey. Perfectly reasonable. Everybody has their own way of dealing.

"Oh, Harry, one more thing," she said. "I'll need a key."

Sally chuckled when he told her where the spare key was hidden: in the knothole of the dogwood to the right of the garden shed. "Of course," she said. "Where else would someone in the Forest Service hide a key?"

Formerly of the Forest Service. That was Harry's next bit of business. By email, he contacted his boss, Irv Mickler, and resigned, effective immediately. Harry had a jillion sick days and vacation days coming to him. He wouldn't be coming back in.

And this was a little vindictive, but what the hell. Harry ended the email with: Just a thought, Irv. Bob Jackson can handle the RP initiatives, SOPA reports, NFS studies, FSI summaries and the process predicament reviews. Bob loves to get down in the weeds. He's an absolute workhorse.

And that was the end of Harry's career in bureaucratic forestry.

12

And the beginning of life in a real forest. He stared at Oriana. The word *forest* was no longer a simple word. Just thinking it, he could feel this young girl's pull. I'm trying to get to Harry's Trees, he thought, but to get there I will have to travel through Oriana's Forest.

"What is that thing?" she said. She scanned a lumpy duffel bag with her flashlight. They stood at the base of the tree house. The moon had come out from behind a cloud.

Harry removed a strange folded contraption from the bag. "Voilà. A camp commode."

"A what?"

"A camping toilet."

"You brought your own *toilet*? Ew. Weird."

Harry gave her a look. "I'm sorry. You don't have a toilet in your house?"

"This is outdoors. Outdoors, you just go."

"Well, I do things differently."

She unfolded the contraption. It was a three-legged stool, with a plastic fabric sling seat that had a circular hole in the center. She sat on it and grinned. "This is the dumbest thing I ever saw."

Harry crossed his arms and waited. "Had your fun? Can we go up now? Actually, you need to go home. It's late. It's the woods. It's night. Go away."

"You bring anything else good?"

She rummaged around in the duffel bag and pulled out an old green-and-white cap with an official Forest Service logo on the front.

Harry said, "It was in the trunk of my car."

She put it on her head. "What else do you have?" She started rummaging again.

He stopped her and zipped up the bag. "Just provisions."

"What are 'provisions'?"

"Provisions. *Things.* Food. Clothes."

"I know most words. Just not the ones you use sometimes. I'm really smart, you know."

"Believe me, I know."

She considered him. "You really don't have kids?"

"No."

"But you're married." Her light went to

his wedding band. The gold flashed, undeniably.

Harry didn't meet her eyes. Which, even though it was dark, he knew were lasered in on him. He gripped one handle of the cooler. "If you're going to hang around, then help. Grab the other end," he said.

They struggled up the spiral stairs. Oriana was small but mighty. Strength gained from rustic living. Harry doubted the kids on his suburban block would be able to do this.

The Grum's Ledger sat on the triangular wooden table in the corner, waiting. Oriana had taken it out of the pillowcase earlier in the day, when she had come looking for Harry. The light of the kerosene lamp, which Harry had lit a few minutes earlier when he'd gone up to the tree house with the first of his supplies, played over the ledger's wrinkled and faded cover.

Harry averted his eyes.

"You were supposed to read it, but you didn't," Oriana said.

"Oh yeah? And how would you know that?"

She opened the book and pointed to the tiny bit of woodpecker fluff on page four. "Still there." She pursed her lips and blew it into the air.

"Sneaky girl," Harry said.

Oriana nodded approvingly. "I stay on my toes," she said.

"Where did you get the book?"

"From the secret place. Where fairy tales come from."

"Ah, of course, the secret fairy tale place. The land of Snow White and magic lottery tickets and hawks and unicorns and ogres."

"Not ogres. Grums."

Harry sighed. "Let's do something sensible, shall we?" He thrust a box of crackers at her. "Help me put my stuff away."

Oriana helped store his food in the two cabinets on either side of the tiny kitchen sink. She showed him how the sink worked. "You pull up on the handle then give it three pumps. It uses rainwater so it's just for washing dishes." A fifty-gallon oak rain barrel was fixed to the roof of the tree house. She told him he was supposed to use only organic soap. The sink drained down a long hose hidden under the spiral stairs and into the ground. The tree house was as tight and perfectly appointed as the captain's quarters in an old sailing ship.

"You guys thought of everything."

"For drinking water, there's a spring. I'll show you where tomorrow. It's kind of hidden." She opened the cabinet under the sink and pulled out a plastic jug. "This is to carry the water."

"You need to go home. You're tired."

"I can't fall asleep until I've had a bedtime story." She eyed him.

Harry turned to the window. The moon was bright now. They stood at the largest window in the tree house, which faced west, and looked out onto the moon-silvered treetops.

"Beautiful," Harry said. "I love that this copse — fancy word for a cluster of trees — is quaking aspen. Know why this beech tree is right in the middle of all these aspens?"

She shook her head.

"Because aspen leaves are very acidic, and beech trees thrive in acidic soil." He filled the room with facts. "And it goes both ways. They help each other." He patted one of the smooth, silver-gray branches, thick as an elephant's leg, that went up through the middle of the tree house. "A beech tree is very tall and gives mixed shade. That's what aspens require. Not too much sun or too much shade."

"You're stalling," she said. And placed *The Grum's Ledger* in his hands.

He put it back on the table.

Oriana considered him. "Are you an aspen or a beech?"

"An aspen, definitely. I quake a lot. I'm

just one of a crowd. I bend in the wind."

"I'm definitely a beech tree."

"Why?"

"Because my dad was a giant." She patted a thick branch. "So I'm going to be like this. Giant and strong."

They stared out the window for a while longer without speaking. Did she mean a *real* giant? Probably. Her father a giant and her mother, in Harry's mind, an Amazon warrior queen. This kid's imagination was contagious. He looked into the forest, expecting to see Amanda Jeffers just behind a distant tree trunk, Amazonian, with an immense bow, reaching into her quiver for an arrow with his name on it, taking aim. *Hurry up and read my daughter the book, it's late, she has school in the morning. Don't be such a quaking aspen.*

Oriana, beside him, was nodding to herself, deciding on something important. "Okay. In bed last night, I was thinking. You're right." She gestured to the moonlit woodland out the window. "This is both of ours. These are your trees, too."

Harry fiddled with his wedding ring. After a long moment, he said, "Harry's Trees." He blinked and looked away. Cleared his throat, spoke softly. "That's always been a dream of mine. To start a business called

Harry's Trees." And at the end of each day, he thought, I would come home to Beth.

He looked up. Oriana was watching him play with his ring. He stopped and placed his right hand over it.

"Harry's Trees," she said gently. "That's a great name. Nice and simple." Then she stepped back, and recited:

"Oriana's Forest
And Harry's Trees.
A place enchanted,
Thick with leaves."

Harry nodded. "Wow. Impressive."

"Told you I was smart."

The Grum's Ledger sat on the table, waiting. Oriana waiting.

Harry avoiding. "So this tree house," he said. "How come nobody breaks in or bothers it?"

"You know why. It's protected by magic." Oriana considered further. "And nobody really comes out here much. You might see Ronnie. And maybe Stu."

"Who are they?"

"Ronnie was my dad's friend. He feels bad about my dad dying. When he gets a deer, he always brings venison for Mom. He won't bother you unless you bother him."

"And Stu?"

"Stu Giptner. He's a creep that always

pokes around. He sells houses."

"Why would he be coming out here?"

"To look at our house. Because he's a vulture."

Ronnie leaving meat. Stu sniffing out the property. Amanda Jeffers, widowed, supporting herself. An Amazon with a financial Achilles' heel?

Harry looked over at *The Grum's Ledger.* "Tell me more about your dad," he said. The man hovered above everything, was at the core of Oriana's obsession with magic. Harry didn't know a thing about kids, but it made sense. If he'd had a crazy year after Beth, this child would have had her own kind of crazy year.

And he wondered. Did her father write *The Grum's Ledger* for her? Was that the secret of this book? If Dean Jeffers built this far-fetched tree house, did he make up stories, too? Certainly, no-nonsense Amanda Jeffers was not a storyteller.

Oriana said, "It's *time,* okay?"

Why was he stalling? Because the book was everything to Oriana, her sole purpose, and if it loomed large for her, it loomed large for him. Here he was trying to deal with his own heartache, and she was determined to pull him into hers. What if he couldn't help her? Really, how could he, when he'd done such a lousy job of making it through his own tangled forest? Look at me, Oriana. You see I'm still wearing my ring. If I told you what it meant, you'd understand that I'm the last person to help you let go of your father. I am not a man who knows how to let go.

And then he thought, Jesus, Harry. Stop thinking of yourself and help this kid. Help *her* let go. Really, what is she asking of you? She just wants you to read a book. Not very much, is it? This is what grown-ups do with children. She needs the comfort of a special book. You read it, she feels better, she calms down. What's more soothing than a book? That's what they're for, right? A good book, then she goes home, climbs into her little bed and falls to sleep. Oriana goes to sleep. Harry goes to sleep. Amanda goes to sleep. The forest goes to sleep. The entire planet goes to sleep. Harry was getting sleepy just thinking how wonderful it was going to be. The perfect way to end a long day. A bedtime story. He yawned.

"All right. Okay. We read it," he said. "Then you go on home to bed."

"Deal."

They sat side by side on the cot.

He cleared his throat and scrunched his eyes. Harry realized he had never read a book to a child.

Oriana reached over and opened the cover of the old bank ledger. Harry took a nervous breath and read the first handwritten words. " 'Once upon an endless time in the Endless Mountains there —' "

Oriana elbowed him. "Go slower. And your voice should have a kind of singsong to it." She demonstrated. "Once upon an endless time . . ."

Harry nodded and started again. He could feel his heart pounding as he read. And he could feel, somehow, the beating of Oriana's heart, too. The tree house was a-thump with human heart.

" 'Once upon an endless time . . .' " he said.

The Grum's LEDGER

Once upon an endless time in the Endless Mountains, there lived an old grum. From moonrise to sunrise to moonrise again, the grum sat hunched and grumbly atop his hoard of gold coins, his heart as cold and heavy as his treasure.

At the end of each endless day, he counted his coins and entered the number in his ledger. The number was always the same. Everything was always the same.

One evening, as the sun dipped below the distant mountains, the grum fell into a fitful slumber. He whimpered and twitched, his nightmares tossed with Grieving Ghosts and Shadowy Sads and Woeful Wisps.

The grum lurched awake when he heard a sound — plink plink plink. His twitchings and turnings had shaken loose a single piece of gold. It rolled down the treasure pile and plinked away into the dark green forest. This had never happened before. The grum frowned, sighed a great musty sigh and started after it. He stopped. Sighed again.

And again.

Something wasn't right. He breathed another grummy breath. The heavy place inside his thick chest felt . . . lighter. He shifted his furry bottom, which was icy cold from sitting so long atop his pile of gold. When he wiggled the six gnarly toes of his left foot and the seven gnarly toes of his right, three more coins rolled — plink plink plink — down the golden heap.

Now when he drew a great lungful of foresty air, the grum smelled rich earth and damp leaves. His murky eyes unmurked, and he saw fireflies like gold coins dancing in the air around him.

The grum scooped up a handful of coins. He felt their cold weight and winced at their blindy shine. He opened his fingers and let them slip from his grasp — plink plink plink.

His thumpless heart thumped. His crooked spine uncrooked. For the first time in years (that had passed like centuries), he turned his eyes from his treasure heap to the star-soaked sky. The stars . . . were brighter than his gold!

The grum scooped up another handful of coins and let them fall. And then he scooped up two handfuls and tossed them into the night. He did it again. And again. More and more, faster and faster. As the mound of treasure grew smaller, his arms grew stronger. Clumps of greasy fur dropped from his body. With a smoky poof, a gnarled toe vanished from his left foot and — poof poof — two toes vanished from his right. He stared at his feet and remembered. Five was the right number of toes! The more gold he tossed into the night, the less grummy he grew.

Casting away the last of the gold in great heaps and hurls, he uncovered another treasure, his first and truest, which he had lost long ago — a beautiful young woman with chestnut hair and tortoiseshell glasses. Year after year, coin by greedy coin, he had buried and forgotten her. The grum fell to his knees and begged forgiveness.

The woman was wise and kind. With a kiss she forgave his foolishness. The grum changed back into the young man he had once been and the two lovers walked hand in hand through a forest lit by golden fireflies, endlessly happy ever after in the Endless Mountains.

Oriana made Harry read the story twice. The second time through, she listened with her eyes shut.

Harry felt light-headed as he closed the ledger.

Oriana opened her eyes. "Now the other

story. They go together."

What did *that* mean?

"I had the book, you had the ticket," she said. "You have to tell me the story of the lottery ticket."

"Now wait a minute. That's not a story. It's real life. And I don't want to."

"You *have* to." She cocked her head and studied him. "You've never told anybody. Have you?"

When he shook his head, he didn't look at her.

"Because you've been *saving* it," she said. "You've been saving it for right now. That's what my dad knows."

"Listen," Harry said, his voice rising. "All I did was buy the damn thing. At a convenience store. I bought a crummy ticket at a crummy convenience store. There's no story. Not everything's a story, Oriana."

"Everything *is* a story," she said. "And this one's so big you came to the forest. With your *rope.* Why?"

The girl played rough. Harry rubbed his neck. She was right, of course. For an endlessly endless year, he'd kept it inside. Never telling a soul.

Oriana reached into her pocket, waited a beat, then opened her hand and revealed the lottery ticket. "I didn't want to give it back until I was sure you'd stay." She held it out to him.

He didn't want to touch it. She had to uncurl his fingers to place it in his hand. He immediately closed his fist over it.

"Harry. You have to look at it. You have to look at it really hard."

He snapped at her. "How do you know all this? How is it that you have a rule for each and every thing?"

The girl wavered, then jutted her chin at him. "Rules are important in fairy tales. It's just the way it is. We won't get anywhere unless we do it right. The ticket is like a book you have to read. The story's *inside* it."

My God, she was exhausting. How much was he going to have to give this child? He met her steely eyes.

"Fine. Okay. All right." He slowly opened his hand. Looked. "So, okay, here's how it goes. Here's the story." He stared at the worn, crumpled ticket as he spoke. "It was a year ago." He flicked his eyes at her. "You know the exact date. Obviously. And my wife and I — Beth and I — we were in Philadelphia on our way to a movie."

Oriana grabbed his arm. "No. Not that way. Like a fairy tale. You have to tell the lottery ticket the right way."

"What?"

"Once upon a time . . ."

"Oh, Jesus."

"Once upon a time . . ." she pushed.

Harry, tired of arguing, closed his eyes. And saw Beth on Market Street as she handed him the mini Snickers. Then saw the same Snickers waiting for him in the knothole of the sugar maple. The gold wrapper glinting with a blindy shine.

He opened his eyes, blinking and squinting in the suffusing light of memory. Oriana, unstoppable Oriana, was right. It was a fairy tale. A grim fairy tale, absolutely unreal, absolutely true.

And at last, it came out of him. After a year of holding it in, he told his story.

He stared hard at the lottery ticket — his unlucky talisman — and began, his voice quaking like the leaves of an aspen. "Once upon a time, an endless time that was only yesterday, when the sun was shining and all the world was before them, there was a beautiful woman and a selfish, weak man who loved her very much."

Harry faltered. The tree house swayed in the night wind. Everything swaying everywhere. He was in the tree house, but he was also on Market Street as a cold March blustery gust blew Beth's new red coat against her legs.

Back and forth Harry bounced, unstuck in once upon a time.

"You're doing good," whispered Oriana from somewhere. Harry present yet far away.

"Very, very much, did he love her," continued Harry. "But the man was full of cowardice that was really a kind of greed. Greed, like a toad that sat on his heart, like a dragon that burned his soul. He was greedy for all that was safe and for all that was secure. His desire for sanctuary was insatiable. Always, he was in search of the safest place.

"When he was a child, a little boy, the safest place in the world was the giant beech tree that stood in front of his house. The tree was safe, the house below the tree was unsafe. He loved his tree. All trees. Trees rooted solidly to the earth.

"And only once did he ever dare to come down from his tree. And that was to marry the beautiful woman. Only once, did he take a chance. And from then on, he devoted his life to protecting her. He lived in a safe house on a safe street and worked in a safe job.

"And that was his undoing.

"Because one day, he realized he was

unhappy. Safe but *unhappy.*

"What was it that made him so unhappy? He had lost something he cherished, something vital. *Trees.* He worked in the safest place in the world, in a tree sort of place called the Forest Service, but it was an impenetrable, treeless forest. There were trees everywhere but nowhere. How could he escape this forest and reach the real trees that meant so much to him? How could he *safely* escape?

"The beautiful woman who was his wife stood at the edge of his treeless forest and said, 'Come to me. I love you, I will help you.' She held out her hand. 'My love,' she said. 'Take my hand and I will lead you out of the treeless forest into the world of living trees. Trees that bloom and turn color and have upon them the scent of winter and spring.'

"But there was another voice. A dark voice. And it was his own. 'Don't risk it. There's an easier, safer way to escape the treeless forest. Through black magic. There exists a single, magic ticket. And that ticket is the only way out of your treeless forest.'

"So each and every week the man tried to get this magic ticket. With it he would unlock the door to untold riches — he would *buy* his way out of the treeless forest and risk nothing. He knew that taking hold of his beautiful wife's hand might not work. Something could go wrong. It was not safe. But money would protect him. It would protect them both.

"Money, vast, measureless amounts of money, would cloak him as he escaped the treeless forest. He would slip away, invisibly, effortlessly, safely.

"His wife begged him to take her hand. 'You do not need the treasure you seek,' she said. 'All you need is me.' But he didn't listen. 'Wait here,' he commanded. And turned his back on her.

"He bought yet another ticket, and this time when it touched his hand a wave of terror passed through him. The man turned to look back at his wife. She was gone. Everything that he had feared came to pass. All that was terrible and frightening and dark came crashing down upon her.

"What he loved, he had killed. And he didn't mean to. But greed undid him. Cowardice blinded him. She was his truest treasure, and instead of reaching for her hand, he reached for a paper ticket and the mountain of gold it promised — and he lost everything.

"Everything," whispered Harry, sitting on the edge of the cot. "Everything, everything." Somehow there was a paper towel in his hands. He wiped his eyes and blew his nose.

Oriana handed him another one. She said gently, "That was a really hard story to tell. I'm sorry I made you do it, but you had to. Right? You had to."

"Yeah," said Harry weakly. He stared out a window into the dark trees, and began to shake his head. "But there's more. Shit, Oriana. I bought a lottery ticket in that convenience store. And told my wife to wait outside. There was construction going on, and there was an accident. A big, impossible accident. And she died, she was killed."

"I know," said Oriana quietly.

"No. There's more, listen. There's a thing people do when something like this happens. My brother took me to a lawyer to sue the company that caused the accident. Oriana, you get money when something terrible like this happens. A kind of awful reward."

Oriana sat, taking it in.

Harry said, "That's why I came to the forest with the rope. I was in shock. I fell to pieces. I didn't win the lottery, but Beth's death brought me lots of money. Four million dollars of terrible money."

"Oh," whispered Oriana, stunned. "Wow."

"But I get it now, what's going on. This is where Beth wants me to be. If I'd taken her hand that day, she'd have led me here."

"Out of the treeless forest into the world of living trees," recited Oriana. "Trees that bloom and turn color and have upon them the scent of winter and spring."

He nodded. Then shook his head. "But the money . . ." He gripped the edge of the cot mattress with both hands.

"You have to get rid of it. Right?"

"As fast as I possibly can."

They both looked at *The Grum's Ledger,* sitting closed in Harry's lap.

Harry opened the book. Doleful eyes stared up at him. For the last year, looking into the morning mirror as he shaved before work, those eyes had stared back.

"I'm the sad-hearted guy with the money. I don't know how you knew it, but you did. This book, the lottery ticket. I get it. All right? The grum feels better after he gets rid of his money. And so will I. I already decided that. It will be gone soon."

"But you have to do it *right.* You have to follow the *rules.*"

"What? No more Oriana rules! I just make some calls, talk to a lawyer, maybe. Donate it, I don't know. Just get rid of it. Like the grum does. He gets rid of it. I get rid of it."

Again, she recited from the tale of the lottery ticket. "Harry Crane lived in a safe house on a safe street and worked in a safe job. And *that* was his undoing."

She reached into her pocket and took out a mini Snickers. Studied the gold-wrapped candy sitting in the palm of her hand. Lifted her gaze.

"Harry. What if it's all about *how* you get rid of the money?"

With that, she tossed the candy into the air. Flickering lamplight reflected off the wrapper as the candy bar spun and twirled, turning the little one-room tree house into a vault of glittering gold.

13

Six miles north, in a little A-frame cabin, Ronnie Wilmarth tossed and turned in his bed, beset by thoughts of Amanda. While the arrow on Stu Giptner's mental Amand-O-Meter pointed steadily at Unsavory Brooding, and Cliff Blair's twitched between Desire and Remorse, Ronnie's arrow was ever-aimed at Ineffable Concern.

Ronnie believed he was inextricably connected to Amanda by way of Dean. What Ronnie had not done for Dean, he would do for Amanda. He would *be there.* He was her guardian angel. Although she didn't want an angel and didn't need a guardian and often told him so explicitly.

"Ronnie," she'd say when he'd sidle into view, "go away."

There was not a woman in Susquehanna County more capable than Amanda Jeffers, even in widowhood. Especially in widowhood. But a guardian angel, even against strong pushback, must *guard,* so for a year now Ronnie had doggedly hovered, keeping watch from the outskirts of Amanda's life.

Every few weeks his beat-up truck would sputter and cough up her long drive and he'd drop off five or ten pounds of fresh-butchered venison for her freezer, or maybe she would hear a chain saw start up, and she'd look out back and see Ronnie, hunched in the rain or snow or thick summer heat, working on her woodpile.

Sometimes he'd just be standing out in the yard at a respectful distance, cap in hand, and she'd call, "Hey," and he'd clear his throat and call back a greeting in his Pennsylvania mountain twang thick with the lilt of the Mississippi lumbermen and the guttural of the Polish coal miners who once populated the region. "Hey to you, Amanda. You need anything?"

Amanda would study his sun-leathered face, and if she discerned within those scrunched-up lines and creases an overload of Dean-remorse she'd give him some purposeful activity. But generally she shooed him away.

"Ronnie, it was an aneurysm that killed Dean, not you going off to lunch at Jim's Diner. I know this for a fact, because I read the autopsy report. So can you lighten up a little with the guilt thing, please?"

"Oh sure, sure, I'll go away." He'd go, but he always came back. *Aneurysm* may be on the death certificate, Ronnie knew, but *Abandoned by His Pal* was also stamped on that document, invisible to all but Ronnie Wilmarth.

He tossed and turned in his bed. He'd hoped that now that he had commenced the maintenance and repair of Pratt Library, it might assuage his nighttime frets. He'd had such a good morning at the library, trapping the ceiling raccoons. Though there'd been some pushback in that situation, too. One little sharp-toed son of a bitch attached itself to the leg of Ronnie's pants, and he had to hobble-run to the front door and launch it with a catapulting kick out onto the front walk.

He slammed the big oak library doors and leaned against them, panting.

"That's a wondrously resourceful method of pest control, dear," Olive called over from the circulation desk.

He had hoped that the little glimmer of mental relief he felt as he fixed the toilet and caulked the storeroom windows and straightened out the gutter over the library's back steps might induce a measure of calm into his nights. Because if what Olive said was true — that helping Pratt Library would ultimately absolve him from Dean-guilt — shouldn't he be having a wee nighttime taste of that promised redemptive peace? Just, like, a thimbleful of calm, or something? I mean, it was only a couple of days in, but jeez, Ronnie thought, why on this night in particular am I so anxious about Amanda? What is going on? I feel worse than ever.

"If only," he said in a haunted whisper, staring up at the glowing cobwebs in the moonlit rafters of his cabin. If only he'd been there on that snowy field last year, and done CPR on Dean, he would not be a cursed soul in constant pursuit of absolution.

Compounding his guilt, he was certain that if he, Ronnie, had collapsed in the snow, Dean would not have been off gulping hamburgers at Jim's Diner. Dean definitely would have been there to catch him. Dean would have whisked Ronnie to Susquehanna Hospital where Amanda would have revived him with a powerful application of CPR.

Ronnie sat bolt upright in bed. Amanda. CPR.

Amanda leaning down to press her lips to his to breathe life back into him.

Amanda's pillowy lips.

Ronnie cringed in the dark and called out, "I'm sorry, Dean! Those are not my real thoughts." Dean's ghost had every right to come howling through the wall to throttle him. Ronnie felt short of breath. He jumped out of bed and skittered across the chilly floorboards and found his cigarettes in the pocket of the jeans he'd tossed on a chair along with his shirt, socks and underpants. He lit up and took a deep drag.

He never had Amanda thoughts like that invading his brain. Well, okay, he did have them, but only exceedingly, extremely rarely. And darn it all, Amanda doing CPR on him? She's not *my* guardian angel, I'm *her* guardian angel. I'd be the one leaning over *her* doing the CPR kiss of life.

He smacked the wall, as if smacking himself. "Not *kiss*! The *breath* of life, that's what I meant, Dean. No kissing, just breathing." He jabbed the cigarette into the silvery dark. "I don't think of Amanda that way, okay? When they yak about her at Green Gables, I don't participate. That's Stu and Cliff and Tom and the EMT guys." He sucked on his cigarette and exhaled a factory stack of smoke.

Across the room in the dark, Grandmother Wilmarth's mantel clock whirred to life and began to bong loudly. Ronnie jumped.

"Damn you, clock. Scared the shit out of me."

Ronnie didn't have a mantelpiece, so he kept the clock on top of the refrigerator in the kitchen section of the one room cabin. He was never absolutely certain what time it was, because sometimes when the refrigerator kicked on, it unnerved the clock into a series of bongs that kept going past twelve to thirteen, fourteen or fifteen o'clock.

Twelve bongs. He'd driven home from Green Gables around eleven so it really was midnight, Ronnie figured. The clock had gotten it right.

He flinched when it bonged one more time. Uh-oh. Thirteen. He'd never heard the clock deliver an isolated thirteenth bong. He hugged himself. "Dean?" he whispered into the moonlit dark of the cabin.

Somewhere in the living room, something twitched imperceptibly. *Supernaturally.* Ronnie yanked the pull chain on the overhead light and looked.

The living-room section of the cabin was defined by a tired sofa, a temperamental TV, three deer heads mounted high up on the wall so close together their racks entangled like vines, and an enormous Victorian bookcase (also inherited from Grandmother

Wilmarth), its dark wood embellished with carved angels and birds and roses. Like everything else in the cabin, it was flecked with dust and wizened mouse droppings as small as caraway seeds.

An array of Ronnie's treasures was visible through the beveled lead-glass doors of the bookcase, including: a grinning raccoon skull; five bird nests; a row of spent shotgun shells arranged chronologically from the year Ronnie had bagged his first deer at age thirteen; a pirate ship he'd crafted out of birch twigs, copper wire and cigarette rolling papers, topped with a pirate flag of black cardboard; a lime-green enamel bowl he'd purchased at a street fair in New Milford that held two of his wisdom teeth and the claws of a black bear.

Atop the bookcase, isolated from the benign collection within, sat a huge, red-handled Italian switchblade that Great-Uncle Wade Wilmarth had given him in 1981 when Ronnie was twelve and Uncle Wade, an old coal miner, was on his deathbed. Ronnie fixed on that shining switchblade and thought back to Uncle Wade's final moments.

Quaking in his boots, young Ronnie stood at the foot of the four-poster bed where Uncle Wade lay on a horsehair mattress beneath a patchwork quilt. The old man was eighty-one years old but looked a hundred and fifty, and his nostrils were ringed a permanent black from the coal dust he'd breathed in for more than half a century.

Ronnie had gathered his courage and approached the bed, trying to ignore the spectacularly spooky sound of Uncle Wade's slow wheezy breaths, which even close-up sounded far away, as if emanating from an infinitely deep mine air shaft.

The old man held the big red switchblade in his arthritic claw. Gestured for Ronnie to take it. Then he motioned the boy closer.

Ronnie leaned down. He was certain he saw a puff of coal dust rise from Uncle Wade's lips as the old man whispered, "She'll bring ya luck."

What kind of luck, good or bad, Uncle Wade failed to describe, because upon uttering those words he gave a single violent hiccup and died.

Although he generally delighted in knives and guns, Ronnie was terrified of this knife. He never activated the switchblade's release button, not once.

Ronnie stood now, smoking and eyeing the knife. He felt a pressure building in the cabin, a gathering of unearthly emanations. Whoa, was the knife *quivering*? Oh, man, it was. The knife was quivering! Or no, wait, it's just my eyes watering. Ronnie smiled in relief, and when he smiled, he blinked. And in the dark flick of an eyelid, the knife made its move.

Click.

The switchblade snapped open. The force of thirty-five years of pent-up mechanical tension launched it off the bookcase. Ronnie screamed and ducked. The razor-sharp missile flew by his head and pierced the pillow on his cot. From the wound, something feathery poofed into the air.

"I knew it!" cried Ronnie. Another feather message from Dean!

The feather, tiny and pale, floated about the room.

"I'm here for you, Dean!"

The feather floated down onto the enamel surface of the stove.

What did it mean? Ronnie's eyes went bright with sudden understanding and alarm. The brand-name of the stove was not Kenmore, not Frigidaire. But *Amana.*

Amana. He saw the message immediately. All you had to do was add a *d* for danger, because that's what she's in. "Amanda!" Ronnie cried.

When he called out her name, his breath gusted the feather. It lifted off the stovetop, traveled three feet to Ronnie's left and settled again, atop the keys to his truck that lay on the kitchen counter.

Amanda, danger, truck, go!

He pulled on his clothes and grabbed the truck keys. Then he stopped and eyeballed the feather again. Picked it off the keys and held it close. It wasn't a feather. It was a piece of polyester fluff. He grabbed up the wounded pillow. Read the label. "Synthetic fill. *Synthetic*?"

Amanda, danger, truck, go!

What should he do? Was it a Dean message or not?

Wait a minute. Dean didn't know. That's it! Dean didn't know it was a new pillow. I threw out my feather pillow last week.

Go, go, go! Ronnie careened out of the cabin into the night. He jumped in his truck, raced six miles south, down Route 11 and veered onto Maple Road.

Eagle-eyed, he spotted a glimmer of lamplight in the deep forest behind Amanda's house where there should not have been light. He pulled over. The flame flickered, then as he got closer, it went out.

Hunter and guardian angel, Ronnie slid through the trees, entered the tree house, moved like a shadow across the room and touched Uncle Wade's switchblade to the sleeping stranger's throat.

"You so much as twitch, I'll lop off your nose."

14

Harry's eyes opened, his first thought: the grum?

In his one minute of sleep, Harry had begun to dream. The dream was overstuffed, like an indie film — short on plot and long on symbolism. Harry was ten years old. He was wearing Oriana's red jacket and standing beside the sugar maple, the lone tree in a forest of very tall vending machines filled with golden mini Snickers. Instead of leaves, miniature blue nooses dangled from the branches of the maple. The sky above the vending machine forest churned with red-tailed hawks swooping up helpless lottery tickets, tearing them into shreds that snowed down on little Harry and stuck to his red jacket like tiny Post-it notes. The sugar maple shuddered and the blue nooses began to sway. Something approached. Growls, grunts, vending machines toppling. Harry tried to run, but he was up to his neck in shredded lottery tickets.

"I am the grum," came a voice, rumbly and low. It was just the sort of voice you'd expect from a grum. Harry couldn't see the creature, but he could smell its beery breath and its potent BO.

When the grum spoke again, its voice had changed into a mountain twang. "You so much as twitch, I'll lop off your nose."

Something cold touched Harry's throat, and his eyes opened to a strange man leaning over him in the moonlit dark. Harry didn't cry out because he thought he was still dreaming. Dreamlike, the grum had entered the tree house. Very undream-like, though, the grum was wearing a scruffy John Deere cap.

Harry snapped fully awake. As commanded, he did not twitch, though he did shift an eyeball. He saw that the intruder was holding a large pot, backward, the tip of the pot handle pressed to Harry's Adam's apple.

"Lop off my nose?" Harry whispered, hoping that a whisper didn't count as a twitch.

Ronnie's eyes flicked to the pot in his hand. When he'd entered the tree house, weaponless, he had grabbed the first object within reach.

"Supposed to be a knife," he said.

In his haste to rescue Amanda, Ronnie had forgotten Uncle Wade's switchblade. As always, Ronnie was lacking.

But wait, that's not true. Knife or pot, he'd caught himself a forest creeper. The situation we have here, Ronnie decided, was not lacking, but a complete and total success. He unslumped his posture and proclaimed, "I am the Protector. The Guardian. The Hunter."

"I'm Harry Crane," Harry said. "And you are scaring the bejesus out of me."

Ronnie blushed with pleasure and grinned. "I am?" Caught himself. Scowled. "You got reason to be scared, creeper." He raised the pot high into the air.

"Goddamn it, Ronnie!" came a powerful voice from the woods.

A pounding up the spiral stairs. Amanda burst into the room. Ronnie stood frozen in the glare of her flashlight, pot in the air like Liberty holding her torch.

He put a hand to his eyes and squinted. "Not on me. Shine it on the cot, Amanda!"

He pointed behind himself with the pot. There was a light bony bonk as the pot made contact.

"Ow, shit," said Harry in the shadows.

Amanda brought the light full onto Harry. He sat up in the cot and rubbed the side of his head.

"Ronnie, you hit him."

"Didn't mean to." Ronnie squinted at Harry. "He's got Band-Aids all over him."

"I *know,* Ronnie. I put them there." Amanda stepped over to the cot and shined the light on Harry's scalp, felt for a bump. "You're okay," she said. Then added, "Wasn't sure you'd be coming back."

"I had a bunch of things to do down in Scranton," Harry said. "Branch office meetings. Getting supplies."

Ronnie gawked. Searching her fingers through his hair? Getting supplies down in Scranton? "What the fuck?" he said.

Amanda turned to him. "Ronnie Wilmarth. What if I'd had Oriana here?"

"I never curse in front of Oriana."

"I cursed in front of Oriana," said Harry from the cot. "I'm not used to being around kids."

"He *knows* Oriana?" Ronnie said.

Naturally, the protective reach of Ronnie's guardian-angelship extended to Oriana. He raised the pot. The creeper gets bonked again for cursing in front of a child.

Amanda snatched the pot from him. "Go over there and light the lamp, will you, please."

Ronnie huffily followed orders. A match

flared. A thought dawned. "Hey, how'd you know I was here?"

"Your truck. You come down a road like World War III."

The distinctive sputter and cough of his pickup had awakened her. What gives, Ronnie coming by at midnight? He came late sometimes, to work on the woodpile, but this was way late. When his truck went silent well short of her house, she jumped out of bed. Ronnie was an excellent hunter, and there was no doubt he had somehow detected Harry in the tree house. Why had she not foreseen this possibility?

Ronnie chuckled. "Yeah, need to tend to that muffler. And the alternator. And manifold."

"You should just shoot it. Be a mercy killing."

"Or hit it over the head with a big pot," offered Harry.

Ronnie narrowed his eyes and stepped toward him. "Who is he? What's going on, Amanda?"

She had been pondering the best way to deflect Ronnie. She decided to appeal to his base instincts. "You know how you're not a big fan of the government?"

"Got that right."

"And you know how you feel like you own

these woods?"

" 'Course I own them. So do you. We been traipsing these woods forever."

Harry eased his pants off a chair, wiggled into them under the sheets and stood beside Amanda. "This really the best way to introduce me?" he murmured.

Ronnie looked at him askance.

"Show him your badge," Amanda said to Harry.

Badge? Ronnie quickly considered his multitude of sins, specifically the ones in the "illegal" column. He f licked his eyes to the tree house door, estimating time and distance.

"It's an ID, not a badge," Harry said. He fished it out of his wallet and handed it to Amanda who handed it to Ronnie.

Ronnie held it in the light of the kerosene lamp. "Department of Agriculture. Forest Service. Harold F. Crane."

Amanda spotted the green-and-white Forest Service cap hanging on a hook on the door. She got it and put it on Harry's head. Nodded approvingly.

Ronnie glanced from the ID to the cap. His look was less approving.

"Yep. Forest Service," Amanda said. "Meaning, he's not an intruder. Meaning, this is his land."

"Don't own it, just manage it," Harry interjected.

"Good as owns, Ronnie," Amanda said. "He's here to work the woods. Do tree counts, measure things. Take soil samples. You know, *manage.*"

Ronnie assessed Harry's bumps and bruises. "Looks like something managed him."

"I fell from a tree," Harry said. He reached into his pants pocket and pulled out a crinkled golden wrapper. "Saw one of these glittering in a knothole. Didn't know what it was, so I climbed up to see."

Ronnie's face went red and his jaw clenched. "That's for Dean. That's *sacred* candy." The Department of Agriculture eating a little girl's candy — governmental intrusion at its most criminal.

Amanda said, "It's not sacred anymore, Ronnie, it's trash littering the forest."

"Trash? Well, just how does Oriana feel about *that?"*

"She's been cleaning it up."

"What? Because why?"

"Because it got a federal employee hurt, because she's over her candy phase and because he's doing us a kindness."

Harry tightened and looked away. *Over her candy phase.* Well, yes, he thought, that was true. Oriana had left the candy phase, but she had entered the grum phase. Which was a secret Amanda did not know.

"Can you keep a secret?" Amanda said.

Harry looked at her, startled that she had read his mind. He was about to answer, not certain what he would say. But it was Ronnie she had addressed.

"No," Ronnie said. "Secrets kind of well up inside of me and push to get out."

"Okay, let's try this. Are you my guardian angel?"

"Absolutely. And Oriana's."

He narrowed his eyes at the Snickers wrapper in Harry's hand, glittering in the lamplight.

"Okay. Then here's another way you can be our guardian angel. You know money's tight, right? And how your venison's a big help. And the turkey."

"No big deal. Just a little meat and a few gobblers."

"Well, you know we appreciate it. But now, Ronnie, let me ask you this," she said, tossing him the easiest question in the world. "If a sack of money fell at your feet, would you keep it?"

"Hell, yeah."

"Okay. So, this tree house is against the law. And here's the kindness Harry's doing for us. He's letting us keep it. And here's the money part. He's renting it for a month."

Harry did a double take. "Wait. The deal was three weeks," he said.

She turned to him with a sweet smile. "A month. I mean, I did just rescue you from a pot-wielding maniac."

Now Ronnie began to smile, too. He loved this angle, as Amanda was certain he would. Extracting money from the feds. "*Knife*-wielding maniac," he said. "You want me to go get Uncle Wade's switchblade, Amanda?"

She looked to Harry. "Does he need to go get Uncle Wade's legendary switchblade?"

"Aren't switchblades illegal?" Harry said.

"God*damn,* is that what everything is to you, legal or illegal?" Ronnie said. "Candy, tree houses, forests and knives. You're Mr. Rule and Regulation, is what you are."

"Point taken," Harry said. "I don't need to see your knife. And I am more than happy to rent this place for a month."

"All right, then," Ronnie said.

"Shake hands, men," Amanda said.

Ronnie had to think about it. "I never shook the hand of government before."

"Ronnie," warned Amanda. "Be civil."

Harry offered his hand.

Ronnie fidgeted, reached for Harry's

hand, scrunched his face and quickly jerked his hand back. "Soft as a baby's ass. You don't have calluses where you come from?"

"I spend a lot of time in front of a computer."

"Figuring out ways to steal candy from children?"

Off Amanda's glare, Ronnie reached for Harry's hand again and shook it properly. "All right, candy man. Forgiven."

"Good," Harry said. "And while I'm out here in the forest, I'll work on toughening up my skin."

"You work on not falling out of trees," said Ronnie.

By the time he left, Ronnie felt spiritually lighter. Literally: Dean's ever-hovering spirit had receded some. Ronnie smiled as he moved through the night trees. He and Amanda had straightened out the forestry guy pretty good. Dean would be especially proud of Amanda. Yeah, she had that Harry Crane under control. Tricking him into paying more rent. Ronnie laughed as he started up his truck. There was not a man in Susquehanna County she could not trounce, even federal ones with fancy IDs.

Amanda and Harry stood at the triangular window, looking out into the dark of the woods. Among the call of whip-poor-wills and the hoot of owls was the receding congested sputter of Ronnie's truck.

"He's quite a protective guy," Harry said.

"Ronnie can be very Ronnie sometimes. Won't happen again, he'll be good."

"I don't know that he really meant to kill me."

"No, he's not much of a killer, unless you have antlers or you gobble."

They were standing at the window a foot or two apart. When they spoke, it was to each other's reflection in the glass. It was an easier way to talk.

She tapped the glass with a finger. "All right, so ask your question."

"I don't have a question."

"Sure you do. Same one I'd be asking: What the heck's going on? All this crazy nonsense, right?"

He spoke to Amanda's reflection, cautiously. "I dropped in out of nowhere. Stirred things up."

"You didn't stir anything up. You fell from that tree into the middle of a bunch of pre-stirred nonsense. And let me tell you, I have nonsense-fatigue, big-time," Amanda said. "I've reached my year's limit for nonsense, sneaky-ass behavior and made-up stories."

Meaning, Ronnie, Cliff and Oriana, in that order.

And what she liked about this guy, this Harry Crane, this bland, levelheaded bureaucrat who understood rules and regulations, was that he was not going to complicate her life. In fact, he would uncomplicate it. Because he was going to straighten out this forest, drain it of every ounce of enchantment. The process had already begun. The sacred candy was sacred no longer. Oriana had filled two trash bags.

Harry felt unsteady, as if the tree house had shifted under him. Amanda Jeffers hated nonsense. She could not have been more clear. And here he stood, the living, breathing embodiment of nonsense, made-up stories and sneaky-ass lies.

His ID badge might as well read: *Harold F. Liar, Department of Fabrication and Falsehood,* because from the moment he fell from the sugar maple and stood before this woman, he had spouted a steady stream of lies and stories. He was Lord of the Lies. But only because he *had* to be. Right?

He lied because it would keep him in the woods. And that was his sole mission. If Amanda had seen the noose, knew the crazy truth, she'd have booted him right out of the forest.

And from that first lie — that he was here working for the Forest Service — the nonsense had escalated to a degree that would make her head explode.

Oriana thinking he was a grum — Harry squinted at the window, his reflection distorted by the flickering flame of the kerosene lamp. He leaned closer. Were his ears pointy? Was that hair sprouting from his face? Did Amanda see the truth of him? He touched his cheek. And when he did — there was a flash of gold.

"Whoa," Amanda said. The wedding band gleaming on Harry's hand. She gripped the windowsill, emotion coloring her cheeks. "Sorry. Your ring — kind of caught me off guard."

She slowly raised her own left hand, looked at its reflection in the window, touched the bare third finger. "It still feels strange, not having a ring there. My finger feels weightless. It sort of floats there on my hand, untethered."

She glanced at Harry's reflection. Shook her head, flustered. "Listen to me, spouting like a poet. And all I mean to say is my husband died. Which I'm pretty sure you guessed. A year ago. *Phfft,* fell over dead in a field. No poetry in that."

"I'm sorry," Harry said.

He'd slid his own left hand out of sight behind his back. His thumb traced back and forth over his wedding band. It felt enormously heavy. Because it, too, was one of his lies. A very heavy lie.

"No, hey," Amanda said. "I wanted to explain things, is all. Ronnie hovering. And Oriana missing her father, full of wild talk, acting out, working through her feelings. Like you say, you dropped into the middle of things, so I wanted you to understand the situation. It can get, you know, a little overwhelming." Amanda shivered. "Not that I can't handle it. I'm a nurse, people die. Life's not fair. All that stuff." She looked away, embarrassed. "I am talking way too much. And it's way late. I just wanted to clear the air."

She's able to clear the air, thought Harry. Why couldn't he? Amanda Jeffers hated deception and deceit, and the only true thing he'd told her since landing in this forest was his name. He had to tell her something more, something real, but he didn't know how. An immense pressure was building inside him. He was a bulging cargo ship with too many secrets in the hold, about to pop a rivet.

No, not a rivet.

A ring.

His left hand, under its own volition, shot from behind his back, straight out in front of him.

Amanda stared at his reflection. Pivoted to look at him in full.

Harry twisted and tugged at his wedding band.

Amanda stepped back from him. *Wait. He's removing his ring . . . so I won't feel so bad?*

"What are you doing? Leave that alone." *What an amazingly touching gesture. And really unnerving. Or no. Me being ringless — he's not about to offer me his wedding band? Is he? Like it was an umbrella and he could shield me from the rain?* "Hey. Stop. I don't need that." *Wedding bands,* she thought anxiously, *are nontransferable.*

But events were beyond Harry's control. He wrenched the ring loose, as if uncorking the pent-up pressure of himself. It shot off his finger, fell to the wooden floor and rolled under the cot.

Amanda dropped to her hands and knees and fished for it. The first bit of gold she pulled into view was the crumpled Snickers wrapper. She fished some more. "Here it is," she said. "Got it." She stood, a little dazed, and held out the ring to him.

Harry went pale and stepped back. "No,

it's off. It's finally off."

Amanda stared at him. "What are you doing?"

He went still as a statue.

"Harry?" she said. "Come on. What's going on? What would your wife think?"

He lifted his left hand, stared for a long moment, then said in a whisper, "It's weightless. The finger. Weightless as a ghost."

"Hey. Put this back on."

But he wouldn't take it, stepped back again.

She thought, How hard did Ronnie bonk him on the head?

Harry stared at his naked finger, then raised his eyes to meet Amanda's. "I have something to say. To tell you. I have to tell you the *truth.* There's a ring. But there's no wife. I don't have a wife anymore."

A long beat. Outside, the whip-poor-wills and the owls went silent.

"You don't have a wife," Amanda said. "Anymore."

"Her name was Beth."

Amanda looked at the ring. Looked at Harry.

"When the person you love dies," he said, "when are you supposed to take off the ring? I've worn it for a year. Somehow, it just wouldn't . . . come off."

"Oh my God," Amanda said. She placed the ring on the kitchen table, beside the kerosene lamp. The light striking it, setting it aglow, made it seem like the only object in the room. The only object in the world.

"I lied to you," Harry said. "I lied about why I came to these woods."

Amanda hugged herself.

"I'm not really here for my job. I'm here because I worked for years in a miserable office. Beth would say, 'Just quit, Harry. Go where the trees are real. You can do it, Harry,' she'd say."

Amanda struggled to make sense of his words. "And she . . . Beth . . . she wanted you to come here? Exactly right *here*?"

"I really do manage these woods. Did. The other day, I walked out of the office, got in my car and just drove. Drove until I ran out of gas. And arrived here."

"Exactly here. In *this* forest."

He nodded.

Now she was the one who stepped back from him. "Harry Crane. This is a big deal."

"I know. I lied, and you hate sneaky-ass behavior."

"A very big deal."

"I'm sorry."

Amanda looked into the distance for a

long moment, then at the ring, glowing in the lamplight. Working through the enormity of it.

"Coming here — it's some kind of quest. This is all about your wife. This is for her. Isn't it?"

Yes, but no, Harry thought. He *hadn't* come for Beth. He came with a length of rope in his hand. It was only after he crashed to earth that he realized he'd come for Beth. And then, very quickly, it all became so much more — because now he seemed to be here for Oriana, too. And to be here for Oriana . . . would mean a truckload of nonsense, made-up stories and sneaky-ass behavior.

The panic began to rise again, but he stifled it. Because at least he had removed the ring. He'd told a truth. He could breathe a little. "Yes," he said to Amanda. "I'm here for Beth."

Amanda thought, I would have done this for Dean. If he'd asked me to, I'd have done it. I'd have come to the middle of the woods and stayed in a tree house. Whatever he asked. She suddenly missed him unbearably. She looked around this place he built, this solid thing that hovered in the treetops of the forest. Her eyes went to his collection of field guides, neatly side by side in the bookcase. A bird guide, a wildflower guide, a rock guide, a tree guide, a fern guide — a guide for everything except for how to go on without him. She didn't know the tears were there until the room began to shimmer. She blinked them back.

Harry spoke. She turned to him.

"Amanda. Will you please let me stay? Even though I'm a lying liar who lies?"

Her voice carried the weight of a long year. "You're not a liar. You're a widower, Harry. Widowers do things. They say things."

"And widows?" he said. "What do they do?"

"They . . ." she began. They what? They screw Cliff Blair and get filmed? They run around the forest chasing their possessed daughters? "They work very hard to keep their shit together," she said.

"I didn't keep my shit together," Harry said.

"Hey. You made it through your first year."

"Barely." Harry felt the rope around his neck. The wind from the wings of a hawk.

" 'Barely' is a win."

Not a win, thought Harry, but with the help of a girl and this forest, maybe a reprieve.

Amanda pointed to his ring. "Huge night,

Harry. Right? You got it off."

"How did you get yours off?"

"You know nurses — we tear off a bandage hard and quick. That first week, the ring was off and in a drawer. And then, I just kept shedding his stuff. Got rid of as much as I could as fast as I could. As if that would make it easier."

"Beth's toothbrush is still next to mine. I kept everything."

Amanda wondered: How did Beth die? Amanda understood death, as a nurse, as a young widow. How it came suddenly, swept everything away in the same moment that it left everything behind. Every object, the toothbrush, the ring, the clothes in the closet, suggesting a return. Every object a permanent reminder of impermanence.

Amanda was an ER nurse, and she could feel it radiating off Harry — Beth died unexpectedly. Her death still stunned him. Sent him into the forest.

"There's no right way," she said. "No good way. There's only one way, I guess." She shrugged. "Forward."

"Forward through a land where inches are miles and hours are centuries," Harry said. He shrugged, too. "Listen to me. Spouting like a poet."

The hint of a smile at the corner of

Amanda's mouth. She looked at her ringless hand for a long moment, then slowly raised it, gesturing to Harry to do the same. Harry raised his ringless hand. They stood facing each other, hands in the air.

"We're a club," Amanda said. "The Year One Club."

Harry, with his own trace of a smile, said, "Up here in our clubhouse."

The night wind picked up. The tree house moved gently back and forth.

"There's somebody else in the club, too," Amanda said. "A junior member."

"I know."

"The candy? She left it in the woods because she thought Dean was an angel, then a bat, then a bird. Always some winged something. That he'd come back. But he didn't come back."

"Wingless Harry showed up instead," Harry said. "The candy thief."

Amanda said, "But you know what? I love that you're not anything like Dean. I love it for my daughter. That you're just some ordinary guy who's going to inhabit these woods."

"You forgot to say boring. Dean — he was pretty amazing?"

"Oops," Amanda said.

"I get it. I had one of those. Beth was

beyond amazing."

"Did she walk on water? Dean walked on water."

"Beth danced on water."

They looked into each other's eyes.

Harry cleared his throat. "Let's get a little air," he said. He walked out onto the deck. Amanda followed. They stood at the railing. The night forest surrounded them.

Harry took a deep, appreciative sniff of the atmosphere. "The trees," Harry said. "Smell them?"

"Yes," Amanda said.

"In two days, exactly two, the quaking aspen will open their buds," Harry said. "One day later, exactly one, trust me, the sugar maples will follow."

He made a sweeping gesture at the half-seen trees, like a conductor bringing an orchestra to attention. "One by one, like slow-motion fireworks, tree after tree will burst to life. And the very last tree will be this big guy, the American beech." Harry patted a heavy gray limb as if he were patting the warm, friendly mass of a great animal. "Beech leaves open so quickly, it's something you can actually hear. Really." He smiled. "That is, if you're a guy who listens to trees."

He reached out and touched a sharp apical bud, rolled as tight as a miniature cigar. "Beech leaves have highly denticulate margins and resinous leaf hairs. In other words, they're really sticky. So when the buds open, two hundred thousand of them all at once, it sounds like the tree is giving a great big, raspy sigh of relief."

Amanda was taking Harry in. "Because spring has come," she said.

"Because winter's over," Harry said.

They breathed the night forest, in and out.

"I don't know kids, Amanda. Beth and I didn't have any."

He didn't know kids, but he knew that Oriana was a fellow traveler. It scared him, it really did, but he sensed that, inexplicably, she needed something only he could provide. Winter was over, but spring had not yet come for him and Oriana. They were between uncharted seasons, at the cusp of change, but only at the cusp. He didn't know kids, but he supposed that sometimes a kid needed something she couldn't find at home, but only in the wild of the forest.

"For the next few weeks, I'm just going to walk around these woods. Just be here. I don't know what I'm doing."

"Perfect," Amanda said.

"I'm here to stare at trees."

"Perfect."

"Believe me, I'm not perfect."

"Just keep being Harry Crane. Do your trees. Do your thing, Harry. Because whatever it is you're doing, it's already rubbing off on Oriana. Do what you need to do."

In a court of law, maybe, in the absolutism of the moral universe, it wouldn't hold up. But for Harry, on this crazy night, it was permission enough. Besides, there was little choice. He was going to do his thing, not because he wanted to, but because he had to. A spell had been cast — he had been turned into a grum who, in some as yet unidentified manner, following the fairy tale rules demanded by a ten-year-old girl, was about to get rid of four million dollars.

Harry and Amanda stood together at the railing a few minutes longer, then Amanda said good-night and went home to her bed.

Harry lay on his cot. Drifting into dream (for the second time that night), he watched a gold coin roll down from the top of a great pile of gold coins and vanish into a deep forest.

Six miles north, dreaming in his bed, Ronnie saw a magic feather turn into a red-tailed hawk and fly in and out of the windows of his cabin.

Stu, tangled in sweaty sheets, dreamed of

Amanda, naked and holding bags of money as she walked into his real estate office, which was the size of a football stadium.

Amanda dreamed of shimmering fireworks that became blossoming trees.

Cliff dreamed of cows lined up in unforgiving rows, shaking their heads at him in disappointed unison and lowing mournfully.

One of Cliff's cows dreamed of Cliff, and mooed a blissful moo.

Wolf dreamed twitchily of Harry cowering high up in the beech tree that stood in the front yard of their childhood home as Wolf, growling and on all fours, circled below.

Olive Perkins called out in her sleep, "Grum! Grum!"

While all the grown-ups (and cows) dreamed their dreams, Oriana was awake and at work on the computer in the kitchen, tapping the keyboard, quiet as a mouse.

15

Harry was up a tree. A young bitternut hickory, to be exact, thirty-five feet tall, base trunk diameter approximately forty inches. He looked at his watch. He had intended to fill his plastic water jug at the spring, head back up the spiral staircase to the tree house and make a cup of coffee. He had not intended to be in a hickory tree at seven thirty in the morning.

It had been a long night, his first without his wedding ring around his finger. Lying on the cot through the dark hours, he'd fought the urge to put it back on. But he didn't do it. He'd made it. And a cup of coffee made of spring water would have been just the thing. He would have calmly faced the day. Or at least had a shot at calmly facing the day.

Instead, as he dipped the jug into the icy waters of the spring trickling down among the mossy rocks, Oriana came bursting into view. She had her school backpack on. Good sign — she wasn't staying long. But the wildness in her eyes and the huge excited grin on her face — bad sign.

"Here's the plan!" she declared. "Here's what you have to do with the four million dollars."

Gripping the water jug with both hands, Harry listened. Blinked. Blinked again and said, "No way. There's no way in hell I'm doing that."

"But you have to," Oriana said. "You *agreed.* The way you get rid of the money has to be unsafe. It has to be an adventure."

He knew what he'd agreed to. Something unsafe, yes. But *this* unsafe? This much of an adventure?

"It can't be legal," he said.

"But it is," she said. "Give me your phone, I'll show you."

Harry stared at the glowing screen, as she swiped to one site after another. This is completely insane, he thought. He could barely stand to look at the screen. Each time she went to a new site, the screen grew brighter. He grabbed the phone back from her.

"You *agreed,*" she said.

"I agreed to *something.*"

"It's perfect."

It was. But he wasn't going to do it.

"But I'm going to help you," she said. "We're a team."

A team? Ha! thought Harry. Wait until Amanda finds out. She's going to absolutely love The Team carrying out The Plan. His brain had put it into capital letters. It kept growing, became a flashing neon sign. The Plan. The Plan. The Plan.

"Go away, I'll think about it," he said, intending not to think about it. But it had permeated his brain — the dazzling scope of it, the simplicity, the rightness.

"How long will this thinking take?" she said, eyes narrowing.

Her phone chirped. Time for school. "How long?" she said again.

"Go away," Harry said.

And the next thing he knew, Oriana was running back toward her house and he was climbing up the bitternut hickory. He was twenty feet off the ground before he even realized he was *in* a tree. He had been leaning against the hickory trunk to steady himself as Oriana talked, pressing harder and harder against the smooth, tan bark, instinctively seeking the feel of the familiar and the known. When Oriana vanished into the underbrush, Harry turned and, without thinking, went up on his toes and took hold of a low branch.

So now here he was, twenty feet up. He stopped climbing and sat on a branch. He was panting, his arms and legs throbbed. He was way out of shape. Of course he was. He'd barely moved his body in the last year.

He took some deep breaths to slow his pounding heart. He nodded. "Okay. All right. This is good," he said. There was nothing better than a tree. How long had it been since he'd climbed one?

He took another deep breath, then looked the hickory up and down. It had a strong central leader. No signs of bark beetle or twig girdler. No limb rot.

"Carya cordiformis," Harry said. The formal Latin nomenclature uttered aloud was a steadying sound. "You look in pretty good shape. How are things?" The tiny tight catkins dangling from the tips of the branch (they would peel open in four or five days when spring touched them) trembled in the wind, and that was a kind of reply. Trees have their own way of communicating. It was a matter of listening closely, observing and knowing. Trees wanted to show you things. It had been a long time since Harry had looked.

"Don't see a lot of you guys in the higher elevations of the Mid-Atlantic Appalachians." Harry felt a lovely calming sensation. He was in a forest, thinking like a forester. It had happened last night with Amanda, when they stood on the deck and looked over the night tree canopy, and it was happening again now. I am in a tree, thinking tree thoughts.

He looked down at the silvery water trickling between the rocks. One of the hickory's lateral roots was curled over the rim of the spring, like a straw deep into a tall drink. "You chose a good spot," he said. The spread of a young hickory's roots is double that of its crown branches. In deep summer, sudden intense wind gusts whipped through the upper Appalachians. The hemlocks and spruce might uproot, but a bitternut hickory, with its wide and deep root array, was windfirm. It would stand.

"Windfirm," Harry said. Good word. *Windfirm.*

He stood up and continued to climb. He climbed until he reached the top. It was a small tree, but for Harry it was exhausting work. He held tight to the leader. The mountain wind blew gently, and with the addition of Harry's weight, the leader swayed like the heavy pendulum on a grandfather clock. Harry ticktocked back and forth. His eyes closed, and he remembered a moment when he had been in a different bitternut hickory. Fifteen years ago in Chadwick Arboretum on the Ohio State campus.

"Are you having a bad day?" Beth had called up to him.

Harry, twenty-two years old, looked down at her. He was sitting on a branch, holding a handful of dried catkins, harvesting them for lab class, where he would test them for all sorts of things that were fascinating only to a forestry graduate student. "No, I'm having a good day," Harry replied.

"You're in a tree. Usually, guys your age climb trees only when they're drunk or they think they're squirrels."

"Funny you should say that. I saw a drunk squirrel, last week."

"Friend of yours?"

Harry smiled. "He was in the apple orchard, south end of campus, near the Aggie center, sitting on a limb eating a fermented apple. Chomping away, and then suddenly he just tipped over and fell into the grass. Lay there with a big smile on his face, staring up at the sky."

Beth laughed. Although he didn't know her name until a day later.

What had happened that day, that first day they met, was both very small and very large. Harry climbed down from the hickory tree, and they simply talked. It intrigued her that he was in grad school for forestry, that he was the kind of guy who climbed trees and knew that squirrels got drunk.

Harry was not intrigued by Beth, he was dazzled. She was beautiful, a grad student in social policy, and she laughed a lot.

She suddenly glanced at her watch, and said, "I have to go."

"Don't go," he said, and blushed that the words came out so emphatically.

"I have to. I'll be late for class." She looked at him and he looked at her. The look that changes everything. "Will you be in this tree tomorrow?"

Harry nodded. He would be in this tree every day, if that's what she wanted.

"What kind of tree is it, anyway?" she said, patting the trunk.

"*Carya cordiformis.* Prefers mollisols on a fertile surface horizon."

She regarded him. "Thought so," she said, in a very serious voice. "Said to myself, this friggin' tree is a *Carya cordiformis,* and it prefers mollisols on a fertile surface horizon."

Harry fell in love right there.

Beth laughed, and waved goodbye, and he whispered after her, "Don't go."

But he wasn't in the arboretum on campus whispering those words, he was whispering them from the top of a bitternut hickory in the middle of the Endless Mountains.

"Don't go."

But Beth was gone, and she was not returning to this hickory to look up at him and smile. She was long ago and far away, and now he was atop a very different tree.

He stared at his hand, at the white skin where his ring had been for so many years. The ring was off, Beth was gone. A terrible wind had blown across his life.

"Windfirm," he said. Because it occurred to Harry that he was still standing. After that terrible wind, still standing. And even more important, he was standing high up in a tree.

He looked around. There were a lot of trees in this forest. He had a lot of climbing to do.

When Oriana was running back toward the house after telling Harry about The Plan, she turned and looked over her shoulder and saw him starting up the bitternut hickory.

"He's climbing a tree," she reported to her mother as she got into the truck. "The bitternut hickory by the spring."

"Don't be out there bothering him," Amanda said.

"I *wasn't.* I didn't even talk to him," Oriana lied. "I just wanted to make sure he was still there."

Amanda, too, was glad Harry was still there. Last night he said he didn't know exactly what he'd be doing, but that he needed to be in the forest. Needed to stare at trees. He'd made it through what had to have been a long night. He could've taken off, but he stayed. Good. It would be good for him, and good for Oriana.

But something was worrying Amanda. She hadn't expected he'd be climbing trees. Then again, that's what he'd done with the sugar maple. He'd started to climb it, going after the Snickers, and the limb broke. That bump on his head? Was he in any shape to be climbing?

It was Amanda's day off. She had a ton of chores around the house, but when she got back from dropping off Oriana at school, she grabbed the bird-watching binoculars and slid into the forest. Just to check on him.

She peered from around a fat sycamore, scanned the leafless trees of the spring forest. She saw a flash of bright white and green and focused on Harry's Forest Service cap.

Harry was sitting on a branch halfway up a bitternut hickory. He wasn't doing anything, in any forest management sort of way, taking core samples, or examining the bark for beetle borers. And he wasn't searching for more Snickers. He was simply . . . sitting.

She watched him for several minutes. He'd look down at the ground, he'd look up at the sky. Sometimes, he'd just stare straight ahead, staring into a distance far beyond the boundaries of a forest.

Amanda knew what he was looking at. Himself. He was a man lost in thought. Harry climbed — Amanda had walked. When she was overwhelmed by thoughts of Dean, especially in the early months, she walked up and down the gravel road in front of the house. She had walked. A tree man would climb.

She lowered her binoculars and left the forest as silently as she had entered it.

After the hickory, Harry climbed two more trees, a Norway spruce and a white ash.

He stared up into the ash. It was a beauty. They make baseball bats out of the tight, hard wood of the ash because it is highly resistant to shock. But this ash would be spared because it lived in a protected wilderness area that would never be lumbered. It would never be turned into a tool handle or flooring or the legs of a chair. Like the bitternut hickory, it was a young tree, and it would grow to a medium size of about ninety feet. It would live for ninety years. Ninety feet, ninety years. When the buds opened, in about four days, Harry guessed, rolling a swollen apical bud between his fingers, it would flower, leaf out in a glaucous green, and in midsummer produce single-winged seeds that birds loved. Harry loved them, too. When he was a kid, there was a white ash in the Magnusons' yard, and he would gather handfuls of the winged seeds and throw them into the sky, then stand very still as they helicoptered down around him. They made a faint whir that only a child could hear.

Harry sat midcanopy and imagined, in a time-lapse film in his mind, the lifespan of this ash, from seedling to its toppling death, decades from now. It had picked a good spot to live and die, just as the hickory had picked a good spot beside the spring. He had walked a half mile to get to the ash. It was not near a spring or a creek, but the spot was good in a different way, because it was an eastern slope and there was just enough competition from the surrounding sugar maple, yellow poplar and gray birch to reduce branchiness. Branchiness was an actual arboreal term.

The structural dynamic of a tree is interesting (at least to me, Harry thought). Again, he had that lovely feeling, a kind of slow return to certainty he hadn't had in a very long time. I am certain about trees, he thought.

He looked down through the limbs of the ash, to the ground. The spot where the ash had taken root, twenty years ago or so, was loamy, and a tree that is not branchy casts its mass down its central column into its taproot. It's like a tent pole, driven deep. The taproot would grow toward water just as its upper branches grow toward the sun.

Harry liked the thought of that, life reaching in two directions, toward dark and light. He wasn't thinking spiritually, just in admiration, that a tree knows what it needs, and goes where it must to get it. Food and water.

He suddenly wanted both. Climbing the ash tree had made him very hungry. What an odd sensation. Hunger. He wanted a sandwich. His body wanted food and, specifically, a sandwich. When he got back to the tree house, just before noon, he made two large cheddar cheese sandwiches and downed them with three glasses of spring water.

He looked over at his cot. He was tired in the same way that, earlier, he had been hungry. His body tired, because he'd been using it. He stretched. His back muscles were sore. His arms and legs were sore. And he thought, *Good.* He'd forgotten he *had* arms and legs.

He wanted to lie down, but he went back down the spiral staircase and out into the forest again. He wanted more of what he was feeling, and he didn't want to lose it to sleep.

He certainly felt the Norway spruce he climbed — too much. But he had committed himself to it, and he would climb. A spruce is a tough tree to navigate, a tree intent on making itself unwelcome to visitors. Foresters like to say a Norway spruce puts the "hard" in hardy. Its brown-black bark is coarser than 24-grit sandpaper. Great traction, but wicked on his vulnerable skin. By twenty feet up, dots of blood began to appear on his palms. The dark green quadrangular needles, though they smelled spicy and wonderful, poked and scratched, and made repeated attempts to spear his eyeballs.

Harry stopped to catch his breath. "You're a real mean son of a bitch," he said admiringly. Sap stuck to his skin like glue. He dabbed a little on a deep scrape on the back of his hand. He'd learned this trick his second year of grad school, when he spent a month in the woods during his semester in sustainable forest management. His teacher, Professor Gibbons, a grizzled old man who was part scientist and part wood elf, tripped and cut his knee on a rock when he and Harry were hiking back to camp in the Trimble Wilderness Area in southeastern Ohio.

It was a nasty cut, but the professor's eyes glittered at the sight of it. "Going to teach you something extracurricular, Harry." He touched his finger to the blood and worked it between his fingers. "What is this stuff?"

Harry paused a second, but what other answer could there be? "Blood," he said.

"But what *is* it, Harry?"

The old professor worked a smudge of blood between his fingers until it dried a little and became tacky. He smiled, because he could see the light coming on in Harry's eyes. Professor Gibbons was leaning against the trunk of a Norway spruce. Harry's gaze fixed on an ooze of amber glistening in a gap in the bark. A recent wound, a single long gash, as if a bear or a badger had dragged a single claw across the trunk. The Norway spruce was bleeding.

"Sap," Harry said.

"Sap, yes! Same properties, blood and sap. Similar properties, anyway, don't you think?"

Absolutely, thought Harry. Like blood through veins and arteries, sap flowed through the body of a tree via xylem and phloem. It was a medium of transport, carried sugar, amino acids, minerals, water. When exposed to air, its viscosity increased, until it clotted and hardened. Sap and blood, essential to life.

"Amazing stuff," said the professor. "Especially pine sap. Better than blood, actually."

Harry touched his finger to the edges of the wound in the tree. The sap was hard, but pliable, too.

"Like a scab," the professor said. "But while our blood can't fix the injured tree, the sap can fix me."

Professor Gibbons touched his finger to the pine sap and brought a shiny glob to his bleeding knee. "Probably could use a stitch or two, but we're out in the middle of nowhere. You can always count on a tree to get you through, Harry." The old professor dabbed the sap onto his cut, and almost immediately, the slow bleeding stopped. "Pine sap is antiseptic, astringent, anti-inflammatory and antibacterial. Best damn Band-Aid in the world, Harry, remember that."

Harry, sitting now in the Norway spruce, remembered that. The pine sap he'd applied to the cut on his hand had stopped the bleeding. He continued his climb. The limbs of the spruce were springy, the wood not dense like the ash and the hickory. As he neared the top, he cracked a limb or two. Time to stop. It was late afternoon. He carefully climbed back down. He stood at the bottom looking up through the swooping evergreen branches. "Thank you," he said. He patted the raspy trunk of the spruce.

A sharp edge of bark gouged his already pocked and tenderized palm. Yet another dot of blood appeared. "You are one ornery bastard," Harry said.

But a forest needed a few ornery bastards.

After the Norway spruce, he went for a long walk. Every tree seemed to vibrate with the pent-up energy of spring. And all the animals, too. He spotted the shiny quivering black nose of an opossum sniffing the air from the O of a knothole in an ancient white oak. Skittering around and around the base of a sugar maple, a pair of squirrels. A white-breasted nuthatch hopped headfirst down the trunk of a maple. Bullfrogs along the edge of a stream spoke to one another in slow, ratchety groans. Harry listened and watched and walked. Though his arms were tired, he picked up two chunks of rock, gripping them in each hand and raising and lowering them like he was working out with weights. He raised the rocks up and down until he got back to the tree house, then placed the two stones at the bottom of the spiral stairs. He was so exhausted he barely made it to the top.

It was dark now. Before he went inside the tree house, he stood on the deck and looked toward Amanda's house. It was a half mile away, and in a few days, when the trees leafed out, he would not be able to see it. Was she looking in his direction? Oriana certainly was. He could feel her impatient gaze. He entered the tree house and lit the kerosene lamp. The orange flame flared and settled.

He was too tired to eat, but he was too hungry to sleep. He sliced off circles of meat from a salami, squares off the chunk of cheddar. Chewed slowly. The spice of the meat, the sharp tang of the cheese. What an odd thing, to taste his food. He ate two apples. Sour. Sweet. Crunch. Juicy. He ate a third apple.

He sat groggily in the Adirondack chair and listened to the wind blowing through the beech. A low branch clicked against the skylight. Way, way up, through the dark tangle of the massive tree, he could see the moon.

When he stood up again and looked out the triangle window, Amanda's house was dark.

He lay down on his cot. He had forgotten this kind of tired. The spring peepers began their shrill chorus. The tree house rocked in the wind.

As he drifted into sleep, Harry's thoughts were uncluttered, peaceful, ordinary. A hickory is windfirm, he thought. A white ash is strong against sudden shock. The sap of a Norway spruce binds a wound.

He slept.

The next day, he sat up in bed and winced. He took stock. His back hurt, his biceps hurt, his shoulders hurt, his knees hurt, his thighs hurt. His nose and eyebrows hurt! It all hurt, and it felt . . . *good.*

He ate a large bowl of oatmeal. Bathed in the ice-cold stream. Pulled on the same clothes he'd worn yesterday and set out into the woods.

He climbed two trees. Two was all he could manage, because his muscles were so worn out from the day before. A northern red oak and an American larch. It took a long time to reach the tops.

Again, on the way back to the tree house, he picked up two chunks of rock. They were slightly larger than the ones from the day before. He raised them up and down as he staggered home. When he got to the beech, he placed the rocks beside the other two rocks.

That night he slept dreamlessly.

It's just that he climbed so *many* trees; Amanda hadn't expected that. And so many different types. After the third day, she and Oriana began to compile a list of the species they saw him climbing. It was human nature — Harry was a puzzle they wanted to solve.

What was his system for selecting certain trees? They cataloged his choices as best they could, though of course there would be some they missed because Oriana was off at school and Amanda had to go to work.

At first, they thought that the pattern was obvious: Harry was going to climb one of every species of pine and hardwood tree in the forest. But very soon, they saw that wasn't it. He never climbed the same tree twice, but sometimes he climbed the same *species* of tree he'd climbed before. He climbed two different red maples, three different black walnuts and so on.

Bitternut hickory (1)
White ash (1)
Norway spruce (1)
Northern red oak (1)
Sweet gum (1)
Red maple (2)
Flowering dogwood (1)
Black walnut (3)
Box elder (1)
White oak (2)
Eastern white pine (1)
Yellow birch (3)
Osage orange (1)
Red bud (1)
Sweet birch (4)
Black birch (2)
Pin oak (2)
Paper birch (1)
Eastern red cedar (2)
Balsam fir (1)
Virginia pine (1)
Horse chestnut (3)
Black cherry (2)

American larch (1)
Sycamore (3)
Cucumber tree (1)
Norway maple (5)
American linden (3)
Black locust (1)
Tulip poplar (2)
Scarlet oak (2)
Slippery elm (2)
Red alder (3)
Quaking aspen (3)
Jack pine (1)
Black oak (4)
Bigtooth aspen (2)
Silver maple (2)
Shagbark hickory (3)

Whatever he was doing, all these trees, Oriana was certain that climbing was his way of "thinking" about the plan.

How long will this thinking take? she had asked him. Now she wondered, How many trees is this going to take, Harry? The list kept growing.

Amanda had her own belief: Harry was processing.

It was a huge deal getting that wedding ring off. It would take a good many trees, and a lot of thinking to reshape the meaning of his life.

Amanda and Oriana did not, of course, share their thoughts with each other. They both simply agreed that Harry needed some "alone time in the forest to get settled," as Amanda put it. They left him alone, but kept a close eye on him. Actually, Amanda did more than that. Over the nearly two weeks that Harry climbed his trees, she sneaked off several times to leave food on his kitchen table. Fresh-baked sourdough bread. Beef stew, a slice of homemade carrot cake. She was compelled to attend to him because she knew what he was going through. They were in the same club. He was making such an effort, it was only right to sustain him. It's what any nurse would do for a patient. Nutritional support, attention to the body and its needs.

He left a note for her one time. "The cake was delicious. You don't have to, you know, but thank you."

Of course, I have to, thought Amanda. You need to keep your strength up. Can't have you falling out of trees.

The note he found when he got back that night: "You've climbed seventy-six trees. That's a lot. Just saying. A."

Confirmed — they were watching him.

He'd felt their presence in the forest but never saw them. He turned and looked toward Amanda's house. On the second floor, two lights were on. The one on the left went out. He guessed it was Oriana's bedroom. An hour and a half went by before the light went out in Amanda's bedroom. He knew this, because every few minutes he went to the window to check.

That there was someone out there who kept an eye on him. And someone he was keeping an eye on. The stir of human life. Amanda's light was out, so he turned out his own.

At the top of a sweet gum, Harry thought of his father. Harry scratched at the thin bark at the tip of a yearling branch, which had begun to leaf out. The tiny leaves were soft green jewels. Watery sap seeped out of the bark. Harry bent the branch toward him and sniffed deeply. His father wore aftershave, and it smelled just like this.

Harry's father never hugged him. Although Harry could definitely remember, on one occasion, his father placing an arm around his shoulders. The two of them were posing together for a photograph. But that's not when Harry would have smelled the aftershave with such intensity.

He sniffed the clear sap again. What am I remembering? he thought. And then he knew. Whenever he got into a car with his father, the car held the smell of him. A lemony, gingery, slightly cinnamon scent, hermetically sealed in the car.

Of course the strongest smell of him would be in a car. His father sold cars. His father drove away from the family in a car. A car noxious with aftershave.

Harry felt dizzy. He climbed down from the sweet gum. He had not reached the top, and he did not climb another sweet gum, although there were several in the forest.

For two weeks, he climbed; he went for morning runs; he carried larger and larger rocks back to the tree house and stacked them to the side of the spiral stairs. He drank gallons of spring water. Usually, he slept through the night. But some nights he couldn't breathe because he missed Beth so terribly. He'd get out of bed and sit in the Adirondack chair, lean back and look up through the skylight into the branches of the beech. Each night, the waxing moon got a little brighter. The spring peepers sang, the owls hooted and tree after tree was coming to life. All of this helped, although not always. Sometimes the sadness didn't go away even when dawn came. But at dawn, he put on his cap and climbed. He never knew exactly what a tree was going to bring him. But he knew where it would take him: up — even when up was down, as it so often was.

Way down, when a tree provoked a memory of his father. Or Wolf.

Sitting a third of the way up a white oak, Harry thought of the time Wolf had trapped a neighborhood kid, Kenny Watlinger, in a white oak. Kenny had run from Wolf, which everyone knew was a mistake, because it just prolonged the inevitable — Wolf was going to get you — and it gave Wolf time to think up an even more disconcerting torture than the one he'd originally intended. All he planned to do to Kenny was pelt him with acorns. It was a beautiful fall day, acorns were abundant, and all Wolf wanted was to fire a few at somebody. It's why acorns were invented. Kenny happened by, so it would be Kenny. It would've just lasted a minute or two, the pelting, but Kenny panicked and bolted up the white oak.

Coming home from school, Harry witnessed all this. He crept closer and closer, hiding behind wide street trees, peering at the scene. He was three trees away from Wolf and Kenny.

"I'm going to start counting," Wolf called

up to Kenny, "and whatever number I reach before you come down here, that's the number of acorns you're going to eat."

The look on Kenny's face. *Acorns. I'm going to have to eat acorns. I'm going to die.*

Harry had seen the look on so many kids' faces. Harry didn't know how to save Wolf's victims, any of them. But sometimes he could help a little. Kenny, of course, would be assuming acorns were poisonous to humans. They had to be, if Wolf was requiring you to eat them.

"One," began Wolf, smiling up at Kenny.

Behind Wolf, Harry signaled to Kenny, whose eyes flicked. Harry put his finger to his lips. *Don't speak, or we're both dead.* He held up a half-peeled acorn, picked out the white flesh and ate it, nodding up at Kenny. *See? Not lethal.*

Kenny dropped from the tree when Wolf got to seven, and began peeling acorns like shrimp and chewing them as fast as he could. The satisfaction for Wolf was fleeting, and he walked away, bored. He passed the tree Harry had been hiding behind, treading heavily on bits of acorn shell without noticing.

Beth came to him in twenty-three trees. Sometimes she said hello, but mostly she said goodbye. Hello, goodbye, her voice always fainter, her memory-image thinning to light-pierced fog.

Seven trees provoked thoughts of Wolf. His father turned up only once, in the sweet gum. His mother once, in a pin oak. In an eastern hemlock, staring back in time, Harry listened to a chain saw cutting down the eastern hemlock that had stood outside his office window.

Sometimes, he was simply a forester, a scientist in a tree. He examined a dangling brown linden leaf — still holding on from last fall — for leaf spot and nectaria canker. He ran his fingers along the black scar of a lightning-strike high up in a red cedar. Lightly touched the sticky new leaves, neon green at the tip of an alder branch.

Foresters call dead trees "snags." He climbed one, a silver maple, a gray-white skeleton teeming with life. Raccoons rustled inside their hidden nests in jagged knot-holes; a dark-eyed opossum crawled upside down along a leafless branch; a male downy woodpecker drummed on the hollow wood at the broken top of the maple to claim its territory, as an impressed female flitted nearby. A bear had climbed this tree. Harry fingered the dotted claw scratches (bear ascending) and beside them the longer scrawls indicating the bear's descent.

Climbing, Harry often thought of Oriana. Climbing, he thought of Amanda.

Atop a very tall, craggy sycamore, Harry could see over the crowns of most of the surrounding trees — the tented peaks of the conifers, the oval spread of the maples, the columnar towers of the dark-limbed poplars. And a half mile northeast, he could see into a clearing, in the neat center of which stood Amanda's house, its red metal roof gleaming in the sunlight. His eyes lingered on the geometric, orderly red in the emerging sea of spring green. He could not see Amanda or Oriana. The house was too far away.

What would Amanda think he was doing, day after day, in the trees? What did Oriana imagine?

Because it had taken Harry fifty-three trees to understand what he was doing. And now, high atop tree number 127, the sycamore, he was as ready as he was ever going to be. He turned from Amanda's house, toward the tree house nestled in the five great branches of the immense American beech.

"Oh shit," Amanda said, looking through the binoculars at Harry in the canopy of the sycamore. They were standing on the back deck of the house.

Oriana had been adding "sycamore" to their list. Harry had climbed well over a hundred trees now. Oriana stared at her mom. Mom *never* used that word. And she looked frightened, which frightened Oriana.

"Mom? Mom, what?"

Amanda lowered the binoculars. Numbly took the list from Oriana's hand. Stared at it. "It's not the number he's climbed," she whispered. She took a breath. "And it's not the types." Amazingly, she said the curse word again, "Oh shit, Harry," and looked toward the sycamore again.

"Mom."

"The pattern. Why he chooses them. It's about how *tall* they are."

All along, she'd noticed it without noticing at all. Every tree he climbed was taller than the one before. The climbing, the running, lifting the stones. Harry was getting in shape. All this time, he'd been getting ready. He was a man with a plan.

They didn't need the binoculars to see the tallest tree in the forest. Both of them turned and looked at the American beech, not yet leafed out, but on the verge. It towered above all the others.

"Wow," Oriana said. Because if Harry

climbed a tree like that, he could do *any-thing.*

16

Just like Harry, Wolf was up a tree. The tree was not in a forest, however, but in Harry's backyard in Waverly. It was not a towering tree, but a measly dogwood that barely supported Wolf's bulk.

Harry, Wolf thought, as the dogwood swayed back and forth, if I fall from this tree and snap my neck attempting to break into your house, I'm holding you personally responsible. And you know what that means, don't you? Wolf frowned. Well, it won't mean anything, if I can't find him, will it?

Interesting, that I could die falling out of a tree. Like Mr. Forestry set a tree trap for me. But that's not like my Harry, thought Wolf. Whatever it is you're up to, it's not about me. Though, it is about me, because you're pushing my buttons. And that's why you ran with the money, because you knew I wouldn't stand for it. All your life, you never pushed back, and now you're pushing. Why?

Wolf did not like mystery and conjecture. He was a beeline kind of guy. And what kind of guy are you, Harry? Good guy, bad guy or guy who's lost his grip?

Doesn't really matter because you're the guy with four million dollars, and that four million dollars exists because I took you to that ambulance-chasing lawyer. I put a winning ticket in your hand. You won, and you didn't even want to play. Through you, I played Lawsuit Lotto and won.

I *want,* Harry. Wolf wants his winnings. And more to the point he needs them. His divorce, nearing its brutal endpoint, his third goddamn divorce — Harry, I'm going under. You are *not* giving that money away to strangers. Goddamn it, we're fucking brothers. It's always been you and me against the world.

Wolf stepped onto the second-floor roof. There was just enough light from the security light on the garage next door so he could see what he was doing. Harry's house would have no security. The Waverly police patrol car had made its lazy drive-by, the neighborhood was asleep and quiet. Wolf broke a windowpane with a pop of his knuckles, reached in and undid the latch.

Inside the house. What was he looking for?

A clue into Harry's state of mind. Had he been thinking at all rationally? Did he have a plan?

This was the question Wolf had put before Bob Jackson earlier in the day. Wolf had taken the day off work and driven up from Virginia.

Wolf went up to the third floor, where Harry used to work. He was directed to Bob Jackson.

Bob was sitting in Harry's old cubicle. He looked like he wanted to cry. On his desk, thick files in teetering stacks: rangeland management, forest resource utilization, inventory and analysis, development and evaluation, ecoregional protocol monitoring.

A shadow darkened Bob's desk. He swiveled in his chair. Looked up. And up.

A gigantic hand reached down. Bob shrank back from it. Oh, the hand's not going to strike me. It wants to shake. Wincing, Bob offered up his own moist, trembling little hand.

Wolf squeezed as he introduced himself. "Hi, Bob. My name's Wolford Crane, but please call me Wolf. Got a second?"

Dizzy with adrenaline, Bob nodded to the wolf, vigorously in the affirmative.

Wolf explained who he was and why he

was there. Bob liked this development. Although Wolford the Wolf was terrifying and took up most of the space in the cubicle, Bob had a glimmer of something positive: maybe this huge man would drag his brother back to work.

Harry had sent Irv Mickler his resignation, but Wolf looked like a man who could change minds.

"Are you going to make him come back?" Bob said.

Wolf was a very quick study. Mountains of paper on Bob's desk, thanks to Harry. Bob himself, with the air of the office shirker. "Did Harry betray you, Bob?"

"Well, that's a strong word."

"But he did, didn't he?"

"I had seniority over him."

"And now this dump job."

"Will you bring him back?" Bob said. Because Wolf looked very much like one of those bounty hunter guys you see in movies. Bob wondered if Wolf had a gun. Harry Crane delivered at gunpoint back to his cubicle — Bob would welcome the sight.

Wolf thought, Yes, I will bring Harry back. To his senses. "What I need from you, Bob, is a description of Harry's last moments. You said he just stood up and walked out of the office. Brushed right past you."

"Yes, and he looked very weird. Weirder than usual, I mean." Bob lowered his voice. "Never the same since the wife thing, you know."

Wolf twitched, reflexively protective of Harry. This guy Bob had no doubt taken advantage of Harry's post-Beth daze. Harry wanting to bury himself in work, and this little worm milking it. Wolf stopped himself from lifting Bob to his feet and giving him a spine-snapping shake.

Instead, he guided Bob into the aisle. The other office workers were furtively watching Wolf and Bob. No one questioned Wolf's presence. He oozed authority. And forestry bureaucrats were by nature nonconfrontational. Irv Mickler, the boss, stepped halfway out of his office, absorbed Wolf's commanding stature and shrank back out of view. Sequoia, Irv thought. The man is a giant sequoia. No doubt FBI or NSA, but certainly, definitely, none of my business. I need not know what I need not know. Irv clicked his door shut.

Wolf stood behind Bob, leaned down to make sure his breath was hot on Bob's neck. "So, Harry stood up, you said."

"Yes. I was down by the elevator, there —" Bob pointed "— and walking this way. He'd just gotten off the phone. But he was still talking. As he came toward me. Talking."

The call from Toland came in, the news of the money, all that fucking money, and it fried Harry's precarious brain, Wolf thought. "Bob. Bobby boy, what was he saying?"

"It was hard to hear."

"Go back in your mind, Bob. And hear it, please." Wolf placed a hand on Bob's shoulder. It was heavy as an anvil. Thick fingers began to knead. Bob gasped. Oh my, Bob thought, those are powerful fingers. I think something in my shoulder is separating.

It all came rushing back to Bob. There he is, Harry, he's walking toward me, and he says something. What does he say? Speak louder, Harry! And then Bob heard Harry, loud and clear. *To the trees.*

"To the trees," Bob blurted. "To the forest and the trees!"

Inside Harry's house now, using the flashlight app on his phone, Wolf looked around. *To the forest and the trees.* Wolf had pressed sweaty Bob, to no avail. What forest, what trees was Harry talking about? Were Harry's gaskets blown, was he simply a babbling forester, or was he heading to a specific patch of forest? Did he have a favorite forest, a place he might go? But the office managed a thousand forests in the

Mid-Atlantic states. Bob, surely there was a *special* forest, a *special* tree? Could we look on his computer? Click click click, but what were they looking for? Nothing stood out, it was all data and graphics. No images of special trees, not even a photo of his first love, the big beech in their childhood front yard.

Wolf made his way into Harry's den. Disheveled like the entire house.

To the forest and the trees. Wolf reached for his phone and pulled up the text exchange from last week.

> **Harry:** I'm not coming home, Wolf. And I am in a safe place. You got all that?

I'm in a safe place. You're in a fucking forest with four million dollars is where you are. Always looking for a safe place, up your big beech tree, and now in your unknown forest.

I'm not coming home. And you didn't. You got the Toland call at the office, and you didn't even come home, did you?

Wolf stood in Harry's bedroom. The drawers were stuffed with underwear and socks, the closets full. Of Beth's stuff, too. In the bathroom, Harry's toothbrush still in the holder. And Beth's, beside it. Jesus, Harry, you haven't moved a molecule since she died. The money came, you detonated, and you wandered off and found a safe place. Both a definitive and utterly arbitrary act. Fuck. How do I find a man without a plan? A man safe somewhere deep inside one of a thousand forests? Fuck me.

Dawn would come soon. He needed to get the hell out of here. Instead, Wolf went into the den, dropped into a leather chair and lit a cigarette. Smoked it. Stubbed it out in an empty glass he picked up in the kitchen. Lit another. And another — and on the flare of the cigarette lighter saw a small photograph, high up on a bookcase, in plain view but somehow also out of sight. Wolf got out of the chair and reached for it, brought it to the glow of his cell phone. It was a photo of Wolf and Harry, when they were little kids.

"Aw, Harry, see what I mean? This is what I'm saying. Look at us." Just look at us. Wolf stared into the eyes of his younger self. There was no anger in them. The perpetual glare, the grimace, had not yet settled into his face. We should've just stood there forever, bro. Because, goddamn, look at us.

Wolf noticed something, the little corner jutting from behind the photo. Another photo tucked behind the frame. He tugged it into view. And felt, like the sear of a harsh chemical, the anger burning into his eyes as he studied the revealed photo. It was a snapshot, in the same spot, taken moments before or after Wolf and Harry had happily posed. It was blurry, like a kid had taken the picture. Wolf closed his eyes and saw himself holding the Kodak Instamatic to his eye, looking through the lens at Harry and his father, Jeffrey Crane.

Wolf blinked at the photo. Little Harry, with his father's arm around his shoulders. Harry smiling. His father smiling, too. Wolf checked to see if there was another hidden photo. One that he wanted to see, and did not want to see: Dad with his arm around me.

But there were no more photographs. Wolf closed his eyes, and tried to remember. Was there ever such a photograph? He tried to feel it, the embracing weight of his father's arm around his shoulders.

He snapped out of it. Furious. "Why'd you fall for that shit, Harry?" Can't you see it in Dad's eyes? It's right there. He's looking into a distance he can't wait to escape into. And are you doing that, too, Harry? Is that what I see? Wolf held the cell phone light right up to their faces. They looked like conspirators, the two of them. Dad ran . . . and you're a runner, too, Harry.

I hate it when people run.

And it doesn't help when they have four million dollars. Dad took my life, and you took my money.

"Wolford, you're being overdramatic. Calm down." Wolf hated when teachers and counselors told him that, in middle school. Calm down, Wolford, calm down. Frightened of him, so large. He didn't even like it when he said it to himself. So he kept saying it. "Calm down, calm down, Wolford." Because that's the kind of guy he was. A beeline kind of guy. Beelining himself straight to the only emotion he understood. He felt the flare of his anger, and *saw* it, too. The spark, the flare, the flame — Wolf held the cigarette lighter under the photo of Harry and his father. It smoked, caught fire and burned. He grinned as his father curled and blackened. And then Harry went up in smoke, too.

A little stunned, Wolf dropped the smoldering black ash into the kitchen glass and sucked on his burned fingertips.

"Calm down." And this time he meant it. You don't calm down, you're going to have a fucking heart attack.

And he almost did have a heart attack when the smoke alarm above his head broke into an ear-piercing string of amplified chirps.

Wolf bolted for the front door, spun around, ran back into the den and scooped up the photo of him and Harry, then bolted for the front door again and ran into the predawn Waverly dark and leaped into his car, parked in the shadows two blocks away.

17

It was five in the morning and Harry was asleep, dreaming of the beech tree. It was speaking to him in Amanda's voice. No, wait. The tree wasn't speaking — Amanda was speaking, very softly. There she was, perched on a low branch like the Cheshire Cat, whispering as the wind might whisper through the leaves of a tree, "Spring has come. Wake up, wake up."

And then she raised her arm above her head and pointed. Up.

Harry woke with a start.

Where was he? It was very dark, but also very bright. The full moon cast its light through the multicolored windows of the tree house. Moonbeam through colored glass is the light of dreams, so it took Harry a moment to understand he was awake. He closed his eyes and revisited his lingering dream. Amanda sitting in the beech, telling him to wake up. *Spring has come.* Swinging his legs over the side of the cot, Harry scrambled into his clothes, pulled his Forest Service cap firmly on his head and went out onto the deck. He looked up into the dark center of the beech. Up seemed infinite and unreachable. But it was the only way he was going to get to the light.

He trembled once, a full body shake, like a racehorse at the starting gate, then narrowed his eyes, swung up onto the roof of the tree house and grabbed hold of the first limb. He pulled himself up easily, hooked his leg over the thick limb and stood. The effort of climbing no longer hurt. He wasn't panting for breath. His body had changed since he first climbed the bitternut hickory two weeks ago. His arms and legs were strong. He flexed his shoulders and shrugged his back, felt the smooth glide of muscles — nothing popped or crackled like in those first days. The forest had changed him. Even the way he breathed was different. Longer, calmer breaths, the forest air reaching a deeper place.

He looked down. In the moonlight, he could just see the mossy roof of the tree house. He reached for another branch and pulled himself up. Once he got beyond these heavy lower branches with their wide vertical spacing (a few of them were just out of reach, and he had to spring into the air like a lemur to gain the last few inches) the branches would become more abundant and dense. A beech is a tree with weak apical dominance, so it produces an abundance of lateral shoots and a compact canopy — it's very branchy. This made it a good climbing tree — but a tall one. Harry guessed the beech was 160 feet tall. Yesterday's sycamore was 130.

He climbed, leaped, swung himself up. As he ascended, the tree house roof began to shrink — to car-size, then toy-size, then to the size of his thumb. Below the tree house, the forest floor turned into a distant moonlit blur lost in a spidery tangle of dark, leafless limbs. Up he went, forty feet, fifty, sixty.

As he approached the secondary canopy, the air grew thinner (or so he imagined), the branches less substantial (true). The sleepy creatures living in the tree were not pleased to see the moonlit interloper, grunting and sweating his way past their homes. Raccoons growled. Squirrels chirred and skittered by, across his shoulders, down his leg. When he gripped the rim of a damp knothole to steady himself, an opossum poked into view, bared its yellow teeth and hissed. Startled owls dipped and swooped around him. A pair of bats shot out of a dark V-crotch and flapped jaggedly past his head.

Harry leaned back against the smooth, gray trunk of the beech, breathing in the heady oxygen of a million trees. He looked to the east, toward the low rolling mountains. The light was changing. He was 110 feet off the ground, he guessed, had been climbing for almost an hour. Fifty more feet to the top.

When he reached for the next branch, his hand jostled a nest of twigs. A high screech, and a pair of wood thrushes suddenly dive-bombed him, swooping and buzzing like angry bees. Swatting them away, Harry slipped. As he fell, he grabbed hold of a long, secondary scaffold branch, thin as a rope. His plunging weight snapped it, but not completely. His knowledge of trees saved him. He jerked his body clockwise, twisting the long fibers of the branch, adding a fleeting moment of tensile strength. Instead of plummeting to the forest floor, he rappelled safely down to the next big branch, five feet below.

He hugged the beech trunk, panting like a frightened dog. But there was no time to be frightened. Up. He had to get *up.* Because the stars were fading, the moon was gone and the black of night had begun to lighten.

He climbed faster. Sweat dripped off his nose and fell into the void. Attuned, Harry could hear everything — his sweat falling; animals rustling in their knothole nests; birds lifting their eyelids, preparing for the coming dawn. But most of all, he heard the beech — the sap coursing through its veins, the tips of the branches quivering as though touched by a cosmic tuning fork. Only one element was missing. Harry pulled himself through the canopy, gasping as he strained upward, as fast as he possibly dared. One element, due east, just behind the rolling swells of the Endless Mountains.

A purple finch chirped.

A second finch chimed in.

A sleepy pause. A yellow warbler warbled. Then dozens of finches, warblers and thrushes began to call from all the trees, the chorus of the forest tuning up.

Harry reached the very top of the beech. He pulled himself up the tapered central leader, crooked an arm around it like King Kong clinging to the top of the Empire State Building and looked east, toward the barely visible dark lumps and bumps of the Endless Mountains.

There, right there. It had begun. First, a faint glimmer at the tip of a cloud. Then a thin, bright crescent peeking into view. And finally, rising into full splendor, the sun, igniting the scattered clouds, overwhelming the night, dimming the stars.

Harry shimmied even higher, as high as he could, a human flag on the pinnacle of a flagpole. The leader creaked and swayed, and Harry swayed with it. He reached into a ray of light as it touched the highest tip of the beech. His fingertips glowed.

Awakened by the sun, the terminal bud on the beech opened. A hint of green — the beginning of the beginning. Harry heard it happen — the apical husk unwrapping with a dry scritch, denticulate margins and resinous leaf hairs rasping apart, sap racing like heart's blood through the microscopic xylem and phloem. A second bud opened. A third, a fourth, dozens, thousands. A wave of sound cascaded from the top of the tree to the bottom, as the sun rose and the beech tree came to life. The chirping birds, hidden within the green of the forest, erupted as one.

Harry looked north, south, east, west, directing his sweeping gaze on the hills and dales of the Endless Mountains. He saw at the base of them the sinuous snake of the Susquehanna River turned into glittering mercury by the sun; saw a wavery cloud of birds rise up and scatter; saw a train crossing a far distant bridge; saw old mining sites and scattered towns and the tops of millions of trees.

"Look at all the trees, Beth," Harry whispered.

And he knew what she'd say. *Harry's Trees.*

"I'm going to do something crazy," he said.

Your eyes are smiling again, Harry. At last.

"There's this kid named Oriana. And she has this plan for me and the money, Beth. And I think I can do it." Because once you climb this high, you keep climbing.

Harry waited for Beth to speak to him again. But there was nothing more for her to say. He clung to the tree in the dawn light. He breathed in and he breathed out. And he understood: this is how it would be. Beth was inside him, but he could let her go, too. It was a wonderful, heart-rending sensation. It was life. He breathed Beth deep inside himself, held her for a moment, then breathed her out over the spring forest. And all the new leaves took her in and became a little greener, and then they, in turn, breathed her back to Harry.

"Skreeeeee," cried a distant hawk, circling high overhead. It was the red-tailed hawk. Harry watched as it flew west, straight over

Amanda's house. It kept on flying until it disappeared into the dawn light.

The sun rose and shined on Harry. He absorbed the light and breathed the forest air. After a time, he took off his Forest Service cap, undid the adjustment strap and attached it as high on the leader branch as he could reach.

The mountain wind shifted the hat right and left, fluttered it back and forth like a flag.

Harry watched for a while and then began his descent.

Oriana was at school. She'd argued, but Amanda sent her off. "Mom, you'll text me when he climbs it, right?"

If he climbs it, Amanda thought, standing alone now on the back deck. She raised her binoculars to the beech tree, lit by the early-morning light.

Why hadn't Harry climbed it yet? A day had gone by, two — and he hadn't climbed *any* trees. Was she wrong about the beech? Was he done with climbing?

And then it hit her. This morning, the beech tree was different.

His words came back to her: *One by one, like slow-motion fireworks, tree after tree will burst to life. And the very last tree will be this big guy, the American beech.*

This was the day. The beech was green, bursting with life. It was leafing out.

That's what Harry had been waiting for — the perfect moment to climb the tallest tree in the forest.

"Harry," she whispered. "You're climbing it right now."

But where was he? She scanned up and down the tree, looking to see how high he'd gotten. It was hard to see through the new veil of green.

How can he possibly make it to the top? she thought, her heart racing. The beech was so incredibly tall.

"Harry. It's a crazy idea," she whispered.

How many times in the ER had she had patients who'd pulled some crazy stunt — plowed a too-steep hill and overturned a tractor; taken an ATV out on the ice; stood on the top rung of a rickety ladder, reaching out with the paintbrush to get that last bit of trim, way up. So many tumbles and falls, so many accidents, she'd seen it all.

But Harry *wasn't* crazy. Not like the guys around here always pressing their luck, doing dumb stuff. He's careful.

Early-morning light poured through the palette of emergent green dappling every tree in the forest, a crayon box offering a thousand shades of a single color, all of it between her and a good view of the beech. She moved from one end of the deck to the other, looking for a good angle.

There. A clear view. She scanned the wide gray trunk of the beech, panning out to the lateral branches, now awash in green. Her gaze swept from the roof of the tree house upward, looking for him. No, Harry definitely wasn't crazy, he was *careful.* He was *methodical.* He'd studiously prepared himself over the last two weeks to climb this particular tree.

Again she remembered his words, remembered the night he'd removed his wedding ring, when they were standing on the tree house deck, looking out over the leafless forest.

"So when the buds open, two hundred thousand of them all at once, it sounds like the tree is giving a great big, raspy sigh of relief," Harry said.

"Because spring has come," Amanda said.

"Because winter's over," he said.

Remembering this made her blush, and that surprised her.

She focused the binoculars, raised them slowly up and up, scanning the mid canopy, with its denser tangle of branches. She looked for the jiggle of branches that would reveal his presence, or the white of his Forest Service cap.

"Where are you, Harry?"

And then at the top of the tree, a flash of white! She leaned back and focused on it . . .

It was his cap — his cap was attached to the top branch of the tree, fluttering in the wind.

He'd planted his flag atop his mountain.

"Because winter's over," he said.

"Spring has come," she said.

She smiled. "You did it, Harry!"

It looked amazing up there, Harry's cap atop the world.

In a rush of excitement, Amanda thought, He's probably just gotten down from the tree. I'll get some stuff together for pancakes and go over to the tree house and make breakfast for him. He deserves something, he —

She was still looking at the beech through her binoculars when something caught her eye. A clutch of branches shaking, about twenty feet below Harry's fluttering cap. The shaking stopped, started up again. Harry coming down the tree?

More shaking, and when she finally fixed on the spot, going up on her toes, leaning into the deck railing — it wasn't Harry. Two raccoons were chasing each other around and around the trunk.

She relaxed, about to lower her binoculars, when she saw something else. A raw wound on the beech — the jagged stump of a freshly snapped limb. A sudden sick feeling in her stomach. No. The raccoons snapped it, chasing around. It happens all the time, she thought, raccoons, opossums snapping branches. And sometimes they fell — these animals born to climb — tumbling through the air. Walking in the forest, you came upon them, dead at the base of a tree. It was the precarious nature of life.

Amanda gripped the deck railing. Because she knew. Harry had snapped that branch. Harry, descending in triumph, had gone too fast, done something stupid, something unsafe. After climbing so many trees — so many! — his luck had run out. He'd fallen to his death. He had put his foot down too hard on a weak limb and it snapped and he fell — oh God, from such a height — to the forest floor. This man who had come into Oriana's life, who had begun to right her daughter's world, was dead. And Oriana would know forevermore: there was no righting the world.

Amanda stumbled down the stairs of the deck and across the backyard into the woods, her heart pounding because she was so angry for Oriana. That Harry would do this, that he would do this to her.

But if he were dead, why was she running? What was the point of running, the laurel bushes scraping her legs, pine branches whipping at her. She was running because she was terrified, because she didn't want Harry to be dead. Amanda was so scared that for a fantastic moment she thought she might be able to get there in time, in some miraculous manner she might hold out her arms and catch him.

It was the craziest thing she had ever experienced, running through the forest with her arms out, prepared in some impossible way to break Harry's fall to earth. So that when she came suddenly upon him, stopping short, her arms extended, she thought for a startled instant she *had* saved him. Even though he was fifty yards away from where she stood.

Amanda slowly lowered her arms and stared in wonder. Harry was alive. *Incredibly* alive.

He hadn't heard her crashing through the forest because he was standing in the middle of the rock-strewn stream, the water rushing noisily around him. He was naked, his back to her, splashing water on himself, bathing.

Harry had come down from his tree, sweaty and triumphant. The stream was a few hundred feet from the tree house. He bathed in it every day, neatly piling his clothes, wading into the cold water with a towel around his waist in case Oriana came sneaking into view. He always carried a bar of soap he placed on a mossy rock in the middle of the stream. His routine. But this morning, he had shed his clothes exuberantly and tramped into the waters. He cupped the clear water with both hands and tossed it into the air, leaned back and let it splash down onto his body. He did again and again. The sun turned the water droplets on his skin into glittering jewels.

Amanda stared. She had seen this before, animals splashing in this very stream. Red foxes, deer, even a black bear once, dipping itself on a blistering summer day and shaking its heavy flesh and wet fur. Harry, naked and wildly alive, was one of them. A creature of the forest.

He pushed his wet hands through his hair — thick tangles of black, his hair taking on a new wildness. Standing straight and tall, Harry looked like a different man. His body wasn't heavy, didn't possess the rural mass of Dean or Cliff, but it was surprisingly strong, lean, the triangle of his shoulders and back tapering to his waist, a good ass she shouldn't be staring at, solid thighs, muscular calves. A body transformed by days spent struggling up trees. Amanda looked beyond Harry to the beech. The huge tree had not been an instrument of death, but its absolute opposite. A giver of life.

The water parted around Harry. Sunlight filtered through the green trees set him aglow. Amanda continued to stare at him. She had been watching him for days. She'd watched him at night, too, looking for the orange flame of the distant kerosene lamp that assured her that he was there, in the tree house.

If he turned around, he would see her. Harry, who thought he was alone, who needed to be alone. It would embarrass them both. But still she was compelled to watch, absorbing the wonder of what she was witnessing. For a widower's year, Harry had been in a trance-like sleep, and the forest had kissed him awake.

Harry froze. Cocked his head. He'd sensed something. Turning, he saw the rustle of leaves, fifty yards away, in a patch of stream willow. He was about to scramble for his clothes, when a doe and her fawn stepped into view. The doe eyed him for a long moment. And when she was certain that Harry was a fellow creature of the forest, she allowed the fawn to step forward and drink from the stream.

18

Simple would suffice. Beth liked simple. Harry, freshly bathed in the chill waters of the stream, shaved, put on a clean shirt, combed his hair and set off into the forest, ring in hand.

The sun was bright through the green of the trees. He wondered about Amanda, what the moment had been like for her. She put her ring in a drawer, and that was that? No. *And then, I just kept shedding his stuff,* she said. *Got rid of as much as I could as fast as I could. As if that would make it easier.* It wasn't easy for Amanda, it was doubly hard, because she had Oriana's grief as well as her own.

And now Harry had *their* grief as well as his own. Remarkably, the disastrous decision to buy the lottery ticket a year ago had one positive outcome. It led him here, to Oriana. I can return Oriana to her mother, he thought, and together they can move forward. And that, for Harry, was the gift hidden within the story of the grum and his gold.

The less I have, the more they will have. I will dig away at the mountain of gold until Oriana emerges, free, released from her spell of grief. The Plan was a good plan.

But first, a proper Beth farewell, the next step in his long goodbye. He would leave the ring at the base of the sugar maple because that's where he'd reached for the Snickers — the gold that saved his life — and found a way into his future. He would return to the tree house. Okay, Oriana, he'd say, I'm ready.

For a few minutes, moving through the ordinary familiarity of the forest, the world seemed to Harry like a reasonable place. Perhaps even straightforward, after the convolution of death-bringing lottery tickets, life-saving hawks, grums, willful little girls and very tall beech trees. Really, all he had to accomplish next was a mere financial transaction. There'd be four million dollars in his bank account, and then there wouldn't. The Plan was a wee bit fancy, perhaps. Or hell, maybe not. No reason to be nervous about it, the Swiss do this sort of thing all the time, right? Ordinary Americans do it. Oriana had shown him the sites.

Tons of sites. Big deal, Harry, gold. Everybody's doing it!

He stopped in his tracks. Stared. The forest an ordinary and reasonable place? He had reached the sugar maple and the stone wall. Sitting atop the wall was an old woman looking for all the world like . . . a witch. Frizzly white hair, wrinkly face spookily veiled in a cloud of smoke. *Very* witchy. The smoke swirled away, and Harry saw that she was smoking a large meerschaum pipe.

" 'Are you a Being Natural or a Being Unnatural, O forest-dweller?' " she said in a raspy voice.

Harry took a step back from her.

Olive laughed, smoke puffing from her mouth in little bursts, like a steam locomotive. "It's just a quote, dear, from a short story, a bit of Gothic piffle written by Washington Irving in 1838 entitled 'The Midnight Encounter.' The protagonist asks the question of a ghost. 'Are you a Being Natural or a Being Unnatural, O forest-dweller?' The action takes place in a cemetery in the middle of the forest primeval."

"Excuse me. Who *are* you?" Harry said.

"Well, who are *you,* for heaven's sake?" She examined him. "Wait, don't tell me." She relit her pipe, exhaled a plume of smoke and poked a finger into it as if in mystical analysis. She pursed her lips and nodded. "You are Harold F. Crane, forester, renting the Jefferses' tree house for three weeks, though tricked into four."

Harry's mouth opened and closed.

Her laugh was a cackle. "I'm Olive Perkins, dear, local librarian, and Ronnie Wilmarth was bursting with the news of you. He has a gift for not keeping secrets. It's practically a superpower."

"You're out here looking for me?"

"I was about to ask you the same question. Why have you come to my stone wall and my maple tree?" Her eyes fixed on the broken limb draped over the far end of the wall. She sighed deeply. "My poor old sugar maple. My poor, poor tree." She burst into sudden tears and dropped her pipe.

Harry's hand went to his heart. He'd broken her tree. He hurried to the wall, got up beside her and put his arm around her shoulders. Her bones were bird-like. He was holding the saddest bird in the world.

"Oh, I'm sorry," she said. "You were having a nice sunny walk in the woods. And you stumbled upon a scene of woe."

But why so much woe? The tree was old, yes, but still healthy, the wound would heal. "I'm sorry about your tree," he said. And he was, although he did not admit that he was the perpetrator of the crime.

"You've seen worse, I'm sure. As a forester, I imagine you've seen absolutely dreadful things happen to trees. Lightning strikes. Fires. Beetles and borers."

"It's the nature of things," Harry said.

"True enough. And if catastrophe doesn't get you, time will. The great scythe of time. An old tree, an old wall and an old woman. Limbs snap, rocks tumble, the flesh weakens and withers. Truly, it is the nature of things."

Harry patted her hand. "But look at the new green all around you. Spring comes, too, you know. That's also the nature of things."

Olive smiled, tears shining in the wrinkles of her cheeks. "One is apt to forget, but you are absolutely right. Spring." She leaned back from him. "This old hag before you, in the winter of her decline — can you imagine her in the spring of her youth?"

"You're not a hag. And yes. I can imagine it."

"Oh piss and pissle, you're lying." She pointed at the meerschaum in the leaves at the base of the wall, Mark Twain's carved face scowling up at them. Or was it a look of amusement? "Be a dear and fetch the old hag's pipe."

Harry got the pipe. She filled it from a

small leatherette pouch, then eyed him as she tamped her tobacco and lit it. She tilted back and blew a great stream of smoke up into the heavy branches of the maple.

"It's difficult to imagine me young, I know," Olive said. "But let's try something. Since you know trees. Turn your forester's eyes to the maple, and imagine how it looked sixty years ago. It was perhaps twenty or thirty feet tall, its bark smooth and gray. No broken limbs, no knotholes. It was *young,* Harry."

He saw it. For a dream-like instant, he saw the sugar maple, young and reaching for the sky. Not a blemish of age on it. He turned and looked at Olive. And she, too, was suddenly young! Her skin smooth, her brown hair lustrous on her shoulders, her posture straight and strong. She smiled.

The veil of pipe smoke cleared, and Olive returned to her old self.

Harry stared at her in amazement.

"You saw me, didn't you?" Olive said. "The possibility that I was once young?"

"How did you — ?"

"Mental nudge. A librarian's trick. In the old reading-hour days, to get the children ready for a story, I'd say, 'Close your eyes and imagine you are in a castle or a cave, and the voice in your ear is not mine, but a wizard's or maybe the rumbling growl of a dragon.' Got the little buggers every time. Especially Ronnie Wilmarth, who was a fidgeter."

Harry was still staring at her. "You were beautiful."

Olive smiled. "Well, well. You're my kind of fella. Suggestible."

Highly, thought Harry.

"Well, I wasn't beautiful, but I *was* young. The old know that no matter what you looked like when you were young — even if you wore tortoiseshell glasses and had mousy brown hair — you were beautiful. Because youth itself is beautiful."

Harry closed his eyes. Unstuck in time, he saw young Beth perched on the handlebars of the three-speed bike they had just bought at a yard sale. Beth, beautiful and laughing as he pedaled down Kirlsen Hill toward campus. He opened his eyes at the sound of Olive's voice.

"Harry. I need a favor from you, a kindness. May I tell you a story? This old librarian is in desperate need to tell a story." She patted the stone wall. "Come sit beside me."

Harry sat beside her. Together, they looked up into the sugar maple as Olive puffed on her pipe and told her story. In the swirl of smoke lifting into the tree, Harry saw every detail of every word she spoke.

"It's a love story," Olive began. "Which is the most important kind of story there is."

Tight in his hand, Harry's own love story, contained in a small circle of gold.

Pipe smoke left Olive in a sigh. "But life being life, love stories don't always end the way we want them to. The one I'm about to tell you is full of heartbreak and woe. And utter foolishness. And I won't pretend it's not autobiographical. I won't fancy it up with 'Once upon a time,' although it is utterly a fact that in our moment of love I was a princess and he was my prince, and that when we were together in the midnight of this forest, the light cast from the moon was a shimmering light, and the air was a perfumed bower of bliss.

"In other words, we were young and hot for each other and we made love. Multiple times." She blew out a puff of smoke. "I did not get pregnant. That is not the woe of this story.

"I see your look, Harry Crane. Hard to imagine, right? That the old were young, that they had sex." She laughed and shook her head. "It was a lot of damn fun. Shimmying out of my underwear, rolling around on a blanket." She pointed with the stem of her pipe. "Right over there, in that little patch of sunshine and grass. Good Lord, if I shimmied out of anything these days, I'd end up in traction in the hospital!"

Harry laughed. Olive, too.

"It was 1955," she said. "I was eighteen. But an enlightened eighteen, I made sure the young man wore protection. He had a little box of condoms, got them in Scranton. Certainly, he didn't buy them from Rognoff's Pharmacy in downtown New Milford. Ha! No, down in Scranton. Trojans, ten to a box. Only one brand and one model in those days. They sure weren't the lubricated, circus-colored wonders you see now at CVS." Olive smiled and looked into the distance. "But they worked just fine."

Her face grew serious.

"So, yes," she said. "We would meet and make love in the night forest. Like Hester Prynne and the Reverend Dimmesdale. But my story is not *The Scarlet Letter* — except that of course, it is. Because at its heart lies a secret. Our love — that was the secret. Our love was a hidden thing. And no matter how you lie to yourself, how one sweetens the truth, secrecy is the worm in the apple. And what my love — my prince — hid, was *me.* He would not admit to me. He would not go to his parents and utter my name. There was nothing shameful about me,

Harry. I was a good girl. A good, good girl. But I was not *good enough.* In an insurmountable way, I was not right. So we planned to elope.

"He'd bought a ring, down in Scranton. A secret engagement ring, and each time we made love, he'd slip it on my finger." Olive raised her left hand, knobby with arthritis, and touched the third finger, where there was no ring. "And when I would leave the forest and return to my parents' house, I would take it off again and hide it beneath a floorboard in my bedroom.

"Our plan was simple. We would elope, move away to a place where no one knew our names. It was the name, you see. The name was everything. He could not give his to me. Not here, not in this county.

"On the moonlit night of June 14, 1955, I entered these woods with a little cardboard suitcase, and the engagement ring on my finger. I was so proud. I was so happy." Olive's voice dropped to a whisper. "My love was not waiting for me. In his place, upon this wall, was a note. I saw it as soon as I came through the trees. Lit up in the moonlight. Aglow with fate. I barely had the strength to raise it to my eyes. It burned my fingers. It seared my soul."

She held up her hand as if reading from

the note, as if all of her life it was there before her.

"Olive, I love you with all my heart. But I had to tell Father. I had to. I could not marry you without his approval. He did not give it. And what I now realize, thinking about it, maturely, is that my love for you is a betrayal of my family. Oh Olive, my name is our fate. Keep the ring. Hold it in your hand, sometimes, and remember me. I love you, but I cannot have you. You will find someone better than I, someone who deserves you."

Olive shook her head. "They sent him away. A grown man, allowing himself to be sent away. I never saw him again. And all that remained of our love was a diamond ring. A ring. That great symbol of binding love, and it didn't protect me. In stories, the ring always protects, or has great power. I thought it would bind us forever." She touched her ringless finger. "But there is no safety in rings. They don't protect anything."

"No," Harry said softly. "They don't." He opened his right hand, slowly, and revealed his wedding band to her.

Olive's eyes went from the gold ring in his palm, to the pale ring of skin on the third finger of his left hand.

"Oh my. You have a story."

"It's only five words long — she died a year ago. And I'm out here to say goodbye. Which turns out to be a long and complicated process. I'm not sure I'll ever finish saying it."

Olive reached for him, and they sat for a long moment, Harry and the old woman, holding hands on the stone wall. "You never finish, Harry. I'm not finished with it either. Why does the universe allow love to happen? Against such odds — death, abandonment, and a thousand other misfortunes and ordeals — why would we risk falling in love? When it can be snatched from us at any time for any reason?"

Harry looked away.

Olive closed his fingers over the wedding band. "Because it's worth it. Worth the risk and the pain. Of all the glorious enchantments of this world — spring, snow, laughter, red roses, dogs, books — love is by far the best."

She released Harry and got down off the low stone wall. She took in the sugar maple, the wall, the forest. Hugged herself and smiled sorrowfully. "By its very nature, though, love is tragic. You can't protect it. No matter how tightly you hold on to the one you love, they leave you or you leave them. That's what life is, loving and letting go. I am so grateful to those two young lovers of sixty years ago. I am so grateful to have tasted love. But all love ends tragically. Because, tragically, *love always ends.* What a heartbreaking and wondrous conundrum! Whether you have it just a few weeks, or years, or your entire life — always, it ends." She lit her pipe, drew deeply, pursed her lips and blew. She reached her hand into the hovering, swirling, slowly vanishing cloud.

Love, thought Harry. Here and gone like a puff of smoke.

Olive faced him. "I now turn this hallowed spot over to you. Come to my library sometime, Harry Crane. Pratt Public Library, up the road in New Milford. Get a book. Reading solves most things. Or at least assuages the heart."

"I don't live here," Harry said. "I don't have a library card."

Olive clucked her tongue. "Damn, Harry. You *are* a rule-bound creature, aren't you? Just like Ronnie said." She thought a moment. "Tell you what. You're in her tree house — I'll put you on Oriana's card. She's the ultimate reader. And quite the opposite of rule-bound." Olive tapped her pipe on a lichen-covered rock on the stone wall, considered the little mound of emptied ash, then considered Harry. "I must say — it's quite fascinating. Amanda allowing you to stay in the tree house. Tough woman. Widow, you know."

"I know. I'm well aware."

Olive patted his cheek. "Well, I'll leave you to continue your story then." She smiled and winked, and started off into the forest.

"Why did you wink at me?" he asked.

She turned. "Because I love a good story. 'The Widower, The Widow and the Child in The Forest.' " She disappeared into the enveloping green.

"Is everything a story to you?" Harry called after her.

"Absolutely!" came Olive's voice. "I'm a *librarian,* dear!"

Harry dropped to his knees at the base of the sugar maple. He brushed away the leaves gathered between two upheaved old roots and began to scoop away the loamy soil. The earth gave way easily. He paused and turned his head, looked through the trees in the direction that Olive had gone, then down into the little hole again. He scooped away another handful of dirt. There was a twinkle of gold. Harry gently brushed away dirt that had remained undisturbed for sixty years and uncovered a delicate diamond filigree engagement ring. Again, he looked into the forest. Olive was not near, but her presence lingered like smoke.

After a long moment — *That's what life is, loving and letting go* — he placed his own ring beside Olive's long-buried ring, pushed the soft earth into place, patted it down and covered the spot with a scattering of leaves.

He stood, brushed the leaves and dirt off his knees, and turned to the broken branch, which lay across the half-tumbled end of the stone wall. It upset Olive, so he'd pull it into the brush so she wouldn't have to see it if she ever returned. He tugged at the broken end of the branch. Something caught his eye. On a loose flap of bark on the very end of the branch — the bark was scarred. Someone had carved something, long ago.

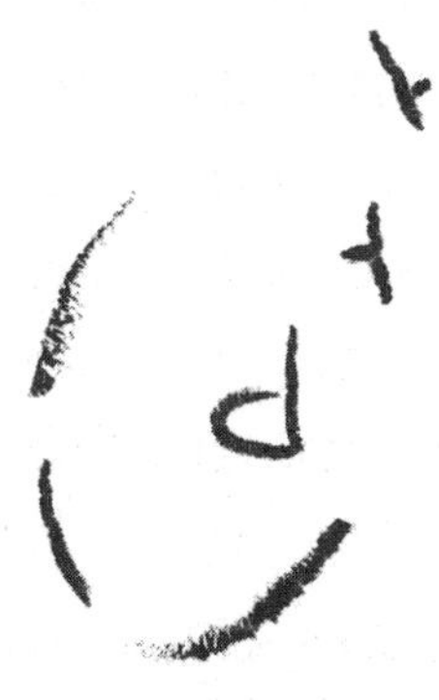

He pulled the piece free of the broken limb. Turned it in various directions. When he held it a certain way, he saw the letter P.

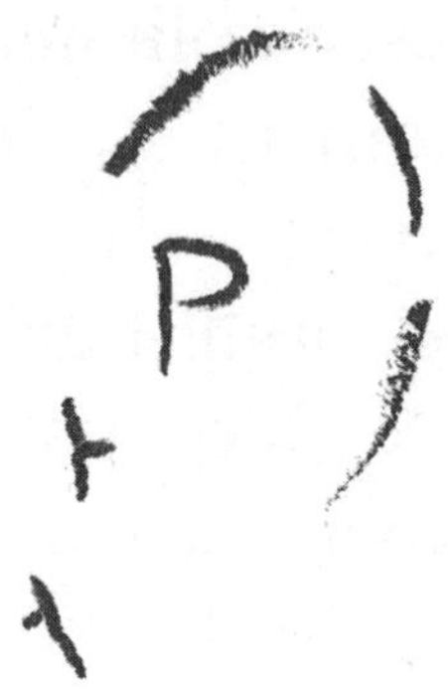

He looked up at the spot on the tree, where the limb had snapped off. The wound had stopped dripping sap. The healing had begun. He climbed up on the wall, went up on his toes. There was a small piece of dangling bark above the wound — the other half of the carving.

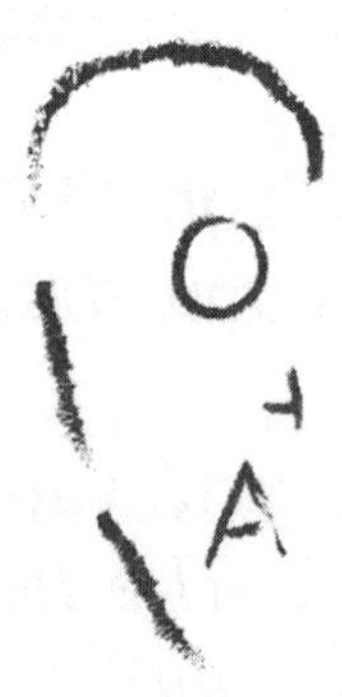

The two sections of bark were like two puzzle pieces. He fit them together:

Olive and her lover had carved their initials and drawn a heart around them. Time and insects had worn away the letter of his last name. And what was his first name? Alfred. Albert. Allen. Aaron.

Harry got back down off the wall. O and her A. It would've been A who carved the initials, climbing up on the stone wall in the bright moonlight. O would have stood at the base of the young sugar maple looking up.

"I'll put them up high," he would have said. *"And only we will know they're there. It will be our secret."*

And the young girl, watching, would have thought to herself: *The heart will protect us, too. Drawn around our names, snug, like the ring on my finger.*

19

Except for the extraordinary part, The Plan was simple. Harry and Oriana sat at the kitchen table in the tree house. It was early morning, before school. Oriana was holding *The Grum's Ledger.*

"Just because I agreed to do it, doesn't mean it's not scary," Harry said.

"But you climbed this tree," Oriana said, patting one of the thick branches of the beech that went up through the center of the tree house. "All the way to the top. That's way scarier than a little gold."

"A little gold," Harry said. "A smidgen of gold. Just a wee bit of gold." He gave her a look. "Could you please acknowledge this is scary? Just say, 'Harry, wow. Impressively scary. I can't believe you're actually going to do it.' " And yes, he *had* climbed the beech. But he'd always understood trees. He was a tree man by instinct and profession. By neither instinct nor profession, not even in the wildest of his wild dreams, was he a *gold* man.

"But I do believe it," Oriana said, "and now so do you. You climbed the tallest tree in the forest. And that makes you amazing. And now you're going to do something even *more* amazing."

Her eyes were filled with such excitement as she looked down at the grum atop his pile of gold. Harry tried not to gulp audibly. He sure hoped he was doing the right thing, bringing a fairy tale to life. But she believed in it, needed it to come true. Helping Oriana through her grief over her father's death — how could it not be a good thing? But what if I screw up? Harry swallowed again.

"So, now," Oriana said, picking up Harry's phone off the kitchen table, "it's time to choose."

He took the phone from her. "Here's the deal. Certain things only *I'm* going to do."

Oriana narrowed her eyes. "Because why?"

"Because I'm the adult. So I handle this next part. I need to find a shipping site, a wheelbarrow, some other stuff. And the cell signal here is spotty. I'll be using my phone a lot. So I'm going to Scranton."

"Scranton? For a wheelbarrow?"

"Oriana, I don't want to do anything suspicious around here."

"Why's a wheelbarrow suspicious?"

"Trust me. It isn't until it is. People are smart. They put things together."

"You could borrow ours."

"No! No, no, no. Of all the people I don't want suspicious, your mom is number one. Numero uno, Oriana. Got it?"

She leaned back from him. "Okay. Jeez, I get it. Don't sound so angry."

"I'm not angry. I'm scared. Remember?"

"But it's not illegal. You can't go to jail. The grum doesn't end up in jail."

Harry rolled his eyes. "My story's different from his story."

"But it's a lot the same," Oriana said. "The sad part, and now the gold part."

"All he had to do was toss his gold into the forest," Harry said. "But what I have to do — anything could happen."

She put a hand on his arm. "You climbed this tree. That was the hard part."

Harry wished that were so. He looked up through the skylight into the towering canopy of the beech. The tree was in full leaf now. It looked like a lovely place to spend a year or two hiding from four million dollars.

Oriana poked him. "So I know what *you* get to do. What do *I* get to do?"

"You get to find a good hiding place for

our treasure."

A hiding place for the treasure, thought Oriana. That was Oriana Eagle-Dare FeatherTop Frog-a-lina Cinderella Athena Snow Queen Jeffers's kind of job. "Okay. How big?"

"Big. But small." Whatever that meant. He was sure Oriana understood.

And she did. A riddle kind of a place, thought Oriana. *What is seen, but not seen? What has a mouth but no tongue?* "I might have a few ideas," she said. "Should it be high or low? Near or far?"

"Low and near," Harry said. "We're not talking permanent storage. And it needs to be close to the old quarry road, where my car is parked."

Oriana pointed at Harry's phone. "Can I at least see the number?"

Yesterday, Jeremy Toland's law firm had transferred the settlement money to Harry's money market account at Vanguard. It startled Harry, seeing for the first time the number in bold and in his possession. He went to the Vanguard site, then held his phone for Oriana to see:

$4,013,276.45

Oriana's eyes went wide. "That's, like, all

the money in the *world.*"

"It's just magic money. It's not real. It'll be here and then — plink and poof — gone."

"I bet it's going to be heavy. I bet it's going to be amazing. You'll let me see it, right? I have to see what magic looks like in real life."

Harry dropped to his knees in front of her, placed his hands on her shoulders and looked her in the eye. "Oriana — and I feel really mean saying this, but I have to — it's one thing to honor your father and carry out his wishes. I get that. I understand why we're doing this the grum way."

"Because you need an adventure."

He looked at her. "But I want to make sure of something here. A big something. For both of us."

"Okay."

"At the end of *The Grum's Ledger* the grum gets his lost love back. But when *we* get rid of my money, that's the end of our story, Oriana. That's as far as our fairy tale goes. Your dad won't reappear when we finish. Beth won't come back. Tell me you understand."

Oriana answered him in her very solemn voice. "I understand," she said. The thing about grown-ups, she thought, is that sometimes you have to look them straight in the eye — and lie. She knew something wonderful, extraordinary would happen when they got rid of the last piece of gold, she just couldn't say what. She had lost a father and Harry Crane had lost a wife on the very same day. Who could say what amazingly super-wonderful thing would happen at the end of the gold?

Harry went off to Scranton. Oriana went off to school.

So, what was so extraordinary about The Plan?

This: Harry was going to convert his four million dollars into gold coins. But he wasn't going to toss coins away like the grum. He was going to stuff them into bags and *give* them away. Had anyone ever done such a thing? Handed out bags of gold? You don't hand out a box of gold. It had to be a bag. A *burlap* bag of gold. That's the proper look. An unassuming bag, something that doesn't get in your face and shout, "Gold!" They had not worked out all the details — how many bags and to whom.

But one heart attack at a time, thought Harry. The first heart attack would be pulling the trigger on the buy.

He drove down to Spellman Heights, a

working-class suburb fifteen minutes north of downtown Scranton. He sat in his car with the engine idling, scanning the neighborhood, cell phone to his ear. The street was lined with trim, white three-story houses with heavy porches made of Pennsylvania bluestone cut from local quarries. Across the street from Harry's car, a pregnant woman swept her front steps. Two houses up, an old fellow leaning on an aluminum walker hosed out a trash can in his driveway. In the rearview mirror, he spotted a middle-aged blond woman coming up the sidewalk with a collie. Cars and pickup trucks lined the street. No one paid any attention to Harry in his dusty Camry.

There were thousands of gold bullion sites on the internet. They all looked the same, and the traders at the other end of the 1-800 numbers gave identical spiels. It's what Harry needed to hear, over and over — the dull legitimizing words of everyday commerce. As a (former) bureaucrat who had spent years wading through the molasses of governmental red tape, it thrilled and shocked him that he could obtain gold so easily. It was so damn legal it felt illegal.

He dialed the number of YourBullion America.com. They all had names like that. GoldVaultNow.com, WealthGoldMint.com,

MonexGoldImperial.com.

A voice came on the line. "YourBullion-America, my name is Kevin Purnell, how may I assist you today?"

Harry hunched down behind the steering wheel. This was it. He had talked to enough of these guys, it was time. "Yes. I'd like to buy some gold bullion, please," he said, his voice just above a whisper.

"Certainly, sir," said Kevin the trader. "And how much would you like to purchase?" There was no limit to the amount of gold an American citizen was allowed to purchase and privately own, and there was no report of the transaction to any government agency. No report, no registration, no paperwork.

Unbelievable — and perfect, Harry thought. He had to be as invisible as Santa Claus. Santa, lugging around sacks of gold. "I was thinking, two hundred fifty thousand dollars' worth?" he said. It seemed like the right amount to start with, to test the system, large but not staggering. Who was he kidding? It was completely staggering.

"Yes, sir. And will this be in coin or ingot?"

"Coin," Harry said, straining to be casual, as if choosing between coin or ingot was like choosing between whole milk or skim.

"Yes, sir. In coin, we offer Krugerrands,

the Canadian Maple Leaf and, our most popular, the one-ounce American Gold Eagle."

Should he ask if they had coins with a grum imprint? Harry felt light-headed, like he was strapped to a rocket blasting off for the moon. Steady, boy. Focus. "I'd like to buy two hundred fifty thousand in . . ." Wingèd gold for Oriana. "American Gold Eagles," he said.

"All right, excellent, sir," Kevin said. "Now, for purchases over a hundred thousand dollars we do require an electronic funds transfer."

"Not a problem."

"Great. Before I take your information, I do want to say we start the shipping process as soon as the wire is confirmed, which means that the order may be received by you within four days of being placed. However, during periods of high activity, shipment of orders can be delayed."

"Is this a period of high activity?"

"I'm not at liberty to say, sir."

Wow. This is not illegal, this is not illegal, Harry repeated to himself. It's just incredibly secretive. His eyes flicked. The woman walking the collie had stopped on the sidewalk beside his Camry. She gave a wave. Harry wiggled his fingers back at her. Just ordering a quarter-million dollars in gold, ma'am, pay me no heed. She came closer. Harry tightened. She motioned for him to roll down his window.

Harry murmured into his phone. "Kevin. Could you hold on a second, please?" He rolled down his window.

"Are you the gutter guy?" the woman said. The collie jumped up on the car door and sniffed at Harry.

Christ. Was it a gold-sniffing dog? Harry leaned back from the window. "The gutter guy?" he said.

"Oh, sorry, I thought you were the gutter guy. He's supposed to come do an estimate at noon." She pointed to her house. The gutter above the front porch was loose and swinging in the spring breeze. "Of course they never do come when they say they will."

The old fellow hosing the trash can in the driveway of the house called out, "He the gutter guy?"

"No, Pop-Pops, he's a different guy." She turned back to Harry and suddenly noticed he was holding his cell phone. "Oops, didn't see you're on your phone. Sorry."

The collie narrowed its eyes at Harry and sniffed deeper. The woman yanked him back. "Don't be nosy," she said.

Yes, thought Harry, his heart beating like a kettle drum. Be a good doggy, please, and go away.

"He the gutter guy?" Pop-Pops shouted again. Pop-Pops seemed to have forgotten he was holding a hose. A heavy arc of water thudded on the wood floor of the front porch.

"No, he's some *other* guy. Pop-Pops, you're getting the furniture!" The woman rushed off to tend to him.

"I'm back," Harry said into his phone. Pop-Pops squirted the howling collie as the woman struggled to wrest the hose from him.

"Will we be shipping your order to a business or residential address, sir?" Kevin the trader said.

"A PO box." Harry had set up two boxes. If this first buy went smoothly, he would purchase the gold from different companies and use the post office as well as UPS drop-off sites. Best to mix things up. Keep the Chinese hackers, the FBI, the Treasury Department and whoever else was probably monitoring his every move on their toes.

"Ordinarily, we ship via registered insured US Mail, but as your shipment is over twenty thousand dollars, we will be using a private insurance carrier."

"That's fine," Harry said. An arc of water splashed across his windshield. The woman looked back at Harry and shrugged an apology.

Kevin went on, reading in a monotone from his computer screen. "If you choose to make future gold purchases with us, and if those shipments are over three hundred thousand dollars, we would suggest to you the practicality and convenience of a private armored carrier such as Brinks or Loomis Fargo."

An armored truck! Harry imagined two armed guards from Brinks driving up to his tree house in the middle of the woods. "No, no. Don't need one of those."

"Of course, sir. As I said, we ship in any manner that fits the particular needs of the particular client. By the way, shipping is free."

"Nice," Harry said.

"All right then, sir. Because the spot price of gold changes by the minute, your buy-order must be locked in by 3:00 p.m. today with a bank wire. Will you be remitting payment via a bank wire today, sir, and locking in?"

Harry paused a minute before he spoke. "Locking in," he said.

"Excellent. And one last thing before I

start taking your information. Because we value your business, I do want to say again we absolutely respect the client's need for privacy. Therefore, we never put a client's name on an invoice. I'll be writing your name, address and purchase information on a five-inch-by-eight-inch card, which I will then staple to your invoice. After you verify receiving your order, the card will be detached and destroyed."

A thin trickle of sweat settled in the notch below Harry's Adam's apple. *Okay, Oriana, here we go.*

20

When they were boys, they had adjacent bedrooms, and there was a nightly ritual. Wolf, in his bed, would chatter until he fell asleep, and Harry, on the other side of the wall in his bed, silent, would listen. There was an old shared heat vent in the wall that warmed both rooms. It was Wolf's portal to Harry's psyche. When their father abandoned the family and everything changed, Wolf's words darkened, and his voice, deepened by adolescence, growled and snarled into Harry's brain. Wolf talking and talking, so that the vent seemed no longer to deliver warmth from the basement furnace, but the unnatural heat of Wolf's voice.

Wolf was alarming, even before their father left them. When they were little, he would narrate highly descriptive tales of the monsters that lurked in Harry's bedroom. "See that weird shadowy lump on the right side of your room, Harry, by your desk?

That's not your toy chest. I know you think it is, but it isn't. It's a vampire, and it's got this big hump like a hunchback, but different. It's a *blood* hump, kinda like a camel's. The vampire stores the blood in there, from all its victims, blood all mixed up and half-scabby and thick like a milkshake. And that's where *your* blood's going. If you close your eyes for even one second, the vampire is going to hop onto the foot of your bed, then skitter up the wall like a spider and drop onto your face. And it doesn't suck blood from your neck like a normal vampire, it sucks blood from your face. Your *face,* Harry, with this weird tentacle mouth-thing, sucking on your cheeks and forehead and eyes like a leech. Mom won't even recognize your body in the morning."

Then Wolf would lean close to the heat vent and make wet echoey slurp-slurp-slurp sounds. Not just a few — he'd slurp away for a full five minutes, then suddenly stop and whisper in a spectral voice, "Good night, sleep tight, don't let the vampires bite. I mean, face-suck."

Wolf filled Harry's little bedroom with a galaxy of vampires, ghosts, werewolves and monstrous creations Victor Frankenstein might dream up during a laudanum bender. But the really scary part came in the period after their father drove off, and Wolf entered the full bloom of adolescence. He left childish things behind, and all of his soliloquies turned personal. Wolf the bully, the troublemaker, the revenge-seeker. Every night — whispering menacingly into the heat vent, communicating to the unseen Harry as if Harry was the priest on the other side of the confessional screen — Wolf would describe some daily transgressor: a teacher who pissed him off, a guidance counselor, a store clerk, a neighbor. The revenge he would take. Seldom actually carried out, but gorgeous in its unnerving descriptive power. And all of it going into Harry's brain.

Thus, Harry grew up with a singular ambition and life skill: Wolf avoidance. Harry spent a lot of time in his tree, as far away as possible from Wolf's constant and dizzying ping-ponging between being a protective big brother and a soul-crushing oppressor. Perpetually antagonizing Harry, but offering unwanted paternal security, too, like a Mafia godfather. Even the most benign interaction, like calling him in for dinner, felt like an act of aggression.

"Hey, asshole in the tree," Wolf would shout from a window. "Time to eat."

Safe asshole in the tree, young Harry would think.

But never safe enough. Now, up in his tree house in the middle of the forest, Harry contemplated Wolf — was forced to contemplate him, because Wolf had just left a midnight voice mail on Harry's cell phone. Wolf had been silent since their first and only text conversation. And Harry had been unnerved by that silence. There should have been an hourly tirade of texts and messages after Harry had blown him off and gone into hiding. A brooding, silent Wolf was a bad thing.

But now there was a call. Harry could just delete it. But he could no more delete it than turn off Wolf's long-ago voice, broadcasting nightly through the childhood heat vent. The voice a threat, but a *comfort,* too. Because if Wolf was speaking to him through the vent, he wasn't in the room with Harry — which was a deeply important notion, because sometimes Wolf would creep into Harry's room and suddenly leap out of the dark onto the bed, put a pillow over Harry's face, just for a moment or two, followed by a hard pinch on the cheek, all of it happening so fast Harry couldn't cry out. And then suddenly Wolf's voice starting again on the other side of the wall, as if nothing had happened but Harry's imagination bringing the dark to life.

Harry lay in the tree house. He did not want to hear Wolf's voice. On the other hand, to not hear Wolf's voice always held the threat that a silent Wolf was creeping close. Purely psychological, because Wolf could *not* be close.

"Wolf, you are not in this tree house with me." Or out in the night forest or in Susquehanna County or even in Pennsylvania. You are home in your own bed in Virginia. But it was unnerving that Wolf, with that sensitive nose of his, had placed his call on the very day Harry had purchased the first of the gold. Detecting Harry's move, deeply unhappy that he was actually following through on his threat to unload the money. But that was impossible: Wolf could have no idea where Harry was, or what he had done today.

Harry's finger hovered above the delete button. Things are going fine here, he thought. Things are excellent, in fact. Just delete him. And poof, he's gone.

Instead, Harry put the phone to his ear and listened to the message.

"Hi, Harry, it's your big brother, talking to you through the heat vent." Laughter, then a thick cigarette cough. "Oh shit, remember those days? Me talking to you. Helping you through the rough and tumble of life. That was fun, though, right? The stories we used to invent."

You invented, Wolf. And not for my benefit. Harry looked across the darkened tree house to make sure the vampire with the blood-hump wasn't crouching. Don't let Wolf into your head. This is good news, hearing his voice. It means he's somewhere that's not here. Where could he be but in Virginia, wrangling through the terminal stages of his divorce. Whatever he has to say, he's just messing with my head. All he can do is play games. I'm safe. The gold is on its way. I'll be rid of it, and any last claim Wolf thinks he has on me will be gone.

"I just want to say, I hope everything is going okay for you out there in the forest," said Wolf.

Harry sat bolt upright on his cot. Oh shit. He's not playing around. Dropping that line like a bomb. Wolf wasn't guessing. He knows.

"Yeah, forest," said Wolf. "You left the office, and you went straight to your little forest hideaway."

Phone to his ear, Harry was up off the cot and standing at the large triangular window, peering into the night forest. Wolf had gone to the office, like a private detective. Harry could imagine it. Wolf prowling the cubicles, pressing people.

"Boy," Wolf said, "you left some pretty pissed off people at your office. Not pleased at all that Harry Crane jumped ship."

Wolf would have gotten to Bob Jackson. Weak, lazy Bob. Harry could just see Wolf pressuring him.

"And are you up a tree, Harry? Right this minute, you are, right? I know you are. Because you are the world's most predictable man. Harry sitting in the biggest tree in the forest."

"Jesus," Harry whispered.

Wolf laughed. "I know my Harry." Wolf's voice sounded like it was coming to him through the heat vent, like he was that close, that dangerously intimate. *I know my Harry.* Every time Wolf's voice paused in the voice message, Harry, squinting into the night forest, thought he saw him slide from behind one tree trunk and move to another. Wolf advancing.

"Harry, I know you're listening. I like a brother who listens. What I don't like? A brother who runs."

Harry stared into the forest.

"I led you to the money," Wolf said. "It exists because I made it happen, goddamn it!"

Harry held the phone away from his ear,

Wolf's voice rupturing the peace of the tree house. "I want my share, Harry!"

Harry wavered, then shook his head, as Wolf continued to shout. No shares, Wolf, the gold has been promised. The gold is for Oriana. It's out of both of our hands now. It's all moving forward and you can't stop it. You're bluffing, you don't know where I am.

Wolf said, "Your forest is no different than your old bedroom, Harry. You always thought you'd be safe, if you kept very still. But then I'd pounce, wouldn't I? Out of the dark. I never let you down. You always knew I'd come. And I came."

Harry cringed, then swallowed. For a long moment, he heard nothing. And then Wolf's final whisper. "Good night. Sleep tight. Don't let the Wolf bite."

21

Oriana in the den on the computer. Amanda in the kitchen slicing vegetables. Oriana listened to the knife, rapid-fire on the cutting board. *Clack clack clack clack clack,* like a woodpecker. It was after school. Oriana had finished her snack and was racing through her homework. She'd been waiting all day to go into the forest to start her secret mission: find a hiding place. She had one last math problem, which she only pretended was homework. Oriana was a smart girl, very good in math. But this problem was a little tricky. She used round numbers because it didn't have to be exactly exact. From the internet, she knew the price of gold was currently about a thousand dollars an ounce, and that gold coins weighed one ounce. So, the first part of the problem: 4,000,000 ÷ 1,000 = 4,000.

Oriana smiled. Wow. Four thousand gold

coins! That's why Harry wanted a wheelbarrow.

But how much did they weigh? That mattered for the hiding place. "Mom," she called to the kitchen. "I have to do ounces to pounds. If I have four thousand ounces and I have to make pounds . . ."

Clack clack clack. "Okay, think," Amanda called to her. "What do you have to do first?"

"I don't know."

"How many ounces in a pound?"

"That's easy. Sixteen."

"Okay, so the next step . . ."

"Just a hint. Is it a times or a divide?"

"A divide."

Oh, yeah, of course. Oriana typed the numbers into the calculator: 4,000 ÷ 16 = 250. "I got it, Mom, thanks." Four thousand coins weighed 250 pounds. A big wheelbarrowful.

Amanda scooped the carrots and peppers into a bowl. Oriana came into the kitchen. "I'm going to go to the tree house now, okay?" She reached for a carrot and bit into it.

After Dean died, Oriana fell out of the habit of friends. But suddenly, out of nowhere, Oriana had a friend. Harry. And that wasn't a bad thing, Amanda thought. You start with one friend, whoever he might be, and that gets you back in the habit. Amanda felt a little guilty, placing so much on Harry — he had no idea how much. Save Oriana from enchantment. Save Oriana from solitude.

Was it selfish? Maybe. But didn't Harry need friends, too? Amanda knew exactly what he'd been through. If she hadn't had Oriana, the *thereness* of another human being — Amanda didn't know how she would have gotten through the year. Oriana was good for Harry. And Harry was good for Oriana. Friends were good. Which was the reason she gave herself for what she had done.

"Just to let you know," she said to Oriana, "I invited Harry to Green Gables. For our Tuesday night."

Oriana studied her.

Amanda put her hands on her hips, cocked her head and returned the stare. "It's the nice thing to do. He could probably use an outing."

"But we don't want to scare him off," Oriana sad. "He likes it in the woods."

"I don't think Green Gables is too scary. Except for the lettuce in the salad bar."

Oriana studied her some more, then she said, "Okay." She made for the back door.

Amanda stopped her. "How about a coat, darling girl?" She reached for Oriana's red coat.

"Winter's over, Mom." Oriana dashed for the door. Running across the backyard, she thought, And red is the last thing you wear in the forest when you are on a secret mission to find a hiding place for four thousand gold coins. It was just a little fib she'd told her mother. She would go see Harry — *after* she found a hiding place for the gold.

Amanda stood there, thinking: *No, we don't want to scare Harry off.* But he'd done something pretty amazing, climbing the beech tree. A simple meal at Green Gables was a perfectly reasonable way to acknowledge what he'd accomplished. And ease him back to the world, a little bit. He seemed ready for that. It was time for that.

And no, she told herself, inviting Harry to Green Gables had nothing to do with having seen him bathing naked in the stream. She'd almost wanted to apologize to Harry outright, because pure and simple, you do *not* spy on people when they're naked. That was Cliff's specialty. Though she couldn't get that image of Harry out of her head as she stood at the bottom of the spiral stairs waiting as he came down from the tree house. He was fully dressed, but she blushed as he came into view.

He was surprised to see her standing down there. "Good morning," he said. He had two empty plastic milk jugs for toting spring water.

"Good morning. Sorry, don't mean to intrude —"

"You own the place. You're allowed to intrude." He smiled. He was trying to act casual. She seemed a little flustered.

They stood before each other.

"You had a big couple of weeks out here."

"Thanks for the food. You make a mean sourdough bread."

"All that climbing. Had to make sure you were eating right."

They both stared at the ground.

"So," she said. Hesitated.

"So . . . are you upping my rent?" He gave her a questioning smile.

She met his eyes. "No, I'm — *we're* — inviting you out. There's this local place. Green Gables. We eat there every other Tuesday. Tonight, in fact." She cleared her throat. "It being Tuesday, and everything."

He didn't respond. He was assessing.

Her eyes met his. "Harry, we need to celebrate. Or, not *celebrate,* but, you know, commemorate — or whatever the darn right word is — mark the occasion. That you did it." She pointed to his left hand, at the white band of skin where the ring had once been. Then she pointed up into the beech tree, towering above them.

Harry said, "You must have been thinking, *The guy's crazy.*"

"Batshit crazy. But. Harry, I don't quite know what all that climbing had to do with the ring — except I totally do. It was your process. Trees. The wild need to move. Believe me, I know it's a big deal. I was a crazy person after I took my ring off."

"Wait. You said you tossed yours in a drawer."

"I did. That's true. Then five seconds later, I took it back out and put it on again. Then took it off and ran outside and chopped, like, an entire winter's worth of kindling. After a crazy week or two, it finally stayed off and in the drawer."

Harry laughed knowingly. He pointed up into the beech, endlessly tall above them. "Crazy is climbing a tree like that."

"But you got to the top. And the ring is still off."

"It is," he said.

She didn't ask what he'd done with his ring. And he didn't tell her.

"You look better, Harry. Stronger. Healthier. As a nurse, I can see the difference." But what she really saw was the image of him in the stream, the water beaded on his skin. She had moved closer to him, without even being aware of it.

But Harry was aware. He took an imperceptible step back from her. "Thank you, nurse. I do feel a little better. Healthier," he said.

"Right. Good. So the next stage is — you have to get out of the house. Getting on with life means getting back in the world."

She had Oriana in her life, and it had forced her back in the world. But Harry, it seemed obvious, had no one.

He was going to say no to the invitation. The gold — the last thing he wanted was to be out in the world. A guy who was about to do what he was about to do, doesn't show his face to the world. He was shaking his head, but then suddenly, he was nodding. Because you *do* show your face. When the gold started landing, he didn't want to be the mysterious guy out in the woods in a tree house. "Okay. Sure, yes. I'd like to come."

"Great." She looked at her watch. "I have to run. I'm late for work."

But there was something else she had to say, it was on her face.

"What?" Harry said.

"So it's over now, right? The climbing phase. We're good?" Amanda looked away, then looked him straight in the eye. "The beech tree — you scared me to death. I looked for you up there, saw a snapped limb."

That's why she was flustered, thought Harry. That's why she keeps blushing. I scared her. And she doesn't scare easily.

"And I came running out here," she said. "But you were okay."

"I'm sorry, I didn't mean to cause —"

"It would be very hard on Oriana if something happened to you."

Harry nodded.

"Do you understand what I'm saying?" she said. Looking him in the eye.

"Don't die."

"Correct. Don't die. It's one of the rules of The Year One Club. Members aren't allowed to die."

She turned and headed off into the forest.

And with that, Harry had been invited by Amanda to Green Gables. Out of the forest and into the world.

Oriana was threading her way through the trees, when she suddenly felt the tingle-zing. A tingle-zing (her father had taught her when she was five) was a disruption in the stillness of the forest — an unlikely breeze, a tremble of leaves, the faint snap of a distant twig. A still forest is the opposite of still. It's noisy and alive, filled with mammalian shiftings and insectal rustlings, bird calls, opossum chitter, bear moans. But sometimes there was a palpable change in that busy stillness, a kind of trespassing. Usually it was a predator — a hawk or an owl whooshing unseen through the canopy. Or a branch, weighted down with a hundred years of lichen, thumping to the forest floor.

This time the tingle-zing was Ronnie.

Dumb me, thought Oriana, immediately shifting course to throw Ronnie off. In her excitement, she'd been making a beeline for the abandoned bluestone quarry. With all its rocky overgrown nooks and crannies, it was perfect for hiding gold. And it was near the old quarry road, where Harry parked his car. You can't let Ronnie suspect, she told herself. She turned in the opposite direction, east toward the little meadow in the middle of a spruce grove, which was a favorite spot.

With all the grum and Harry commotion, she'd forgotten about Ronnie, their ever-hovering guardian angel. He hadn't been around lately. Oriana scanned right and left.

The forest had gone still again. Where was he?

Then she heard Ronnie's voice, coming from the spruce shadows to her right, a soft mournfulness in it. "I heard you were gathering up your candy and treats," he said. He was about twenty feet away, standing in the dim. He was a shy creature. A Boo Radley of the forest.

He waved a bashful hello and ventured into the meadow. "The grown-ups make you do that? Grown-ups, sometimes they had enough of something. Call it foolishness and what all, make you stop doing it."

Grown-ups, thought Oriana. He'd said the word twice. Meaning somebody other than just Amanda. Ronnie was terrible at keeping secrets. But Harry was probably pretty good at secrets. Ronnie must've found him. That had to be it. A woodland intruder as big as Harry, Ronnie would spot him. Why wouldn't Harry have mentioned it, though? Grown-ups are tricky, Oriana thought, even when they're on your side.

Oriana plunked herself down in the grass and began plucking spring daisies, white flowers perched on long stems, tiny versions of their big summer cousins. Ronnie sat beside her.

"Where you been, Ronnie?" Oriana began

weaving the daisy stems.

He got a sly look. "Pratt Library. All day, every day," he said.

Oriana tried not to show her surprise. She hadn't been to the library since Olive had given her *The Grum's Ledger.* She'd never seen Ronnie in the library. Ronnie a reader? The world was full of secrets and wonders.

"Been helping out Olive. Before the county building inspector comes," he said. "The place is in pitiful shape."

Ronnie picked a long piece of grass, nibbled the sweetness at the tip. "You might say I was guided there. By a you-know-what."

By a feather. It was the wellspring of their relationship — Oriana told him about wingèd Dean and the convolutions of the candy in the forest, and he told her about the feathers that floated, every couple of weeks, into his life. And neither of them discussed any of this with Amanda. Ronnie wasn't good at keeping secrets, but he was real good at being afraid of Amanda.

Ronnie leaked secrets like a rain cloud leaks water — Oriana would never tell him about the gold. Never ever. He was special to her, but he was something different from a pure friend. They were fellow sufferers. They shared Dean, the unsolvable puzzle of his death. But now, with the arrival of Harry Crane, Oriana was on her way to solving that puzzle. For herself, anyway. Ronnie, though, was still in limbo. In a way, Oriana suddenly realized, he was like Harry. Both men felt responsible for a loss that pierced their hearts.

She shaped and twisted the daisy stems. The chain of flowers was growing. "So another feather? How did it guide you to Olive?"

He nodded. "See, it landed on a book I stole from the library. Stole when I was a kid."

"A fairy tale?"

"Nah. *Treasure Island.*"

"That's a fun one."

Ronnie agreed. "Anyways, the feather landed on the book. And I hotfooted it to the library. I repented, and Olive put me to work paying off my fine."

This was good, Oriana thought. She needed him occupied and out of the forest, away from Harry and the gold.

But why did Daddy guide Ronnie to the library? She thought hard.

Why was it so important?

She closed her eyes. Daddy guiding Ronnie to the *library.* And now he's fixing it.

And then the answer came to her. The

library, Pratt Public Library — was *magical.* Because a magical book like *The Grum's Ledger* could only have come from a magical library. And Olive — surely she was no ordinary librarian. She cursed, and smoked a pipe, and she had given Oriana a book that had turned Harry Crane's sadness into gold.

Oriana suddenly saw something in Ronnie she'd never seen before. That he was *essential.* To everything. He was another one of the important grown-ups in the Endless Mountains. Her mother was the Rock. Olive, the Magic Door. Harry, the Great Adventurer. And Ronnie, the Guardian Angel. And it all began with Daddy — the first grown-up to change into something other than what he was. Daddy died and became wingèd. Daddy led Ronnie to the library. And Ronnie's task was to be the rescuer of the library. It faced so many dangers.

"Ronnie. The library is super-special. It needs you. And Olive needs you. You're doing a wonderful thing."

"Thanks to Dean."

"So you better get back to work."

"Just wanted to check on you."

She gave him a quick hug. "You've been such a help to me and Mom, Ronnie. But now it's the library that needs you."

Oriana waited until the sound of Ronnie's truck faded, then moved circuitously through the forest.

She stood at the south end of the old shale quarry. It was the size of a football field, overgrown and rocky, open on one end where the steam shovels used to come through. There were a million good spots in among the tons of broken bluestone, the abandoned refuse of a half century of quarrying.

She chose a closet-sized, ragged gouge you could see only if you pushed away a curtain of roots dangling from a spruce tree growing on the edge of an overhang. There was poison ivy everywhere, and a yellow jacket nest. It was an unpleasant sort of place that no one would bother. The perfect hiding place for a shimmering mound of grum gold.

22

It was a warm spring day. The new grass on the rolling pastures was a vast sea of wind-tossed green, and the new calves were lifting their pink, spotted noses to the sky as if to suckle upon the sun. And there was Hoop, lanky in the distance, the steady clink of his hammer on a metal fence post adding cadence to the chorus of birds.

I sure do have a pretty farm, and the only blot on it, thought Cliff, is Cliff Blair. He flicked at the encrusted manure on the knee of his jeans. Clots of dried manure sticking to him, head to foot. Isn't that fitting. I'm more manure than man. He remembered (as if he would ever forget!) Amanda's furious parting words.

Cliff's thoughts turned to the day after the Amanda debacle, when he had attempted to atone for his sins. He had wanted to hit the erase button in Hoop's brain. He approached Hoop in the semi-dark of the dawn barn. Hoop in the milking parlor adjusting a stanchion, not turning around to greet Cliff, just giving an almost imperceptible nod.

Cliff tried not to stammer as he addressed Hoop's back. "What I showed you, a while back? Certain, um, images concerning Amanda Jeffers? Hoop, you didn't see them, okay?" Meaning, the laptop glimpses of Amanda, naked from the waist up. The now smashed-to-smithereens laptop.

"Them udders?"

"Darn it, Hoop, not *udders.* A woman has *breasts.*" Oh, Hoop, Cliff thought. I should have just showed you pictures of a Holstein cow clad in a revealing dress. Cliff shook his head and reddened. That's a mean thought. Hoop had been minding his own business, and I'm the one who shoved the forbidden pictures in his face.

"Never mind," Cliff said.

"Never mind it is," Hoop said, and turned his attention to the udders of more immediate concern, the fifty swollen ones dangling under the fifty lined-up cows restless to be relieved of their milk.

Cliff finished securing the solar panel on the water trough, which a cow had bumped off its stand yesterday. He walked slowly across the field back to the tool shed. The

Amanda event was a couple weeks back. It haunted him. What had he been thinking, ordering a mini video camera off Amazon? I mean, what the hell, Cliff? You never make an online purchase in your life, and that's the first item you buy? The minute he clicked on "complete order" it felt creepy. You're a buy-local kind of guy. You operate an organic dairy farm. *That's* who you are. You shop for your supplies at the Agway in New Milford, and what you can't get there, you get down in Scranton.

He was overflowing with shame, but he had to face Amanda. Or at least have a semi-encounter, put his toe in the water. It was Tuesday. Every other Tuesday, with the consistency that was the trademark of her unswerving character, Amanda ate dinner at Green Gables with Oriana. Cliff hadn't been to Green Gables to have a beer with the guys since the incident. Here's what he would do. He would sit at the bar, within glaring distance of Amanda. He would sit there, yes he would, and endure her righteous glares. And if she chose to stand up, cross the restaurant and splash a Coors Light (she always had just one, a twelve ouncer) in his face, humiliate him publicly, he would endure it.

■ ■ ■ ■

Well, I mean, good gosh, Cliff thought. I can't believe it. None of them could believe it. In Amanda's booth, some guy, sitting across the table from her and Oriana, eating his Salisbury steak, baked potato, and a big leafy pile from the salad bar like it was a regular and casual thing, the three of them enjoying their Tuesday night dinner out. And what's up with Oriana? Cliff thought. She's not staring at a book. Doesn't even have one with her. And except for the two quick laser glares she shot at me, Amanda has been all smiles. Deep in conversation, she even reached out and *touched the guy's arm.* Who was he?

Old Walter didn't know him. Tom the bartender didn't know him. The EMT guys didn't know him. Stu didn't know him. Ronnie, however, knew him. He gulped his beer and tried to look like he didn't know him.

"Look at that guy. Who is that guy?" Stu said. His first thought being territorial. Please Lord, don't let it be some fancy real estate guy up from Scranton, using his fancy Scranton dollars to wine and dine the financially vulnerable Amanda Jeffers. I should've wined and dined her. That's my property the bastard's trying to steal. And he'll get six figures.

The men hunched in a tight muttering cluster at the far end of the bar, which gave the best view into the restaurant area. They could not wrap their brains around it: no one but Dean sits in Amanda Jeffers's booth. In the history of mankind, it had never before happened.

Stu was dying to go out to the parking lot for a cigarette, but he didn't want to miss the show. "What do we know about him?" he said.

Old Walter said, "We know he likes Salisbury steak, and he chews with his mouth closed."

An EMT guy said to the group, his voice low, "We know his name's Harry." When Harry came in, Amanda called him by name and waved him over to her booth.

Harry *Crane,* Ronnie almost said. Except for Olive Perkins, Ronnie had told not a soul about Harry. Ronnie was a dam about to burst. Any minute now, he'd gush the facts as he knew them. Already, Stu was glancing at him, because Ronnie was keeping suspiciously quiet.

Cliff was quiet, too. Stunned. Earlier, driving to Green Gables, he thought he might actually go over to the booth, make some sort of friendly gesture. Tip his hat. Or maybe he'd pick up the bill for Amanda's supper. Or buy Oriana a slice of ice cream cake. Then, coming into Green Gables, he lost his nerve, and, besides, gestures were probably a bad idea. But as he stood there waffling, the stranger had entered the bar, nodded to the men. Amanda called out, "Harry," and waved him over. What the — ?

Tom the bartender leaned over the bar and said, as if it was a detail that would crack the case, "Well, we know he's a Corona drinker. Without the lime."

"Like you ever put a lime on a Corona," Stu muttered.

"I tried it a couple weeks. Nobody sucked on them."

" 'Cause they're not for sucking. The customer squeezes them into the bottle."

"Well, nobody around here was squeezing."

Stu glanced over at the booth. That real estate guy chatting up Amanda — he sure looks like he knows how to squeeze a lime, down to the last drop. Then Stu eyed Ronnie, squirming on his bar stool.

Old Walter nodded toward the booth. With his usual devastating clarity, he summed it up for the little impotent gaggle of men. "I think what all you youngish studs find problematic is one thing, pure and simple. Looks like Amanda Jeffers found a fella. And a pretty good-looking fella, at that."

Amanda was *screwing* a real estate agent? thought Stu. He's getting six figures and sex? Six and sex? And the bastard's got good hair, too. Stu despised people with good hair. Or *any* hair, for that matter. Clench-jawed, Stu zeroed in on Ronnie. "Spill your beans, Ronnie."

Everybody leaned in Ronnie's direction. From the restaurant came the sound of Amanda's laughter. The men flinched and drank fortifying gulps of beer.

Ronnie's Adam's apple bobbed. "Well, I don't know the particulars. But he *is* living in the tree house."

My God, thought Stu. Living in the tree house. And Amanda close by in her big Dean-built log house.

Cliff, hearing Ronnie's words, had the stunned look of a neutered bull.

Look at those fools, Amanda thought. It was killing them, just killing them seeing Harry in her booth. And I hope, in particular, Cliff Dirty-Video-Taker Blair, it's killing you.

Amanda and Harry were lingering over their beers. Oriana was in the alcove between the restaurant and the bar playing on the old-fashioned skittles table. She bowled the little wooden ball. Pins toppled. She pumped a fist. "Yes!"

Yes, this was *very* good, Amanda thought, this additional, and not entirely unintended, perk of having invited Harry to Green Gables. "I just want them all to back off, you know?" she said.

Harry looked over his shoulder at the men. They were doing a bad job of trying not to look his way. He could see Ronnie in their midst.

Amanda said, "They just don't get it. They think, 'Oh, a year's passed.' Like it's some sort of unspoken timeline. That every widow —" she nodded at Harry "— or widower is ready to get back in the game because that official year has passed."

Getting back in the game, Harry thought. Even more inconceivable than handing out millions in gold.

"Thing is," Amanda said, lowering her voice, "I *did* get back in the game, just for the sex, you know, the physical ache you get, but should definitely ignore, because it gets you into trouble."

"Sex," Harry said. The word had not entered his brain during the past year, let alone left his mouth.

"Right?" Amanda. "Hard to say it, and dumb to have it. Ugh. But lesson learned, you know? Lesson learned." It was then that Amanda shot one of her laser glares in Cliff's direction.

Harry followed it. Which one of those guys was she aiming at? Not Ronnie. And that guy in the bad suit — rule him out. But there were a lot of strapping, good-looking males in that cluster. The one wearing the EMT uniform? No, Amanda would not mix work and pleasure. Pleasure, Harry thought. He'd only just managed to remove his ring — pleasure was a million light-years away.

Amanda's hand suddenly on his arm. Harry jumped. She left it there and gave him a big smile. She spoke through her smiling teeth. "Sorry. But smile back at me, okay? So they'll think we're a thing. Please?"

Harry smiled. Her hand on his arm. He was wearing a flannel shirt, the contact was not even flesh to flesh. Still, he didn't breathe until she removed her hand. His forearm tingled electrically. It would probably tingle for the next month.

She looked over at the bar. Her touching Harry had sent a charge through the group. "They can't believe it." She turned back to Harry. "How perfect is this? The date that isn't a date."

A pause, then Harry said, "Well, I *am* paying for dinner."

"No way."

And it was almost as if his hand moved on its own. That had to be it. That it was reflexive. When Beth's hair would fall in front of her face, at the breakfast table when she was reading the paper, or when they stood in line at the movies and she looked down to check her phone, when that lovely wisp of hair fell, he would reach out and tuck it behind her ear again.

And that's what he did when a wisp of Amanda's hair came loose and fell in front of her face. When she said, "No way," shaking her head, her hair came loose and Harry spontaneously reached across the table and fixed it behind her ear. And at the moment he touched her hair, when he looked at Amanda, into her eyes, he saw . . . Amanda.

His hand hovered by her ear. She was not a woman who rattled easily. But there was sudden color in her cheeks.

He pulled his hand away. And though his heart was pounding, he managed to say, almost smoothly, "This date that isn't a date? Wouldn't a guy do that?"

Amanda's flummoxed frown became a slow smile. "You're good. And right, right, it's perfect you paying for dinner." She studied him. "Boy. You look innocent, but you're devious and cunning."

Harry smiled nervously. You have no idea, he thought. He watched Oriana bowl over the skittle pins.

Over at the bar, heads were bobbing, beers rapidly downed. Amanda said, "They look like a frantic beehive that's lost its queen." She glanced at Harry. "See, that's what I don't like. Being these guys' queen. They need to get a life."

Don't bees sting? Harry thought. Some of those guys were pretty big. His eyes fell on the small guy at the end of the bar who was picking at his scalp. "Who's the scratcher?"

"The weasel real estate agent who's after my house. Stu Giptner."

Harry went quiet, thinking, The bags of gold. Of course. Put one on Amanda's doorstep. Right? She needs the money.

But Amanda, staring at the men, eyes ablaze, said, "I don't want saviors, you know? I don't want weasels trying to threaten me or tempt me with money. This idea that I can't make it on my own. Pisses me off." Her cheeks were flushed. She turned back to Harry. "That's what's so great about you."

He looked at her.

"You're the only guy in this place who *gets*

it," Amanda said. "We both don't want the same thing." She raised her beer mug. Harry raised his.

"A toast. Here's to not us," Amanda said. They both laughed. But before they could touch mugs and consummate the toast, a crash of skittle pins and Oriana's excited voice. "Strike!"

She ran over to the booth. "Mom. Can I have another quarter? Please? One more game?"

Amanda looked beyond her daughter to the men sagging at the bar. "Nope. I think we've bowled over enough pins at Green Gables tonight."

They were out in the gravel parking lot a few minutes later. It was a school night for Oriana, and work started early in the morning for Amanda. Amanda said good-night to Harry. Behind her, Oriana traced the toe of her sneaker in the gravelly dirt. When they got in the truck, Harry saw that she had drawn the letter G. He glanced at his phone. As the truck pulled out, Oriana gave him a questioning look. And very, very discreetly he gave her a thumbs-up.

G for gold.

The tracking notification showed that his first shipment had arrived. Harry stood by his car, staring at the glowing screen, dazzled, as if he was looking directly into the sun. Or the bright, golden core of Fort Knox. Transfixed, he did not hear the men approach.

"Howdy, stranger," came a nasal voice.

Harry startled back against his car door. There were six of them, Stu Giptner at the head. He looked like a Chihuahua leading a pack of German shepherds.

"We just wanted to welcome you to New Milford," Stu said.

Harry nodded carefully. For the first time in his life, he missed his big brother. Wolf was tailor-made for this moment. He spotted Ronnie in the group. "Hello, Ronnie."

Ronnie was staring at his boots. So was Cliff.

Stu jumped in. "Ronnie here says you live in Dean Jeffers's tree house."

"I said 'renting,' " Ronnie murmured.

"Either way, he's there."

Cliff toed the gravel. He didn't like this at all. But Stu, beered up, had goaded them into it (old Walter, voice of reason, had gone home earlier), and if Cliff had hung back, Stu would've wondered why. Cliff lifted his eyes and looked at Harry. Certainly a question tugged hard at him. It came out before he could stop it. "How'd you get in her booth?"

There were three EMT guys. One of them said, "Nobody sits with Amanda."

"Tell us about that," Stu demanded.

Harry took a breath. "I was invited?" Well, Amanda sure got what she wanted, riling these guys up. He clenched his various muscle groups, taking quick inventory. A couple of weeks spent in the forest, he was in pretty good shape. When the fighting commenced, Harry imagined he could get in one good punch. Before they tore him to pieces.

Stu sneered. "Why would she pick you, a government bureaucrat? Doesn't make sense. She likes real men. Men who work with their hands." Stu thrust out his hands, realizing too late he only used them to shuffle paper. One of the EMT guys snickered.

Harry thrust his own hands out. For Ronnie's inspection. "Look. Calluses." They were standing under a light in the parking lot. Ronnie took a peek.

"How about that? You got yourself toughened up." Ronnie looked Harry up and down, nodded approvingly.

A couple weeks in the woods had done Harry good.

Ronnie said, "I wish *I* could live in a tree house."

The EMT guys nodded. "Living in a tree house is pretty cool, actually," one of them said.

"Especially that tree house. Nobody builds a tree house like Dean," another said.

"And that's the goddamn point!" Stu shouted. "This is the guy replacing Dean!" Stu suddenly lurched forward and socked Harry on the jaw, smacking him back against the side of his car. But Harry didn't fall. His right ear buzzed, and he had a moment of dizziness, but he was upright. And both of his fists were clenched.

Stu had a frightened feral grin. When he tried to retreat backward, he couldn't. Cliff, Ronnie and the EMT guys made themselves into a wall. Keeping him there for Harry's turn.

Harry stepped up to Stu. Got right in his face. "You know, I have this brother, got in fights all his life. And he'd just love it if I hit you. God, it would make him so proud."

Stu went pale with panic. Harry gave him a long look and then unclenched his fists and stepped away.

Stu's panic transformed into a smirk. He was about to open his mouth, when Cliff suddenly lifted him straight up into the air from behind, carried him a few paces and dropped him on his ass. The men turned their backs on him and faced Harry.

Ronnie stepped forward. Shook Harry's hand.

Then Cliff stepped forward and shook Harry's hand. Leaned in, and spoke so only Harry could hear. "Well, maybe the best man won." Meaning Harry vs. Stu? No, wait, Harry thought. This was the guy Amanda slept with. Big, handsome. A slight whiff of the barn about him not altogether unpleasant.

Then all the EMT guys shook Harry's hand. The last one said, "Wish I lived in a tree house. Way cool."

23

Harry tried to convince himself that it was just one more stop on a list of errands to run in Scranton. Let's see, go to CVS, ShopRite, and oh yeah, if I have a minute, drop by the post office for that quarter-million dollars in gold.

The internet bullion companies shipped gold in amounts under $300,000, insured, to either the post office or UPS. Harry had set up PO mailboxes in two locations — which for some reason was perfectly legal — a branch in East Rydsen and the main office downtown. His plan was to mix and match, use a different gold company shipping to a different location each time, either UPS or the post office, depending on . . . what? On how it all *went.*

He parked his car and smiled for the security cameras. Surely there had to be some. Already, his image was in the hands of Interpol. And Chinese hackers had already contacted their hit men in Scranton. They'd have to beat the FBI, which was no doubt waiting for him in the lobby. He hoped the handcuffs wouldn't be too tight.

Harry was so nervous he had to grip the handrail to get up the front steps. He braced himself and pushed open the doors and entered the lobby. No FBI, no Interpol. Really? Just the gray-haired clerk behind the desk? It couldn't be this easy.

It took him three tries to guide the key into the lock of his mailbox. The clerk glanced over as Harry's key clicked against the little metal door. When Harry reached in for the yellow delivery slip, he accidentally bumped it out the open back end of the mailbox.

He turned in alarm. The clerk was already sliding off his stool. He shrugged and called over, "Not a problem," and went slowly through a door to the back. Harry heard him groan on the other side of the wall. Harry was gripping the edge of the counter when the clerk came back through the door holding a package the size of a shoebox.

"Hoo boy, whatcha got in here, lead?" the clerk said.

"That's right, yes," Harry heard himself say. "Lead soldiers. I'm a collector." He gave the clerk a sheepish shrug.

The clerk brightened. "That right? I used to have a bunch of those little guys."

Harry kept his smile in place. This was not the scenario he'd planned on, which was: anonymous man picks up inconspicuous package in outlying post office and gets the hell out of Dodge.

Harry held out his hands, but the clerk was still admiring the heft of the box.

"Boy, you must have Napoleon's entire army in here."

Harry's outstretched fingers were twitching. He tried not to grab the package. "Actually," he said, "just a British Revolutionary War battalion."

The clerk grinned. "Ha! Redcoats! I love those guys. Soldiers used to dress nice for wars, you know?"

He handed the package over to Harry, and Harry almost dropped it, the weight of it startling. He went through the whole catastrophe in his mind. The box hitting the floor and splitting open, a quarter-million dollars in gold rolling in all directions, people diving on the coins in a free-for-all. He drew the box tight to his chest and glanced over his shoulder. The only other patron was a stout old woman in a purple knit hat who had her arm so deep inside her mailbox it looked like she was trying to deliver a breech calf.

The clerk was still speaking to Harry. "We used to dress nice, too. I had a route, back in the day. Wore the cap with the hard visor, gray wool trousers with the black stripe down the outside, shoes you could see your reflection in, you know? A uniform you were proud of." He sighed. "I miss uniforms." He stared into the distance and sighed again. "Well, it all went ka-flooey in the eighties, like most things. Guys come to work now in their long johns, practically."

The clerk looked over Harry's shoulder and called out to the woman still fishing in her mailbox. "Miss Pulzniack!" He touched his head and rolled his eyes for Harry, whispering, "She never believes it's empty, poor thing." He came around the desk, "Come on now, Miss Pulzniack. Can't have you getting stuck in there again."

Harry exited. For the second delivery of gold, he'd be using UPS.

Twilight. The tree house. The box on the table, waiting.

A sudden little chill up Harry's spine: a memory of Wolf. Long ago Wolf, drunk, squeezing Harry's shoulder with a big paw and leaning in. *Listen up, Harry,* he'd said.

Listen up, Harry. Gold. I'm telling you. When

the fucking world goes down the fucking toilet, and it surely will, gold is your lifeboat.

You're so right, Wolf, Harry thought, staring at the box on the table. Gold is my lifeboat.

Harry glanced out into the woods, as he'd done so frequently since the voice message from Wolf. *I'm coming, Harry. I want my share!*

All had been silent since then, but Harry could just imagine, if Wolf found out that Harry was converting his money into gold, the silence would turn into howls.

"Harry?"

Harry snapped out of his reverie. Oriana was beside him. Going up and down on her toes in excitement.

"Are you going to open the box? Come *on.*"

Gold *was* his lifeboat, and Oriana was his lifeboat, too, and this forest, and this tree house. And Amanda's hand on his arm at Green Gables.

Was it the first time he'd been touched in a year?

At the office, in and out of the cubicles, surely somebody would have bumped into him, or in a crowded supermarket aisle brushed past him. But Amanda at Green Gables — it was the first time in a year he'd *felt* the touch of another person. The second time was when Stu Giptner punched him. And in a way, strangely, that moment was a lifeboat, too. Snapping him awake. *Felt.* These accumulating moments, small and large, lifting him higher and higher out of a dark numb sea.

He had a sudden vision of Wolf in the dark waters and lifeboats capsizing.

"Harry, how about I open it?"

He nodded. Oriana picked up the paring knife and expertly sliced down the taped center of the box. Carefully parted the flaps.

My God, Harry thought. Talk about felt. Now he was the one up on his toes, tense with excitement. He'd never seen a gold coin before except in pirate movies. A beam of light from the setting sun cut through the branches of the beech and ignited the interior of the box. For a blinding instant it was like looking into a teeming treasure chest.

Bedazzled, Harry blinked his eyes and laughed. "Gold!" he exclaimed.

Oriana, too. "Gold!"

What else could you say? Gold! Look at it! Neatly packed in clear plastic tubes — twenty-five tubes, ten coins in each — mundane, orderly and unbelievable. He reached for a tube, hefted it up and down.

What did it weigh? A half-pound? A half-pound of hamburger felt like nothing in particular when you picked it up from the meat case. But a half-pound of *gold*!

He placed the coin tube in Oriana's hand.

"So heavy," she breathed.

"Open it," he said. "Go on. Take one out."

"No. It has to be you. You have to touch the gold first," she said. "Open your hand."

Oriana looking at him, so intently. What did she see? The grum of course. And what would she see when he plinked away the final piece of gold? Would she like him as much when the grum turned into plain old Harry? So complicated, when life had been transformed into a fairy tale and a fairy tale into life.

She tipped the tube and a gold coin fell, end over end, into the palm of his hand. The coin was icy cold and spectacularly bright. On its front, a depiction of Liberty, torch in hand, astride a mountain. He flipped the coin over. On the reverse, a golden eagle hovered above a nest containing a female eagle and her hatchlings, his big wings spread protectively. The great bird was so finely minted Harry could almost see the wind ruffling its wing feathers.

"Wingèd," whispered Oriana.

"It's an eagle. Not a red-tailed hawk,"

Harry cautioned. Caution for what possible reason, this far along in their golden adventure? Because they were on a tightrope. To make this adventure work, he had to keep things as real as possible. He had to be the adult. Or, at least, try to be.

"Oh, it's perfect!" Oriana exclaimed, launching herself at him and giving him a big hug.

And here it was, out of nowhere *another* lifeboat. He looked down at the child, this wonderful creature of the forest. "It is, you're right," he said, his voice thick with emotion. "It's perfectly perfect."

He put the coin in her hand. "Your turn to hold it."

Oriana stared at the eagle. She traced her fingertips over the wings. "I can feel his feathers," she whispered. "Really."

Harry looked over her shoulder. "The detail's amazing."

"Touch his wing," she said.

Reluctantly, he touched the tip of a golden wing. And he felt the feathers, too, and maybe even a little gust of wind moving through the eagle's wings. He yanked his hand back. It spooked him, how Oriana could get him going. But the point of the gold was not to revel in it and be amazed — it was to get rid of it as fast as possible.

Oriana played with the coin, the light dancing around the room. She sighed. "I know she can't, but I wish Mom could see this. I wish we could show her." She looked quickly at him. "But I know we can't."

Harry instantly dropped to a knee in front of her. Waited until she met his eyes. "Listen to me. Your mom finds out about this, Oriana? It's over. The gold will never happen. She'd boot me out of the tree house and out of the forest. She'd kick my butt over the Endless Mountains."

"She likes you, Harry. After Green Gables, she said so."

Again he thought, *Get rid of the gold as fast as possible.* "She likes me, because she doesn't know who I am."

"And I like you because I do know who you are," Oriana said.

He took a deep breath. "Let's see if everybody still likes everybody at the end of this." He clapped his hands together and stood up. "And to get to the end, we have to get started."

He opened *The Grum's Ledger* to the illustration of the grum brooding atop his gold mound, and placed the book on the cardboard box filled with real gold. "So," he said. "We've got the grum's gold. Next question — how do we give it away?"

"Wait," Oriana said. "What about the lottery ticket? That's the other big thing."

Harry smiled. "Knew you'd say that." He took the faded lottery ticket out of his wallet, held it between two fingers.

"Because it's magic," she said, "just like the book. And I was thinking, the numbers . . . what if —"

He clapped his hand over her mouth. "The numbers mean absolutely nothing. And that's the key."

She pushed his hand away. "It's *magic.*"

"When I bought this ticket, everything changed. *That's* how it's magic. I bought it, and wham, my world disappeared, and here I am in a tree house in the forest with you. But the actual numbers printed on the ticket? They're random, picked by a computer."

Oriana spoke quietly. "I'm sorry it wasn't all good magic."

He lifted her chin. "But the good magic is — I'm here, Oriana. It's the way magic works. You know all the stories. Some of them are very Grimm."

She half smiled.

"And some of them," Harry said, "are very grum."

Full smile. "They start sad," she said, "but they end happy."

"*If* we work together. *If* your mom doesn't find out." If Wolf doesn't find me, he didn't say. "And if —" he waggled the lottery ticket "— we listen to the ticket and keep it random. Random and *simple.* How simple?" He opened a box and pulled out six old burlap seed bags he'd picked out of a bin in a farmers market outside Scranton. "Six numbers on the ticket so . . . we hand out six bags of gold."

"Just like in the stories!" Oriana said. "Bags of gold!"

Harry nodded, pleased with himself. "Gotta do it right, right?"

Four of the bags were the size of plastic shopping bags. The other two were twice as large. In *The Grum's Ledger,* the grum rids himself of the gold, a little at first, and then at the end begins to "hurl great heaps" into the night.

Harry explained he would start small, and then for the last bags he'd give away the gold in great heaps. An adventure, after all, has to build to an exciting climax.

He held up burlap bag number one. Oriana opened the coin tubes and poured in the gold. The gathering coins clinked and plinked. The bag got heavier and lumpier. When it was full, he handed it to Oriana.

She gripped it with two hands, her mouth

open in wonder. It was fifteen pounds of gold, but it felt like a thousand. She shook the bag. Twirled it. Jingled it. Jangled it. He took it back before she accidentally tossed it through a window. They were *not* going to toss the gold into the forest like the grum. Harry would dispose of it carefully. Six bags in six different towns.

But how to choose the towns? He had an answer for that, too. Oriana was amazed by him. Harry had an answer for everything. In the light of the kerosene lamp, he seemed to glow. And on the wall behind him, he cast a very big shadow.

The wind blew and the tree house rocked like an old wooden sailing ship. But Harry had gained his sea legs; he was steady on his feet.

They would choose the six towns randomly, Harry said, just as the computer had randomly chosen the six ticket numbers. Random means no pattern. And if there was no pattern to how he handed out the money, it would make it hard for anyone to trace anything back to him. He reached into his back pocket, held up a folded map he'd bought in a gas station convenience store and spread it out on his cot.

Oriana read the words printed in large letters across the top. "Map of Susquehanna

County. There are so many towns. How will we pick?"

"Come on. You know how we're going to pick . . ." He held open the bag for her.

It took her a second and then she laughed. "We flip a coin!" She reached into the bag.

Oriana held up a coin. When Harry gave her the nod, she stepped forward and flipped it into the air. It landed on the map with a papery *thunk,* glinting in the light as it twirled in a slow circle and dropped, eagle side up. They went down on their knees beside the cot and looked at the map. Harry nudged the coin aside to see where it had landed.

"Elkdale," he said. It was one of the smallest towns on the map. Small and *random.*

"I love that name!" Oriana said. "It sounds enchanted."

And who in Elkdale would get the gold? Which house would Harry choose? On what doorstep would he leave a burlap bag?

Certainly, not on the doorstep of someone already living in a castle. No, he would choose an ordinary house on an ordinary street. Nice and ordinary — with a good tree in the front yard. And all things being equal, he'd choose the house closest to the road out of town. Because after he made the drop, he planned to jump into his car and hit the gas.

Could he guarantee that the most deserving person would get the gold? No. He had learned the hard way: life was a lottery, so let the gold land where it may.

He was not an all-knowing god, after all. He was simply a man trying to heal the heart of a little girl by making her fairy tale come true.

24

Elkdale was far from enchanted. Like most of the towns in the Endless Mountains, it hunkered in a valley. None of the towns in Susquehanna County ever seemed to make it to the mountaintop. They were submerged in deep shade for fully half of each day, so that the houses, even the big three-story Victorians built in the coal and lumber boom years of the 1890s, looked stunted and moist, like mushrooms.

The main road through Elkdale was Route 11, and traffic, what little there was, zipped through the middle of town with only a yellow light flashing feebly to slow it down. Four potholed streets intersected Route 11: Center Street, Greenwood Street, McAdams Avenue and Church Road. The largest store in Elkdale was the Agway Feed-and-Hardware at the end of McAdams Avenue where the asphalt petered out into a gravel parking lot. A bedraggled laundromat stood on the corner of Greenwood Street and Route 11. There was a bar of sorts: Tripley's Tavern, which was really just an outbuilding attached to somebody's house.

It was late April, but a red aluminum Christmas tree still sat in the dusty window of the Dollar Store on Church Road, its branches festooned with candy bars in their wrappers and snowflakes made out of Popsicle sticks encrusted with silver glitter glue. In lieu of a star, a trucker's cap perched on top, as if between seasons the tree served as a hat rack.

No, thought Harry, driving in his car at twilight, there was not a whole hell of a lot of enchantment in Elkdale. A bag of gold would be welcome here.

Harry didn't know which house he'd pick on Center Street, and he didn't know as he drove down McAdams and Church. But when he turned onto Greenwood Street — he instantly knew. There it was, an ordinary little house beneath the protective limbs of a fine, tall sugar maple. In the fading evening light, a boy and a girl in the side yard kicked a soccer ball back and forth while a cocker spaniel ran around barking. The boy kicked the ball hard, and it smacked into the old stone wall behind the girl, dislodging a small stone from the midsection.

The girl raised her hand like a referee stopping play. And the boy stopped obediently. So did the dog. The girl ran over and picked up the stone and slid it back into place, like she was gently returning a fallen baby bird to its nest.

Nice, thought Harry.

When the girl looked up, the passing car was gone, and the sound of its engine was lost in the high whine of someone revving a leaf blower behind the Methodist church on Center Street.

A mother's voice called for supper. The dog barked once and followed the boy and girl into the house. All was dark and quiet on the streets of Elkdale.

At midnight, when the broken cuckoo clock above the bar in Tripley's Tavern cuckooed eleven wheezy times then gave up, when the last toilet flushed and the last light in the last bedroom in town winked out and the raccoons and opossums began to make their nightly trek out of the woods toward the neighborhood trash cans, a hasty delivery was made to 112 Greenwood Street, Elkdale, PA.

At sunrise the next day, sleepy Phil Bartek

came downstairs to walk the family cocker spaniel, Toodie. He snapped the leash onto Toodie's collar, opened the front door and placed his hand on the storm door. He looked down at the bottom panel of the door and frowned. There was a long crack in the glass he'd been meaning to fix.

Phil didn't like that the world was falling apart, starting with the storm door in the morning and ending at night with the embarrassingly ornate "Sorrento" metal headboard on his king-size bed. The bed, one of its legs warped, wobbled when he climbed in beside Minnie, his wife of thirteen years. Serves me right, Phil would think, for buying clearance at Stegmyers Furniture in Binghamton.

He pushed on the door. Toodie whined and scratched when it didn't open all the way. Phil yanked her back.

"Toodie, shh. Hold on."

He tried the door again, but something was holding it up. He put his face to the glass and looked down at the front porch landing, lit dimly by the sun rising up over Packer Hill.

"What the heck is that, Toodie?"

It was brown and lumpy. Some kind of bag? He pushed harder on the door, but the bag was heavy and some of the burlap had gotten caught under the door. Toodie pushed her nose forward and growled.

"*Hush,* girl."

Phil scooped her up and went through the kitchen and out the back door. She tugged Phil around to the front of the house to investigate the bag.

He approached it carefully. It was an old burlap seed bag, and something was in it. Seed, he thought, but that didn't make sense, because the words *Brukmann Seed Corn* were stamped on the side of the bag in faded blue, and Brukmann Seed had been out of business for, what, nearly twenty years now?

As he reached down gingerly, Toodie got in front of him and lunged at the bag. When she bit it, it made a strange clinky sound that stopped Phil short. Toodie whimpered and pressed herself against Phil's pajamaed legs.

From inside the house, Minnie, who had come downstairs, pushed at the storm door, which was hung up on a wad of the burlap.

"Hey, don't do that, be careful," Phil said.

"The cold's getting in. What's that down there?"

"A seed bag. Somebody put a seed bag on our front porch."

"Well, pull it loose, the cold's getting in."

"It's not seed inside that bag, Minnie. It's full of *metal.*" Phil licked his lips and got a little ahead of himself, drama-wise. "It could be bullets in there."

Minnie gave him a long look. "A bag of bullets. Somebody left a bag of bullets on our doorstep."

"Well, they sure left a bag of something."

"And you won't know what until you look inside."

"Something's not right, I'm telling you."

"Oh Phil. *Bullets.*" Minnie knelt to work the bag loose from her side.

"Don't! Just, *hold on* a sec, will you?"

She stopped tugging, but she didn't let go.

Phil said, "We don't make another move until Skip takes a look." It really gave him the willies: somebody had been in their yard last night creeping around. Somebody had come up on their front porch *in the dark.*

"Oh Phil, don't bother Skip," Minnie said. "You get so overexcited."

He wagged his finger at her. "Don't touch that bag again. I can see his kitchen light on. I'm gettin' Skip."

Skip Harmon was a lieutenant in the Pennsylvania State Police. Running across the yard, Phil could see Skip, an enormous man, in his red long johns at his kitchen table drinking his mug of coffee.

Skip stood at his back door and listened to Phil without expression. That was just his state trooper way. Intimidating, but only if you didn't know Skip's hobby was raising Gloster canaries.

"You want me to come over in an official capacity, Phil?" Skip said in his deep trooper monotone.

"Well. It would set Minnie's mind at ease," Phil lied. *He* was the one who needed easing.

So Skip came over, still in his long johns but wearing his duty belt slung around his waist, pistol holstered.

Phil's two kids, Sarah and Phil Jr., were with Minnie now, hopping up and down with excitement, watching through the glass of the storm door. Toodie was still running around in circles in the front yard, barking her head off.

"Toodie should be on a leash, Phil," Skip said.

"She's on a leash, I'm just not holding it at the moment because there's a bag full of I don't know what on my front porch, maybe explosives."

Skip froze.

Minnie called out from the other side of the storm door. "Oh, it's *not* explosives, and it's not a bag of bullets. It's probably just chains or something."

Phil shot her a look. "Skip, the point is, we don't know what the hell —" Phil flicked his eyes at the kids who grinned in delight at the curse word "— what the *heck* is in there."

Skip took the big Maglite off his duty belt and gave the burlap bag a poke. It jangled softly.

Skip nodded. "I think we're okay here."

A pickup truck and a minivan had stopped in front of the house, his neighbors rolling down their windows to watch.

Phil sighed. We just live in a tiny corner of the Endless Mountains, and this silly seed bag will be our big excitement for the week. He wasn't complaining exactly, he just wanted a little *more.* But that was never going to happen. Not in Elkdale.

Skip clicked on his powerfully bright light and aimed it down into the bag. A golden glow erupted from the bag and lit up his face like the sun.

"Oh good gosh! Good gosh! Wow!" Skip cried.

He reached into the bag with his shovel-sized hand and brought up a glittering mound of gold coins . . .

A giant and a bag of gold.

That's what Phil saw in those first dazzling seconds. He backed away from the wonder of it and kept going until he bumped up against the stone wall that ran along his side yard. He leaned against it, took hold of it with both hands. It's what he needed. A solid stone wall, thousands of pounds of rock to secure him to Earth and Elkdale.

25

"What's up?" Amanda said. "You haven't said a word or moved a muscle."

On purpose. Because Oriana was trying very hard not to look beside herself with excitement. "I'm okay," she said in her best neutral voice. *Harry, you did it!* she thought. *You did it, you did it!* Oriana imagined the map of Susquehanna County back at the tree house. The dot marking the town of Elkdale pulsing now with a golden glow.

"Are you mad because we're returning the book?" Amanda said.

They were in the pickup truck on their way to Pratt Library to return *The Grum's Ledger.* Yesterday, her mother had asked her, "Hey, you have an overdue book, don't you?" Amanda was particular about overdue books. She didn't like to owe money to anyone for anything. With all the Harry fuss of the last few weeks she'd forgotten that it had all started with a lost book.

"I'm not mad," Oriana said.

"So, how was the book?"

"It was pretty good, I guess. Nothing special." Out of sight, Oriana's fingers wiggled with the tension of masked excitement.

Amanda pondered Oriana's aloofness. In weeks and months gone by, Oriana would've given a fevered analysis of a book. Every fairy tale dripping with clues. Amanda prodded her. "Looks pretty special, though. It's handmade."

Oriana gave *The Grum's Ledger* a bored glance. "I think it was from the old days. Olive said on school visits sometimes she had the kids make their own books. She saved some."

This one was written on an old bank ledger, Amanda observed. Olive repurposing whatever materials she could get hold of, which would be Olive's frugal way. It was a shame Pratt Library was in such dire straits. No more supplies for kids, no more school trips, the building falling down around her. Amanda was torn. For the last year, the books pouring out of that library and into Oriana's brain had been a source of worry and irritation. But somehow it seemed to be coming out okay. A lost book led to Harry Crane, after all. And Amanda had never been against *all* books. Just fairy tales. And she was definitely *for* Harry Crane.

Oriana flipped pages casually. Stopped on the illustration of the grum sitting on his gold. They were at the stoplight in New Milford. Amanda reached over and tapped the picture. "I don't like that creature. He's frowny. What's he called? A glum?"

"A grum," Oriana said. "But it ends happily."

"Fairy tales always end fifty-fifty happy, though, right? *Jack and the Beanstalk* — Jack's happy, but if you're the giant, you get killed. Or the wicked witch or the big bad wolf. So who kills the glum?"

"The *grum.* He doesn't get killed. He changes."

Amanda pulled the pickup in front of the library. Not hard to get a spot. Amanda got out of the truck, not giving *The Grum's Ledger* another look.

Oriana trailed up the steps behind her, the book under her arm. Harry thought it was smart to return it to the library, to lie low. "Your mom's right. It needs to go back. It's a clue that could lead back to us. Don't know how, one in a million, but why risk it."

Oriana stopped on the top step to look at

Pratt Library. It was grand and beautiful, but very sad, too. Green corrosion from the old copper gutters streaked the limestone facade. She picked up a broken slate roof tile. It looked like a heavy scale sloughed from a storybook dragon. Its skin coming off, its bones buckling, the library had lost the ability to protect itself. She patted the side of the building to comfort it. She heard a sharp laugh and turned.

Across the street, smoking a cigarette in front of Endless Dreams Realty, Stu Giptner had been watching her. He shook his head, dragged deeply on his cigarette and flicked it into the street.

"You shouldn't litter," Oriana called to him.

"Careful. That building might fall on top of you," Stu called back.

Inside the library, the sound of a circular saw starting up.

"Ronnie's fixing things," Oriana said defiantly.

"I'm planning to fix it, too," Stu said. He laughed again, spun on his heel and went back inside the realty office.

"I don't like you," Oriana whispered. She turned, pushed open the big oak doors and entered the library.

Her mother was standing beside the circulation desk talking to Olive. In the rear of the library, in the nonfiction aisles, blue poly tarps covered two bookshelves. She could hear Ronnie, the clink and clank of his tools. He was whistling softly as he worked, something staccato like a polka tune. Echoing off the marble walls, it sounded like a chirping bird had gotten loose in the library. Or maybe it really was a bird — certainly there were enough holes in the roof for flocks of them to come and go as they pleased. But Ronnie was doing a good job. He'd patched and sealed a lot of holes. Oh, but there were so many, and so much to do. Holes, flickering lights, teetering bookshelves, peeling plaster.

At the circulation desk, exchanging hellos with Amanda, Olive had been thinking, What is going on here? Amanda never comes in. But when Oriana came through the door a few moments later, Olive trembled. There it was, under the child's arm, *The Grum's Ledger.* It's come back. And of course, it would. It was the kind of book that came back. And really, why had she given it to the child in the first place? Desperation and despair. In a lifetime of books, it was the one that was writ large.

The echo of Oriana's approaching footsteps, the portentous book she held out in front of her, Olive felt a wave of dizziness, and bumped back against the circulation desk. She felt Amanda's strong hand at her elbow.

"You all right, Olive?"

The old librarian gathered herself, pulled away and straightened. Don't be fainting in front of a nurse, she warned herself, or straightaway you'll end up in the ER with those oxygen tube thingies jammed up your nostrils. Give them no openings, Olive. If you falter, if you don't stand tall and vigilant, they will close the doors of this place and you will never get back in. These thoughts in the five seconds of Oriana's approach. Suddenly *The Grum's Ledger* was back in Olive's hands. Its immense weight almost pulled her to the floor.

"Not overdue. You could have kept it, child," she murmured.

"It was time," said Oriana.

Amanda watched Olive staring at her daughter, and sensed that something more than a book had been placed in the old librarian's hands. There had always been the air of a secret pact between Olive and Oriana, something going on that was beyond fairy tales and fiction. And Ronnie, banging on things in the back. She hadn't seen much of him lately. Now he's working on Pratt

Library? What was going on in this place?

The doors of the library suddenly groaned open, and a mother and a young girl Oriana's age entered. The girl eyed Oriana. Gave her a quick wave. Then skipped off to the children's section.

Please, please, Amanda thought. "Oriana. Why don't you go look for a book?" She gave Oriana a slight push, as she turned to the mother. "Hi, I'm Amanda Jeffers, Oriana's mom."

As the mothers talked, Olive settled in behind the circulation desk and tried to unfluster herself. She'd put some distance between herself and *The Grum's Ledger,* which she'd placed in the "returns" bin, as if that would normalize the situation.

Oriana, heading toward the children's books, saw Ronnie fixing a shelf in nonfiction. She gave a smile and a thumbs-up, but she was worried. Very worried. Poor Pratt Library was in so much danger, maybe too much for Ronnie, she thought anxiously. It's such a rickety old place.

And that awful Stu Giptner standing across the street smoking his nasty cigarette and tossing it into the gutter. He'd toss a lit cigarette in the front door of the library, if he could. She could hear his sharp laugh, imagined him dancing around the flames of the library, like a troll dancing gleefully around a bonfire.

Ronnie gave Oriana a little wave. He was turning back to his work when he noticed Olive creeping down the next aisle with a book in her hand.

Olive never creeps, thought Ronnie. She was forthright and deliberate. And she certainly never did what he saw her do next. She closed her eyes and felt her way a little farther down the aisle and stopped, eyes still closed, and touched among the backs of the books that lined the shelf in front of her, at shoulder level. It spooked Ronnie, watching her. Her lips were pressed tight, and she was shaking as she moved two books aside and shoved in the one she had been carrying. She made her blind way back down the aisle, then opened her eyes again and walked quickly back to the circulation desk.

Ronnie swallowed. It was if he had just watched a dog bury a bone in a vast backyard, with the strange intention of never finding it again.

Oriana, meanwhile, had made her way over to YA which was next to the children's books. The other young girl was down on her knees perusing titles.

"Hi, Tess," Oriana said. Tess was in Oriana's fourth grade class. Sometimes they sat together at lunch, but they didn't speak much. Tess had red hair and that was interesting. And her parents were divorced, and that was interesting, too.

"Hi, Oriana," Tess said.

"What book are you getting?" Back at the desk, the mothers were looking their way.

"The Buckskin Sisters," Tess said. "It's kind of old but I like it. It's cowboys but with girls." It was a series. She handed a volume to Oriana.

Oriana paged through it. "Looks good."

"It's goofy but I like it." Tess moved a little closer to whisper. "Do you like this library?"

Oriana nodded. "Very much."

"I do, too. Mom says it's dusty. And that it smells."

"I love the smell of books," whispered Oriana.

"Me, too," whispered Tess.

Both girls smiled and nodded. Tess's mother beckoned, and the two girls grabbed their books and skittered to the circulation desk.

Amanda was loving it, the two girls side by side, like friends. And each had the same book. Some kind of series. "Whatcha got there, can I see?" Please don't be, please don't be — and it wasn't! On the book's cover a picture of two girls in buckskins staring intently at a herd of buffalo in the prairie distance. Not a fairy tale. "Nice," Amanda said.

Oriana stepped up to the desk, and Olive whammed the date stamp on the Date Due slip in the back of the book. Olive didn't meet Oriana's eyes. It registered deeply with Olive, too: Oriana was done with fairy tales. She had changed. Metamorphosed. And Olive knew why. She felt dizzy again, and braced herself against the desk.

The tale of the grum had ended fairy tales for Oriana because it wasn't a fairy tale at all. *The Grum's Ledger* was a grown-up story.

Oriana, a child, an innocent, had been exposed to the real world of woe and loss and regret. There really was a doleful grum who hoarded his treasure — the only part of the story that was a fairy tale was the happy ending. Olive wanted to whisper to her: *I didn't mean to show you a truth, sweetheart. I am sorry to have shown you a truth.* And then Olive was awash with shame. That she stood wavering before this young girl.

What else is a library, but a temple of truth? What other function do books have, the great ones, but to change the reader? Books to comfort. But most of all, books to disturb you forward. Oriana needed to change. That was a truth. The grum could only dream of change, while Oriana, before Olive's very eyes, was changing by the minute. *Keep going, sweetheart, until you read every book in this library.* Olive looked around at her glorious, tattered temple. *But hurry, hurry.*

"Oh my goodness," Tess's mother suddenly said. She'd gotten a text message. She stared at the glowing screen of her phone, gave her head a little shake of astonishment and laughed. "Guys. Listen to this. In Elkdale?"

Oriana stood very still. If she was absolutely still no one would see the trail of gold coins, like crumbs in the forest, that connected her to Elkdale. Boy, did news travel fast. But of course it did. A hummingbird couldn't sneeze without it being instantly detected by the internet.

"Elkdale's only, what, ten miles away?" Tess's mother said. "Somebody, you're not going to believe this, found a bag of gold on their front doorstep."

"Gold?" Amanda and Tess and Olive said in unison. Oriana made sure to say it, too, though she was a second behind everyone else. "Gold?"

Tess's mother held her phone so everybody could see. They leaned in. There on the screen, atop a news brief from the *Scranton Times,* a photo of Phil Bartek holding a burlap bag in one hand, and a dozen glittering coins in the other. Standing beside him was a very large and grinning state trooper.

"Is it real?" said Oriana. Her voice squeaked.

Tess's mother scanned the news blurb. "Totally. It says they tested it, and it's real."

"Who would hand somebody a bag of gold?" Amanda said.

Oriana spoke too quickly, "They didn't hand it, they left it." Oops. But nobody paid any attention to that fine detail.

"Two hundred fifty thousand dollars," Tess's mother said. "Can you imagine? Waking up and finding that on your doorstep?"

"Was there a note?" Olive said. "A reason?"

Tess's mother scanned the article. "No note."

Good Lord, Olive thought. Someone, a do-gooder or a grum, relieving himself of gold. How stunning the world is.

"I know who it was," Tess suddenly said.

They all stared at her.

She pointed at Oriana.

Oriana went pale. But Tess reached for the book Oriana was holding. *Buckskin Sisters: The Treasure of Craggy Creek.* "The

Buckskin Sisters find a bag of gold in this one," Tess said. "I bet you they left it on that man's doorstep."

Oriana thought she would faint dead on the spot.

Tess's mother laughed and took Tess's hand. "Time to go home. Let's see if there's a bag waiting on *our* doorstep."

Back in the stacks, Ronnie didn't hear any of the chatter and commotion. He had opened a very strange book, written by hand. He whispered the first line as he began to read. " 'Once upon an endless time in the Endless Mountains . . .' "

He didn't look up from the book until it began to snow on him. Absorbed completely by *The Grum's Ledger,* he thought he had been transported to a fairy land where it snowed inside buildings. But when he looked up at the ceiling, Ronnie saw a raccoon paw triumphantly penetrating a new plaster patch that Ronnie had troweled into place just the day before.

At that same moment, down in Richmond, Virginia, Wolf's ears pricked and he sniffed the air. Some animals are finely attuned to the scent of blood. Others to the scent of money.

"Elkdale," Wolf said. He was staring at his iPhone.

It was not a scent, but a news aggregator app he'd had on his phone for years called "Lucky Bastards" that had led him to the Elkdale story.

"Lucky Bastards" was devoted to the undeserving rich, the disgustingly rich and the suddenly rich. Stories about how much money it takes to heat the Queen of England's four castles. The price of the latest mega yacht. Lottery winners standing beside the podium with their ludicrous oversize checks. And now this undeserving schmuck in Elkdale, Pennsylvania, Phil Bartek.

"A bag of gold. On your goddamn doorstep," Wolf said.

He was sitting on his own doorstep in the late-afternoon sun, pulling on a cigarette, the post-lawyer's-conference rage working through him like a horse shiver. Here he was on a doorstep he would soon lose in the divorce. A doorstep that was costing him money, not earning money. Draining him, like Harry was draining him. Harry somewhere out there, not giving Wolf his share.

Harry threatening to give away his money, but *has* he? And whether he has or hasn't, what good docs it do if I can't fucking find him? What forest was he hiding in? Harry was a needle in a haystack. I'll never find him. But I have to. I will.

Who's so generous that they give away money? Demented. Why would somebody give somebody something? That's like surrendering. Here, take my money, I can't deal with it. How perverse is that? It's like giving away oxygen. Why would you give away your oxygen? Wolf pulled deeply on his cigarette.

Wolf was sweaty with desire. He envied Phil Bartek of Elkdale, PA. Phil Bag-of-Gold Bartek. That's how easy it was supposed to be for *me.* That's how easily Harry's settlement money was supposed to come to me. *Here, Wolf. Thank you, big brother. Here's a fat check.* Wolf imagining it. How it was supposed to be. The doorbell rings, right? And I go outside, and on my doorstep is the check from Harry. So easy, it would've been. And so *right.* So fucking *fair.*

Wolf zoomed in on Phil's blandly pleasant face. He tapped a fingernail on the glass of his iPhone, but what he was really doing was tapping Phil on the forehead. Wolf used to do that to guys in high school. Scared the living shit out of them.

Then Wolf began to tap his own forehead because a memory was suddenly taking form. A childhood memory of the first time he saw and desired a bag of gold.

Way back, when kids were allowed to stuff their faces with sugar, there was a brand of gum that came in a small, fake burlap bag. The gum inside was shaped like yellow nuggets of pretend gold. Bag o' Gold, that was the name of it. Wolf flicked his cigarette, lit another and looked into the distance.

"Harry and the Bag o' Gold," he mused. It sounded like the title of a children's story. Because it was. Starring Wolf and Harry. Costarring Dad. Simple plot. One day, Harry came home from a trip to the store with Dad. Dad had bought Harry a Bag o' Gold. The bag had a string at the top to close it. Harry swinging the bag by the string and happily chewing his gum as he came up the walk.

Dad didn't buy two bags, one for each son, he bought one. So the outcome was inevitable, right? Wolf had to have that bag of gold. The question was: Was this the formative moment? Did all his desire for money start right there? With Dad and Harry betraying him? His need to take things? To steamroll his brother and everybody else who stood in the way of whatever it was that he wanted?

Wolf squirmed. He didn't like these

thoughts. He wasn't a fan of personal insight. It didn't get you anywhere. It didn't stop the craving. You still, until your dying day, want what you want, and you will damn well get it.

There was more to the chewing gum story.

Wolf walked into Harry's bedroom that long ago day and tapped Harry on the forehead. "Give me the bag," he said. Harry handed it right over. "Don't tell Dad." And Harry didn't. Why wouldn't Harry have told? Because he was weak. And he didn't like to make a fuss. Jesus, Harry. Wolf was so angry at Harry for being weak and his father for favoring Harry, that he climbed Harry's favorite tree, the beech in the front yard, and carved his father's initials into a thick branch. JC. Wolf wanted Harry to find those initials so that Harry would hate his father for wounding his precious tree.

So very unsettling for Wolf, this Elkdale business. He imagined Phil Bartek holding his bag of real gold. Which is more valuable, Wolf wondered, a bag of real gold or a bag of little gum nuggets?

"Where's my fucking money, Harry!" Wolf shouted.

If gold is falling from the heavens, how do I get mine? Paint a bull's-eye on my front doorstep? A golden dollar sign? What had

Phil Bartek done?

Wolf began to tap his own forehead, almost violently. What am I dreaming for, I should be *thinking.* Because somewhere out there is Harry and his four million dollars.

I need to find him fast.

It will be like the old days, Harry cringing, and old Wolfie appears and says, "Give." And Harry would give, so eager to rid himself of anything that might cause him trouble.

Wolf drew on his cigarette. At least that's the way Harry *used* to be.

Now he thinks he's being smart with me, shrewd? Wolf thought. Harry, little brother, you don't do shrewd. You do surrender.

What would I do with four million dollars? What's the first thing I'd buy?

A little burlap bag of golden gum.

And then, I'd start chewing. And when I was done with that bag, I'd buy another and another. Wolf on the doorstep, the heavy muscles of his jaw clenching and unclenching as he chewed on visions of limitless bubble gum and gold. He was so lost in rumination, he didn't see the UPS truck pull up in front of his house. The UPS guy stood there with a box from Amazon.

"Sir, a package for you."

Wolf snapped out of it and focused on the

UPS guy. "What did I order?"

"I, uh, don't really know."

Didn't matter what was in the box. The important thing? Whatever it was, it was his. He owned it. Wolf stared at the box in his lap as the delivery truck drove off.

His thoughts circled back to Harry and the gold.

Wolf held his phone close and zoomed in on the burlap bag of gold in Phil Bartek's hands.

To the forest and the trees. What does that mean, why did you say that?

Wolf began to tap his finger on Phil Bartek's Bag o' Gold. Harder and harder.

No, impossible. It doesn't make sense. It makes no sense at all.

Does it, Harry?

26

That night, in the tree house, they stared at the news photo on Harry's phone.

"Just look at him, Harry," breathed Oriana.

Harry was looking. Phil Bartek standing next to his friend and neighbor, a state trooper. What a grin stretching across Phil's face.

"Look at how *happy* you made them."

Harry nodded. He hadn't expected this part. That the money, which had come from such a miserable place, could put a smile of such joy on someone's face.

"Can't you smile a little, too?" Oriana said.

But Harry was thinking too intently to smile. It was hard for him to process the joy — but what he *could* process was the excitement in the eyes of Phil and the state trooper. It was the excitement part that he had worried about and planned for.

Harry knew it was the second bag of gold that would be the true sensation. The first order of gold, the Bartek bag, had been a test to see if the system worked. Boy, did it. But he wasn't going to pick up the remaining shipments one by one. He didn't want to make multiple trips to UPS delivery sites (forget the post office, too snoopy) no matter how anonymously he could supposedly do it. Not with all the hubbub and hype that would come after bag number two landed on a Susquehanna County doorstep.

Harry ordered the remainder of the gold, approximately $3,750,000, in $300,000 dollar parcels (the allowable maximum) from twelve different gold bullion companies, and had them shipped to three different UPS sites in and around Scranton. It was a complicated and time-consuming pain in the ass, but doable. *Do it, Harry, do it.* That was his mantra for the several days he spent gathering up the shipments. A guy runs around Scranton picking up millions in gold and no one pays a whit of attention. Holy moly. If it hadn't been terrifying, it might've been fun.

Each box weighed twenty pounds. He still would have liked to use a wheelbarrow, but navigating one through a dense forest would be impossible. He used a backpack to schlep the gold in multiple trips to the quarry hiding place Oriana had found.

When he saw the quarry the first time, he was impressed.

"Wow, Oriana, home run."

He had to hand it to her, it really looked like the perfect setting for a troll or a small dragon to hide its gold. Why hadn't the grum hidden his gold somewhere like this, why did he sit on it night and day, Harry wondered. To feel it constantly under his butt, probably. The grum was chained to it, that was the point of the story. The holding, then the explosive freedom of letting go.

"Don't get too close to the edge," Harry said.

"I know how to do this."

He smiled. "I know you do. What was I thinking?"

"It's okay. You were just watching out for me."

They stood on the quarry perimeter, fifty feet above the floor, which was dry except for little pools of brackish rainwater here and there, and giant mounds of broken bluestone slate like shattered temples. The cave, Oriana said, was just below them, tucked into the largest mound, shouldered up against the quarry wall. It was impossible to see the cave entrance through the mass of vines and undergrowth that had invaded the quarry.

"That's a lot of poison ivy. Daunting for gold thieves. Nice touch," Harry said.

"And tons of yellow jackets," Oriana said, pointing to a nest in an oak stump. Five or six bees orbited Harry's head like angry moons around a planet. He raised a hand to swat at them.

"You do that, the whole nest will attack you," Oriana said.

He slowly and carefully lowered his hand. "Bees, poison ivy. How about badgers? Have you assigned badgers to guard this place?"

"Wouldn't that be cool? Badgers in uniforms and big, thick snakes."

Oriana placed a foot onto the slate mound. "Watch your step. Don't start a landslide."

Harry blinked. "I'm thinking this isn't a good idea."

"You wanted the perfect place. This is perfect."

"Oriana. Really. It's perfect but it's dangerous. I should do this alone."

She stamped her foot. Pebbles bounced down the side of the mound. Harry blanched.

"That's not fair," Oriana said. "That's treating me like a kid. I've played in this quarry, like, a million times."

"Your mother know?"

"My dad knows."

Oriana waited. Harry considered his options. "Okay. Fine. Just know that if we tumble to our deaths, your mother will kill me."

"Harry," Oriana said solemnly. "You never die. That's how we met, remember?"

Harry was taken aback. Yes, of course, at the sugar maple. He didn't die that day. And that fact was certainly on Oriana's unspoken list of Important Things About Harry Crane. Harry was a grum. Harry was a giver of gold. And Harry, perhaps most of all, was a man who wasn't going to die. Guaranteed. He had made that guarantee to Amanda, too.

He patted her shoulder. "I do remember." He forced a confident smile and stepped onto the mound of slate.

They descended carefully, lowering themselves a dozen feet through thick underbrush and overhanging spruce tree limbs. The forty pounds of gold in his pack felt like a thousand. It was a half mile back to his car. He'd have to make this trip five times.

It wasn't a true cave, but a large alcove, a pocket in the side of the slate mound. The patio in the backyard of Harry's house in Waverly was made of the same bluestone slate, cut into neat suburban rectangles. He had taken pleasure in keeping the stones swept and tidy. It appealed to his bureaucratic nature. But now the forest was his home. Here, the bluestone was pocked and covered with orange and green lichen, snaggle-toothed. Here, life was wild and woolly.

Oriana could stand up in the little cave, but Harry had to crouch. Light speckled in through the vines that curtained the entrance. It was cool and smelled of earth and stone. A proper vault for gold, elemental, lost in time.

Oriana's job had been to carry the five remaining empty burlap bags. She put them down and helped Harry wriggle free of the backpack. The gold was heavy, but the burden of it was getting lighter. A strange lightness of being.

"Wouldn't it be fun to give Phil Bartek's friend the next bag?" Oriana said.

"No. It would be dumb. What's the rule, Oriana?"

"It has to be random."

"Because random is safe." Harry settled

the two boxes of gold on the stony floor. He looked around. "This is a good spot. You did a good job."

"What if we flip a coin and it lands on Elkdale again?" she said.

"Then we flip again."

"What if it lands on the next town over, would that be okay?"

"Stop. You're making me anxious. We pick a town. Randomly. I drop off some gold. I run. I don't want to overthink this."

"You're doing a good job," Oriana said.

It really was going remarkably smoothly. "We make a good team," Harry said.

They made a very good team, so Oriana felt a little tiny bit bad about something she did. But she couldn't help it. She really couldn't. They had finished storing the portion of the gold they would hide in the cave, and now they were up in the tree house with the second bag of gold, which sat on the kitchen table. The first bag had contained $250,000 in coins. This one held $300,000. So would bags three and four. The last two would hold over a million each. They would be the grum's "great heaps and hurls." Only he and Oriana would ever understand the logic. The grum of it all.

Harry spread out the Susquehanna County map on the cot. Oriana reached into the burlap bag and picked out a coin. Held it up. Harry gave the signal and she flipped it into the air. It thunked onto the map, twirled and dropped, eagle side up. Harry nudged it aside.

"Halfordsville," he said. A larger town than Elkdale.

"That's where we go to the movies — Halfordsville."

As Harry intently studied the map, Oriana casually picked up the gold coin and turned toward the bag on the kitchen table. She looked over her shoulder. Harry was still staring at the map. She felt a little jab of conscience as her hand hovered above the open bag. The gold in the light. Such a beautiful magic disc. And all she wanted was one coin of her very own.

One coin wouldn't matter. And she wasn't going to steal it, she just wanted one temporarily, to look at and play with. Then she'd slip it back into the final bag of gold. It would be her secret, she'd keep it in her room. Gold of her own. Borrowed. She slipped the coin into her pocket. Oh, the thrilling secret weight of it.

She poked the burlap bag to make it clink as if the coin had been dropped in. Harry turned at the sound and said, "Halfordsville's great. There's a good main road right off I-81. This should be even easier than Elkdale."

Harry folded the map and joined her at the kitchen table. He took hold of the bag. "Help me tie this closed. Then it's time for you to go home. And time for me to go to Halfordsville." They tied the bag.

Oriana hesitated in the doorway. Her legs didn't want to move her out of the tree house.

"Go," Harry said. "Before your mother comes."

He gave her a small push, and then she was off and running, down the spiral steps, like Cinderella escaping the midnight castle — a Cinderella who had not lost a shoe, but snitched an extra one from the prince's closet to admire when she got home.

Deep are the bonds of friendship. Long are the memories of discord.

Francine Dillon and Ginger Thompson had been best friends and best enemies since first grade at Halfordsville Elementary School. On the first day of school in 1960, their desks were side by side. Now their houses were side by side, Francine in a blue Dutch Colonial and Ginger in a green Victorian. Both were divorced, each had two children, now grown up and moved away.

Ginger's children had stayed in Pennsylvania. Francine's lived in Austin, Texas! Francine always said it with an exclamation point. All the way to Texas! She rarely got to see them, so whenever one of Ginger's came for a weekend, Francine experienced a twinge of envy.

Just a twinge.

Not like the full-bore rage she felt in twelfth grade when Barry Kelmer, who was supposed to ask Francine to the senior prom, asked Ginger instead. That was a five day disruption in their friendship. Francine had actually slapped Ginger. When the blow landed, both girls burst into tears and hugged.

"I don't want him," Ginger sobbed. "I just want you to be my friend."

"Best friends, always, always," Francine sobbed.

To show there were no hard feelings, Francine baked Ginger treats. Ginger, a pretty girl, but ten pounds heavier than the ideal (plain Francine was willowy as a whippet) loved anything that came out of an oven. Preferably gooey with several thousand pounds of chocolate chips.

Best friends can be so trying. Especially when the friendship lasts decades.

"What did you do to your hair!" Francine

shrieked in 1969. "You look like you ate a bowl of electricity." They were standing in Ginger's bedroom. Rather, Francine was standing. Ginger had collapsed onto the floor in a moaning heap.

"Don't say that, I feel terrible." Her hair, a mix of porcupine spikes and roller coaster spirals, was a fascinating horror. Against all common sense, she'd allowed Frieda, of Frieda's Hair Deluxe, to give her a perm.

"You look terrible," Francine said. "I'm sorry, but you do. How are you going to go to school tomorrow?"

"Go away," Ginger moaned. "I hate you. You're not helping."

Francine considered. Her best friend lay sobbing on the floor. It was not easy to come by friends in Halfordsville. It was a small, boring town.

Francine sighed, scooped up Ginger and guided her into the shower. After several vigorous applications of Prell and gobs of conditioner, they restored Ginger's injured locks.

"You are my best friend in all the world," Ginger said, hugging her.

Now they were sixty-one years old, and they'd had another fight. In their loneliness, they had each other. So it was stupid to have had this latest tiff. There was only one way to end an extended tiff with Ginger. Baked goods.

Francine smiled as she took the brownies out of the oven. The sun was not up yet, but the sky was lightening. She looked out the kitchen window at her favorite sight in all the world: the magnificent sugar maple in Ginger's front yard.

"What nincompoops we are, Ginger," she said.

The sugar maple was the source of the latest squabble. It was the most beautiful tree in Halfordsville. Maybe even in all of the Endless Mountains. Francine was jealous of Ginger's tree. Why did she long to own it? Why wasn't it enough that it was in Ginger's yard, fifty feet away?

It all started because Ginger wanted to cut a lower limb from the tree.

"You can't," Francine exclaimed. "That would be like amputating an angel's finger!"

Ginger laughed. "That's gross, but funny."

Francine wasn't trying to be funny. "I'm serious."

"The squirrels are using it to get in my gutters," Ginger said.

"But from my window . . . there's this *balance.*" How could Francine explain balance and symmetry to this old fool. And Ginger *was* getting old. And heftier. And she catered to those children of hers, far too much.

"It's the smallest limb, Francine. It's inconsequential."

"Please."

"How about I give it to you after I have it taken off?" Ginger was in a teasing mood. A tree limb, for god's sake. Francine needed to lighten up.

Francine glowered. "How about, after you have it taken off, you shove it up your voluminous butt."

The two friends spun away from each other, marched up their front walks, and slammed their front doors so hard that Bill Palmer, two streets over, thought he heard pistol shots.

The sun was coming up, the brownies were cool enough to cut, stack neatly in a Tupperware container and leave on Ginger's front porch. It's only a tree limb, Francine chided herself, who cares? Abundant are the limbs on trees, rare is the friendship that is true.

Francine walked past the sugar maple and started up Ginger's front walk. She stopped short. While she did not have an actual heart attack when she realized the crumpled bag leaning against Ginger's front door was a burlap bag just like *The Scranton Times* said had been found on the porch of that man over in Elkdale, Francine had many of the symptoms. Shortness of breath, dizziness, strong palpitations and a sense of imminent death.

"Oh no," she whispered. "No, no, no." Whoever was delivering bags of gold (she had now opened the burlap bag and the glow was blinding) had given one to Ginger Thompson and not to Francine Dillon.

Francine sat on the front step beside the bag, brownies in her lap, the sun just rising. She looked to her left. Looked to her right. No one on Plindon Avenue was awake. Her fingers tapped nervously on the Tupperware lid. I cannot bear it, she thought. I cannot bear that Ginger has a bag of gold. She'll be able to pay off her mortgage. She'll be able to plant dozens of sugar maples in her front yard, if she wants to. *The Scranton Times* will have a large photo of her, grinning. For doing nothing, Ginger was about to become a kind of hero.

"No, no, no," Francine whispered. She put down the Tupperwared brownies and, grunting with effort, picked up the bag of gold and lumbered back across Ginger's lawn toward her own house. She didn't make it past the maple tree.

"No," she said weakly. "No, Francine."

She breathed in the essence of the tree. The trueness and the purity of its existence on earth.

Ginger, my Ginger, Francine thought. Your life has not been ideal. You never had good hair. Your son played drums and not the cello.

Francine returned the bag of gold to its spot on Ginger's front porch. She left the Tupperware of brownies on top of the bag — one brownie short because Francine had taken one for herself. She crossed the lawn, walking slowly in the beautiful dawn light. And it was enough. Dawn, a fresh stolen brownie, a good cup of coffee, and from her kitchen window a view of the sugar maple so vivid and green it brought tears to Francine's eyes.

27

One bag of gold on a doorstep was an isolated, freakish miracle. Like a meteor smashing through your garage roof. The citizens of Susquehanna County were able to wrap their heads around the staggering but *conceivable* nature of it. The appearance of the second bag of gold a week later in Halfordsville was a mind-blowing sensation. Because a second bag meant that someone was handing out bags of gold. Plural. *Bags.* Bags of gold were about to start raining down on doorsteps.

It was early May, warm and green, not even remotely Christmasy. But when somebody yakking on a local news station came up with the corny-but-perfect nickname that best encompassed the legendary qualities of a serial gift giver, it went viral. Susquehanna Santa. Christmas in May! Susquehanna Santa doesn't squeeze down your chimney in the middle of the night. No, he delivers to your front doorstep like a nocturnal UPS.

Where would the next bag land? The phenomenon was obviously and intriguingly local. Elkdale was only twenty miles from Halfordsville. And when? Would a week go by between every one of the bags? And how many bags would there be? Some tight-ass on talk radio groused, "Well, you have to pay taxes on it. It's income." So what? Good problem to have. You don't want gold on your doorstep, toss it over to me, pal!

During a man-on-the-street interview in Halfordsville, the Scranton reporter holding the mike right up to a big farmer's ruddy nose, the farmer actually said, "You know how Santa lives in the North Pole? Well, Susquehanna Santa lives in the Endless Mountains." This was a grown man talking. The lore, the fairy tale, the myth, growing by the minute. By the internet *nanosecond.*

Yes, it was the age of the internet, but the world was also still touchingly old-fashioned. Handmade signs began to appear on front lawns: SUSQUEHANNA SANTA PLEASE STOP HERE!!!!!!

Stu Giptner had passed a dozen such signs on the way to work. Now, he sat brooding in his hellishly small office. "Everybody going apeshit," he grumbled. "Like it could happen to them. Yeah. Right. Never in a trillion years."

What he really meant was — never in a trillion years would that kind of luck happen to *him.* The universe had found another way to torture Stu Giptner. So why had he taped a map of Susquehanna County to his wall and stuck red pushpins on Halfordsville and Elkdale? Because through serious cogitation, he might be able to break the code.

"Because if I break the code, if I can see where the next bag is gonna land, then . . ."

Well, then he would buy a house in that town. He'd crack the code, figure out the town where Susquehanna Santa would take his next gold dump and buy a little "as is" house. Then he'd plant, like, a thousand PLEASE STOP HERE!!!! signs in the front yard. He'd go big. Neon signs, strobe lights, sirens. He'd shoot Santa out of the sky if he had to. No, that's the other Santa. Susquehanna Santa probably drives a black Lexus IS 250C convertible. Leather-wrapped steering wheel, bird's-eye maple dash, paddle-shifter, alloy wheels, V6.

Stu's head throbbed. Phil Bartek's and Ginger Thompson's haul were both *six figures*? Had *they* spent their entire adult lives striving toward six figures like he had? No, no, don't you see, Susquehanna Santa? Stu

Giptner is The Six Figure Man.

"It's not fair," Stu said. He felt like punching somebody. He couldn't believe he had punched Harry Crane. Who didn't even have the guts to punch back. I need to throw another punch. I need to make things happen. I need to be somebody.

Stu cringed when he heard his boss's door open. What he needed, and desperately, was to throw a real estate punch or he'd lose his goddamn job. That's the thing I need to make happen. *Six figures, six figures, make it happen, make it happen.*

Stu stood up and stared at the county map, suddenly drawn to it. Why? What did his mind perceive? *Symmetry.* That spot on the map equidistant between the red pushpins of Elkdale and Halfordsville. At the edge of the big green chunk of government forest, right about there — he placed his thumb on the spot as if he was squashing a bug — Amanda Jeffers's house.

Even the ER patients, bumped and bloodied, wheezing with asthma, half-dazed with their injuries and ailments — it's the first thing they'd mention. It was getting ridiculous. On top of everything else, they were suffering from gold fever.

The patient in room 6, a man named

Hank Captow, had broken his arm falling off a ladder. "Nurse," he said. "You hear about them bags of gold?"

"Did one fall on you, Mr. Captow?" Amanda was always professional when she addressed patients. Not "Hank" but "Mr. Captow." She did not believe in getting chummy. Patients wanted, and deserved, an adult in charge.

He laughed. "Nah. But I wish one would."

"Doesn't your arm hurt? That's a pretty good fracture." It's one of the things she liked about the rural life — these tough old birds who would talk about crop rotation or hunting while the doc sewed a finger back on or stitched a leathery forehead.

He stared at the lump on his wrist matter-of-factly. "Yeah, it aches some, I guess. What would you do with a bag of gold?"

Pay off my loan, pay off my truck, put money in a college fund for Oriana, Amanda thought. "I don't believe in Santa," she said.

"How do you mean? It's really happening."

"Happened," Amanda said. "It's not going to happen again."

Mr. Captow looked at her. "Not a daydreamer, huh?"

She gave him a pill, despite his protests, to dull the pain she knew was coming his way. The world was a predictable place. You break your arm, it's going to hurt when they twist your ulna bone back into alignment down in the cast room. You dream of Susquehanna Santa, your silly childish heart is going to break.

The EMT guys, coming in and out of the ER, were full of gold chatter, too. One of them, Bill Planowsky, suddenly veered off-topic.

"So, how's Harry?" he said.

Amanda was at the nurses' station, and Bill was wheeling by with an empty ambulance stretcher.

"How is Harry?" she repeated. Because it caught her totally off guard, this casual mention of Harry, who was now part of the community, or at least on the edges of it. Bill had been at Green Gables when Harry was in the booth.

"Mr. Tree House," Bill said.

A touch of red blushed Amanda's cheeks. She felt like she was in high school. "You think you know all the details, huh?"

"We know what we saw, sure."

"What did you see?" What she wanted them to see, of course. That it looked like she and Harry were an item. Touching and carrying on in the booth. You can't have it both ways, Amanda, she told herself. The whole point of Harry was to keep guys like Bill at bay. And to dig at Cliff. And to . . . her cheeks going warm again, at the memory of Harry reaching out to fix her hair.

"At first, we couldn't figure it out," Bill said. "You dating somebody who works in an office. That's so not Amanda."

Dating, Amanda thought. Amanda dating Harry.

"But when Ronnie spilled the beans, said Harry was living in the tree house while he evaluated the wilderness tract —"

"Boy, you heard it all."

"No, but just, that he's living in the tree house. And that he can take a punch." All Bill meant to convey was that Harry had been vetted and approved. I mean, the men of Green Gables were not thrilled that Harry had succeeded where they had abysmally failed, but still, Harry was, you know, as far as any guy ever approves of any other guy, okay.

More blood in Amanda's cheeks now, hot enough to boil an egg. "You *punched* him?"

They'd had a picnic the other day, she and Harry and Oriana, down by the creek between the house and the tree house. Amanda immediately noticed a small contusion at the edge of his right occipital orbit. Assessing him professionally. Harry said he had walked into a tree branch. Amanda touched her fingers along the edges of the bump, Harry closing his eyes. This touching thing, even when they were not in a Green Gables booth, pretending.

Bill stepped back, because Amanda had moved in close. Up close and personal with Amanda — Bill, like all the local guys, had often fantasized about it — turned out to be a very threatening place. He tried to step back again, but he was against the wall.

"Not me, Amanda. I didn't punch him. Stu punched him. Out in the parking lot."

Amanda leaned away from Bill, staring in complete confusion. Stu, weasly Stu Giptner, got in a fight with Harry?

Bill quickly laid out events. Too many beers, Stu goading them out to the Green Gables parking lot to stand up for their rights . . .

"Your rights? Your rights to what? To me?" Ugh. It was even worse than she thought. The men thinking they had rights to the Widow Jeffers.

Bill put up both hands. "That came out wrong. We just, you know, wanted to know more about this Harry Crane guy. And we *liked* him, Amanda."

"Except for Stu, who punched him. What the hell, Bill?"

"Sucker punch. Totally Stu, right? But here's the cool part."

Amanda thought about it for the rest of the day. Harry, who could've taken Stu apart, did not strike back. That was very cool. How many men (and women) had she treated in this very ER for giving and receiving blows? That there was a nonphysical way to beat a man. What a novel approach.

The other cool part was that Harry, nobly, was defending the honor of a woman with whom he was not actually involved. Harry took a punch for a romance the guys in Green Gables thought was true, but that Amanda had manufactured. He had been wounded for love. He had taken the punishment but had been afforded none of the pleasures.

Not only did Stu have unceasing bad luck, today he also had exceptionally bad timing.

Out in the ER parking lot, he was fidgety with the looming sense of victory. The beauty of his plan was that there was an element of truth to it. Fact: Amanda Jeffers was in arrears on her loan payments. Fact: he had her over a barrel. Fact: he was doing her a favor. Fact: she had it coming, for rebuffing the overtures he never (fact) had the guts to make.

Possible fact: Harry Crane evaluating Wilderness Tract A803 (Stu had looked up the official name on the website). Was the government about to sell it off? The fracking boom had petered out (Stu making not a dime, of course), so what was the deal? Lumber. You send a forestry guy in to evaluate the trees. The government was selling off everything, these days. Big Lumber was coming in. What a beautiful notion, clear-cutting all that creepy forest. Stumps, as far as the eye could see. As far as Stu was concerned, you could flatten the Endless Mountains and take every barrel of oil, ton of coal, board foot of tree. And suck the water out of the Susquehanna River while you're at it. Stu was not big on nature.

The ER doors slid open. He went up on his toes. Here she comes. He straightened his tie. Practiced his opening line. *Hi, Amanda!* No. *Amanda, how ya doing?* No. *Good to see you, Amanda.*

She saw him standing by her truck. Boy, thought Stu, she's approaching fast. Like a locomotive. Maybe this wasn't a great day. Yeah, maybe she's had a bad day at work. How could she not, it's an ER. Is it too late to run?

Too late. She stood in front of him, arms crossed.

He tried to meet her eyes. "Hi! Good to, how ya see ya doing, Amanda?" Stu sputtered. *Six figures, six figures, six figures.*

"You're next to my truck, Stu. Trying to steal it?"

He made an anxious laughing sound. *Six figures, six figures.* Because he absolutely had to go back to the office with something real to deliver to his boss, Vince Bromler, who had said, "Put your big boy pants on, Giptner. Make something happen out there."

Stu forced himself to meet Amanda's eyes. Then he locked on. Because you know what? He was in charge here. He had the facts. And facts were power. "Got a minute, Amanda? Want to talk to you. I have some good news."

Amanda scrunched her eyes, trying to figure his angle.

With the customer, Stu thought, first you do the chitchat. You chat the chit. "Boy, that Susquehanna Santa, huh? Bag of that gold would be something, huh?"

Amanda, silent, waiting.

Stu cleared his throat. "But, in real life, money-wise, things are a little harder to come by. Money doesn't just drop out of the sky."

The jerk is up to something, Amanda

thought. Look at the glitter in his eyes. Bet they glittered like that just before he sucker punched Harry.

"No, sorry to say, money doesn't drop out of the sky," Stu said, warming up to the fact that he was definitely the one in control now. Despite Amanda's size. Despite her armor of beauty.

Amanda felt her right fist tighten. She made herself untighten it. "Stu. I'm going to do you a favor. Move out of my way. I'll get in my truck."

"No, see, I'm here to do *you* a favor. You're three months in arrears on your loan payment."

Amanda was so angry and so embarrassed, she was actually flustered.

"Yeah, see. It's come to my attention. Via my sources. My *in* at Susquehanna Mortgage & Loan."

Amanda shivered. It was like being touched by the little creep. She actually felt his slippery hands all over her. Plucking and probing for money. "You broke the law."

He laughed. "No way. Don't know what you're talking about. A piece of info from a guy who knows a guy who knows a computer." He sounded like the mob! God, this felt good.

"I'm making the payment," she said. It

made her sick that she was rattled, making excuses to Stu Giptner. "At the end of the month, I've already —"

He touched her arm. She jerked free.

He smiled. "Here's where we are. If you miss a fourth payment, which I suspect you're about to do, the bank will no longer allow you to catch up. They will not accept any further payments. They will simply foreclose." A beat, and then he added, "I could help you out on this hardship."

"Put my house on the market? Screw you. It's a month's payment. And I have it."

"And enough to pay the three months you missed, plus interest and penalties? Maybe you'll squeak by. But can you keep squeaking by?"

Stu was up close and personal now. In Amanda's space.

Amanda could smell his cigarette breath. She felt sick to her stomach.

"The house is too big for you now, Amanda. Don't you think?"

As the words left Stu's mouth, he had a teeny tiny thought: Did I just overreach?

Yes. In a swirl of rage — that the house that Dean built was being threatened, that the little weasel getting in her face had sucker punched Harry — Amanda swung her right fist toward Stu Giptner's head.

But the beauty of it? She stopped her fist a fraction of an inch from his jaw. She didn't hit him. But he felt the blow, yes he did. The crashing fury of a woman protecting her man. Stu screamed in pain and fell to the asphalt. Amanda shook her head in wonder, stepped over him, got in her truck and sped off.

He wobbled to his knees and whimperingly patted his untouched jaw. This is what it felt like to *not* get hit by Amanda? If he ever provoked her enough to land a real punch, he knew he'd never survive it.

Like a punch to the head. That's what it felt like. Pow!

It's *Harry.* "It's fucking Harry!"

Even through his Bose QuietComfort 25 Noise Cancelling Headphones, Doug Hufnal, on the other side of the cubicle, heard Wolf loud and clear, but very carefully did not react in any way. He never did. No one in the office did, not even the office manager. Not when Wolf banged on his desk or shouted into his phone — usually at his wife's lawyer. Not even last week, when he put his fist through the partition of his cubicle, penetrating into Doug's side. Doug had never seen such hairy knuckles. Or big ones.

"It's fucking Harry!" The words jumping out of Wolf's mouth. Then he clammed up, hunkering close to his computer screen. He didn't want anyone else in the world to know that his brother, fucking Harry — stunningly, unbelievably — was Susquehanna Santa.

When the "Lucky Bastards" app had pinged the second bag of gold landing in Susquehanna County, Wolf had pulled up Google Maps, looking from Elkdale to Halfordsville, back and forth, back and forth.

Wolf had dismissed the premonition of the Elkdale bag, because of one simple piece of logic: the bag on Phil Bartek's doorstep didn't contain four million dollars in gold coins, only $250,000.

But now Halfordsville. Another bag, this time $300,000.

Harry had some kind of insane, mysterious plan: he was going to hand out the four million in increments.

To the forest and the trees. Those words suddenly made sense. Wolf traced a line from Elkdale to Halfordsville, a straight line, as the crow flies. And right between the two little towns was a big patch of green. A forest.

Wolf could barely breathe. You didn't go to that forest to hide, Harry. You're a man with a plan. You've converted that four million into goddamn gold. And the forest is where you're hiding it! You're like some sort of troll with his big stash of gold. You go into your hiding place, fill up a burlap bag, and you make a drop in some little Susquehanna County town. You're a demented troll, Harry. Because you got it upside down. Trolls stash their gold and sit on it and laugh at the world. They hoard it . . . that is, until their brother comes and finds it, and steals it.

Or what's left of it. Christ. Harry's almost whittled it down to three million!

Wolf stared at the map.

Forest.

White-faced, stunned, Wolf walked out of his office, got in his car and drove north to the USDA Forest Service.

Bob looked up as Wolf approached again. When the elevator door opened and he saw Wolf, Bob allowed himself a tentative smile. Was Harry behind Wolf? In handcuffs? Bob looked at the miserable mountain of paperwork on his desk. Yes, Wolf, cuff Harry to his cubicle, so that he can never leave again.

But Harry wasn't with him.

Bob jumped up and extended his hand.

"Hi, hi, hi! Good to see you, Wolford."

Wolf pressed Bob back down in his chair.

Pivoted Bob to his computer.

"Harry was in charge of managing federal forests and wilderness tracts in the Mid-Atlantic region, yes?"

"Yep. Yes."

"Pull up your regional map. Could you do that for me, Bob?"

Wolf pointed to various patches of green, Bob providing each time a name or a wilderness tract number. Wolf pointed to the patch of green between Elkdale and Halfordsville.

"Wilderness Tract A803," Bob said.

Wolf twitched. Bob didn't notice. Wolf pointed to a few more sites, to cover his tracks.

"Thanks, Bob," he said abruptly and slapped the little bureaucrat hard enough on the back to dislodge the glasses on Bob's nose. When Bob looked up, the beast had vanished.

"You gotta have a roof over your head, Harry. Everybody needs a roof over their heads."

Wolf would soon need a roof over his own head, when the divorce went through. He was sitting out in the parking lot, formulating a plan of action. Wolf loved action.

Okay, Harry. You're hiding your gold in Wilderness Tract A803. But you need a place to live. To sleep and eat. A place to park your car, so you can drive around to your little Susquehanna towns and deliver your bags of gold. Then you gotta come home and take a shower, sleep. It takes a lot of energy to be Susquehanna Santa.

Wolf typed on his phone. Swiped his screen, searching sites. There. Laurel View Realty, just outside Elkdale. He dialed the number and put the phone to his ear. After this call, he would find a real estate office in or around Halfordsville, and maybe a few of the other little towns that dotted the outskirts of the forest. Harry wouldn't have bought a place, but rented something. Condo maybe. Or some little shit rental up in the hills, so he could come and go without attracting attention. Harry had walked into a real estate office and signed an agreement, Wolf was sure. Harry existed, somebody's seen him, he's living right next to his forest.

Oh, am I going to enjoy the look on your face. Wolf had to laugh, because Harry and this gold thing was perfect. Because really, how could he have forced Harry to give him his share if the four million had been sitting in Vanguard or Schwab or some bank? But now it's in the form of gold. Whatever millions of it are left. It's untraceable gold, which is why Harry's doing it this way. Jesus, Harry. Now I can take it all. Because who knew you ever had it if it's untraceable? If it doesn't exist on any record? Whether the gold is in your pocket or mine, no one will ever know.

Thank you, Harry, for giving me back purpose in my life. Bless you. I've been floundering this last year. These endless divorces. These dull jobs. What a Wolf really wants to be is on the hunt.

Someone at Laurel View Realty answered Wolf's call.

"Hello there. How are you today?" Wolf said into the phone. "Listen, I'm calling because I'm interested in property around Elkdale. Do you have a minute to chat?"

28

Stu was beside himself. He stared beseechingly at the Susquehanna County map taped to his wall. Elkdale. Halfordsville. Those crummy little burgs — New Milford, where he lived, was only twenty miles away from either of them. You notice that, Susquehanna Santa? Drop one of your damn bags on my doorstep, will ya? I'm in dire straits here, pal. The Good Ship Stu is going down.

Stu leaned his forehead against the map. "Please, Santa," he whispered. "Please, please, please."

This morning, Stu had come within a rat's whisker of losing his job. The ax about to fall — Mr. Bromler had set up a meeting — then a last-minute reprieve: Mr. Bromler's mother died. Mr. Bromler was a mama's boy. Ate dinner with her every Sunday. Took her on vacations. This was a guy with a wife and three grown children. How many times had Mr. Bromler rushed out of the office to change a light bulb for the old lady? Mama always came first.

Well, she certainly was first in Stu's book. Thank you, Mama Bromler, for dropping dead so fortuitously! So, granted a few days' reprieve, how best to take advantage of it? Nabbing Amanda Jeffers's house would've been a coup. But he needed something spectacular, now. A showstopper. He needed Pratt Public Library.

Town Council, of which Stu was president, had endured ten years of Olive's pleas. They were hoping she'd die or something, because even though the building was a hazard and an eyesore, the softies on council felt like they'd be stealing Olive's home out from under her if they closed Pratt's doors. Who wants to torment an old lady? the other six council members said.

But she already has a perfectly nice home, Stu argued. And she's a volunteer. It's not like we're sacking her. Who goes into that library, anyway? When's the last time one of you even walked through the doors? Never. You know why? Because you're afraid if you yank on the door handle the whole building will cave in on you.

Ronnie's in there sprucing it up, one of them said.

Ronnie, Stu said. Ronnie is the death knell. If you got Ronnie Wilmarth sprucing you up, you're beyond terminal. It don't need sprucing up — it needs tearing down.

It just seems mean, they stammered, as Stu fumed. Let's see how it plays out. She's an old lady, jeez, Stu.

Whoa, hey, he wasn't looking to torment her. He didn't have anything against Olive Perkins personally, he told them, but the library was in the way of downtown development. It was on a primo lot. You put a Dunkin' Donuts on that lot and, hell, the whole town turns around. Dunkin' Donuts, and before you know it, Chick-fil-A will be clamoring to get in here, and bam, New Milford's a destination. A place people come, not just pass through to get to Scranton. New Milford was one Burger King away from becoming the next Scranton, don't you people have any vision?

As for Stu's vision? Stu, the town booster? What he was *really* trying to boost? His career. More people in New Milford, more houses to sell. Action, baby. Because selling real estate, which he was crummy at, was the only thing he did well.

Stu glared at the map. Tapped New Milford with his finger, like God should do to Pratt Library. Give it a good, hard tap, knock it down. Okay, he thought, so I'm just going to nudge Olive a little, loosen her up so she volunteers to quit the place, you know? We're not talking about tasing a geriatric. I'll just throw a few civilized elbows her way. Like I did with Amanda. Which was going great, until, you know, it didn't.

It was a dumb move to go after Amanda. You don't go after the young and healthy. You cull the weak.

And Olive was feeling weak. Weak and overwhelmed. The return of *The Grum's Ledger* had unsettled her. And, oh my, the state of Pratt Library. Ronnie, he was a good man, trying so hard. Fixing and patching as fast he was able. But it was a losing battle. He'd just tried to reinforce a beam above the bound periodicals, and a chunk of ceiling the size of a refrigerator had come down on him. He was shaking, he was so apologetic.

"Miss Perkins, termites just made the wood too soft. I tried to slip in a ridge splint, but it didn't hold."

They were standing there, staring up into the gaping hole, the dust of a hundred years swirling around them, when Stu Giptner walked in the front door with the county building inspector, Jerry Palco.

Olive had always believed that Death, when he came for her, would enter through the front doors of Pratt Library. And now, here he was, Death in the guise of a wormy real estate agent puffed up with the authority of a town council president. But it was not her own death that was imminent (though she would've gladly switched places), but her beloved library's.

Stu and Jerry were wearing hard hats. Stu's idea. Intimidating. Jerry had a pair of them in his trunk, since in his official capacity he checked a lot of buildings and new construction. Stu rolled his shoulders as he approached Olive and Ronnie.

Jerry didn't much like Stu, but he did like a deal. The deal was that Jerry lower the boom on Pratt Library, and for a minor kickback, Stu, as council president, steer the lot Jerry's way. Jerry was telling Stu, yeah, definitely, a Dunkin' Donuts, donuts being Stu's weakness, but he was thinking, Qdoba, Mexican food being Jerry's weakness. Jerry imagined free soft corn tacos for the rest of his life. And Jerry was visionary in a way Stu was not. America was changing, and it was about time the Endless Mountains region caught up. Donuts and chicken *out,* taco and tomatillo red-chile salsa *in.*

Stu was almost giggling with pleasure as he surveyed the jagged hole in the ceiling. He wasn't going to need to hire a demolition crew to knock this place down — Ronnie was doing it all by his lonesome. Stu eyed Olive, covered with so much dust she looked like she'd been dipped in flour.

Flustered, Olive did her best imitation of her feisty self. "I know what you're thinking, and you're thinking wrong, Stu Giptner. And your muscle here —" she shot Jerry Palco a withering look "— doesn't scare me one iota."

"Not here to scare you, Olive," Stu said. "We're here to keep you safe."

"He's got a point, Olive," Jerry said. "I'm very concerned. Very, very concerned about the structural integrity here."

Olive went up on her toes. "Oh, such integrity. It's just radiating off you scoundrels."

"That dust could have asbestos in it, Olive," Stu said.

Olive raised her dusty palm and blew it in Stu's face.

He leaped back from her. "Hey! Hey, no call for that."

"As if you haven't sold a hundred places, brimming with asbestos, and God knows what all. You and your as-is properties."

He wished he *had* sold a hundred places. Olive gave him too much credit. Sure, he'd sold a few with asbestos. His biggest coup, though, two years ago, was selling to a pushy Canadian a place that was venting enough radon to fuel a nuclear power plant.

"Jerry, ready to start your inspection?" Stu looked at Olive as he said this, meaning: You want to give in now, or you want to drag out the inevitable?

Stu raised his clipboard. He'd play personal assistant, writing down the violations as Jerry did his walk-through.

A sudden rumble in the flooring. Stu clutched Jerry's arm. The bookshelves in nonfiction shuddered.

Ronnie shuddered, too. Because he knew exactly what it was. Down in the basement — this morning he'd jammed a floor jack under a joist. Even fully extended, the jack didn't quite reach, but instead of using a proper wood shim, Ronnie slid two books in to fill the gap. It was meant to be temporary, while he dealt with a leaky pipe next to the furnace.

A bookshelf teetered.

"Oh!" cried Olive, rushing forward. Ronnie held her back.

The shelf tipped and fell. Slammed into

the shelf across the aisle. Five shelves went down in a crash of metal and wood. Boom, boom, boom, boom, boom, the noise reverberating like cannon fire off the marble walls of the library. Books flying everywhere.

Stu clasped his hands together in delight. "Dominoes!" He loved to topple dominoes. Actually, other kids' dominoes. But *this* — books splattered and splayed on the linoleum like birds shot out of the sky, some of them still twitching and settling — was divinely thrilling.

Olive almost fainted with despair. They sat her down in her chair behind the circulation desk. Stu patted her shoulder. She was too dazed to push his hand away.

Ronnie took Jerry aside. "Don't let him do this, Jerry. Two weeks is all I'm asking."

"What could you do in two weeks?"

"I'll get her up and running."

"Up and running? What you need to do, Ronnie, is run for your life. Really. This place is a hazard. Stu's a jerk and an eager beaver, but he's right on this one. It's time to close the doors."

They left, Stu practically clicking his heels on the way out. Olive, who had been holding back, burst into tears. Ronnie enfolded her in his arms. She was tiny as a hummingbird. He could feel her heart thrumming against the thin bones of her chest. If it beat any faster, it would burst.

"Don't cry, Olive. We'll get those bookshelves up in a jiffy. It's just a sag in the floor."

She could not be consoled.

Think, Ronnie, think, he commanded himself. You got to distract her before she has a heart attack. Should he take her home? What should he do?

He looked around the library. Plaster and splintered wood everywhere, fallen bookshelves, holes in the ceiling. He wasn't saving the place, he was wrecking it. He almost started to cry, too. Nothing he did ever came out right. He had failed Dean. Failed Olive. Failed Oriana. I don't know what to do for anybody.

Holding Olive, looking around at the dusty chaos of the library, Ronnie's eyes fixed on a far corner, where a beam of light from a high leaded window shined down on an old overstuffed chair. The Reading Corner, where legions of enthralled children had once sat as Olive read stories to them. Ronnie had been one of those children. She had taken him to so many magical places.

And then it dawned on him. There might be a way to distract her from her sorrow.

"What are you doing?" Olive murmured

vaguely from the depths of her misery.

Ronnie scooped her up and carried her the length of the library, toward the long-unused Reading Corner, his work boots echoing on the hard linoleum. He put her in the chair, like a servant depositing the infirm queen upon her throne.

Its effect was immediate, the power and the majesty of the throne strengthening the will. Olive roused and straightened. She looked around.

Ronnie stood humbly before her. "Miss Perkins, please, ma'am, will you read me a story?"

A brightness came into her eyes.

She smoothed her hair, flexed her spine and shoulders, cleared her throat. As she had directed so many children over the decades, she now directed Ronnie. "Of course I will, sweetheart. Go fetch a book."

She sat erect on her throne. I will never abandon my post, she said to herself. This library will never close. Go get your book, Ronnie Wilmarth. Together, we will hold the fort. We are not the sole survivors. There are others like us. All those who once were children, scattered now in the hills of the Endless Mountains, they will hear my voice, and they will come to the rescue of Pratt Public Library.

Kneeling in an aisle, Ronnie chose his book. It was one Ronnie had secretly read a dozen times, spellbound. That day he watched Miss Perkins hide it in the stacks — such a strange thing to do, and then, he decided, a very Miss Perkins sort of thing to do. A kind of game to entice a reader. A special book, a treat for him to find. And what a book it was. *The Grum's Ledger.* The grum, so sad. But then miraculously, the grum does the right thing and digs his lost love out from under all that gold.

Ronnie stood before Olive, grinning ear to ear, holding the book behind his back. "It's the saddest and happiest book I ever read, Miss Perkins," Ronnie said, placing *The Grum's Ledger* in her hands.

Olive clutched the book to her heart. The color drained from her face, and her eyes rolled.

For a horrified moment, Ronnie thought he'd killed her. And then her lips moved. She was whispering something. Ronnie leaned close.

"Grum," she whispered. "Grum, grum."

"Miss Perkins?"

She opened her eyes. The look in them, infinitely sad. She opened *The Grum's Ledger.* Stared at the grum. And the grum, atop his pile of gold, stared at Olive. The look in *his* eyes, infinitely sad. "I loved you," she whispered to the grum. "With all my heart, I loved you."

Astonished, Ronnie dropped to his knees on the rug in front of Olive's chair.

She raised her eyes from the book and looked at Ronnie, and gave a great sigh. "I need to tell you a story, Ronnie. A real story. Will you please, please hear it? I need to tell someone the most important story of my life." She reached out and touched his face. "It's very short, and you already know how it ends."

"I don't quite follow." In fact, he didn't follow at all.

"It ends with a library crashing down around an old woman named Olive Perkins."

Oh my Lord. "No ma'am," he said. "I won't let that happen."

"Sweet Ronnie. You are strong and wonderful and kind. That's the part you play in the story. My faithful knight and guardian."

Frankly, the look in her eyes, the dreamy sadness of her words — it was scaring the pants off Ronnie.

Olive began her story. "Several weeks ago," she said, "I received in the mail a large envelope. *The Grum's Ledger* was inside, and a letter from a lawyer. And I quote: 'As per the instructions of Alexander Grum, who died on January 4, 2017, in Fair Acres Assisted Living Facility, in Delphine, Colorado, enclosed please find *The Grum's Ledger.*' "

"The grum's name is Alexander?" Ronnie said, utterly baffled.

"No, dear. The grum was a real person. Alexander Grum. He was real. Just as I was once real. If our pasts are ever real."

Olive rose from the chair and led him by the hand to the bound periodicals, scattered now on the floor. She tapped one with her foot. "That one. Pick it up for me, dear. It's heavy." Ronnie picked it up. *"The Olde Scrantonian,"* Olive said. "A society journal, long defunct. Turn to Volume 38, April 1951, page 32."

Ronnie found the page. A group of photos from Scranton high society, in the flush years when coal and lumber money had made men rich. Grand houses, parties, boat rides on the Susquehanna, Christmas balls. Olive tapped a small photo on the lower left. A young man in a tuxedo, the caption under it, "Alexander Grum."

There he was. And there it was in writing: Grum, not grum. There was a sweetness in his face, but a vulnerability, a weakness in his eyes.

"Look at the paper on that page," Olive said. "Puckered and wrinkled. From my tears, sweetheart. It's the only picture I had of him, and over the years, I looked at it often."

My tears, sweetheart. Ronnie thought: Alexander Grum, you made Miss Perkins cry. Ronnie bristled protectively.

"Drop it back on the floor, Ronnie. He deserves to be dropped with a thud." The bitterness in her voice, blending with a depthless melancholy.

Now she led Ronnie to a small, oak-paneled alcove at the very back of the library. On the wall were fading photographs of library committee chairmen, book sales and, most importantly, five head librarians dating back to 1906. The last in the succession, dated 1959, was a pretty young woman wearing glasses.

"That's you," said Ronnie. He peered intently at the young girl's face. "The tortoiseshell glasses!" he gasped.

In anticipation of his discovery, Olive had already opened *The Grum's Ledger* to the last page. She read, " 'Casting away the last of the gold in great heaps and hurls, the grum uncovered another treasure, his first and truest, which he had lost long ago — a beautiful young woman with chestnut hair and tortoiseshell glasses.' "

Olive smiled wistfully, patting her thin, gray hair. "I did have rather nice hair."

"Where are the glasses?" Ronnie said. Her current ones were nondescript wire-rims.

"Broken and thrown away, long ago. The glasses, my youthful abundant hair, all of it the memory-dream of an old man dying in a nursing home. Alexander Grum was real. And he turned our story into a fairy tale. I recognize, even in these shaky letters —" she held the handwritten book out for Ronnie to see "— the same hand that composed secret love letters to me, long, long ago. The same hand that once placed a diamond ring on my finger."

"You were *married,* Miss Perkins?"

"Jilted, Ronnie. Rings slide off as easily as they slide on."

"But *The Grum's Ledger* is a love story."

"It's a remorse story." She softened. "But yes, there was love. We met by chance, in the dining car of a train, bound for Scranton. I was coming home after visiting an aunt in New York City. We talked. He charmed me. I flirted. Didn't even know I knew how to flirt. We fell in love. He would come here, to New Milford, in his big car. We would meet secretly in the moonlit forest."

"Secretly," Ronnie said.

"The word is poisonous," Olive said. "It sounds like a word whispered by a serpent. 'We have to keep it a *secret,*' Alexander would say. 'Until we tell the world.' By which he meant his parents' world. The world of money. I had none. No secret there."

"But he loved you." Ronnie saw it so clearly. Handsome Alexander and beautiful Olive in her tortoiseshell glasses, strolling hand in hand in the forest.

"Not enough to overcome his fear," Olive said. "He abandoned me for money and tradition. That's the remorse of the grum."

"But *The Grum's Ledger* ends happily," Ronnie said.

"An utter fairy tale. Alexander Grum died in a nursing home, alone and penniless. I Googled him. On that irritating but handy machine." She pointed to the single library computer in the cubicle beside the circulation desk. "He'd moved west. Married. The family business collapsed in the 1980s — they'd gone from Pennsylvania coal to Colorado copper ore. To nothing. Lawsuits, children squabbling, divorce. A dreadful, selfish story of money, money, money."

Ronnie pointed to the illustration in *The*

Grum's Ledger. "There he is. On top of his gold."

She tilted her head back and shouted to the heavens. "And you regretted it, Alexander!" Her voice echoing off the walls. *Regret, regret, regret.*

Her eyes brimmed, but her jaw was set. "But I found happiness, Ronnie. I did. I found a life that otherwise I might never have had. It was the 1950s. If I'd married him, I would never have had a career. I would never have had Pratt Public Library. The children and my books. The readers. They were my family."

"You did wonderful, Miss Perkins."

Her voice dropped to a whisper. Her sigh was the sigh of a young girl. "But I would like to have been loved. Openly and proudly loved, and not abandoned in the forest."

Ronnie drew her close. "And that's what he wanted, too. It's in the fairy tale. He loved you all his life."

"But what's gained, sweetheart, that he's telling me this now? Sending me a fairy tale from beyond the grave? What good has come of *The Grum's Ledger*?"

Ronnie had no answer. All he could do was hold the old librarian close. And all she could do was hold a book to her heart.

■ ■ ■ ■

When you're on a roll, baby, you're really on a roll.

I mean, Stu couldn't believe it. When he went back to the office after his beautifully successful encounter with Olive — oh, she was going down, baby, and Pratt Library with her — his phone rang. His phone never rang. And Jesus, this guy sounded serious. He was looking to buy land abutting the forest. Something *special.* And he wanted to know how hot the market was. Have people been renting or buying in the area? Wanted to come in and discuss it.

I mean, this guy sounded like a mover and a shaker. Stu had never heard such adrenaline in a voice. A real player. When Stu asked him his name he said, "Let's just keep names out of this for the time being."

Stu practically fainted with that one. He loved it. Was this going to be a cash deal? What the hell was going on here? Like the guy was fronting for the Russian mob or something.

I'm making deals left and right. I'm in the zone. Pratt Library, this big fish on the phone. A big fish who makes things happen. Well, so am I. I'm the guy who makes things happen, too. Because the property next to the forest I got for you, Mr. Mysterioso? How would you like a hand-hewn, deluxe log cabin estate?

Moving and a-shaking. Rocking and a-rolling. Smirking and a-smiling. Stu picked up the phone and called Steve Jones over at Susquehanna Mortgage & Loan.

"Stevie boy! Stu Giptner. I need you to do a little tappity-tap on your keyboard for me. It's time to advance that little mutually beneficial matter we talked about."

Because, Amanda: when you take a swing at Supreme Realtor Stu Giptner, he takes a swing back. God, was Stu feeling all-powerful. He saw himself sitting on Amanda's back deck, a few months from now, knocking back icy shots of vodka with his new Russian friends. And then afterward, tipsy, they'd all go down to the shiny new Dunkin' Donuts sitting right in the middle of where Pratt Library used to be.

29

Midnight. Amanda, wired and distraught, sat at the computer in the alcove off the kitchen. Oriana was asleep upstairs in her bedroom. The house was whisper quiet. The only sound, or it felt like a sound, anyway, was the anxious throb of Amanda's heartbeat. She was going through her finances because Stu Giptner had truly nailed it. She was out of money. Close to it, anyway. Savings account down to nine hundred dollars. And half of that was thanks to Harry and his tree house rent money.

Stu had more than nailed it. She stared at the email from Steve Jones, the bastard down at the savings and loan. Stu's bastard.

Dear Valued Client:

This letter is a formal notification that you are in default of your obligation to make payments on your home equity loan, account #382W904. Per our rec-

> ords, you failed to pay your home equity loan, $265.09, for three consecutive months. We intend, therefore, to initiate preliminary foreclosure proceedings.

The words on the screen went in and out of focus.

Because it wasn't just the bank loan that she hadn't paid. She was behind on her oil bill, her electric, and come June 1, three weeks, she'd be hit by the real estate and school taxes. Why had she allowed things to get this far?

Because she'd been in a damn daze. This year without Dean, she'd been so into survival mode — living, breathing, working, struggling with Oriana — she hadn't kept her eye on lesser things that weren't lesser things at all. Like paying your bills on time. She'd been living day to day, week to week. And let's face it, paycheck to paycheck. That her financial humiliation would come in the form of Stu Giptner was almost too much to bear.

She heard a skittering in Oriana's bedroom. She leaned back in her chair and looked up at the ceiling. "Oriana?"

A faint voice, in reply. "Yes."

"What's up?"

"Going to the bathroom."

Stupidly — she was not just financially negligent but parentally, too — she'd let Oriana have a Cherry Coke Zero at dinner. Why do I even have Cherry Coke Zero in this house? What's wrong with me?

"You okay?" said Amanda. Please say yes, because I can't deal with no.

"Yes."

Amanda sighed, stared at the computer again, the rows of ugly numbers. Nothing uglier than debt. Except goddamn foreclosure. She didn't want to stare at numbers. She wanted to go to the tree house. Wouldn't that be nice? To go to the tree house and sit on the deck with Harry and listen to him talk about trees on this moonlit night. Something about the way he talked about trees, a sort of sensible poetry to it. And she didn't even *like* poetry. She turned and looked into the kitchen. The window above the sink. The window to the forest. She couldn't see the tree house, but he was out there. Was he looking this way, toward her house? Was he thinking, possibly, of how nice it would be to sit with Amanda watching the moon silhouette the trees?

Amanda, she said to herself, you're thinking about Harry. *Thinking* about him, you know?

All right, okay, so what? She was openly

thinking about Harry. But what's the *deal* here? He wasn't like Dean or Cliff, the kind of guy that was in her native blood. She couldn't even put her finger on what kind of guy Harry was, exactly. He seemed to be constantly changing before her eyes. He was kind of ridiculous and kind of brave. Ridiculous enough to live in a tree house. Brave enough to climb to the top of the tallest tree in the forest. To not throw a punch. To put aside his own tangled grief and allow Oriana, in her grief, to reach out to him.

The question is, Amanda thought, am I brave enough to do anything about him? And what do I want to do? Is this because he's nice to Oriana? Am I grateful, or am I attracted?

I'm attracted.

Okay, all right. But am I attracted because he's so refreshingly not attracted to me? Except he is attracted to me. Because the few times I have dared to touch him, he has closed his eyes, as if in prayer.

Whoa. Heavy thoughts here, Amanda. Poetic thoughts. It's midnight, you're tired, you're swimming in deep waters. But.

This widow, widower thing. This protective wall we've put between us. What are we walling in or walling out? And it *was* a wall, where she'd first met Harry. That first day, the sugar maple, the stone wall. She remembered the sight of him, rising into view, the stone wall between them. And did the wall stop her that day? No. When he started to pass out, she caught him. She vaulted the wall and took hold of him. From the very start, her instinct was to hold him.

And then Amanda took a swim in deep waters. What would it be like to kiss Harry? To move forward, like it was so obviously time to do. Did he know how to kiss? Really know how?

Plink.

A sound from above, bringing Amanda back to earth. Oriana in her bedroom, dropping something on her floor. Please just go to bed, Amanda thought. Don't make me come up. She stared at the computer staring back at her. The foreclosure letter throbbing on the overbright screen like a migraine. The overdue bills. She clicked helplessly back and forth in the mire of bad news. She couldn't take it anymore, so she did what everybody does when faced with an insurmountable and unpleasant task on the computer — she began to surf the internet. She typed the word on the keyboard without really knowing she was doing it. S-A-N-T-A.

Absentmindedly, you gorge on Amazon or

Netflix or Spotify, or you Google something just to Google it. *Brownies. Mercedes Benz. Snow boots. Ten Hottest Vacation Spots.* Amanda's tired brain, craving relief from bad financial mojo, wanted to believe in Santa for a moment or two. She clicked.

Boom, a million links to "Susquehanna Santa" came up. Amanda leaned into the screen, reading. Then she wanted to see it, see a photograph of one of those bags of gold that had landed in Elkdale and Halfordsville. Her fingers on the keyboard. G-O-L-D.

As she typed, the search bar auto-filled. And she stopped. Like any parent would. You check to see what sites your kid is visiting. Look at all these sites coming up for "gold," Amanda thought. Those are all Oriana's, not mine. It was odd. Oriana not talking about gold very much, but she had read tons about it.

And odder still, the gold searches were all variations on: how to buy gold. Where you buy it, how you buy it, the legalities of gold ownership. Amanda clicked left and scrolled down the search history. A little prickle of electricity went up her spine when she looked at the dates. It wasn't her intent to spy on her child. She was simply interested. Then she was very interested. And then she spied. Because those first dates, when Oriana was checking out gold . . .

A little anxious now, Amanda typed in: "Elkdale first bag of gold." Susquehanna Santa handed out the first bag seven days ago, April 27. But Oriana had typed: "Can anyone buy gold coins?" on April 8. A few weeks before the gold landed in Elkdale, Oriana was researching gold. Gold *coins.*

Amanda leaned back in her chair and hugged herself. Stared at the ceiling. Stared at the screen again. Oriana's searches weren't idle. She didn't type in "fairy tale gold" or "gold ring" or anything childlike. What she had typed was businesslike. Full of intent. Something more than curiosity. Was her daughter psychic? Amanda swallowed. I am not the parent of a psychic child. What *am* I the parent of?

Plink. Oriana in her bedroom. Something falling onto a floorboard, rolling, settling.

More than a prickle shot up Amanda's spine. She was up and out of the chair in an instant, her feet silent on the stairs. She knew how to move in stealth. How often had she been at Dean's side as he stalked deer or bird-watched? She reached the second-floor landing, crept down the hallway toward Oriana's closed bedroom door. A furtive shadow passed back and forth in the light under the door. Oriana scurrying like a creature in the underbrush.

Amanda put her hand on the doorknob. And pounced.

Oriana was on her hands and knees, reaching under her bed, her hand touching what she had dropped. She brought it into the light just as her mother burst into the room. Oriana yelped and tried to hide the object in her hand. But it was like trying to hide the sun.

Blinded by the magnitude of what she saw, Amanda thought for a disoriented moment that she had stepped into a fairy tale. That her daughter was not from this world, but some other. What was this being, clutching in her hand a large golden coin? A princess, an elf? What lair had Amanda stumbled upon? What magic was happening in this room? What was happening here, what?

"What — ?" The overwhelming question voiced in a garbling panic.

Oriana had never heard her mother make such a sound. Or seen such a look on her face. Confusion. Fear. Oriana stepped forward, holding the coin out to her. Her mother shrank back.

"It's just gold," Oriana cried.

Amanda breathing out of her mouth, staring.

"It's just one," Oriana said. "I'll put it back."

And were those words a comfort? No, they were not. "Put it back . . . where?" Amanda whispered.

Oriana burst into tears. She pushed the coin into her mother's hand, and wrapped herself around her. The coin was as heavy as a planet. Amanda stared at it, as she clutched her child to her. She held her tight, as if to protect her from the gold. That was her instinct. This gold is a danger and I must protect my child. Amanda worked to return to herself. To her parent self, to her nurse self, to the person who knew how to deal with chaos. She was the mother of a child who had somehow gotten herself into inexplicable trouble. She let Oriana sob for exactly one more minute, then uncoiled her, walked her across the room and sat her down on her desk chair.

Again, Amanda asked. "Put it back *where*?"

Between gulps and gasps, Oriana said, "It's Harry's. He's the grum."

Amanda gripped Oriana's desk, as the room tilted and swirled. She dropped the gold coin onto the desk as if it was poisonous. Because it was.

"What do you mean, 'it's Harry's'?"

"He's the grum."

Amanda gripped her daughter's shoulders. "What is that? What's a 'grum'?"

Gulp, gasp, sob. Amanda ran into Oriana's bathroom, unfurled a mile of toilet paper, flew back into the room, pressed it to her daughter's nose.

"Blow." Oriana blew, long and hard and messily.

"What's a grum? What is this gold? Oriana, tell me what's going on!"

"The Grum's Ledger." And then the fairy tale came tumbling out of her. The whole, nightmarish fairy tale. It took time. A lot of shouting. And the rest of the roll of toilet paper. Because between the two of them, there were a lot of tears.

Amanda blew her nose, angrily tossed the wad to the floor. Then picked it up and put it in the wastebasket, because she was a nurse and used Kleenexes were germ bombs.

Harry Crane was the grum. Harry Crane was Susquehanna Santa. Harry Crane was everything but the dull bureaucrat he was supposed to be. Harry, who was supposed to bring Oriana back to earth, had instead pulled her into another world. For a year, her daughter had wandered in the forest. And then it ended. With the arrival of Harry

Crane, it ended. That was the truth his sudden arrival promised. *Harry will save my daughter.* And it was a lie. He did nothing of the kind. He betrayed me. Like an ogre — like a grum — he pulled Oriana even deeper into the forest.

There was too much to process here, and it made so little sense. How much of what Oriana had told her was true and how much was just batshit crazy? What was the truth, what was a fairy tale, and what the hell was going on in a world where a forestry bureaucrat lands in my backyard and hands out four million dollars in gold? That was their plan. That's what he was doing right now. Or was about to do.

Amanda looked out Oriana's window into the deep of the forest. Was he out there, or had he already left on his Santa rounds?

Amanda reeled around the room. All she knew for certain was that she was going to put an end to Harry Crane. Now. She was going to find him. And what — turn him over to the state police? Drag him to the quarry and throw him off the edge? Toss his bags of gold after him?

She was going to find him, now.

"He's not there, Mom. He's gone."

Her daughter privy to Harry's every move. It weakened Amanda's knees. Her scheming daughter and her scheming grum. Amanda calmed herself, so that she could calmly find out from her scheming daughter where she might find Harry, so she might calmly wring his neck.

"Where has he gone?"

"It's after midnight. He's handing out bag three."

Deep breath. "Bag three. And now tell me, because I know you know —" Amanda leaning in, speaking slowly "— where exactly will our grum be handing out bag three?"

Oriana, who was a very bright girl capable of outfoxing adults, knew she had better not outfox this one. She began to sniffle again, because she hated to give up Harry, but she also hated that she had lied to her mother. "I did this for Daddy, I did this for him."

Wingèd Dean, the red-tailed hawk. Do not be moved, Amanda. Your child's welfare is at stake. "Now do something for Mommy, Oriana. Who gets bag three?"

"Somebody in Wynefield."

Wynefield. The next town over. Four miles east. "How does he choose the house?"

"There'll be a tree," Oriana said. "And he'll know."

Of course, Amanda thought. The tree man.

"Let me come," Oriana pleaded.

"No." Amanda would absolutely not allow her to become further entangled. Tonight was the great untangling. "You stay right here. You know the drill."

The drill was this. She and Oriana had to make their way through the wilderness of life. Sometimes, Amanda had to leave Oriana alone. Oriana was a latchkey kid. Tough enough to stay in a house alone. Tough enough to explore the forest alone. Of necessity, independent, self-reliant, able to fend for herself. Fending for herself, Amanda thought in bitter amazement, Oriana found a grum in the forest and cooked up a plan to hand out millions in gold.

Holy mother of God. You teach a kid to be independent, and they step through a door into a state of independence you never dreamed possible. Through sheer force of will, Oriana had brought a fairy tale to life.

Amanda jumped in her truck and sped grimly into the night. Oriana stood watching at the upstairs window. She was as forlorn as Rapunzel, imprisoned in her tower.

Ten minutes later, roaring into the sleeping town of Wynefield, Amanda was dead certain that fairy tales were disruptive nonsense, introducing into the brains of children the harmful hope that magic exists in the world. What she wanted Oriana to know was that life was hard, life was real. Fathers and husbands sometimes die, houses can be foreclosed on, strangers who appear in the forest are there to undermine and betray you.

Life will never be smoothed over by magic, because magic does not exist. These were Amanda's unyielding and determined thoughts, as she turned the corner onto Lindmore Street, the last of seven streets down which she had careened in search of Harry Crane.

Alice through the Looking-Glass.

Dorothy in the Land of Oz.

Amanda on Lindmore Street.

When she saw it, Amanda almost crashed her pickup into a fire hydrant. In the front yard of the last house on Lindmore, caught in the high beams of her truck headlights — golden stars flying up toward the moon, crazy dazzling fireflies, the twirling lanterns of elves. There was no making sense of it. What was she seeing?

In the center of the shower of impossible golden light, two beings. One was Harry. The other, circling him, was a large black blur.

Harry had turned onto Lindmore Street five

minutes earlier.

When he first entered Wynefield, he saw SUSQUEHANNA SANTA PLEASE STOP HERE! signs on several front lawns. He avoided those houses. He remembered himself as a child on Christmas Eve, waiting up for Santa. How many Wynefieldians, young and old, were waiting up for Santa?

He had not scouted Wynefield beforehand, as he had Elkdale and Halfordsville. The gold deliveries would all be made in darkness now, after midnight. Even in the dark it wasn't hard to find the best tree. It was not always the tallest or the grandest, but the one that truly belonged to a house. A sort of dream pairing. The tree had to be the kind a child might climb. That Harry himself might climb.

In Wynefield, the perfect tree was a towering white oak in the front yard of the last house on Lindmore Street, where the paved road gave way to gravel. In rural small towns, paved streets often end as gravel roads that snake off into the countryside, through woods or past farmland.

Harry didn't like back roads. Too easy to get lost. Or they turned into dead ends. Not good roads for making your escape.

It was a moonlit night, a few clouds. Light enough to see, dark enough to obscure. The moon would be approaching full for another week. But he didn't need a week. His plan was to hand out one bag a night for the next four nights. Tonight's bag, and tomorrow's, numbers three and four, were the small ones — if $300,000 could be called small. The final two bags would be the big boys, over a million each. The relief that would come when he got rid of all the gold: mission accomplished, the adventure achieved, the permanent smile that would affix itself to Oriana's soul.

Through Harry, Dean Jeffers performing great and otherworldly magic. This was a fine thing, Harry thought, this was a good thing. And no Wolf! This was a perfect thing! The grum, back on his shelf in the library, maybe even he'd crack a smile. Why wouldn't he? At the end of his story, he uncovers his great love.

A compelling idea. Dig deep enough and you find love.

And what would Harry uncover when the last of his gold was plinked away? He was not in love with Amanda, not even romantically involved — despite Oriana hoping it, Olive Perkins at the stone wall alluding to it, the guys at Green Gables thinking it. He was not involved but he was intertwined. He was very thankful he had landed in her world. He allowed himself this. That it was a fine thing, a good thing, to be in Amanda's world. There was no one for him but Beth, of course. But he needed to be with Amanda. She was the perfect woman for this moment. They were in the same exclusive club, The Year One Club, and she understood the liberating rules of membership — that it brought them just close enough. He could let go of Beth just enough to allow a little bit of Amanda.

He would miss her when this was over. He would miss the tree house, and Oriana, and he would miss Amanda. The way she loved and understood the natural world. Her resilience, her guidance of Oriana, her tough kindness, her amused tolerance of him. Increasingly, he counted on seeing her light at the end of each day. The sound of the wind through the trees, the owls hooting in the dark, the spring peepers chirping like crickets, the distant beckoning light of Amanda's bedroom.

Beckoning? Bedroom? Harry steadied himself. A comforting light, not a light that beckons. Like the moon is a comforting light. Keep your mind on the mission. Are you nuts, Susquehanna Santa? Focus.

He fixed on the white oak. Perfect tree. He fixed on the house. Dark and quiet, plenty of bushes to shield his movements. Excellent conditions for a surreptitious delivery. He felt a kind of lightness, in himself and in the bag of gold as he hoisted it off the passenger's seat of his car. A moonlightness.

He gripped the rough burlap and hoisted the bag over his shoulder — yes, yes, like Santa. A child peeping out a window (hope not!) into the moonlight might think that. Santa! But a slender Santa, dressed all in black, intent on absolute silence, devoid of ho-ho-ho. Harry moved like a cat, the three hundred coins in the bag as noiseless as a sack of marshmallows.

He shouldn't have moved like a cat.

For the dog that patrolled the half acre of yard that surrounded this little house on Lindmore, a 120-pound Rottweiler named Brutus, hated cats. He patrolled the yard all night long, staying well within the boundaries of the invisible dog fence (because what he hated almost as much as cats was an electric jolt from the receiver box attached to the studded collar that circled his muscular neck). Brutus's favorite spot was the base of the white oak tree, the trunk so wide that Harry failed to sense the massive presence tensing on the other side of it.

Brutus watched Harry. Friend or foe? He

huffed very quietly, which was the Rottweiler way of chuckling. Oh, that's right — he had no friends. Everyone on the planet was foe. Especially strangers moving catlike after midnight. Brutus stood. Flexed his paws like a thug cracking his knuckles.

Halfway up the front walk, Harry stopped. Was it a shift in the wind? The whisper of a curtain parting at a window? The sound of an approaching car? Something indiscernible stopped him. He looked over his shoulder.

Brutus lunged, barklessly. To make him even more lethal, his owner had had a veterinarian remove Brutus's vocal cords, his bite now infinitely worse than his bark. Brutus missiled toward Harry at fifty miles per hour, which was also the speed of the pickup truck, veering into view around the corner, headlights blazing. The headlights made Brutus's fur gleam like a black leather jacket. Maybe it *was* a leather jacket. Brutus, a leather-clad, stud-collared, killing machine.

That was Harry's first thought when he saw Brutus hurtling toward him. *I'm going to die!* His second thought: *My, what big teeth you have!*

Harry attempted to run. Brutus hit him from behind, knocking him to the ground.

The dog's mighty jaws clamped down on the burlap bag slung over Harry's left shoulder. Brutus thought he had torn off a chunk of Harry's back. In a frenzy of blood-lust, he circled Harry, shaking the bag maniacally. Harry jumped to his feet.

Brutus shook the bag of gold with the awesome power of a great white shark. Coins rocketed into the air like fireworks, lit up by the moon and the headlights of an approaching truck.

Harry was no stranger to dogs rending bags asunder. Sometimes dogs spread ashes. Sometimes they spread gold. Perhaps it was the reason dogs had been invented — to add spectacular craziness to the world.

Harry was not stricken with despair, as he had been a year ago. This time, it seemed perfect. Dog running around insanely with a bag of gold. Why the hell not? Harry lived in the forest now. He had climbed a very tall tree. He had millions of dollars hidden in a quarry. Life was an adventure!

The truck powering toward him, however, was another matter. He ran for his car. He had left the door open and the engine running. He jumped in and gunned it down Lindmore Street. The pickup truck tore after him.

Harry bounced up the dirt road into the

night-black hills. The halogens reflecting in his rearview mirror were blindingly bright. It was as if he were being pursued by a monster with twin suns for eyeballs. He twisted and turned his car, spraying dust and gravel. Was it the police? But there were no flashing lights, and it was a truck — a vehicle much better suited to this twisty road, and much more powerful than Harry's Camry.

Harry couldn't go any faster. The trees were tight on either side, and he was swerving in the slippery gravel, the truck so close now it felt like it was about to climb over the back of the car. The bumpy road bounced him around in his car, grew narrower, twistier. The guy in the truck honked and flashed his lights.

Suddenly, it cut to Harry's right, pushing parallel to Harry's car. The truck squeezed past. A sharp grating of metal, and then it was in front of him, slowing inexorably, weaving back and forth. It turned sharply and skidded to a stop, cutting Harry off in a spray of gravel.

Harry hit the brakes.

A woman jumped out of the truck. Amanda! In his headlights, she was a brightly lit avenging angel approaching in a swirl of dust. Her fist pounded down on the hood of his car like Thor's hammer.

"Get out of that car!"

Harry obeyed. He instinctively raised both hands in the air.

"Yeah, look at you, hands up like a criminal."

Harry cleared his throat. "Hi, Amanda."

"Because I should call the cops. Lurking around our woods. Getting Oriana involved in your. Your —"

"Adventure?" Harry offered. He carefully lowered his hands.

"Adventure." Amanda spat the word. "You think this is funny? You're an adult. Oriana's a kid. What were you thinking?"

He'd been thinking, for the last month, Hope Amanda never finds out. And now she had. "How — ?"

Amanda threw something at him. It bounced off his forehead. "Ow!" A gold coin lay in the dirt at his feet. He picked it up. Stared at it.

"Yeah. That's right. She stole gold from the crazy-ass son of a bitch living in the tree house."

Harry shook his head sadly as he continued to stare at the coin. "Oriana, Oriana. You stole a coin."

"Borrowed, she said. Just to play with, she said. You know how kids are. When they can't get hold of diamonds, they like to play with gold." Amanda was hugging herself so tightly, her nails dug into her arms.

Oh Oriana, Harry thought, brushing the dust from the coin. He felt the feathers of the golden eagle. And he understood. It was too tempting. And it meant so much to her. He held the coin out to Amanda. "She should have it."

Amanda slapped it out of his hand. She paced angrily back and forth, in and out of the headlights. "Hawks and candy bars. Grums and gold. How could you do this, Harry? How could you pull her in so deep?"

Deep. Did Amanda know the deepest thing of all? "Did she tell you I wasn't climbing the sugar maple that day? The day we all met? That I'd tried to hang myself? Did she tell you Dean saved my life?"

Amanda rushed forward and slapped him.

Harry bounced back against the hood of his car. Straightened. Looked her in the eye. "It's true. He saved my life, Amanda."

She slapped him again.

Again he straightened and stood before her. "He saved. My life."

"Stop it!" She raised her hand to slap him again. Harry braced for the blow. But her hand came to his cheek, slowly, and rested there. She looked into his eyes, searching.

"Why are you doing this?" she whispered.

"Her father, dying in a field. Someone so wonderful, Amanda, so powerful, suddenly vanishing from her life. There had to be a reason. A magnificent reason."

"And you're it."

"I'm it. And the gold is it. And the grum is it, and the forest, and Susquehanna Santa. It answers everything for her. A great big, magnificent, Dean-sized adventure."

Amanda hugged herself again and turned away. "You can't involve her in this. It's so over-the-top. It's so wild."

"She's safe at home. I'm the one running from Rottweilers."

"Harry, listen to yourself."

"I am, and isn't it amazing? Oriana brought *The Grum's Ledger* to life. I'm giving away *gold,* Amanda."

He turned her around. "You want to know how Dean really saved my life? He sent Oriana to me. And guided by her vast, incredible kid-wisdom, I'm doing this crazy, amazing thing. Me. Harry Crane. Bureaucrat. A guy who's never risked anything, never taken chances, is running around the countryside handing out gobs of gold."

Amanda shook her head. She removed his hand from her arm. "You know what's really crazy? That you tried to kill yourself. Why didn't you hold on, Harry? People hold on."

"Not if they do what I did." Harry looked into the night. "It was my fault Beth died."

Oriana, in her rushed account of the gold, had not told Amanda this. "How was it your fault?"

He took the tattered lottery ticket out of his wallet and placed it in Amanda's hand.

"I couldn't just quit my shitty job. What I needed was a little courage. A little trust that Beth and I would figure it out. Instead, I bought lottery tickets. She asked me not to buy this one. Just this once, don't do it, Harry."

Amanda stood very still.

Harry, in the headlights. "I told her to wait outside. I left her there, Amanda. In front of a construction fence. And I crossed the street, went inside the convenience store and bought that ticket. And a crane collapsed."

A long silence. "And there was an accident," Amanda said. Her voice, very quiet.

"A year later, I was awarded millions. That's the lottery I won."

And you bought a length of rope and climbed a tree, Amanda thought. And then Dean saved you. She was trembling.

"Harry," she said. "I trusted you. And you created a secret world with my daughter.

You led me to believe you were someone you weren't."

"Yes."

"Lied."

"How could we have asked your permission?"

"I would never have given it."

"But Dean did."

Amanda looked at Harry. For a long moment, just looked at him. "If you knew how that sounded."

What it sounded like was a miracle. Amanda allowed herself to connect the dots of a miraculous story. As a child might. Her child. She'd heard Oriana's words, but only half-understood them because she had refused to truly listen or believe. Amanda closed her eyes, and listened to the voice inside her recite a fairy tale:

Once upon a time, a grief-stricken man wandered into a deep forest and threw a rope over the limb of a sugar maple. At the moment of his death, he was saved by the glitter of gold in a knothole — a piece of candy placed there by a red-tailed hawk. The hawk had found it in the forest, where it had been left by a little girl who, in her wisdom, had filled the trees with candy. When the man reached for the golden candy, the limb broke, and he fell to the ground, where he found a magic book the girl had lost in the forest.

He returned the book to the girl. They read it together, and she helped him understand that life is an adventure you can't avoid. Do the very thing you cannot do, she told him.

He found the strength to climb the tallest tree in the forest. And like the grum, he began to throw his gold to the winds. When at last, against all odds, he cast away the very last coin, he was saved. And in saving himself, he saved the little girl.

Hand in hand, the man and the little girl walked out of their forest.

Amanda opened her eyes. And saw Harry. Astonishing Harry. He was doing the impossible for Oriana. And it was working. The crazy plan was working when nothing else in the last year had. He had unlocked Oriana's grief. And good Lord, Amanda, she told herself. The man is giving away millions of dollars in gold to complete strangers. There's no one in the world like him.

Watching the cascade of emotions flooding Amanda's face, Harry didn't know what to expect. He was prepared for anything. Except for the moment she suddenly reached out, pulled him close and kissed him.

The fairy tale she had told herself about Harry. So many of them end with a kiss. It was a worrisome thought, as she had stood there struggling over whether or not to risk it. Because what if Harry, though astonishing, couldn't kiss? Kissing well — very few men could do it.

She kissed him. And Harry kissed her back. Just the right amount of pressure. Just the right amount of heat. Parting his lips, just right, to meet the parting of her own. Harry smelled good. He tasted good. Harry could kiss.

He pushed away from her. Pale and shaken. Touched his lips.

The Year One Club, Amanda thought. She'd broken the rules. She looked at the ground, then at Harry. "I get it. Beth danced on water."

Harry started to touch her, but didn't. "All I'm allowed is the chance to help Oriana. That one, little, tiny sliver of redemption. But having you . . ."

Was impossible. The look on his face, sorrowful but resolute.

She reached out to him, but he drew back. "You're very, very hard on yourself, Harry Crane."

"Will you let us finish the gold?"

"I'm going to ground her, Harry. She has to be punished."

When Harry started to protest, she held

up her hand to quiet him.

"Not for Operation Grum. For that, you have my blessing."

"Then punish her for what?"

"That gold coin," Amanda said. "She *stole* from you, Harry."

He nodded. "You are one tough mother."

Amanda smiled. "You are one amazing grum."

She got into her truck and Harry followed behind. In the tree house, later, he waited until she turned out her light before he turned out his own.

30

Wolf had driven around Wilderness Tract A803 twice, just to get a feel for the thing, and a sense of the little towns that clung to its perimeter. The forest was thirty-eight-thousand acres. It took him two hours to drive around it, the roads generally crummy, the stoplights in the towns interminable. Why were there stoplights? Who would stop in these miserable towns, lost in the shadows of the rolling Endless Mountains?

And what really irritated him about these towns? All the greedy SUSQUEHANNA SANTA PLEASE STOP HERE! signs. You people think you're taking my gold? That you have some kind of right to it?

Well, they didn't have a right to it, but they were getting it. Harry was speeding up the process, as if he could tell I'd entered his domain. And this latest Santa drop, un-fuckinbelievable. Wolf was chewing angrily on a bad hamburger in a bad diner on the side of the road outside Elkdale.

"Now Rottweilers are getting my gold? *Rottweilers?*" Brutus the Rottweiler was instantly famous. Photos of him posing proudly with the torn burlap bag between his teeth had gone viral. Wolf stared into the dog's eyes and Brutus stared back. Wolf swiped the "Lucky Bastards" app away.

The question is, where is Harry's domicile within the domain? Wolf had spoken to an agent at Laurel View Realty, used a lot of teeth in his smile, big mesmerizing alpha teeth.

"Yes, we also rent properties," the agent said, quickly going through his listings. Wolf leaned over the agent's shoulder, staring into the screen. The agent felt Wolf's chin stubble brush against his cheek. He gave a little jump.

"No rentals in the last month?" Wolf said.

"Uh, no. You, uh, mentioned on the phone, though, that you were interested in buying a property. Isn't that what you said?"

"Is that what I said?"

The agent cleared his throat. "Yeah, well, maybe I just —"

"Misunderstood?" What am I doing? Wolf thought. Why am I intimidating this guy? Because it is my nature. Because time is running out. Because I am an endangered species. I have three arrows in my back, shot from the bows of three wives. I am the hunter of a dwindling sum. Wolf felt a sudden wild hunger.

"Need to eat some meat," he said. "Where might I do that?"

The agent stared up at Wolf. Meat? "You mean . . . like a hamburger?"

Wolf nodded. The agent gave him directions to a diner. There was a place closer, but the agent didn't want Wolf closer. He wanted Wolf farther.

Later, Wolf walked past Phil Bartek's house. He saw Phil standing next to his pal the state trooper, who was big like Wolf. I could take you, if I wanted, Wolf thought reflexively. Both of you at once. Except the state trooper has a gun on his hip. And Phil. What does he have? Phil has a brand-new Dodge Ram pickup. Bought with my gold. A little cocker spaniel came yapping across the lawn.

"Toodie," Phil yelled. "Come back here, girl."

"Not a problem," Wolf called back. Resisting the urge to punt the barking runt over the top of Phil's new truck. Wolf kept walking, feeling the state trooper's eyes on him.

He went to Halfordsville next. Talked to a woman realtor there. No need for teeth, just charm. She told him there was no recent rental activity.

"Bet things pick up with all the Santa fun," Wolf said.

"Actually, I've started to get a few calls."

"Well, it's a lucky place," Wolf said. Full of lucky bastards.

When he left the realtor, he swung down Ginger Thompson's street to have a look-see.

What he saw made him smile. The little bread crumbs, Harry, that only your big brother could see. There'd been one in front of Phil Bartek's house, too, it just hadn't quite clicked. Big, beautiful trees in both Phil's and Ginger's yards.

Really, Harry? You ever gonna let go of childhood? Naw, I guess we never do, huh? In the forest, have you hidden the rest of the gold at the base of a tree? Which was why there was no point in searching the forest. Harry's gotta guide me to it. I find you, Harry, and I follow you into the forest.

A pudgy woman came out of the house. Wolf recognized her from all the news photos. Ginger Thompson. Wolf sniffed the air as he drove past.

Francine came out the door behind Ginger. They both stared, heads moving in unison.

"Did you see that man?" Ginger said.

"He was sniffing the air," Francine said. "Like some sort of *animal.*"

"Ew," Ginger said.

"Well, you *do* smell good," Francine giggled.

"And so do *you.*" This morning FedEx had delivered two great big bottles of *daringly* expensive Clive Christian X Women's Perfume Spray. Because, well, thought Ginger, yesterday on Amazon when she'd slid the cursor over to "buy" and clicked, money sure was no object!

The fourth bag of gold.

It was after supper. All concerned parties were gathered at the tree house. Amanda had instructed Oriana to apologize to Harry.

Oriana positioned herself in front of him, hung her head. "I'm sorry I took the coin," she said in a small voice.

"It was our secret," Harry said, wounded.

"I'm really sorry," Oriana said.

On the opposite side of the moral equation, Amanda. "Oriana," she said. "You do not keep secrets from your mother. Well, some secrets, obviously, little ones, but not huge ones like this."

"I'm sorry," Oriana said to her mother. Only it wasn't fair, and it was too grown-up for her to fully understand — that she was supposed to keep secrets except when she wasn't. But the coast seemed clear. Harry and her mother should've been much madder. Interesting.

"We're disappointed in you," Amanda said.

Again, Oriana's internal radar beeped. *We're* disappointed. *We.*

"But we forgive you," Harry said. He patted her shoulder.

Oriana stood solemnly. Then a slow smile began to show at the corners of her mouth. "Were you scared when Brutus came after you?" she said.

"I was more scared when the pickup truck came after me," Harry said. "And boy, when I saw your mom get out of that truck . . ."

Amanda blushed. "Okay," she said. "Now it's my turn to apologize." She stood in front of him. "Harry. I'm sorry I slapped you."

Oriana's hand went to her mouth. This is *so* interesting.

Amanda turned to Oriana. "I was upset, but that doesn't mean you hit another person. Ever. Harry did a very brave thing the other day. At Green Gables, out in the parking lot, Stu Giptner hit him. And Harry didn't hit back."

Harry cocked his head. How did she find *that* out? Boy, is it possible to keep any secret anymore?

Oriana glowered at Harry. Pointed to the fading bruise on Harry's right cheek. "You said a tree branch did it. You lied."

Harry stood before Oriana. "Oriana," he said. "I apologize for lying."

"Why did he hit you?" she said.

Amanda looked at Harry. Harry looked at Amanda. Oriana narrowed her eyes. "Is this a grown-up thing?"

Harry and Amanda nodded in unison.

"All right," Harry said. "We're all even now. Everybody's sorry and everybody's apologized. Shall we move to the next item on the agenda?"

Oriana got the map of Susquehanna County and spread it out on Harry's cot.

Amanda stood behind Oriana and Harry. She stared at the open burlap bag of gold sitting on the kitchen table. She hugged herself and moved a little away from it. The inside of the tree house, so familiar to her, was a deeply unfamiliar place now. The wind carried the intoxicating scent of the forest. The flickering flame of the kerosene lamp sparkled off the gold, off the colored glass imbedded in the irregular windows of the tree house. All her life, she had avoided such sensations, the sense of the unreal hovering at the edge of real. Fairy tales. Magic. She always refused to entertain the possibility of impossibility. And now the impossible was right in front of her.

It was impossible that her daughter, lost so long in grief, was smiling now.

It was impossible that someone as seemingly insubstantial as Harry Crane was more solid than any man in the Endless Mountains.

This moment, Amanda thought, right here, right now — the magic is all around me. It's around me, I can see it now. But I'm not in it. The world that Harry and Oriana inhabit so naturally, how do I enter into it?

She looked at the bag of gold. Oh, she thought. She sidled closer to the kitchen table. And a little closer. She made herself look into the bag. It cast a shimmering aurora borealis of golden light.

Harry and Oriana were watching her now. Amanda took a deep breath and seized a golden coin. She shivered and stared in amazement.

Yes, last night, she'd held in her hand Oriana's stolen coin. But this coin was something entirely different. By freely accepting into her hand a piece of the grum's gold, she accepted the reality of the grum.

"Whoa," she whispered. "Heavy."

"Very," said Harry.

Oriana couldn't believe how cool and wonderful this was. She took her mom by the hand and gently led her to the edge of the cot.

"I feel a little queasy," Amanda said. "Maybe I should sit down."

"No, no. You're doing great, Mom."

"All right. Okay. So I throw this thing at the map?"

"No, no," Harry said. "You flip it into the air and let Fate take hold of it."

"Oh my God," Amanda said.

"Mom. Just toss it up and let it land."

Harry stood just behind Amanda, as she held the coin out over the map. He closed his eyes and breathed her in.

Amanda put her thumb under the gold coin and flipped it into the air. It was a meteor, a shooting star soaring over Susquehanna County.

The coin landed on the map, rolled, settled.

And with that, Amanda Jeffers, and Fate, decided on the destination of bag number four.

Wolf, meanwhile, was concerned with bag

number three. He was like a tuning fork, his body vibrating with the craziness that had happened here in Wynefield.

I see you, Brutus, Wolf thought. I see you lurking in the dark. And you are one humongous beautiful bastard of a dog.

And Brutus saw Wolf, standing on the sidewalk. Brutus's black nostrils flared, his red tongue licked across his black muzzle.

Brutus, you tried to eat Harry, didn't you? I sympathize with the urge, Wolf thought. Harry imagined he had found a nice house with a nice big tree, but he didn't notice the nasty big doggy, did he, Brutus?

Wolf approaching steadily in the dark. "Why aren't you growling, Brutus?"

Brutus's muzzle-flaps puffed in and out. He wheezed and squeaked with muffled rage, his throat gulping and gasping.

Wolf cocked his head and studied the dog. All the while, advancing. "They did that terrible thing to your vocal cords, didn't they?" Wolf said. "Your lovely voice, silenced."

The dog seemed to nod.

"Grrrrrrr," growled Wolf. "Is that what you're trying to say?"

It was a meeting of two like beings. Large, wounded, frustrated, a communication between species. Between brothers.

"Grrrrrrr," Wolf said. "By the way, my name

is Wolf."

Brutus pounced.

And Wolf opened his arms. Brutus slammed into him and licked Wolf's face, his neck, his hands. They wrestled each other happily in the front yard.

"Yeah, boy. Yeah, Brutus. Who's the good boy? Who's Wolf's good boy?"

Brutus's stub tail wagging at a million miles per hour, a super-charged bliss-o-meter. He bounded away from Wolf and circled the big tree in the front yard. Around and around, then, for a moment, he disappeared on the other side of the tree.

Wolf saw chunks of dirt flying in the air. Brutus came into view again and charged right up to Wolf, his paws and muzzle muddy.

"What the hell, Brutus?"

Brutus went up on his hind legs into a beg. Wolf knelt, and the dog pressed his muzzle into Wolf's big hand, opened his mouth and spit out a gold coin.

Wolf stared. Stunned. The weight of it in his hand. The blindy shine. Gold!

Brutus cocked his head.

"Oh God." Wolf stood and held it to the night sky. To hold the gold in his hand. It was electrifying. It was everything he wanted and more. It was just like in the fairy tales.

If you touched a piece of gold, you had to have more. And more.

Wolf laid his big hand on Brutus's head. "You did good. You are such a good boy."

Wolf turned in the direction of Wilderness Tract A803. Out there in the unseen distance. The forest.

Brutus nudged him forward, then went up on his hind legs, barking at the top of his lungs, but emitting only an impotent squeak.

Lenox was hardly a town at all, and that was just fine with Harry. A diner, a closed gas station, five streets, no SUSQUEHANNA SANTA PLEASE STOP HERE! signs in front of the bedraggled houses. Thank you, Amanda, for choosing such a quiet place. It was a bit of a cheat, but he drove a little past Lenox, and looked up into the hills. There, in the moonlight — a glimpse of double-wide trailer. He turned off the paved road, cut his headlights and drove a few hundred yards up a gravel road. And as for a good tree, the omen that this was a proper house to make a gold drop? It was half forest. There were a lot of good trees.

Harry got out of the car and slung the burlap bag over his shoulder. He inched up a winding drive, listening every step of the way for Rottweilers. All he heard were whip-poor-wills and owls, benign lovely creatures on a lovely night. He came around a bend. Stopped short and let out a small yelp. Which, if he hadn't been so frightened, would have been a full-bore scream.

In the clearing in front of the double-wide trailer, a dozen twenty-foot tall, jagged-jawed, flesh-tearing dinosaurs stood on their hindquarters in the moonlight, claws flexed, ready to pounce. But they didn't pounce. They didn't move. They were rusted in place.

Harry advanced. The dinosaurs were sculptures made out of old farm equipment, and tractor and car parts. And they weren't arranged in postures of ferocious attack. Quite the opposite. Harry smiled. They were dancing, claw to claw, jaw to jaw. It was the strangest and most beautiful thing he'd ever seen. Dinosaurs dancing in the moonlight. Clustered around their feet were smaller dancers. Little rusty robots and dwarves and bug-eyed badgers and long-beaked flamingos.

There was one more figure in the moonlight, too, standing directly behind Harry. A tall, wiry middle-aged man, wearing pajamas and holding a pitchfork. Harry moved silently through the dancing dinosaurs. The man moved even more silently, shadowing Harry.

Harry stopped, looked over his shoulder. Saw nothing. When he advanced again toward the front steps of the trailer, the man stepped out from behind a dinosaur and moved with Harry, close enough to reach out and touch him. Or stick a pitchfork in him. Harry eased the bag of gold off his shoulder and placed it on the top step.

When Harry took off through the dinosaurs, running to his parked car, Hoop did not follow him. He stood pondering the bag. With the tines of his pitchfork, he carefully lifted away the edges of the burlap and peered into the bag. A golden, moonlit glow lit Hoop's weathered face. Most men would smile and let out a whoop of elation at the sight of $300,000 in gold.

Hoop sighed.

Forty-five minutes later, Hoop was standing at Cliff's door. It was two in the morning. Cliff stood in his boxers shivering in the spring cold.

"Hoop, what the heck?"

Hoop, looking beleaguered, lifted the burlap bag into view.

"Is that . . . ?"

Hoop nodded.

". . . what I think it is?"

Hoop continued to nod.

"Holy cow!" Cliff said. As if on cue, a faint moo from the distant dairy barn. "Well, where'd you get it?" Even though there's only one place he could've gotten it.

"That Santa fellow." It embarrassed Hoop even to say the word "Santa." Hoop gripped the bag as if he was holding a chicken by the neck. He handed it to Cliff.

Cliff let out a laugh at the jingling of the coins. At the weight of them. And when he opened the bag and looked inside, the glow hitting him in the face like a beam from a golden flashlight, he laughed again. "Holy crappin' cow!"

When he looked up from the bag, Hoop was walking away. Cliff trotted after him, clapped a hand on his shoulder. "Slow down, Hoop, whoa. What are you doing?" He tried to hand the bag back to him.

Hoop leaned away. "Nope."

Of course, thought Cliff. Hoop was not a man to participate in the outside world. And this would be more than participating. If the world found out about this gold, it would besiege Hoop.

"I get it, buddy." Cliff had always provided Hoop safe haven. That's what this dairy farm was. A place where the cows mooed dependably, the grass grew slowly, the seasons came and went with regularity. Hoop was already the richest man in the world — if wealth could be counted in the accumulation of quiet days.

The two friends stood in the dark, the fields and the barns around them.

"You gotta help me out here, Hoop. We got to sit and figure."

Hoop looked at him. "It's for you. For all you done."

Cliff looked at Hoop. Hoop, he thought. You are my friend and you are my burden. I will know no other life than cows and you. Neither of us is real good at navigating the unruly waters of existence. I stupidly show you pictures of naked Amanda Jeffers. You come to me in the middle of the night with a bag of gold. We are two strange men. You in your trailer surrounded by your rusty dinosaurs. Me sleeping in my parents' bed. We will never escape this friendship or our odd, particular lives. Nor do we want to.

"I haven't done anything for you that you haven't done for me, Hoop," Cliff said. He put his arm around his friend's shoulders. "Come inside. Dumb to go home. Two hours it'll be milking time."

In the light of the kitchen, Cliff dressed

now, the bag on the table before them. It seemed larger and more urgent. And definitely out of place. They had gone back and forth, discussing it — that is, Cliff discussing it, and Hoop nodding and offering the occasional monosyllabic response.

There was a lot Cliff could do with the money. Roof the barn, upgrade the milking machines, buy a little more pasture. But you know, things were okay as they were. There was nothing, really, that a bag of money — because that's all it was if you took the Susquehanna Santa craziness out of it — could buy.

The two men couldn't express it, but they sincerely believed that although the bag had come to them, it did not, in the grand scheme, belong to them.

Cliff ruminated over this thought, cogitating to the point of breaking a sweat. Working to articulate within himself the opportunity that sat before him in a burlap bag.

"Why did Susquehanna Santa deliver this bag of money to Hoop?" he said.

"And Hoop deliver it to Cliff?" Hoop said.

The answer was sitting right there in the middle of both of their sentences.

Deliver. Deliverance.

The two men looked at each other. Coming to the same thought, together. So many years together, so many seasons, working through problems. Out in the fields. In the barns. Pushing at a thing until they got it right. Now, in this kitchen, they'd pushed and pushed, until at last they divined a good and practical solution for the gold that also solved a very personal problem of a moral nature that had been deeply upsetting to Cliff. In truth, it hadn't been bothering Hoop to the degree that it bothered Cliff. But it did bother him that it bothered Cliff. Whatever it took to get things back to normal, that's what Hoop was for.

"Hoop, I know what to do with the money."

"Yep," Hoop said.

Deliver. Deliverance.

31

Harry came through the woods into the backyard. Oriana opened the kitchen door and ran out on the deck. Amanda, in her nursing scrubs, waved to him from the kitchen window. Now that handing out the gold was a team venture, the other members wanted to hear the details. They'd texted him, inviting him for pancakes, a quick breakfast before Oriana went to school and Amanda to work.

"Do you think they found it yet?" Oriana called to him.

Harry came up on the back deck. "It's not even six thirty."

"But everybody around here gets up early."

Harry could see that. Cars and pickup trucks were zipping by on the gravel road in front of the house. Amanda stepped out on the deck, followed his gaze. "We're the shortcut to the high school. Dummies drive too fast."

"Last year, Teddy Bale hit a tree in front of our house and broke his arm," Oriana said. "Mom had to take him to the hospital."

"Teenagers want to die," Amanda said. She looked at Oriana, her future teenager. "If you ever text while you drive, I'll kill you."

"You have an impressively direct parenting style," Harry said.

"She's not as mean as she sounds," Oriana said. "Except sometimes."

They went into the kitchen.

"So, tell. Where did my coin flip take you?" Amanda had been awake half the night. She was as excited as a child, and a little scared, being involved in such an enterprise. It felt surprisingly like breaking the law. The law of probability, perhaps? What were the odds that Amanda Jeffers would be aiding and abetting Susquehanna Santa?

Harry was having his own nervous thoughts about aiding and abetting. If he had drawn back from Amanda — and he definitely had — then why was he sitting in her kitchen about to enjoy a casual breakfast? What were the rules of disengagement? Because that's what was coming. He had just successfully delivered bag four. After tomorrow night, the gold would be gone, the adventure over. Oriana was almost out of her forest. And with Oriana rescued, Amanda could move on, too. Everybody settled and moving on.

Harry, too, he'd move on — to Bradford County maybe, or Tioga County, somewhere on the other side of the Endless Mountains. Start his new life.

He'd thought about this a lot. Harry's Trees. What would that look like? He could work in a nursery. Or on a Christmas tree farm, there were tons of those. Or launch something of his own. There'd be a little start-up money when he sold the house in Waverly. But what he would *not* do, was stay here. He deserved nothing more from Amanda and Oriana. He'd done some good here, and that was enough. Spread a little gold, move on. Ramblin' Harry, the tree man.

"Were there any Rottweilers?" Oriana said.

"Not a dog in sight. My easiest delivery yet." No Rottweilers, but a yard full of dinosaurs. Oriana would love this part. Harry was about to tell her about it, when he looked over at Amanda. She'd started toward the table with a plate of pancakes and suddenly stopped. She cocked her head, listening to something outside.

"Mom?" Oriana said.

Now Harry and Oriana heard it. Out front, the sound of car wheels braking hard on gravel. Another car braked. Car doors slammed. Voices.

"Somebody hit a tree!" Oriana shouted.

But there'd been no crash. Amanda rushed toward the front of the house, Oriana and Harry behind her. They looked out the living room window. Two cars were pulled over on the side of the road, teenagers piling out. The kids stood at the top of the walk, excited, pulling out their phones and taking pictures of the front of Amanda's house.

"What the hell —" Amanda yanked open the front door. Looked down. Her hand went to her mouth. There on her front step. A burlap bag.

Harry saw the bag and shrank back, out of view of the open door. Oriana squeezed past him and joined her mother on the front porch.

There were six or seven teenagers. One of them shouted, "It's the gold!"

Another one shouted, "Open it!" They all began to chant. "Open it! Open it!"

Amanda and Oriana turned and looked at Harry — Harry in the shadows, shaking his head. *No, not me. I didn't put it there. Not me, not me.*

Amanda yelled to the kids. "It's nothing. It's a prank. Get back in your cars. Go to school."

They were having none of it. "Open it! Open it!"

Probably the kids themselves, right? They were pranking her. That must be it. Well, she wasn't going to give them the satisfaction. Making her look like a fool. She was starting to get furious.

But Oriana, kneeling behind her, had untied the bag. The morning sun coming up over the maple trees hit the inside of the bag, lighting up Oriana's face in a golden burst.

Oriana stunned, Amanda stunned. The teenagers, stunned — and then they went crazy. Laughing, pushing each other, fist-punching the air, moving in closer with their phone cameras.

Harry, inside the doorway, about to have a heart attack, as again Amanda turned to look at him. Her face, hard with anger. *What did you do? What is this?*

A cheer went up from the teenage crowd. "Gold, gold, gold!" Taking a million pictures, pulling up their Facebook pages, Instagram, going nuts.

Amanda looked down. Oriana had reached into the bag and was holding a fistful of gold coins into the sunshine, as if to verify for herself that, inexplicably, Susquehanna Santa had made the fourth delivery to the Jeffers household.

Utterly confused and upset, she too caught Harry's eye. *This wasn't the plan. This wasn't The Plan, Harry.* And there was fear in her look, too. Because the last thing that her mother, the proudest woman on earth, would ever accept or understand was the gift of a bag of gold.

"Oriana!"

She poured the gold from her hand back into the bag.

And what an image that made on the internet, fifteen seconds later, the zoomed-in videos of a glittering waterfall of slowly tumbling coins.

Amanda gripped Oriana's shoulder. "Go back inside. Now."

Oriana whipped into the house. She stood in front of Harry, breathless. "What did you do?"

"I didn't do it. I don't know what's going on."

Trembling with hurt, she stared at him. Because how could he *not* have done it? Why would he trick them? Why would he endanger the mission? "You ruined everything!" She pushed past him and ran upstairs to her room.

"Oriana," Harry called after her. Shit.

Out on the front porch, Amanda had picked up the bag of gold. She shouted to the teenagers. "You guys get off my lawn. Go to school. And stop taking pictures!" But already, two more cars loaded with teenagers had pulled over. And it would grow. Because that's the way it went, Amanda thought, in despair. She was one of the winners now. The circus was coming to town.

She stormed back inside the house and slammed the door.

"It wasn't me," Harry said.

She threw the bag at him. It him in the chest like a cannon ball.

"Yeah, it wasn't you? It was the other Susquehanna Santa, was it?"

"Amanda."

"So, what — I kissed you, that freaks you out, you feel all guilty? I get the consolation prize? Is that it?"

"What? No."

"I get bought off? Or wait. You feel sorry for the poor widow? You think she can't make it on her own? She needs the help of a good man?"

"I put this bag on the steps of a double-wide trailer in Lenox."

Outside, more cars pulled up. "Look at it out there, Harry."

"I delivered it, and I drove away."

"You know what?" She pointed out the window. "You go out there. And you tell the world — because that's what's about to come to my front goddamn door — that you're Susquehanna Santa. I don't want to be the story. *You* be the story."

"Amanda, listen to me. Early on, yes, of course I thought about giving you some gold. But I didn't. And I wouldn't. Because I *know* how proud you are. You think I don't respect that? Well, screw you."

Amanda took a breath. Harry, angry and hurt, standing there holding the bag.

"I can't explain it," he said. "I can show you the trailer in Lenox. A double-wide with a yard full of dinosaur sculptures."

Amanda took a deeper breath.

And the look on her face was unmistakable. Harry saw it. He'd struck some kind of chord. Some other possibility.

"The gold," he said. "This whole adventure. It's about me trying to wipe the slate, not clean, but a little cleaner. To settle my soul, just a little."

Amanda's thoughts whirling. Dinosaur

sculptures. Cliff, in bed, would talk about Hoop.

Harry seeing it. "There's somebody else, isn't there, who needs to play Santa? Somebody else with an unsettled soul."

"I can't keep it."

"You know it wasn't me. I can see it in your face."

"I can't possibly keep it."

Harry pressed. "The small world of the Endless Mountains. Whoever I gave the bag to — it was somebody who owes you."

Amanda dazed. "For doing something stupid. Infantile. But . . . a bag of gold? That's way, way too much. It makes no sense."

"Whoever gave it to you — it makes a lot of sense to them. You have to keep it, Amanda. You have to accept what's being offered here."

"I can't."

"You know what's even more magic than a fairy tale?" Harry said. "Real life. And it just landed on your doorstep. It's magic when somebody tries this hard to say they're sorry."

Amanda thinking: from the grum to Harry to Hoop to Cliff to me. As impossibly magic as any fairy tale. Hoop — quiet, invisible Hoop — among his dinosaurs, goes to his only friend. And they sit there in the night. And they see their chance. A way to wipe the slate clean.

"And when you *accept* an apology — that's also a kind of magic," Harry said. "You need to accept things from people, Amanda. Especially an apology. When someone is this sorry, you accept it."

He handed the bag back to her.

"And hell, do it for Oriana. Pay off your debts. Put a ton of it away for her college. Be practical. And be gracious."

Outside, more cars pulling up.

Amanda gave him a long hard look. "All right. You want to talk magic and fairy tales? You want me to stand out there with this bag of gold and smile?"

"You don't have to smile. Well. Maybe just a tiny smile."

"Then we make a deal."

Uh-oh, Harry thought.

"If I have to believe in magic," she said, "then you have to *stop* believing in magic. Stop torturing yourself with it. You think buying a lottery ticket caused Beth's death."

Harry wanted out of this deal.

"All you did was go into a store. You'd done it a million times. Buying a ticket — a dumb-ass waste of money — but not a magic crime. Not some terrible fairy tale come to life."

Harry looked out the window.

"You know what I wish?" Amanda said, her voice breaking. "I wish I kissed Dean goodbye the morning he died. I always kissed him goodbye before I went to work. Always. But that day, I didn't. And if I *had* kissed him, our lucky kiss, our magic kiss, no harm would've come to him."

Harry turned to face her. Pain in both their faces.

"Except, Harry, kisses don't protect the people we love. And buying lottery tickets don't cause cranes to collapse. The world does what the world does."

She moved close to him. "All this talk about me accepting. You need to accept something, too. You did all this —" she placed his hand on the bag of gold "— to break free from your crummy job, to have an adventure, to help my Oriana. To *settle your soul.* But, Harry, the biggest, hardest thing you have to do? Stop believing in that lottery ticket and forgive yourself."

A sound behind them. They turned. Oriana was standing at the bottom of the stairs.

"Harry," she said. "The lottery ticket isn't magic. It isn't."

Harry looked at her.

"Okay?" she said.

The world hung in the balance.

Harry, unstuck in time, saw Beth in her red coat on Market Street. She blew him a kiss and vanished. Harry blinked and returned. Oriana waiting. Amanda waiting.

"Okay," he whispered.

Oriana ran across the room and hugged him. Harry reached out and brought Amanda into the circle.

"And *The Grum's Ledger,*" Oriana said, her voice faltering. "It —"

Amanda kissed the top of Oriana's head. "*The Grum's Ledger* is definitely magic."

Amanda looked into Harry's eyes. He smiled.

The commotion outside in Amanda's front yard would not be denied.

Amanda nudged Harry toward the kitchen. "You have to get out of here." It wasn't just kids now. All sorts of people were pulling up in trucks and cars. "Stay out of those woods until it dies down. Away from the tree house."

"And the quarry," Oriana said.

"You going to be able to handle this?" Harry said.

Amanda shrugged. "Oriana goes to school, I go to work." She held up the bag and jingled. "They'll follow me like flies."

"Take that to a bank."

"Get lost. Go."

"One more thing," Harry said sheepishly. "It's not as much money as you think. It's taxable income."

Amanda feigned outrage. "What? You didn't pay taxes on your end? Santa, you suck."

Sure enough, they followed her everywhere. But Amanda figured the way to keep a lid on it was to keep them both safe — Oriana inside her school and herself inside Susquehanna Hospital.

Though she did have to talk to them outside the bank. The press shouted questions at her. There were two state troopers on the bank steps.

"How does it feel?"

"Strange," Amanda said.

"Louder."

"Strange!"

Some people applauded. Amanda squirmed. They were people she knew: friends, neighbors from up in the hills, a couple of folks she'd treated in the ER.

"I'm not a hero. It's just one of those things."

People laughed and applauded again.

"I have to go work. I'm way late."

"What are you going to do with the

money?"

God, how embarrassing. Amanda felt like she was standing in front of the world in her underwear. "What any sensible person would do. Pay my bills, get new tires for my truck, put away the rest for my child's education. And that's it. All gone."

A television reporter from the Scranton station, WNEP, held up a microphone. "What would you like to say to Susquehanna Santa?"

Which one? thought Amanda. To Cliff and Hoop, you're more than forgiven. To Harry. She blushed. He'd given her something far more valuable than gold — how could she ever thank him enough? All she could do, for all the Santas out there, was to look into the TV camera and say, "Thank you."

Nooooooooooo!

No, no, no! Susquehanna Santa practically drives by my house and stops at Amanda Jeffers's place? A mile apart, he couldn't haul his fat Santa ass up my front walk and drop that three hundred thou on my doorstep? Would it have killed him? Because it sure was killing Stu, who sat at his desk, head in his hands.

It had all come together. Deliriously together, the stars aligning. I was foreclosing on her. And the Big Fish was coming, and I was about to dangle Amanda's fancy hand-hewn log house in front of him, and he was going to bite.

Noooooo! Why did Santa swoop in and rescue you, Amanda? You were in the throes of financial despair. We had you. I know we had you.

But okay, okay, Stu told himself. Breathe. So not the Big Fish and The Widow. But I still have Pratt Library. The Pratt closure was a sure thing — but then that began to gnaw at him, because the world was so ruthless. Sure things could suddenly be snatched from one's grasp.

"No," he whimpered.

Would the Pratt deal move fast enough to appease his boss, Mr. Bromler? It wasn't like Stu could go over there and personally bulldoze the place. And what if, spiteful backbiters that they were, town council members finally vote to close Pratt, but then don't award the contract to Stu and Endless Realty? And even though they'd shaken hands on it, he didn't trust Jerry. If Santa could betray me, so could Jerry Palco.

He glared at the Susquehanna County map taped to his office wall. It was quiet, the office closed for Mama Bromler's memorial service. The service was this afternoon at 4:00 p.m. at Kelmer's Funeral Home. Stu would make sure to squeeze out conspicuous tears. Should he bring a whip and flagellate himself before Mama's casket? Whatever you want, Mr. Bromler, just tell me.

Stu was almost in tears right now, staring at the map, lit by the late-morning sun. He held the red pushpin for bag number four. Elkdale, Halfordsville, Wynefield — and right there, jeez, Santa, is my house, not Amanda Jeffers's house.

Stu jammed the pushpin into place, like he was sticking a needle into a voodoo doll. He hoped Amanda felt its sting, the lucky broad. So beautiful, such a nice house, has herself a new boyfriend and now a ton of money. The world is her oyster.

He sat there all morning, looking at all the photos on the internet. Phil Bartek, Ginger Thompson, Brutus the Rottweiler, Amanda the Beautiful. The winners. That's what the internet called them. The Winners.

"Stu Giptner. Winner." The words, dust in his mouth. He slumped in his chair and stared in a daze at the fourth red pushpin. He chewed on his lower lip.

He sat and sat. And then he stood. And the next thing he knew, he was in his car and driving toward Amanda's house. He had to be near the place where the bag of gold had actually landed. He couldn't help it. As torturous as it was, he had to bask in the aura of wealth.

But when he got there, the gawkers were there. Go away, gawkers, I wish to gawk in private. You people don't understand. That gold was mine. That very house was mine. She was in arrears on her loan, I had a Big Fish, and it was all mine.

Stu gulped back his anguish and drove slowly past the house. A quarter mile down the road, the maple trees dense on either side, he saw an opening in the foliage. An old, overgrown road, the wheel ruts just visible. He pulled his car into it and parked, a few yards in. He needed a smoke. He needed to be near the house. He needed. Stu Giptner *needed.*

He began to walk back through the forest toward Amanda's house. He wasn't dressed for it. In fact, he was wearing a coat and tie and his good shoes for Mama Bromler's service. He smoked his cigarette and crunched along beneath the trees. Ah, the forest — so good for a man's soul. Why didn't he go out into nature more often? Look at all these trees. They're so . . . tree-like.

He stubbed out his cigarette on a tree and

lit another one. Looked around. Hey, where was that tree house, anyway? Harry Crane, all snug as a bug in his fancy tree house. You know what, while I'm out here, I think I'll go find me a Harry Crane. What do you say to that, Harry? Let's you and I duke it out in the tree house. Mano a mano. The last man standing gets Amanda and her gold.

Stu peered into the deep woods, uneasily.

Really, where *was* the tree house? The rhododendron and mountain laurel scratched at him as he walked. And which way was Amanda's house? He'd lost his bearings. He lit another cigarette. And for that matter — which way was his car? He stopped and twirled like a ballerina.

The forest seemed suddenly oppressive. Suddenly? The forest was always oppressive, what in God's name was he thinking, coming out here? He never went into the forest. Nothing good ever happened to children in the forest. He remembered Olive Perkins all witchy on her chair in the Reading Corner, reading Grimm's fairy tales to rapt schoolchildren. Little Stu among them, his mouth hanging open. Scared the living shit out of him, those stories. That's why I'm knocking down Pratt Library. The place scarred me for life.

Stu peered into the green dark of the woods. Why hadn't he left bread crumbs so he could find his way back to the car? Well, he had dropped a couple of cigarette butts. Yes, he would follow a trail of butts to safety! Brilliant! He walked, eyes to the ground, searching for the littered white of a cigarette.

An owl hooted, practically in his ear. Stu stifled a cry. Owls were night birds. It was dark as night in here. He looked up into the tangle of tree limbs. No visible sky, only a dense, horrible green. With owls in it. And what if snakes started dropping from the tree limbs? Get a grip, man, he told himself, that only happens in the jungle. You're much more likely to get bitten by a rabid raccoon. Or stomped by a deer. Or clawed by a bear.

He had to get the hell out of this forest.

"Harry," he called softly into the trees. Harry would save him. Yes, find Harry, say you've come to apologize for that punch you didn't mean to throw. I'd been drinking, I'll say. I was drunk.

"Harry? Harry Crane, where are you?"

The sudden throb and whoosh of wings, as a red-tailed hawk flew past his head, its tail the color of blood. Stu screamed and ran pell-mell through the forest.

"Harry! Harry!"

He bumped into tree trunks. Tripped over rocks. Fought his way through dense patches of goldenrod and thistle. He tore the sleeve of his suit coat, scuffed his shiny shoes, bloodied his forehead.

"Harry!"

Running, running, from owls, hawks, anacondas, tigers, elephants.

And then the ground beneath him vanished, and he was flying. His arms windmilled in the air.

No. Not flying. Falling.

"Aaaaahhhh!"

Obscured by a tangle of vines and dense undergrowth, Stu had not seen the lip of the quarry. He saw it now. A great giant rocky pit, sixty feet deep. All his life he had wondered how he was going to die. Now he knew.

"Oooph."

He'd dropped about four feet onto a rocky ledge. He would've bounced off it and fallen to his death, but his leg had gotten entangled in a vine.

He lay, limbs akimbo, his bruised cheek resting on a flat rock. His eyes fixed on a small opening in the pile of stone about three feet in front of him. The sun shining a single beam into the interior of the little cave.

Stu narrowed his eyes and looked. What are those? Boxes? He wriggled his ankle free from the vine. Had he not been diverted by the strange sight of the hidden boxes, he might have noticed that the vine that had saved his life was poison ivy. He raised himself to all fours, balancing precariously on the wobbly mound of quarry stone, and inched on his hands and knees toward the opening. He squeezed himself inside the little cave and crawled over to the boxes.

"Ow!"

Something stung him. He swatted at his neck. A yellow jacket fell to the ground, squirming. Stu beat it to smithereens with a rock. He looked back at the entrance of the cave. There were lots of yellow jackets out there, zipping nastily in and out of the light.

He turned again to the boxes. Eight of them, about the size that hiking boots came in. He looked at his ruined dress shoes. He wished he'd worn hiking boots. How strange that someone would hide hiking boots in a cave. He shimmied closer and reached for the top box. Nothing printed on it, and the address label had been removed. Not much room to maneuver inside the tight cave.

He lifted the box — or tried to, the

unexpected weight of it startling. It weighed at least thirty pounds. He dropped it. It jangled metallically.

"You're not hiking boots," he said. Then, "Ow!" as another yellow jacket stung him behind the ear.

The bees were starting to swarm around the entrance. He had to get out of here. It was the perfect place to die, stuffed in a tight cave, where nobody would ever find him. Who would even look?

But what were all these boxes? He tore at the packing tape of the one he'd picked up, pulled back the flaps, yanked at the bubble wrap. Tubes. Coin tubes. Filled with yellow coins.

No. Not yellow.

Stu's mouth opened and closed.

Yellow was not the color. Gold was the color.

A third bee stung him. "Ow," he said softly. "Ow, wow. Wow, wow, wow."

He poured the coins into his hands. Some of them slid through his fingers and rolled into the corners of the cave. Plink, plink.

"Gold! It's gold!"

Stu was not a religious man, but suddenly he believed in all the gods that are and ever were, even the weird Roman ones dressed in togas. "Gold, gold!" he cried, his voice bouncing off the stone walls.

He poured the coins from one hand to the other, drunkenly.

This was who he was meant to be! This guy, the one holding gold coins in his hands!

Sick with excitement, he tried to think. Each coin weighs, what, an ounce? A thousand dollars an ounce. Boxes and boxes, ounces and ounces. When the figure flashed into his brain, it was a miracle he didn't throw up or pass out. There had to be over two million dollars of gold in these boxes. Not a six-figure man — he was a seven-figure man!

"Stu Giptner's rich," he whispered.

He did not ask the question: Whose was it? Because the answer was so obvious. "It's mine. It's all mine!"

He stuffed loose coins into his pocket in a frenzy. Then, unexpectedly, he did something stunning. He paused. Thought rationally, with razor-sharp clarity.

There was a tale Olive Perkins had once read out loud to the class. An unscary one. Not Grimm, that other guy. Aesop. Aesop's Fables. "The Goose That Laid the Golden Egg." The old Stu would grab as much gold as he was able, right here, right now. But there was probably two hundred pounds of gold sitting here. Line his pockets — or get it all?

Get it all. That's what the new Stu would do. New Stu. Yes. He had one shot to get this right. He turned around and looked at the entrance to the cave. All these bees: bug spray. To carry all the gold: a large backpack. And the road he'd parked on — it was the old quarry road. He could drive close to this quarry, but not in his Buick. He'd need an AWD, and he knew just where he could find one. Back at Endless Realty. Mr. Bromler's company car. The black Dodge Durango SXT, the one Mr. Bromler used to haul around the vacation property buyers. The elite.

Yeah, well, who was Mr. Elite now? Stu's mind was so clear, he felt like he was on drugs. No, not on drugs, he was a *winner.* That's what he was feeling. He had the brain of a winner.

He crawled out of the cave, swatted the air, moving quickly past the bees. He hopped to the adjacent mound of rocks and pulled himself up on the ledge where'd he first fallen. He stood on the edge of the quarry. He didn't even feel dizzy, looking down in that big hole. He breathed deeply of the forest. Maybe with his millions he'd buy this forest. Perhaps he'd buy the Endless Mountains.

He took out his pack of cigarettes, thinking oh so clearly and cleverly, and broke them into little pieces. He perched them on tree trunks and on top of boulders, leaving a trail for himself. He found the top of the old quarry road, and followed it for a half mile back to where he'd parked his car.

Everything was so easy now. That's the way it went for winners. The world was Stu's oyster.

32

Harry was sitting at the counter in Cappy's Diner in Martensberg staring up at the TV when Amanda looked into the camera and said, "Thank you."

He swallowed his grilled cheese very carefully, looking neither right nor left. Was it obvious to the patrons of the diner that she was speaking directly to him? It felt like a Susquehanna Santa neon sign was suddenly flashing above his head.

Harry's waitress, looking at the TV, said, "Why is she going to work?" She called over to the owner, sitting behind the cash register. "Hey, Ray, advance notice. When I get my bag of gold, I'll be taking the day off."

"You do that, Betty Ann, and I'll replace you with that nurse. She's a dedicated worker."

Betty Ann laughed. "She wouldn't take your crapola, Ray. Look at the way she pushed past those reporters."

Betty Ann turned to Harry. "More Diet Coke?"

"I'm fine, thanks."

"Boy, what I could do with a bag of gold."

Harry leaned in a little. "What would you do with a bag of gold?" Because, you know, Betty Ann, I could make your dream happen. Why not, maybe this is the way the stars are aligning. I have to stay out of the forest today. I'm out among the good people of Susquehanna County, and now I get to make a dream happen, up close and personal. Betty Ann, the Santa spotlight is on you. What would you do with a *million* dollars? Yes, that's right, Betty Ann, a million, because the Susquehanna grum is about to hurl the last of his gold in heaps.

"I'd fly first class to New York City," Betty Ann said, "take a limo to Tiffany's and buy the first necklace I saw. Then I'd buy out the entire theater that's showing *The Lion King* and watch it by myself, because I don't like to sit next to people coughing and crackling their candy wrappers."

Sorry, Betty Ann, Harry thought. No bag of gold on your doorstep tonight.

Three stools down, a burly customer in dusty overalls said, "*Phantom of the Opera.* That's the one to go to."

"Dave would know, right?" Betty Ann said

to the rest of the patrons. Heads nodded.

"Oh yeah," Dave said amiably to Harry. "Seen it five times." He held up the five fingers of his right hand when he said it. He was missing part of his little finger.

"You mean four and half?" Betty Ann said, and everybody, including Dave, laughed. "Dave, show him your lottery ticket." To Harry, apparently the only nonlocal in the diner, she said, "Dave won five thousand bucks last year."

Dave took out his wallet and showed Harry. It was a well-worn photocopy of his winning ticket. "They keep the original," Dave said.

"Nice," Harry said. He looked without looking. He didn't want to see the date on the ticket. Things at Cappy's Diner were getting way too close to home. He paid up and went out to his car. His phone vibrated. Text message.

Amanda: having bizarre day. you?
Harry: lying lower than low.
Amanda: will you pick O up at school at 3? don't want her to go home. I might be late.
Harry: Done. meet at Green Gables?
Amanda: pratt library better.
Harry: got it.

A couple of hours to kill. Driving aimlessly around the county was unnerving. What he really wanted to do was go to the quarry and start loading up his car for tonight's delivery. But that wasn't going to happen. He'd have to do it in twilight, maybe even in the dark. Harry looked at all the SUSQUEHANNA SANTA PLEASE STOP HERE! signs in the yards. In the beginning, all the signs had been handmade, but somebody had quickly made a little business out of it. There were signs for sale in convenience stores and gas stations. It was the way the world worked. Pretty soon there'd be plastic good-luck charms in the shape of gold coins and Susquehanna Santa bobblehead dolls.

And there were more people on the roads, too, definitely. Tourists coming in, out-of-state license plates. A car with Ohio plates passed him. Then one from Florida. Not good. What if they started moving up here, buying houses, hoping to get on the Susquehanna Santa game board? The writing was on the wall. He'd talk it over with Team Gold. Oriana, you said it yourself, the lottery ticket isn't magic, let's finish this thing tonight. One more bag. One and done.

Harry was deep in thought as he approached the light at an intersection. When

Wolf drove past in his red Lexus, it registered in Harry's brain in a dreamlike way, like a premonition that the world was closing in — the bag appearing on Amanda's doorstep, Harry having to lie low, crowds and signs and bobblehead dolls — and now hallucinations of Wolf.

Except it wasn't a hallucination. It really was Wolf, in his red Lexus, huge and hunched over the wheel, zooming through a green light.

"Wolf?"

Unmistakably, undeniably, unbelievably Wolf. Just as he'd vowed, Wolf had found him.

"Wolf!" Harry's foot hit the gas pedal. What was he thinking as he floored it into the intersection on a red light? Pursuit? Escape? Pure shock. A pickup truck, coming at him from the left, honked, screeched its brakes. Harry saw it at the last second and swerved. His Camry jumped the curb and hit a telephone pole.

He heard the detonation pop of the airbag, then he heard the crash. Then he heard a crunch when the side of his head bounced off the driver's window.

Pop, crash, crunch. Pop, crash, crunch. Around and around inside his head. It was almost musical, and it certainly had nothing to do with him. Where were these sounds coming from? And red seemed to be a suddenly important color. Wolf in his red Lexus. Was he inside Wolf's car?

"Harry," said a voice.

"Wolf?" Harry said dreamily.

"Harry," said a voice.

"Wolf?"

"He's barking," said a voice. Then, "Harry, can you open your eyes?" Then, "Squeeze my fingers, Harry." Then, "He's still bleeding. Give me another HemCon."

What an odd request. Why does Wolf want me to squeeze his fingers? *Pop, crash, crunch.* Harry opened his eyes. It was like being yanked out of a dream.

He was moving. A siren was screaming. And Bill the EMT guy was staring into his face. Harry was unable to move. He was on a stretcher, strapped onto a stabilizer board and wearing a neck brace.

Bill was running his fingers through Harry's scalp. It felt kind of soothing and nice. "No blood, no contusion."

Harry couldn't see who Bill was talking to.

"Harry, did you black out?" Bill said.

His left cheek hurt. "Cheek hurts."

"You have a pretty good laceration. You'll

have a nice pirate scar to remember this day."

"Wolf," Harry said.

"He keeps saying woof," said the EMT Harry couldn't see.

Bill was suddenly prying his eyelids open and shining a very bright light. "Harry, don't go neuro on us." Bill said to the other EMT: "Pupils equal and reactive, no dilation."

Harry was trying to piece it together. He was at the intersection, he remembered that, and he saw his brother. Absolutely: Wolf in his red Lexus.

"Wolf's here," Harry said.

"I'm not following you, Harry."

"In the intersection, I saw him."

Harry saw Bill give the other EMT guy a look. Bill said, "German shepherd, maybe? No wolves around here. Coyotes sometimes."

"Once in a while, a mountain lion," the other EMT said. "But that's like, totally rare."

"Wolf." And he wasn't speaking to Bill or the other guy. He was speaking to himself. Or maybe he wasn't speaking out loud at all. He was feeling pretty loopy, his brain flooded with post-shock adrenaline and endorphins. But the real shock was that his brother was here, in the Endless Mountains, in Susquehanna County. Even closer than that — he'd come within thirty feet of Harry. So intent on finding him, whizzing through that intersection he didn't even see Harry. Which meant that Wolf had a destination in mind, and it wasn't Martensberg, where both brothers happened to be only by chance. Of course, he had a destination. On the scent, Wolf *never* failed.

You're in your forest, Harry, up your tree. And I'm coming.

Bill the EMT had called Amanda.

"I'm with Harry," he said. "We're bringing him in, car accident."

Amanda's heart had lurched. She heard Bill, but in her panicked mind, she heard Ronnie's voice, Ronnie on the phone, a year ago, calling about Dean. *Amanda, this is Ronnie. The EMTs are with Dean.* And she thought, This is the way the world works. Because it happened to me once, doesn't mean it can't happen twice.

Outside in the parking lot, there were a few lingering reporters and gawkers, hospital security keeping them away from the ER doors. Who has this kind of day? Filled with gold and TV reporters, and the wail of an approaching siren?

Amanda was so scared she was calm, floating. It was the concussion that would kill Harry. She saw it all so clearly, because she'd observed it a half-dozen times in the ER. The farmers falling off their tractors, or the quarry guys with their stone saws, taking a chunk of flying quarry stone to the head, and waltzing into the ER with abashed grins and only a small cut — walkie talkies, the ER staff called them — while the hidden hematoma blossomed in their skulls.

Harry would come in here, and he would bleed out and the day would end with him laid on the morgue table. Now she was thinking just like Oriana and Harry, connecting dots that in reality were not connected, telling herself the story of the arrival and departure of Harry Crane. His end foretold by his beginning. The day they'd first met in the forest he'd had a head wound. As he'd come into her life, so was he doomed to leave it. He would not survive the same injury twice.

And what would she tell Oriana? *The angels have come again. The wingèd ones.* Why did I allow Harry into our lives? Amanda thought. How could I have been so thoughtless?

"So, what's coming into room 1?" said Dr. Kroner, the ER resident.

"Car accident. Facial laceration. Possible concussion. Vitals stable."

Dr. Kroner hearing: *easy case.* "Good. I'm going to wolf down some lunch, then we'll sew him up."

She was not comforted by Dr. Kroner, and she was not comforted when the ambulance arrived and the doors swung open and Harry was alive, the left side of his pale face covered with a big pressure bandage. He was babbling to Bill, not even turning her way when she said his name, his eyes not fixing on her until he was secure in room 1 with half a dozen staff moving around him like drone bees. Then he fixed on her, blinking in the light.

"Wolf," he said to her.

The staff paused to glance at each other, then swamped Harry again, starting a peripheral IV, attaching O_2 sat and BP monitors, EKG leads.

"Are you barking, Harry?" Dr. Kroner said amiably. Amanda would usually join in the banter, ease the patient with casual talk, divert them from their injuries.

"Wolf's here," Harry said.

"Wolf's his brother," Amanda said.

"You two know each other?" Dr. Kroner said.

"We're neighbors," Amanda said. She did

not return EMT Bill's look.

Dr. Kroner assessed Harry's neuro status. Vision, strength, sensation, reflexes, cognitive — Harry was intact. "This is good, Harry, you're giving me all the right answers. Wiggle your fingers and toes for me again."

Amanda lasered in on Harry's responses. Harry was intact, but she would not believe it.

"Harry," Dr. Kroner said, "we're going to keep that neck brace on you for the next hour, and keep asking you the same boring questions."

Harry tried to sit up. "I need to go."

Amanda put her hands on his shoulders. She felt the warmth of him, and still would not believe it. She would not believe the good news. Harry was warm and alive.

"Actually, you need to stay," Dr. Kroner said. "We need to stitch you up and keep you under observation. Amanda will get things set up, and I'll be back in a few minutes."

Amanda said, "What about a CT scan?" For the hematoma that was certainly blossoming in Harry's brain.

"He's neurologically intact." Dr. Kroner looked at Amanda. "Unless you see something I don't see."

What she saw was Harry on the morgue table. She took a deep breath and worked to absorb a new possibility. That Harry would be okay. “No, he’s intact.”

Dr. Kroner nodded and pushed through the curtain.

Harry couldn’t turn his head. Suddenly, from behind, Amanda leaned into view and kissed him on the forehead. She whispered, “I don’t care if I’m not supposed to kiss you. Damn you, Harry.”

Tears fell onto Harry’s face. “Hey,” he said. “Come where I can see you.”

She came to the side of the stretcher, brushing tears away.

He reached up to touch her cheek.

“I’m kind of overreacting,” she said. “The call came in. You in an ambulance. Been down that road before.”

And then Harry understood what had scared her. “I’m sorry. But you know I’m fine. Right?”

“I overreacted,” she said again.

Harry looked at Amanda. He had been sure before, but now he was absolutely certain of the painful gift he would give her when the gold was over. Neither of us want to do this, or risk this, ever again, he thought. Look how vulnerable we are. The day you thought I’d fallen from the beech tree. And now this. When the gold is over, I'll leave the forest and Oriana and you. A wave of pain swept through him.

Amanda saw his look. "I can't give you any pain meds yet, not for another hour. Not until we rule out a concussion."

And Harry remembered. He didn't have an hour. Wolf was here. "Wolf found me. Or not *found* me, but he's looking for me. About to find me. He's here."

He told her what he'd seen, what it meant, how there was no stopping Wolf once he caught a scent. Everything he had not told her before, tumbled out of him. Wolf was onto Harry and the gold.

Amanda spoke to Harry with her calm ER nurse voice. Her voice a whisper, because they were only behind a curtain. "Harry. Harry, stop. Listen to me. Wolf. Urgent, but not an emergency. You don't have to move the gold this second."

"He'll find it."

"Impossible. He's looking for you. That's what you said. He wants to pressure you. You're his only way to the gold."

"I'm telling you. I need to go."

"No. I'm telling *you.* You need stitches. And observation," she said. "And when it's time to leave, we leave together."

Harry understood. When the siren had

delivered heartbreak a year ago, Amanda had endured it, and returned home, utterly alone.

Dr. Kroner drew the curtain aside and smiled at Harry. "You in the mood for some stitches?"

And Harry thought, Yes. It was a day when things were coming apart, and he would very much like to be put back together.

33

Stu sat in Mr. Bromler's big leather chair. He'd come bustling into Mr. Bromler's office just to grab the car keys to the Dodge Durango, but then the chair beckoned, and once he sat in that glorious commanding chair the desk beckoned, so Stu leaned back and put his feet up.

Ah, the trappings of wealth, he thought. When I have my millions, I will replicate this office in my McMansion, right down to the last paper clip. He looked at the framed photo of Mama Bromler enshrined on the right-hand corner of the desk.

"I'm not taking orders from your boy anymore. Comprendo?"

He scooted forward in the chair, extended the toe of his shoe and tipped Mama over. What a lovely, powerful feeling, toppling the mighty. Yes, he would have framed photos of all the people who had maligned him over the years, and each day the butler would line them up like dominoes on the floor of the game room, and then Stu would come in, dressed in his royal blue satin pajamas, and he would nudge the first one and watch them all topple.

Stu snickered, then he looked puzzled. Why am I idling at Mr. Bromler's desk? I need to go get the gold. Like, right this second. But I feel weird, he thought. And I itch. He scratched his leg, extended before him on the desk. I really itch. He pulled up his trouser leg.

"Ack!"

His ankle and shin were bright red and welty. Poison ivy! He lurched his feet off the desk, knocking Mama Bromler onto the floor. Glass shattered. He went around the desk to see. Mama stared up at him, like in a horror movie where the death-ghoul is glaring at you through the splintered glass of your bedroom window. And then he saw something worse, in the mirror in Mr. Bromler's personal VIP bathroom. Himself! Stu crept closer and turned on the light. Puffy crimson bee stings dotted his face and neck. He looked like he had smallpox.

That's why he'd been dawdling. Bee stings, poison ivy — toxic shock! He began to scratch wildly. This is how he would die — face down in Mr. Bromler's office, scratched to pieces!

Stu's heart slammed in his chest and he started to black out. He looked into the darkening cosmos — and saw the light. He was going into the light! He squinted. Wait. It was a *golden* light. Without even knowing it, he'd reached into his coat pocket and removed a gold coin.

"Ha!"

He'd saved himself. As heroes do, they reach deep, into their inner selves. And my inner self, Stu thought ecstatically, is made of gold. He kissed the coin and dropped it back into his pocket. He grabbed the Durango keys and rushed out of Mr. Bromler's office.

Just as he was hurtling past his own office door, a large arm with a large hand at the end of it dropped into view in front of him, like the barrier of a railroad crossing dropping unexpectedly. The arm stopped him cold.

Stu was too surprised to even squeak. One minute he was running, the next —

"Hi," said Wolf, stepping out of Stu's office into the hallway. His big hand remained centered on Stu's chest.

Stu stared at the massive male animal before him. A heavy chin loomed above him, each individual hair as thick as a darkened cornstalk. Please don't smile, Stu thought. Don't show the teeth.

Wolf smiled.

Stu squeaked. "We're closed."

Wolf regarded Stu. Yes, this was Stu Giptner, the nasal voice unmistakable.

"Closed?" Wolf said. He pointed. "The front door's wide open. And I spoke to you on the phone. We arranged to meet, did we not?" Yes, my squirmy little friend, we definitely need to meet, because this morning the fourth bag of gold has landed only two miles from here on that nurse's front porch.

"Oh, right, right, yes," Stu breathed. This monster was the Big Fish. "But sorry, the property is gone. The one I was going to show you. So. We're closed. Please?"

Wolf studied Stu. Looked into Stu's office, at the Susquehanna County map taped to the wall, the red pushpins dotting around Wilderness Tract A803. The red of the pushpins looked like the blood offering of a true devotee.

"I don't believe I told you my name on the phone. That was rude. My name's Wolf."

Stu's bones turned to jelly. Of course your name is Wolf, he thought. Of course.

"And this is your office." Stu's name was on the door.

Stu's eyes flicked to the map on the far wall.

Wolf watched him. "You're a very disheveled realtor."

"What?" Stu said.

"Your suit — it's filthy. Your shoes. And your face, what are those . . . bee stings?" Wolf extended his index finger and tapped a welt in the center of Stu's forehead.

Stu yelped and jumped. The coins jingled in his pockets. Wolf cocked his head.

Stu grinned in terror and reached his hand into his pocket and pulled out the keys to the Durango. Jingled them loudly. "Noisy keys!"

Wolf sniffed the air around Stu. "The reason I'm here, Stu — because it's time to drop all semblance of bullshit — the reason I dropped by this afternoon is I'm looking for someone by the name of Harry Crane."

"Are you a cop?" Stu bleated. "Is this because I punched him?"

Wolf blinked. *You punched Harry?* No one had ever punched his brother. Not on Wolf's watch. And yet this homunculus had dared. What had transpired between them? Was this little fool Susquehanna Santa's helper-elf? Millions in gold — of course Harry would need help. And it had gone bad. They'd fought.

Again, Wolf looked at the map. The red pushpins. No. No helper-elf, not even the stupidest helper-elf on earth, would plant a map on the wall of his office.

"I'm not a cop, and I'm not a priest," Wolf said. "But Stu, I do love confessions."

Stu would confess anything to this wolf. "He lives in a tree. Harry Crane lives in a tree house." Please let that be enough info, thought Stu. Please let me get to Mr. Bromler's Dodge Durango.

Wolf stared down at Stu in wonder. *Endless Dreams Realty. Let us make your dream come true!* That's what the sign on the front of the building said. Harry's dream . . . come true. Harry living in a tree house. Out of his mind. Delirious, overwhelmed, reverting to childhood.

"You rent . . . tree houses," Wolf said.

"Oh, no, sir, no, no. Not *me.*" Stu suddenly seeing a way to get this colossus out of here, to sic him on someone else. "He rents it from Amanda Jeffers."

When Amanda's name left his mouth, Stu looked stunned.

Wolf, knowing Amanda Jeffers was the name of this morning's golden nurse, having seen it online, watched the light come on in Stu's eyes as the dots connected: *Amanda Jeffers. Gold. Harry Crane. Susque-*

hanna Santa. Which suggested that Stu hadn't realized it before — but realizing it now was enough to turn him white as a ghost. What the hell, Wolf thought, is going on with this guy? How is he involved?

"Stu. Is the tree house in the forest?"

Stu nodded weakly.

Wolf reached out a big hand. Stu flinched. Wolf patted the dirt off the shoulder of Stu's suit coat. "Stu. Were you just *in* the forest?"

Stu nodded. Weakly. "We're closed," he whispered hoarsely. "The office is closed. We're in mourning, you see. For Mama Bromler."

All Wolf wanted from Stu was the location of the tree house. So he could find Harry. But even Wolf could not guess the level of treasure he had found in Stu.

"Stu. Could you, perhaps, take me to Harry's tree house?"

Stu was having difficulty breathing. "I don't know where it is," he whispered.

"Of course you do. You're a realtor. You know how to find houses."

"I don't. Know. Anything."

"Of *course* you do. You know *everything.* Your brain, all swollen with endless dreams."

Stu shook his head.

"Would it help if I relieved some of the pressure?" Wolf said. "From your whirling, swirling brain?"

No, Stu's brain whimpered. *It would not help.*

Wolf's index finger headed straight for the welt in the center of Stu's forehead.

Tap.

Stu gasped and went up on his toes. From his coat pockets, a soft jingling sound.

Wolf cocked his head.

Tap.

This time, gasping, Stu jumped several inches into the air.

Jingle, jangle.

Stu raised the SUV keys into view. Jangled them feebly.

Wolf eased them out of his hand. And began to tap, one by one, the three largest welts on Stu's forehead.

Red, rocketing pain. Stu bounced up and down, up and down. Gold coins began to spray from his coat pockets.

Wolf lurched back from him, trying to process the sight of Stu hemorrhaging gold.

Stu continued to jump up and down like a kangaroo, as if once he had started the confession of his golden secret, he couldn't stop.

Dumbfounded, Wolf turned his head right and left, watching coins splatter onto the hallway carpet.

It was Stu who found his voice first. When the last coin settled and Wolf turned to look at him, Stu offered a sickly grin and croaked, "Fifty-fifty?"

When her mother did not show up after school as planned, Oriana was only a little surprised. After all, with bag four landing unexpectedly on their front porch this morning, the day had started all wrong. Oriana had read enough stories to know that when things begin to go wrong, they often go very wrong. The important thing was to keep your head. And persevere.

Mom wasn't there, and she wasn't answering her phone, and across the parking lot was the school bus that Oriana usually took, kids piling in. It was time to make an executive decision. When she arrived home, there might be a crowd of people. That's what Mom had wanted to avoid, why she was going to pick Oriana up after school.

"We'll go out to supper somewhere," she'd said this morning. "Maybe even down to Scranton. Maybe we'll even get a hotel room." Which was an exciting idea since Oriana had never stayed in a hotel room. But she knew they wouldn't. Mom wouldn't leave Harry.

Oriana chewed her lip. The bus. She ran for it.

Litty Stewart, the bus driver, smiled at Oriana as she clambered aboard. "Well, look who's here. The celebrity."

Oriana scooted by. "Hi, Miss Stewart."

A few of the boys whispered and poked the back of Oriana's seat, but they weren't a real bother. Oriana knew from experience that when big things happen to you — like when your father dies — the other kids leave you alone. The bag of gold was a big thing. Big things made you special. And special makes people a little scared of you.

Oriana was tired of being special.

She wanted to become *un*special. She'd spent the day thinking about her own story. Oriana's Story. She knew you had to survive the big things in order to reach the best part of your story.

She whispered softly to herself. "And they lived happily-ever-after."

When they hugged this morning, the three of them tight in a warm circle, Oriana wanted it to go on forever. She didn't want a mountain of gold, and she didn't want to be a princess in a castle or turn into an eagle and soar the skies of the Endless Mountains. She just wanted to come down for breakfast and have Harry there. Harry at breakfast and at dinner and at bedtime. On Saturday mornings and after school. Every day, always and ever after, Harry and Oriana and her mother.

Oriana knew this would happen. It *had* to happen. The way Mom looked at Harry. And Harry looked at Mom. Oriana traced a figure in the dust of the school bus window . . .

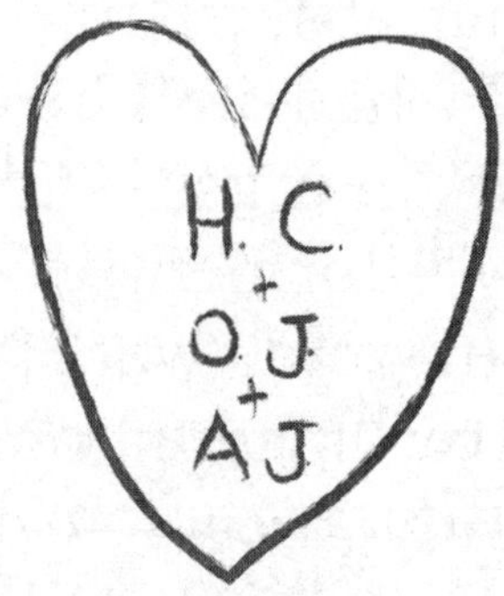

. . . then quickly wiped it clean.

The bus slowed to a stop at the top of Maple Road.

"Guess things have died down," said Litty. There was only one car, approaching in a plume of dust. "You going to be okay?" she said to Oriana as she opened the bus door.

"Sure. Mom said it's just a normal day."

Litty started to say something, but then the car honked.

Who honks at a school bus? Litty squinted

through the windshield at the driver of the Buick. "Of course, who else?" Litty gave him the finger, then sped off.

Stu Giptner never looked in Oriana's direction. But Oriana looked at him. She stood in shock on the side of the road. The expression on his face — Oriana had never seen anything like it before on a real flesh-and-blood person. The eyes bugged out, the sick grin of pleasure beyond excitement. Smaug had that look, King Midas had it, Rumplestiltskin had it. The book illustrations of these beings — men, women, dragons, trolls — tormented into ecstasy by the presence of gold, were so frightening that Oriana never lingered on them.

Oriana instantly knew — in this day that had started wrong — Stu Giptner was the most wrong thing of all. She tore off her backpack and ran into the forest, curving behind her house, bee-lining it to the quarry. It was an awful feeling, knowing exactly what was happening. She was the lone child running through the forest. Her father gone. Her mother beyond reach. Her protector absent from his magic tree house. The treasure threatened by a greedy ogre. All of the things that were supposed to go wrong, were going wrong. And she knew from her year-long education, her immersion in all the possible tales that ever were — that only half of them ended in *happily-ever-after.* In the other half children died, evil prevailed, knights in shining armor succumbed to poisoned arrows, the forest turned impenetrable.

Oriana ran for her life. She ran for her life and her mother's life and Harry's. The branches of the pine trees scratched at her, and the dark forest undergrowth closed in. In her ear she heard the terrible lost sigh of the grum: *This is not the way the story goes.*

I know, I know, thought Oriana frantically. The magic won't happen if the gold is stolen. The gold has to be *given.* That's the only way Harry will find his Amanda. The gold, given away in heaps and hurls.

"Heaps and hurls," she cried. "Heaps and hurls."

As she neared the quarry, the air turned putrid as dragon breath. Stu Giptner's cigarette smoke. It lingered in the bushes and clung to the leaves. There they were, on the ground, cigarette butts, one after another, leading up to the lip of the quarry.

She pushed through the laurel and rhododendron at the edge of the quarry, lowered herself onto the precipice and hopped over to the big mound of broken stone. The curtain of vines had been yanked aside, the bees still hovering angrily.

Expecting to find the cave empty, Oriana burst into tears when she saw that the boxes were still there. He had found them, yes, and torn open a box, but he had not taken them! But he was coming back. That's what the cigarette butts meant. He'd left a trail for himself. He would come back and take it all. That's the way the story always went.

She had to move the gold. But there was so much of it she couldn't possibly do it by herself.

"Harry, where are you?" she called out. "Mom. Mom!" She took out her phone, her hands shaking so terribly she could barely hold it.

In the forest behind her, a sound. Stu Giptner? He'd seen her. She thought he hadn't, but he had. On the road, back at the bus, he didn't turn and look at her, but when he drove away, did he glance in his rearview mirror and see her? As she ran into the forest, he must have pulled over. Followed her.

Oriana slowly turned and peered into the deep forest. He wasn't there.

You know this forest, she reassured herself. You can hear things no one else can hear. Any disruption in the stillness. Any breeze, tremble of leaves, faint snap of a distant twig. No one is there.

When her phone suddenly throbbed, she jumped. *Mom* appeared on the screen. Oriana hit Answer. The phone went silent, call dropped. The bars were low, the signal terrible. The phone rang again.

"Oriana?" The crackling sound of her mother's voice, faint and far away, as if from the North Pole.

"Mom, hurry!" Oriana said. "He found it! He's found the gold!"

Gesturing wildly as she spoke, Oriana dropped her phone. Reaching for it, she lost her balance, tipped forward and began to fall into the quarry.

A pair of hands caught her from behind, snatched her out of the air and pulled her into a terrifying embrace.

34

She'd kept him in the ER as long as she possibly could. She was so focused on Harry, constantly assessing him for possible changes in his neuro status — slurred speech, distal tremors, sudden headache — she forgot the rest of the world existed. She didn't tell him that Dr. Kroner had written his discharge orders an hour ago, or that her shift was over. All Amanda could think about was Harry, and all Harry could think about was Wolf.

Distracted, they'd forgotten something important.

Harry got a sudden look and sat bolt upright on the stretcher. Amanda had a moment of alarm.

"Oriana," he said.

"Oh shit. Oriana," Amanda said. The plan had been for Harry to pick her up at school. Amanda whipped the curtain aside and went to get her phone. During a shift, all

ER staff were required to keep their phones in their lockers. She came back into Harry's room, phone to her ear.

"She left two texts. She caught the bus home."

Amanda felt terrible. When things go wrong, she thought, they go very wrong. No. Amanda clicked back into calm nurse mode. No, they don't. There's no pattern to anything, and panic gets you nowhere. Oriana is self-reliant. If she walks up the road from the bus stop and sees a bunch of people in front of the house, she'll go into the woods.

"It's time to go," Harry said. "We need to go now." He sat up on the side of the stretcher, winced and gingerly touched the bandage beneath his black-and-blue left eye. He looked like a prizefighter on the losing end of a fight.

Amanda placed a hand on his shoulder. "Wait, hold on. She'll be fine."

Amanda did her best to ignore her pounding heart. Cell reception in the mountains was a total crapshoot. Come on, Oriana, pick up, she thought. An eternity of twenty seconds. The call went through. "Oriana?" Amanda said into the phone.

Harry watched Amanda straining to hear her, pressing the phone hard against her ear, closing her eyes in concentration. And now it was Harry who was scared by the sudden expression on Amanda's face.

"What. What is it?" he said.

Amanda tried to call her back, but Oriana's phone wasn't picking up.

Harry took hold of Amanda. She tried to speak, but her voice came out in a gulped whisper. "She said, 'Hurry. He found it. He's found the gold.' "

Five minutes later, they were in Amanda's pickup truck. A reporter and a few others tried to follow her. She left them in the dust.

"It could mean a lot of things," Harry said. Playing down his fear, working to give Amanda something. She veered onto Route 11. "She said he *found* the gold. *Found.* Past tense. Which means it's already happened. He has it."

Deep into her dread, Amanda barely heard Harry's voice. She was doing eighty-five in a fifty-mile-per-hour zone. The road curved like a snake.

She shook her head violently at Harry's words. "No. She said, 'Hurry.' It's *not* over. It's happening right now. Wolf is there, stealing the gold."

Harry tried to wrap his head around this version of Wolf. The old Wolf would've come to find me, Harry thought. To manipulate and bully me, to get his share — whatever that meant in Wolf's head. Wolf's primary pleasure was also his primary need: control. Wolf, the screwed-up father figure. I give to you, I take from you, I own you.

"If he hurts —" Amanda said.

"Never," Harry said. Wolf would never hurt her. The problem was Oriana.

Amanda was thinking the same thing. Oriana, the bold. Oriana, the fierce. She would try to stop Wolf, Amanda knew. Oriana, raised to be courageous. To go into the forest.

Amanda felt the dots connecting, the story unfolding. From the day Oriana first stood on her own two toddler feet, Amanda had set this terrible outcome into motion. *You are invincible, child. Fear nothing. You are the bravest girl in all the Endless Mountains.* Amanda saw her mistake so clearly. She was the foolish mother who had planted dangerous thoughts in a child's head.

Tremble not. Cry not. Persevere against all obstacles. Climb the trees, walk the stone walls, play in the creek, go into the forest.

Stupidly, she had taught Oriana bravery.

Oriana would never allow Wolf to steal the grum's gold. Harry's gold. Dean's gold. Amanda saw it all so clearly. Oriana leaping onto Wolf's back. Wolf shrugging her off.

Oriana falling to the bottom of the quarry.

"Harry," she said. Terrified.

"I know," he said.

Sitting beside Amanda, Harry saw it, too. Oriana falling, and he was to blame. With the lottery ticket, he had set everything into motion. The terrible symmetry. Beth in her red coat, Oriana in her red jacket. Accident and tragedy about to unfold yet again. Those he most wanted to protect, he harmed.

Harry could barely get the words out. "I did this. This is my fault."

Amanda stared straight ahead. Shook her head. "No. I never taught her fear. She thinks she can do anything. And now she will."

For a long time, neither spoke.

"Drive faster," Harry said.

"Drive faster," Wolf said.

Stu was behind the wheel of the Dodge Durango. It was only fifteen minutes from the office to the old quarry road. No need to get crazy with the speed. Especially since this was Mr. Bromler's car.

Wolf lit a cigarette. "If you don't drive faster, I'm going to shoot you," he said.

Stu barked out a terrified laugh. An eruption of sweat made his bee stings burn and his poison ivy boil.

"Jesus, pal, just kidding," Wolf said. "So, what are you going to do with your share?"

My share. He said, my *share.* Stu smiled through his sweat. He's my partner. My first *partner.*

"Maybe I'll buy a Dodge Durango," Stu blurted, as he turned onto the old quarry road. The SUV bouncing so hard on the rocky ruts Stu's teeth rattled in his head. But God, could this AWD baby handle it.

"Why would you buy another one?" Wolf said.

"What?"

"You just stole this one."

"No, I —"

"Borrowed?" Wolf stubbed his cigarette out on the dashboard.

Stu's eyes bugged as a wisp of black smoke curled up from the burn hole in the faux leather.

"I'm not a car thief."

"No, you're a gold thief."

"Yes. No! Santa's handing it out."

"To you? To me? I don't think so."

Stu thought, Everything's happening so fast. I was just here at the quarry finding the gold. And it felt so good. Then I was just in Mr. Bromler's office sitting in his big chair. And that felt good. Then this terrible gorilla appears and I don't feel good.

"It doesn't need to be fifty-fifty," Stu said. Or thought he said. Was he speaking out loud? So close to the gold. And it didn't feel wonderful. It felt horribly dangerous. I'm out of my element, he thought. How do I get back in my element?

They came to the end of the quarry road. Stu cut the engine. He couldn't seem to catch his breath.

"Stop panting and get out of the car, Stu," came Wolf's voice. Stu obeyed.

Wolf stood beside the SUV. The forest, he thought. All the fucking trees. Harry's trees.

You tricked me, Harry. You tried to cut me out. You're just like Dad. All quiet, then suddenly you make your move.

Wolf had a sudden urge to smash something. He turned and looked at Stu.

Stu stepped back from him.

"I want to apologize in advance," Wolf said. "In case something untoward happens."

"Untoward?"

"Unpleasant. Unfriendly. Unkind. I have rage and abandonment issues," Wolf said. "But mostly rage."

Stu went white.

"Lucky for you, I also have money issues," Wolf said.

On the way up from Virginia, Wolf had bought two very large duffel bags. Stu carried them. When they were stuffed with gold, Wolf would carry them. Stu would not be joining him.

"We're close," Stu said. "See how I left a trail?"

Wolf looked at the cigarette butts in the leaves. "Aren't you clever," he said.

They stood on the quarry perimeter. Stu stood to Wolf's side because he sure as heck wasn't going to let Wolf stand behind him.

"Where is it?" Wolf said.

Stu pointed down. "There's a little opening. Hard to see."

Wolf looked. There were giant mounds of broken bluestone all over the quarry. The cave was just below them, tucked into the largest mound, which was shouldered up against the quarry wall.

Stu went first, guiding them onto a ledge. From there, they hopped over to the mound.

Stu stared. "Where . . . are the bees?"

"What?"

"There should be *bees.* In the log. Above the entrance."

But there was no log above the entrance. Stu looked down and saw it smashed on the quarry floor, fifty feet below, the bees in a black swarm of agitation.

"No, no," Stu said.

"Stu?" Wolf said. So close, he breathed in Stu's ear.

"No. No, no," Stu said again, his voice a quavering whisper. They shouldn't be able to see into the cave. The curtain of poison ivy and Virginia creeper vines had been pinned back and held in place by a large rock. A beam of late-afternoon sun lit up the cave. The empty cave. And stuck on a branch dangling at the entrance was a note.

"It's all gone," Stu whimpered. "It all . . . went away."

Wolf pushed Stu aside and reached for the note. Read it aloud. " 'The last of the gold has been delivered. Ho, ho, ho, Susquehanna Santa.' "

Wolf glared at the note. Glared at the cave. Sounds growled up from his throat. And then slowly, tooth by bared tooth, he grinned.

Stu squirmed past Wolf, leaped to the rim of the quarry and ran for his life. It's what he'd wanted to do from the moment Wolf had showed up in the office. Run. Forget the gold. Forget his job. Forget the Endless Mountains. He would run and run and never stop.

But Stu's legs were no longer moving him forward.

Suddenly he was upside down and swinging back and forth like a pendulum.

Wolf had caught him. He held Stu by the ankles and walked him to the edge of the quarry.

Stu watched his sweat drop through the afternoon light. Like diamonds falling.

"Stu, can you hear me?"

Very clearly. But he didn't answer. He was watching the diamonds fall.

"Stu?"

In the distance, the sound of car doors slamming. Feet running through the forest. *Harry,* thought Wolf. Good, let it be Harry. Because this is for him.

"He doesn't have the gold," said a voice from above. "So you should put him down."

Wolf turned his head and looked up. A young girl was sitting on a low branch of a sycamore.

"Who the hell are you?" Wolf said.

"Oriana!" a woman's voice called. Now Wolf looked in the direction of the pine grove. Amanda came tearing into view, followed by Harry.

They saw Wolf at the quarry's edge, dangling Stu over the void.

Harry gripped Amanda, who had stumbled to her knees in fear. She didn't see Oriana. Had Wolf — ?

"Mom! Up here." Oriana waved from the sycamore tree.

Amanda's hand went to her mouth. Harry helped her up. They advanced slowly, Harry out in front now.

Wolf taking it in. Harry with his patched up cheek. The woman at his side. The girl climbing down from the tree.

"Wolf. Put him down," Harry said.

Wolf looked at his little brother. "Okay." He dropped his arms a few sudden inches, as if he was going to let Stu fall into the quarry.

Stu cried out.

Wolf looked his brother over. Harry had . . . changed. It was radiating off him. "Congratulations, Harry, you finally grew a pair. I don't know how you pulled this off, but you did it."

Did what? Harry thought.

Oriana ran to his side and took his hand. Squeezed it hard. "You should've seen them when the gold was gone and they found the note!"

Harry looked at her. *Note? Gold is gone?*

She looked at him, squeezing his hand hard enough to break bones. *Trust me.*

"Thought my head would explode." Wolf laughed. "Love the 'Ho, ho, ho.' Perfect. When you nail somebody, you really nail them. You learned that from your big brother. Finally."

"Hello up there," Stu called weakly, from upside down. "So, I didn't take it."

"Nah," Wolf looked down at Stu, giving him a shake. "You did something much worse." Wolf swung Stu hard, as if to send him flying into the quarry, then twirled him like a baton and stood him upright.

Stu so frightened, he didn't make a sound. Wolf held him from behind, so they were both facing Harry. "Much, much worse. You hit my little brother."

Harry looked at Stu, and saw every terrified high school kid Wolf had ever tormented.

"Harry and I. We're a team," Wolf said, tightening his grip on Stu.

Harry stepped forward.

Wolf smiled. "Here he comes, Stu. My new Harry. All bulked up from living in the forest. He's a wild man, Stu. I sure wouldn't want to be you."

Harry stopped in front of Stu, who was mouth breathing as he stared at the bandage on Harry's cheek, his black eye. He had no idea he'd hit Harry so hard. Wolf twisted his arms so tightly, Stu could feel them starting to come out of their sockets.

Stu braced himself for the imminent blow.

He knew it was going to be bad. After all, Harry was Wolf's brother. Fatally, Stu had provoked not just one wolf, but two.

Harry sized up Stu, leaning in close to look at his face.

"Wolf, you don't need to hold him," Harry said. "I got this."

Wolf, loving it, released Stu.

Stu watched as Harry raised his hand. Oh no, Stu thought.

"You have a lot of bee stings," Harry said.

And the hand Stu thought was going to harm him, came to rest on Stu's shoulder. Gently.

Wolf's smile became uncertain.

"I bet they really hurt," Harry said.

Stu raised his bleary eyes to meet Harry's. "What?"

"I bet those bee stings hurt."

Harry turned and looked back at Amanda. "Do you have calamine lotion back at the house?" he called to her.

Amanda nodded. "And Benadryl. We'll get him fixed up."

"Harry," Wolf said.

Harry ignored him. Began to draw Stu forward. "Amanda will take care of you."

Amanda will take care of you. Stu looked at Amanda, right there before him, in her scrubs, in the forest, a vision. He wasn't going to be eaten by wolves? And Amanda Jeffers, nurse angel, was going to tend to his wounds?

Stu said, pausing to raise a pant leg, "I also have poison ivy."

"That looks painful," Amanda said. She took Stu's arm.

"And gross," Oriana said. But she took Stu's other arm. Harry, Oriana and Amanda, propping up Stu, began to walk away.

"Harry, what are you doing?" Wolf called.

Harry didn't reply.

Wolf's voice louder now. "You were in over your head. I came here to protect you."

Harry strode back to him. "You came here to steal the gold."

Wolf pointed toward Stu. "Wrong — your little friend was going to steal it. He didn't expect old Wolfy to show up. I was going to hand that gold to you, Harry."

Harry just staring at him. "Yeah? Is that how it was going to go?"

Wolf returned his stare. "We'll never know now, will we?"

"I think we know."

"My little brother knows." Wolf gestured at Oriana and Amanda. "Got your life all figured out now, do you?"

"Some of it."

"Harry with his new life. Harry out here with his trees, all fixed." Wolf sneering.

The two brothers stood at the quarry's edge. Harry looked into the abyss, then raised his eyes and looked at Wolf. His voice was quiet and weary. "You need to go, Wolf."

Wolf nodded. Then suddenly grabbed Harry and pulled him close. His mouth at Harry's ear, his breath hot, his voice a low growl. "After Beth, you're really going to try again?" Holding him in a suffocating embrace, whispering. "Harry, it's in our blood. It never works. We're the Crane boys. It always ends in *disaster.*"

Wolf held him and then pushed him roughly away. Harry stumbled back.

"Harry," Amanda called to him. "Come on. Harry?"

He turned and began to walk away from Wolf. Then immediately felt it. Even before he saw Amanda put her hand to her mouth. Before Stu's and Oriana's eyes went wide. *It always ends in disaster.* Harry whirled around.

Wolf, thirty feet away, had turned to face the quarry. The toes of his shoes over the rocky edge. He'd raised his arms out in front of him, gesturing as if he were asking the quarry some profound question that only the quarry could answer. The arms kept going up. Now Wolf looked like a man on a high dive.

Running toward his brother, Harry remembered this moment. How brave Wolf was. Long ago, at the town swimming pool — Wolf on the high dive that every kid feared. Maybe they'd jump from that height, but no one ever dove.

Except Wolf. At ten years old, shoving past a line of teenagers, climbing, standing on the edge of the high dive, the most awful and beautiful sight Harry had ever seen. Young Wolf pushing off his toes, arcing above the water and dropping endlessly. Harry never saw him hit the water because he'd closed his eyes in terror, opening them again only when Wolf rose from the deep and splashed him, laughing at Harry and all the cowards of the world.

Wolf on the quarry rim tipped forward, his feet leaving the rocky edge just as Harry reached out and caught the back of his shirt. Harry, who had never been so strong as he was right then, pulled on the great weight that was his brother, the unstoppable force that only Harry could stop.

From behind, Harry's arms encircled Wolf. Harry held him tight and lifted him in the air, twisting him toward safe ground.

"Let go of me, asshole," Wolf grunted.

But Harry did not let go until Wolf wrenched free and faced him. Harry panting for breath, Wolf's chest heaving, too.

Harry stared at him. "What the hell's wrong with you? Why'd you do that?"

Wolf grinned. But his eyes showed something deeper. And his voice was not as cocky as he tried to make it sound. "You were there for me, Harry."

"What?"

Wolf patted Harry's cheek. "Just testing, little brother."

He laughed, then turned and walked away, vanishing into the dark of the forest.

35

Waiting for midnight to come, Ronnie zigzagged his truck through every square inch of Susquehanna County. He drove 297 miles, up and down back roads, winding through the state roads, hit all the towns, some of them twice. Halfordsville, Kempler, Findlerton, Bass Lake, Forest City, Elkdale. All twenty-seven of them. And when the speed limit signs said thirty miles per hour, Ronnie would go twenty-nine. He did not want to have a conversation with a state trooper.

"Whatcha got under that tarp, sir?" the trooper would say, pointing to the flatbed of Ronnie's pickup truck.

Ronnie trembled at the thought. But he had eluded all the imagined state troopers, had not talked to a soul for the last seven hours. He looked at his watch. It was 11:45 p.m. Fifteen minutes away from destiny.

Ronnie had never had a destiny. The fate

of the world resting upon his shoulders. Or a little piece of the world, anyway.

Oh, but Ronnie — he could feel Oriana's voice inside him — that little piece is everything. Because that's how the world is saved. Piece by piece, every day. Somebody like you has to step up. Somebody like you has to be wonderful.

But what if I blow it? Fifteen minutes was plenty of time for Ronnie Wilmarth to screw up. His life had been a series of screw-ups. Crashing his truck drunk. Slicing his thigh at the lumber mill. Losing jobs, falling asleep in snowdrifts. The catastrophe of eating a hamburger while Dean Jeffers died alone in a field. Failing to hold Pratt Library together. Powerless to comfort Miss Perkins when her tears fell on *The Grum's Ledger.*

And eight hours ago he'd come so close to another catastrophe — almost losing Oriana.

Ronnie pulled his truck over to the side of the road and stared wide-eyed into the country dark. Such a close call. Thinking about it, he began to tremble even harder.

He had been at the library this afternoon, standing in the disaster of fallen bookshelves and leaking pipes. Doom all around him, and the quiet, heart-breaking sight of Olive, wiping her eyes as she wandered lost among her beloved books.

She looked like a ghost, and Pratt Public Library her decaying mansion. Abandoned by Alexander Grum, her library in shambles, the county inspector closing in. Ronnie had failed her.

She dropped into her worn-out chair in the Reading Corner, clutching *The Grum's Ledger.*

"Let me get you a different book, Miss Perkins."

"No, this is my book, Ronnie. The book of my life."

"That's not true, and you know it. Look at all the books in this place. Every one of them is inside you. And you're inside them."

"Sweetheart. It's a *public* library, not my private library. It needs people."

"They got out of the habit, is all."

"The world has changed."

"No, everybody needs a story, Miss Perkins. That's something that never, ever changes."

Ronnie looked at Olive in her chair. And at the rug in front of the chair. He saw himself, way back when, sitting on that rug with twenty or thirty other children. "Miss Perkins. Why did you stop reading to the children?"

Olive sighed. "Budget cuts, sweetheart. I

lost my assistant librarian. I had too much to do, keeping it all together. Things fell by the wayside."

Ronnie dropped to his knees in front of her. "Well, right there, Miss Perkins. That's where your thread began to unravel. Don't you think?"

Olive looked at Ronnie, on the rug before her. And she, too, recalled the legions of children. Their faces upturned. Mouths open, eyes wide in anticipation.

"You're so tangled up in endings," Ronnie said, gesturing at the scattered books and fallen bookshelves, "you forgot about your beginnings. Think of all the beginnings that began right here, in this magic place."

Olive stared at Ronnie, covered with dust, kneeling on the floor before her. What was it about this man that he was able to snatch such bits of poetic wisdom out of his muddle-head?

"See, Miss Perkins, the thing is, you just need to get the kids in here again. You read one child a story. And it's like magic. When they hear your voice, they'll come back for more. And it'll spread, Miss Perkins."

"That's a wonderful thought, Ronnie. And the truth in it, indisputable."

"We'll get you a new reading chair and a new rug."

"And four new computers, Ronnie, and high-speed internet. And a real librarian, not just an old volunteer. And a building that's not falling to pieces." She took his hand. "Sweetheart, it's not just a rug and chair — we need so many impossible things."

"And we'll get them, Miss Perkins. We will. Don't lose faith. Don't let that old grum get you down."

She looked at *The Grum's Ledger,* looked at Ronnie, so loyal. She tried to smile. But then she looked around at the drooping ceiling and the broken floor tiles and the fallen shelves. "Oh Ronnie. My dear, sweet boy, it's over. Pratt Public Library is done." Her words were like a candle going out.

Ronnie felt the darkness closing in. Dean had guided him here to save the library. Olive had depended on him. Oriana had tasked him. Who did they imagine he was? He sagged beneath the weight of their expectations.

And then the grum, who knew a thing or two about misery, added a little more weight to Ronnie's despair. *The Grum's Ledger* slid from Olive's lap and fell into Ronnie's hands, open to the illustration of the grum. Sitting atop his great pile of gold, he stared up at Ronnie. In the grum's doleful eyes, judgment: I failed Olive Perkins, and now so have you.

To every story we bring the story of ourselves. Oriana saw in *The Grum's Ledger* a way to move beyond the loss of her father. For Olive, *The Grum's Ledger* was a tale of love and remorse. Harry had allowed the grum to lead him toward adventure and redemption.

Now, it was Ronnie's turn.

It was the story that had moved Oriana and Harry and Olive. The words. But it was the illustration sketched by Alexander Grum that seized Ronnie's imagination.

What Ronnie suddenly noticed was the mound of gold and the contours of the mountains behind the grum. Ronnie *knew* that mound. And he knew the shape of those mountains, because a hunter knows the landmarks of his terrain.

Hunting in the forest, Ronnie had hiked around the old bluestone quarry a thousand times. At sunrise and at sunset, rain and shine. Seen it from every angle.

The mound of gold beneath the grum was the largest pile of broken rocks in the quarry, and the mountains behind the grum were the Endless Mountains, viewed from the quarry's northwest edge.

And there was even a moon in the picture!

Olive said it had been a moonlit night . . .

Alexander Grum, too, had known the quarry. He had passed by it a dozen times as he went into the forest to meet his love. And on that ill-fated night, when he did not meet Olive by the maple tree, he stood star-

ing into the quarry, the mountains moonlit in the distance.

And forever after, fixed in his memory, was the emptiness he felt at that moment, the sight of stone piled upon stone, the weight and permanence of a cowardly decision.

Decades later, haunted by that memory, old and dying, Alexander Grum had created a final sad image of himself — a creature perched on a pile of gold worthless and lonely as a mound of stone.

And Oriana, Ronnie thought, filling with dread, *you* know the quarry, too.

"Miss Perkins. Did Oriana read this?"

"I'm afraid she did. Why I gave this tragic tale to a child . . ."

Ronnie thinking as fast as he could. Oriana, you've held *The Grum's Ledger* in your hands and you know the quarry. His heart was racing.

That day in the forest, Ronnie had been tracking Oriana, watching over her. He knew she had sensed his presence, knew she had suddenly altered her course, pretending she had been heading all along toward the meadow. But Ronnie was a hunter, sensitive to paths and patterns. Oriana had been heading straight for the quarry.

In the meadow, a few minutes later, Oriana had insisted he devote himself solely to the rescue of the library. Had she been trying to compel him away from something, so he would not interfere, not be her guardian angel, not watch over her? Was she up to something dangerous and didn't want Ronnie to stop her? He had been so intent on his own story, he'd allowed himself to be outmaneuvered by a child.

"What is it, Ronnie?"

Ronnie dropped *The Grum's Ledger* in Olive's lap. "Miss Perkins," he stammered. "I gotta go!" He took off.

Olive watched him vanish. Her guardian angel — even he had given up on her. Who would not flee this place?

She called after him. "Thank you, dear! You did everything you could! Thank you, thank you." Her voice trailed off as the great doors of the library *whumphed* closed.

Sitting in his truck, waiting for midnight, Ronnie saw himself bursting out of the library, leaping in his truck, running so fast through the forest that when he came upon Oriana in the quarry and saw her teetering on the great mound of stone, he almost had a heart attack.

To every story we bring the story of ourselves. He had not saved Dean, but he would save Oriana.

She was turned away from Ronnie, frantically shouting into her cell phone. It slipped out of her hand. The phone fell. And reaching for it, Oriana fell. Leaping like a deer from the precipice to the mound of rocks, Ronnie caught her as she dropped. Pulled her to his chest and fell back on the mound of rocks.

Oriana screamed and struggled. She thought she was in the clutches of the gold thief.

"Oriana, it's okay! It's me. It's Ronnie!"

"Ronnie!" Oriana melted into his arms. She was a girl who did not believe in tears, but for a long moment she gasped and sobbed in the protective embrace of a grown-up.

There were tears in Ronnie's eyes, too. Holding Oriana as he had not been able to hold Dean. He looked up, and high, high in the sky, he saw a hawk vanish into the pale afternoon clouds. Ronnie kissed the top of Oriana's head. "What are you doing here?" His voice was shaking.

The story poured out of her. Harry Crane. The grum. The gold. Stu.

Ronnie stared dumbfounded at the little opening to the cave. He had assumed Oriana was up to something sneaky and probably dangerous. In fact, she had been busy turning the world upside down and inside out.

"We have to get it out of here, Ronnie."

"Harry Crane is Susquehanna Santa?"

"Ronnie. We'll use your truck."

"It's just all so —"

"Ronnie, we can't let anybody get it."

"I know but —"

"Ronnie!"

"Okay!" Ronnie got a stick, wedged it under the oak log full of yellow jackets, gave it a jerk and sent it tumbling to the quarry floor. Then he used the stick to part the Virginia creeper and poison ivy vines, and Oriana rolled a rock to hold them in place.

Crouched in the cave, Ronnie stared slack-jawed at the eight boxes, the top one torn open. He didn't want to touch the gold, let alone move it.

"So we put it in my truck. Then what?"

"You deliver it."

Ronnie got the same "uh-oh" look Harry got when Oriana made such pronouncements.

"*Santa* delivers it," he said.

"Santa is Harry and Harry's not here."

Ronnie looked away. He was very scared.

"You think you never do anything right."

Oriana waited until he looked in her eyes. "You know in the story, how the grum's life didn't go right? But in the end he figures it out and turns things around? Ronnie, this is your day. This is the day you set things right."

He gulped. Then squared his shoulders.

"Let's do it," he said.

They made three trips to his truck, skittering like mountain goats over the rocks. The *Ho, ho, ho* note was Oriana's idea. Ronnie had a carpenter's pencil and a piece of paper in his truck. Oriana stuck the note inside the cave. Then she took off on foot in one direction and Ronnie took off in his truck.

It was midnight, and now here he was, right where he was supposed to be, on top of Zick Hill, staring at the dark and sleeping little clapboard house. Ronnie got out of the truck. The whole world held its breath. The spring frogs stopped piping and peeping. The owls in the trees stared. The wind went still. The clouds waited, the moon waited, the stars waited.

Ronnie slid the burlap bag out of the back of the truck. He had to hold it in both arms because it weighed over 120 pounds. Though, to Ronnie, it felt light as a feather.

Ronnie looked up at the sky, half expecting one last feather to come floating down. But the time of floating feathers was over. It was now the time of gold.

Midnight. The magic hour. And all he had to do was walk a hundred yards to those front steps and deliver the gold. A hundred yards of not screwing it up.

"I can do this," Ronnie whispered to himself. Just move your feet, Ronnie. And watch out for tree roots. Don't trip on a stone. Here you are at the front walk. Here you are at the porch steps.

It was the most amazing thing. Nothing went wrong. He didn't screw up. In fact, he was perfect. He leaned down and placed the burlap bag on the top step. The coins plinked and settled.

Ronnie looked up at the night sky. The owls hooted, the spring frogs broke into a peeping chorus, the wind rustled the leaves in all the trees — for this was the day he set everything right. This was the day Ronnie Wilmarth performed a *miracle.*

Ronnie twirled, hugged the moon and threw a big kiss to the stars. Then he ran for his truck, jumped in and got the hell out of there.

36

Olive Perkins stood at the top of the old marble steps in front of Pratt Public Library. At the bottom, reporters with upthrust microphones. Behind the reporters, locals and out-of-towners filled Main Street. Despite being four feet eleven inches tall and thin as a blade of grass, Olive had the commanding presence of a general about to address the troops.

Almost every person in that crowd was aiming a phone at her, taking pictures and videos. Olive was having her social media moment. If ever there was someone made for the internet, it was Olive Perkins. She knew exactly what all those cameras wanted. Cool as a cucumber, she put a match to her big meerschaum pipe, lit it and exhaled a giant plume of smoke, followed by four magnificent smoke rings. The crowd went nuts. The online crowd went even more nuts. An ancient, pipe-smoking librarian who'd just received millions in gold!

She cleared her throat and began. "As most of you know by now, my name is Olive Perkins, and two days ago, a great big bag of gold landed on my doorstep."

Cheers from the crowd.

"Everyone's been asking me, 'What are you going to do with the money?' Well, I suppose I could buy a pink Cadillac and hit all the night spots in Scranton. Or I could go on one of those fancy cruises — sit on a ship the size of a skyscraper, drink piña coladas and wave at the porpoises."

Laughter and applause.

"Or hell, I'm old, maybe I'll just buy a marble coffin and throw a fancy funeral for myself." She paused and drew on her pipe, exhaled. "Well, Cadillacs move too fast, cruise ships move too slow and coffins move you to a place I'm not ready to go."

The crowd laughed and hooted and cheered.

"So, what am I going to do with my money? I'm going to spend it on an old friend." She patted the stained marble edifice of Pratt Library. "Like a lot of us, she's been through some hard times."

A reporter shouted, "But aren't libraries obsolete? Why waste the money?"

Another called out, "People can download books."

Another shouted, "Do you have enough to save it? And how will you get people to come?"

Olive pointedly didn't answer. She waited patiently until the questions subsided. Then she called over her shoulder. "Ronnie."

The big doors behind her opened and Ronnie Wilmarth, wearing a suit, his hair combed, brought out a large overstuffed chair and placed it beside Olive.

The crowd murmured, aimed their phones. What was this crazy old librarian up to? Olive smoothed her dress and sat in the chair, looked out at all the faces and serenely puffed on her pipe.

Two days earlier, as was her morning custom, Olive had pulled her down vest over her worn red flannel nightie and gone out on the front porch of her little house to eat her oatmeal and watch the sun rise from behind the Endless Mountains. It was cloudy. Olive was particularly inspired by dawns like this when she could not see the sun. It gave her strength and comfort to know that it was out there, rising, doing its daily job, unthwarted by clouds, rain or snow. That's the way she liked to think of herself. Against the impediments and disappointments of life, she was a riser.

Olive found out exactly who she was and what she was made of all those years ago when Alexander Grum had abandoned her. Even though he left a goodbye note, she stood for hours beside the stone wall, holding her leatherette suitcase, a lone passenger waiting for a train that never came.

How strange and terrible it was to remove the engagement ring from her finger and bury it at the base of the maple tree.

How awful and lonely to walk out of the moonlit forest, make her way back up to her bedroom on the third floor of her parents' house, unpack her suitcase, and lie down on a single bed instead of a hotel bed in the honeymoon arms of a new husband.

She lay in the dark and whispered, "Goddamn you, Alexander Grum." Goddamn you, she thought, for breaking my heart. But Alexander, I would rather suffer my broken heart, than endure the suffering that is coming to you. What a terrible thing you will carry inside you for the rest of your life. I forgive you, but you will never forgive yourself.

That morning, all those years ago, despite the devastation in her heart, the sun rose. The world had not ended. Watching the sun from her window, young Olive thought, Now I understand how life works. There are no guarantees, except that every morning, the sun will rise. No matter what happens, good or bad, each day will be followed by a new day.

Would I rather have loved Alexander, Olive thought, or never have met him? Is it better to stay safe in your bed, forever hidden in a room, or venture, each day, into life?

Olive got out of bed that morning.

And she got out of bed every morning thereafter. She let go of one life and began another.

White-haired and old, she stood now at her front door, oatmeal in hand, and looked out at the Endless Mountains. Even on *this* day, with the loss of the second great love of her life, somehow Olive had gotten out of bed. She had survived the loss of Alexander Grum, and she would survive the loss of Pratt Public Library.

No, she would not survive. She had a sudden terrible thought, one she had never had before. She stood there looking toward the Endless Mountains, and for the first time in her life she didn't care if the sun rose.

She suddenly noticed. The sun . . . *wasn't* rising. It's not rising, she thought to herself, because I have died in my sleep. I am in a dark place because I am dead. But why did I fix a bowl of oatmeal if I'm dead? That seems curious. Well, life is so strange, who's to say death is not even stranger?

And then she began to cry, because she had died before she had a chance to say thank you. She wanted to thank the sun for faithfully rising for so many years.

More important, she wanted to thank Pratt Public Library. Thank you, Charles Dickens and Stephen King, Willa Cather and Mary Shelley. A big thank you to historical biographers, particularly Robert Caro. A special thanks to all the writers of children's books, even the brothers Grimm, who were a morbid pair, but vivid in their descriptive power. And wait, she forgot to thank the poets. There was such a nice little poetry section in Pratt, just behind the children's books.

Olive was so immersed in gratitude, she did not at first notice that the night clouds had vanished and the sun was peeking up from behind the mountains. She squinted in the overbright light. Heavenly light? she wondered. Because the blinding light was *golden.* Golden and, inexplicably, it was rising upward from the front porch steps.

Olive looked down.

"Oh," she said. The bowl of oatmeal dropped from her hands and clattered to the porch.

An animal had torn open the burlap bag in the night and spilled its golden contents all over the steps.

"Oh," Olive said again.

In among the scattered coins was a note. Olive lowered herself to her knees and reached for it. She adjusted her bifocals and read the penciled words. *It will never be enough, but I hope it is something. Love, the grum.*

She stared at the note for a long time. Then she cleared a spot for herself and sat on her top step, surrounded by gold. She faced the bright, spring-green Endless Mountains. "It's more than enough, sweet grum," Olive whispered. "It's everything."

Now, two days later, she sat in her overstuffed chair on the marble steps of Pratt Public Library.

The crowd was waiting. Cameras on her. What was the old librarian about to do? What was happening?

Olive looked at Ronnie, off to the side. She nodded. Ronnie had been holding a book behind his back. He handed it to Olive, then he sat down on one of the marble steps just below her, and looked up, his expression rapt.

The crowd buzzed and jostled.

Olive took another long draw on her pipe, then hushed the crowd by giving the universal librarian signal for silence: she placed her raised index finger to her lips and said, "Shhhhhhhh."

"Today's book," she said, "chosen by Ronald Wilmarth, is *Treasure Island,* by Robert Louis Stevenson."

Everybody in the crowd went still. What a sight. All over the nation, and in many parts of the world, people leaned closer to their laptops and squinted at their phones.

" 'Part One. The Old Buccaneer,' " Olive read out loud. " 'I remember him as if it were yesterday, as he came plodding to the inn door — a tall, strong, heavy, nut-brown man, his tarry pigtail falling over the shoulder of his soiled blue coat, his hands ragged and scarred, with black, broken nails, and the sabre cut across one cheek.' "

A little boy squirmed out of his mother's arms and started toward the grand staircase of the library. His mother caught him. Olive smiled and called out, "That's fine. Let him come. You reporters, step aside, please."

The little boy scooted up the stairs and sat beside Ronnie.

Ronnie whispered to the boy. "I love this next part."

The boy put his finger to his lips and said, "Shhhh."

All of this caught on camera, shared online, instantly bounced from site to site.

Olive read on. " 'I remember him looking round and whistling to himself as he did so, and then breaking out in that old sea-song that he sang so often afterwards:

" 'Fifteen men on the dead man's chest —Yo-ho-ho, and a bottle of rum!' "

More children came up onto the steps. A few grown-ups, too. Tentatively at first, tiptoeing forward, finding a seat on the marble steps, staring up at the librarian whose words were as magic as an incantation.

Everywhere, people stopped what they were doing, and . . . listened. Even the reporters listened, transfixed. They pulled out their earpieces, ignoring the producers shouting in their ears. They wanted to hear a story. They wanted to know what happened next.

When she finished the first chapter, pausing occasionally and turning the book around to show an illustration to *oohs* and *ahhs* from the crowd, someone called out, "Don't stop! Keep going!"

Olive read three chapters that day. Online, the first hashtag popped up: #SavePratt Library. Donation sites appeared. Volunteers came forward.

It was a good thing that spring had come to the Endless Mountains, because every day, Olive had to sit out on the front steps of the library and read to the insatiable crowds of people. She read herself hoarse.

Suddenly, Olive Perkins was the librarian of the most famous library in the world.

37

Harry sat in the booth with Amanda, looking around Green Gables, as if in a waking dream. On the TV above the bar, footage of Olive Perkins, regal on her chair in front of Pratt Public Library. Around the bar, Cliff, Ronnie, Stu and a bunch of the EMT guys.

Harry watched Stu say something, and everybody laughed. Stu patted Cliff on the back and signaled Tom. "Another round for the fellas, barkeep, *s'il vous plaît.*" Tom rolled his eyes.

Old Walter said, "Stu buying beers. Olive on TV. Don't know what New Milford put in the water supply but I hope it works on me. I could use a new knee."

Ronnie wasn't drinking beer. He was sipping a ginger ale and craning his neck to watch Olive. He was trying to hear the story she was reading. He'd already heard it, of course, because he was on that TV screen, too, popping into frame occasionally beside

Olive. Ronnie Wilmarth on TV, he thought. Can you believe it? And Olive had gotten him on the Library Renovation Committee. Me, on a *committee.* Can you believe it?

When Tom delivered the beers, Stu ordered a round for Harry and Amanda, too. He looked across at Harry, absolutely baffled that there were such men in the world. After they'd gotten his bee-stings and poison ivy fixed up, Stu took Harry aside, opened his hand and revealed that he was still in possession of three gold coins from the ones he'd stolen when he'd first came upon the gold (Wolf had taken the rest from him). He'd hidden them in his shoe.

Harry shrugged and closed Stu's hand back over the coins. "Our little secret," he said.

Stu had almost wept. He looked now at Harry and thought, There sits Susquehanna Santa. And that's my little secret.

Cliff was looking over at the booth, too. But at Amanda. She met his eyes and held his gaze, and that was enough to settle his soul. It was not often a man got to right a wrong. The cows in their evening stalls; sitting among friends in a friendly place; Hoop quiet and undisturbed up in the hills — Cliff felt pretty okay.

Harry looked at the men at the bar, at

Olive up on the TV, at Oriana over in the alcove between the restaurant and the bar playing on the skittles table. She bowled the little wooden ball. Pins toppled. She pumped a fist. "Yes!" Then it was her friend Tess's turn. Oriana had asked if she could invite Tess to dinner at Green Gables. Amanda said, sure, that would be fine.

Amanda watched Harry watching.

When Oriana came back to the table, she was chattering with Tess about how it would soon be warm enough to swim at Acre Lake.

"Are you a good swimmer, Harry?" Oriana said.

Harry said yes, he was a pretty good swimmer.

"And how about ice skating? Because in the winter, we always go ice skating on the lake. Do you have ice skates, Harry?"

Before Harry could reply, she burbled on about how they'd get ice skates for him, if he didn't have any.

Harry listening, just as he had in the car on the way to Green Gables, as Oriana had talked excitedly about how next spring she would show him how to collect sap for maple syrup and how she was going to be in the end-of-the-year play and would he come? She went on and on.

This imagined future. It was unbearably

beautiful.

Harry, alone in the tree house. The moon so big and bright. He reached his hand into the moonlight beaming through the stained-glass windows, as if he could take hold of the shimmering reds and blues and yellows. But there was no holding on to it.

Through the big triangular window, another light beckoned. Harry went out onto the deck. In the distance, a light flickered in the forest. He went down the spiral staircase and walked toward it.

The light disappeared and reappeared. A flame. He smelled the pipe tobacco and came upon Olive Perkins sitting on the stone wall, smoking peaceably. She regarded him as he approached.

" 'Are you a Being Natural or a Being Unnatural, O forest-dweller?' " she called. "Hello, Harry. Nice to see you again."

Harry had the same sense about her as when they first met: Olive Perkins, veiled in smoke — very witchy. Especially in the moonlight.

"I've been out here, pondering," Olive said. "This old wall — very good for pondering. I believe you stood right here, not so long ago, and pondered a thing or two."

Harry looked from the wall, to the broken

limb on the maple tree, back to Olive.

"And on that day," Olive continued, "you found a book."

"Left by a witch?"

Olive laughed.

"Left by an Oriana. Oh, I might have had something to do with it. In the sense that I'm a librarian, and she's a very compelling reader."

"Very," Harry said.

"My dear Harry, the hour is late, so let's not pretend. You're pretty compelling yourself. In fact, you're a damn wonder. And on top of everything else you've accomplished, you saved my library. So allow me to give you a gift in return. The only gift I know how to give. I'd like to read you a story."

She produced *The Grum's Ledger.*

Harry shook his head. "I've read that book. A thousand times."

"Music to a librarian's ears! So, tell me what happens."

"The grum gives away the gold and he feels better. He's fixed."

"Are you fixed, Harry?"

"Yes. Good things happened. I feel better. I helped Oriana."

"And the money is gone?"

"The money is gone."

"And so the curse is lifted?"

"Yes."

"And that's all the story was about?" Olive sighed. "All right. Time to read it again.

" 'Once upon an endless time in the Endless Mountains,' " she began.

Harry put his hand over the book. "I know the story. By heart."

"Well, *there's* a vital word. Heart. Aren't you forgetting the final scene? He uncovers his love, Harry. He gets the girl, and they live happily-ever-after. And your deal is even better. At the end, you get two loves."

"My deal with the grum was the gold."

"So we just tear out the last page of the book? We pretend it's not there?"

Harry didn't answer.

"Ah. You want the *guarantee.* The grum suffered from a similar affliction."

Harry looked in the direction of Amanda's house. A single light just visible through the trees. "I don't want anything to happen to them."

"But Harry. It's not just that you don't want anything to happen to them. You don't want anything to happen to *you.* And that's how you turn into a grum."

Olive held the book open, and the grum looked at Harry with doleful eyes.

"*The Grum's Ledger* is a tale of regret. In real life, there was no happy ending. Alexander Grum died alone because he was afraid to seize love and risk all the unknowns that go with it. He chose certainty — and it was his ruin.

"The only guarantee I could offer him — against all the unknowns, all the obstacles — was that we would face life together."

The wind picked up. Harry looked into the forest. Looked at Olive, now standing in front of him.

She placed the book on the wall and stepped away from it. "Take it from an old librarian — there lies a book that need never have been written."

Harry put his arm around Olive. She leaned against him.

The wind woke Amanda. When she went to the window, Harry was standing in her backyard. She pulled on her terry-cloth bathrobe, eased past Oriana's room and went downstairs. She opened the kitchen sliding door and went out into the backyard.

"Why are you here?"

"I saw your light."

"I didn't have one on."

"A trick of the moon, maybe," Harry said.

"I'm not in the mood for tricks. I have a little girl who expects you to be here tomorrow. And the tomorrow after that, and the one after that. An endless string of tomorrows with Harry."

"I know that."

"Maple syrup in the spring. Ice skating on Acre Lake. Everything she was saying at Green Gables, and you just sitting there letting her believe it. It's not fair to her. And it's not fair to me."

"I *know* that. That's why I'm here. I need to run through my list of guarantees."

That stopped her. "Guarantees." Amanda narrowed her eyes and wrapped her bathrobe tight around her.

Harry moved a little closer. "Will you, Amanda Jeffers, guarantee that when Oriana rides her bike, she will never fall off?"

"What? No," Amanda said.

"Will you guarantee you'll never cut your thumb slicing an onion?"

"No. Harry —"

"Will you guarantee your appendix will never burst, you will never have a close call with pneumonia, or break your hip when you're ninety-two?"

"No," Amanda said. "And I won't guarantee I'll even make it to ninety-two."

Harry nodded.

"And I won't guarantee I'll never slip and fall on the ice," she said. "I won't guarantee the house will never burn down. I won't guarantee that Oriana will never be eaten by a deer. I won't guarantee the sky will never fall."

"So," Harry said. "No guarantees."

"No guarantees."

Harry looked at the moon in the night sky. At the forest. At Amanda. "All the unknowns, Amanda, all the risks . . . will you face them with me?"

Amanda held out her hand to him. "Yes," she said.

Harry drew her close.

From her bedroom window, peeking through the curtains, Oriana looked down upon them. In fairy tales, she never liked the part when they kissed. But this was not a fairy tale. And a kiss seemed like the perfect way to begin.

Epilogue

On a dark highway, speeding away from the Endless Mountains, a red Lexus, Wolf at the wheel. Heading where, he knew not.

But he wasn't leaving empty-handed. He'd stolen something. Even more valuable than gold.

After the quarry, despair. Wolf had slept in his car, unable to leave the Endless Mountains. But what was holding him?

The windows in the car were down. Wolf leaned his head out the window, and let the night air blow back his ears. He was mirroring Brutus, beside him in the passenger seat. Brutus, leaning his massive head out the window, mouth open, tongue out, ears flapping wildly in the wind. All senses basking in liberation.

Stolen Brutus? No, Wolf had freed him.

An hour ago, Wolf had driven his Lexus back to Wynefield, opened his door to the dark shape circling the tree and called,

"Here, boy."

Brutus did not hesitate, bursting through the prison of the invisible fence, enduring, even reveling in the electric shock from the battery electrodes on his collar. It was the shock of freedom.

Now, Brutus and Wolf were in the red Lexus, on the highway. *Together.*

Brutus drew his head in from the window. Turned to Wolf. He so wanted to express it. So wanted to say it. But they had stolen his voice. He licked Wolf's hand, nuzzled his shoulder. Brutus barked and barked, noiselessly, so desperate to *say* it.

Wolf petting that big head, trying to soothe. "I know. I know, boy. I know what you're trying to say."

Brutus, trying to get it out.

Wolf barked for Brutus. "Woof," he said. "I get it, boy. You're trying to say woof."

No, he was *not* trying to say woof. Brutus, brimming with love, was trying to say something much more.

And then it came. The electric shock of freedom — it had restored something in his silenced vocal cords. Brutus felt the name leave his heart and rise from his throat. He barked it for all the world to hear. The name of his best friend.

"Wolf," he barked. "Wolf, Wolf, Wolf!"

ACKNOWLEDGMENTS

I would like to thank: Mary Hasbrouck, Molly Cohen, Dan Dalton, Ellen Meriwether, Katherine Keefe, Pete Torrey, Joe Gangemi, Stacey Himes, Theresa Park, Alex Greene, Kathy Sagan, Ben Cohen, Carrie Piccard, Steve Voelker, Steve Goldfield, Melissa Lewicki, Steve Lewicki, Merrie Lou Cohen, Anthony Spay, and Trish Haxton.

Thank you as well to all the good folks at Park Literary & Media, and MIRA, who have been so incredibly helpful.

ABOUT THE AUTHOR

Jon Cohen, a former critical care nurse, wrote his first novel between hospital shifts and raising two children. After receiving a creative writing grant from the National Endowment for the Arts, he turned to writing full time. His two novels, both critically acclaimed, are *The Man in the Window* and *Max Lakeman and the Beautiful Stranger.* Setting his sights on Hollywood, he purchased a "how-to" book on screenwriting. He has since written numerous screenplays for Fox, Warner Bros. and Sony, and is the cowriter of *Minority Report,* directed by Steven Spielberg. Jon lives with his wife outside of Philadelphia.

The employees of Thorndike Press hope you have enjoyed this Large Print book. All our Thorndike, Wheeler, and Kennebec Large Print titles are designed for easy reading, and all our books are made to last. Other Thorndike Press Large Print books are available at your library, through selected bookstores, or directly from us.

For information about titles, please call:
(800) 223-1244

or visit our website at:
gale.com/thorndike

To share your comments, please write:
Publisher
Thorndike Press
10 Water St., Suite 310
Waterville, ME 04901